The Dragons of Incendium

THE FIRST COLLECTION

DEBORAH COOKE

AUTHOR OF *KISS OF FIRE*

The Dragons of Incendium: The First Collection
by Deborah Cooke

Cover for the collection by Kim Killion
Covers for the individual books by Frauke Spanuth.

More Books by the Author

Writing as Deborah Cooke

Paranormal Romances:
The Dragonfire Series
KISS OF FIRE
KISS OF FURY
KISS OF FATE
Harmonia's Kiss
WINTER KISS
WHISPER KISS
DARKFIRE KISS
FLASHFIRE
EMBER'S KISS
THE DRAGON LEGION COLLECTION
SERPENT'S KISS
FIRESTORM FOREVER

The Dragons of Incendium
WYVERN'S MATE
Nero's Dream
WYVERN'S PRINCE
Arista's Legacy
WYVERN'S WARRIOR
Kraw's Secret

Urban Fantasy Romance
The Prometheus Project
FALLEN
GUARDIAN
REBEL
ABYSS

Paranormal Young Adult:
The Dragon Diaries
FLYING BLIND
WINGING IT
BLAZING THE TRAIL

Contemporary Romance:
The Coxwells
THIRD TIME LUCKY
DOUBLE TROUBLE
ONE MORE TIME
ALL OR NOTHING

Flatiron Five
SIMPLY IRRESISTIBLE

✳

Writing as Claire Delacroix

Time Travel Romances
ONCE UPON A KISS
THE LAST HIGHLANDER
THE MOONSTONE
LOVE POTION #9

Historical Romances
THE ROMANCE OF THE ROSE
HONEYED LIES
UNICORN BRIDE
THE SORCERESS
ROARKE'S FOLLY
PEARL BEYOND PRICE
THE MAGICIAN'S QUEST
UNICORN VENGEANCE
MY LADY'S CHAMPION
ENCHANTED
MY LADY'S DESIRE

The Bride Quest I
THE PRINCESS
THE DAMSEL
THE HEIRESS

The Bride Quest II
THE COUNTESS
THE BEAUTY
THE TEMPTRESS

The Rogues of Ravensmuir
THE ROGUE
THE SCOUNDREL
THE WARRIOR

The Jewels of Kinfairlie
THE BEAUTY BRIDE
THE ROSE RED BRIDE
THE SNOW WHITE BRIDE
The Ballad of Rosamunde

The True Love Brides
THE RENEGADE'S HEART
THE HIGHLANDER'S CURSE
THE FROST MAIDEN'S KISS
THE WARRIOR'S PRIZE

The Champions of St. Euphemia
THE CRUSADER'S BRIDE
THE CRUSADER'S HEART
THE CRUSADER'S KISS
THE CRUSADER'S VOW
THE CRUSADER'S HANDFAST

THE DRAGONS OF INCENDIUM: THE FIRST COLLECTION

Table of Contents

✸

WYVERN'S MATE

Once, in the Kingdom of Incendium, there were twelve princesses of the realm, each a dragon shifter. Each fiery and passionate. Each possessed of an appetite for pleasure that only her destined mate can satisfy. Twelve men are expected in Incendium, each with special powers of his own, each with the gift to claim one dragon princess's heart forever.

Troy will do whatever is necessary to earn his freedom from solitary confinement on the penal colony of Xanto, even assassinate a princess of Incendium. Being a MindBender, he has a serious advantage as a predator and thinks the princess in question doesn't have a chance. Only one of them can survive and Troy knows who it will be—until he meets Drakina.

Royal dragon shifter Drakina has a quest of her own, to seduce her destined mate and conceive the crown prince of Incendium. Her father will free her from all other responsibilities if she completes this one task. Drakina craves her independence enough to seduce the unattractive Terran who is the Carrier of the Seed. She's sure it will be a quick seduction—until she meets Troy.

Worlds collide when Troy and Drakina meet, and passion flares. The attraction is so powerful that they both choose to put their goals aside for one night of passion together. When their respective secrets are revealed, will the truth turn one against the other? Or will destiny allow this star-crossed pair to save each other and their unborn son?

PROLOGUE

Thursday, August 18, 2016 — the town of St. Anthony, Canada

THE NIGHT SKY WAS FILLED with shooting stars. There weren't many residents here, in the smallest town on the "wrong" side of Dinosaur Provincial Park, but the local population always swelled for the Perseid Shower Festival in August. It was dark in St. Anthony, far beyond the light pollution of any metropolis, which provided the best viewing conditions for meteor enthusiasts. The festival had been held the previous Saturday, the biggest ever, but now most of the visitors had departed.

This was the night of the full moon, the least optimal time to watch the meteors, after all. Most residents had had their fill of meteors and were watching television instead. The local bar, MacEnroe's Pub & Eatery, had closed down at midnight and the streets were empty.

By the wee hours of the morning, all four hundred and twenty residents of St. Anthony were asleep and the meteor shower illuminated the sky unobserved. No one noticed that a single larger meteor hurtled toward the earth. It streamed white fire across the sky and crashed into the badlands not far outside of town with a thunderous crash.

Even that didn't rouse any townsfolk from their sleep.

The ball of flame rolled a distance, then stopped. The meteor was in fact a ship, a ship carrying a MindBender, the most powerful MindBender ever born in the galaxy. He had cloaked the ship in invisibility, a wasted effort since there was no one in the vicinity.

He wanted to arrive without notice.

When the ship halted, the flames were abruptly extinguished. The sphere cracked in half, revealing a seam too straight to have been naturally forged, and the lone occupant stepped out. He stretched when he stood on the ground, then surveyed his surroundings.

Didn't it figure that they'd sent him back to Earth. Troy shook his head. The sneaky bastards. The gamblers of Xanto always kept a few aces up their sleeves. He hoped this was the only surprise, but doubted it.

He was going to win, even so.

Anything he had to do was better than being executed.

Troy had never imagined he'd return to Earth, but here he stood, on terra firma once again. He studied the town and felt surprise. Not just on his home planet, but outside the town where he'd grown up.

Two surprises in as many minutes. They really were trying to stack the odds against him.

And thanks to the High Priestess of Nimue, no one would recognize him. Was that good or bad? Troy knew that no one would believe where he had been.

There were times when he didn't believe it himself. If it hadn't been for the ship—which was already decomposing—and the persistent ache in his muscles from working in the mines of the penal colony of Xanto, he might have thought he'd never left St. Anthony, that he'd just taken a walk on this night in the wilderness.

But Troy knew better. He was changed. He was bitter and he was angry. His heart had turned to stone at the injustice done to him. He had one chance to make it right, to earn his freedom, and even if they stacked all the odds against him, he was going to win.

Or die trying.

It had to be better than execution.

Troy had forty-eight hours in local time to succeed in his mission. Two rotations of the Earth to kill a dragon shifter princess. A simple transaction. His life for hers.

He had no idea why anyone wanted to have the princess Drakina executed, and he didn't particularly care. If he cared, he might not be able to finish the job. Caring was a luxury Troy couldn't afford.

He was here and he had a job to do. He started walking.

Earth might be less developed than the other civilizations he'd come to know, but the planet itself wasn't bad. The temperature and humidity were pleasant, the air smelled good, and the oxygen balance was excellent. The force of gravity was a little lighter than Troy had become accustomed to, but he'd get used to it again easily enough. Out here, far from most humans, it was perfect.

Funny how he hadn't thought that when he was younger. He'd thought himself trapped and hadn't been able to get away. As he strode toward slumbering St. Anthony, Troy appreciated what he'd left behind.

He had one chance.

He had it all planned. He'd MindBend her, disarm her, and finish the mission. His gift would mean that he'd be able to anticipate her, even read her mind. Troy would do whatever he had to do, and not regret it one bit.

He wasn't going back to Xanto.

The gift that had gotten him off this planet would save his butt now.

When Troy reached the perimeter of St. Anthony, he was glad to be unobserved. The sight of the familiar jolted him with emotions he didn't need to feel and he fought to be impassive again. But the Grand Hotel was just the way he remembered. MacEnroe's Pub & Eatery where Ruby used to give him extra fries. Old man Wilcox's garage, where he'd left his beloved Harley. His parents' graves were in the cemetery behind the church on the far side of town. He remembered those funerals all too well. He'd gone to school over to the left and turned, haunted by happier memories. He'd ridden his bike down that trail and out to the badlands.

Hunting dragons.

Some things didn't change.

Home was home, even if he couldn't stay.

Troy felt the hairline crack in the surface of his heart like a wound and set his jaw. It was all part of the game. They were deliberately messing with him, trying to undermine his abilities with sentiment.

The gamblers of Xanto weren't counting on Troy's desire to survive.

He would win.

"I WON'T DO IT," DRAKINA insisted, folding her arms across her chest. She was in the royal audience chamber of Incendium's main palace, confronting her parents yet again. The chamber was large and luxuriously appointed, even the walls touched with gilding. The floor was a mosaic pattern that was actually a puzzle, made of inlaid stone from every territory governed by the monarchy of Incendium. The power and expanse of her father's domain was evident in every detail of his palace and, as leader of one of the most advanced societies in the galaxy, the claw of the King of Imperium reached far across the universe.

His influence within his family, however, was often challenged.

Usually by his oldest daughter, Drakina.

Drakina stood tall before her father, undaunted by his glower of disapproval. Her eleven sisters hovered behind her, watching avidly.

Twenty-two royal advisors and astrologers hovered around the perimeter of the room, also observing, but they were more wary of the king's wrath than his brood of daughters. There were already sparks in the air, leaping between father and daughter.

"I won't," Drakina repeated. Sparks shot from the tips of her long red hair, circling the pair like brilliant butterflies before they fell to the floor and blackened to ash.

"Of course, you will," Ouros countered. Drakina's father was regal and commanding, but he had been king of the realm for five centuries. Getting his own way had become a habit.

It was also Drakina's habit. Oldest of the brood, she was the most stubborn.

"It's your destiny, dear," her mother said, her tone soothing. "You can't escape a prophecy."

"That's what you said the last time," Drakina replied tartly. "It's your own fault I don't believe it now."

Her mother shifted shape in her agitation and fluttered at the reminder of the fiasco. In her dragon form, Ignita was a thousand hues of mauve and pale blue, as ethereal as a morning mist. She liked to disguise her will of iron behind her feminine wiles. "There was no need to create a diplomatic incident," she said.

"I tried saying no," Drakina replied. "That didn't work."

Her mother's expression became exasperated. "Well, we had signed the betrothal agreement."

"You should have asked me first."

"You are a royal princess!" her mother cried. "No one asks royal princesses who they wish to marry."

"They should," one of Drakina's sisters whispered. It was impossible to tell which one, but Drakina would have bet it was Gemma.

She'd been quiet since her betrothal to Prince Urbanus of Regalia had been announced. Drakina would have bet that her sister was planning something. Revenge? Rebellion? With Gemma it was always hard to guess.

Their father heard the words. Drakina could tell by the way his eyes narrowed.

"Did you ask me first before you responded?" He glowered at his disobedient daughter, clearly seeing that she was sowing dissent in the ranks. Drakina could see that he, too, was on the cusp of shifting. Her father changed shape to ensure that he got his way. She bounced a little on her toes, ready to go one-to-one over this and more sparks took flight from her hair. "No one says that destiny is always easy, Drakina," he said, as if trying to make peace. She wasn't fooled. He didn't believe in doing anything against his own will, either.

"You must have needed that humiliation," her mother argued. "There must have been a point."

Her mother had been talking to the astrologers again, it was clear.

"Obviously, she's much more humble," her youngest sister Peri whispered behind her. Peri was the mischievous one and the pretty one.

The other sisters giggled and jostled for a better view.

The results of Drakina's defiance were often spectacular.

Their father's nostrils flared and a small puff of smoke emanated from one of them. "Drakina did not learn from the experience, because she was too impatient!" he declared. "Too impetuous."

"Too hungry," added a sister. Again the words came from their ranks but couldn't be readily attributed to any of them. Flammara, Drakina thought. The outspoken one.

Ouros seethed that the defiance was spreading.

"I don't want anything to do with destiny," Drakina argued. "I just want to choose for myself."

"Then think of this as a way to achieve that," her father countered. He sounded reasonable but his eyes were glittering. "Do this for the kingdom, then you can do whatever you want." He held up a finger. "One concession and your life will be yours."

Drakina regarded her father with suspicion. Ouros did have a reputation as a slippery negotiator. "How exactly would that work?" she demanded, hearing all the skepticism of a wyvern much younger than herself in her own tone.

Her father smiled, showing a vast collection of teeth. He was doing that annoying thing again, the one that really irked Drakina, of hovering on the cusp of change. If she looked at him with one eye, he was in his human form. With the other, she could see his majestic dragon form, all imperial blue and gold. With both eyes open, the view was troubling. Many people agreed to whatever he requested when he did this, just to make him stop.

"This could be the last errand you do for me and for the kingdom," he said smoothly, sounding like the voice of reason. "Do this and I will never ask another thing of you."

"I don't believe it. You're exiling me. It's punishment."

Her father's eyes flashed and the dragon was briefly ascendant. He remained in human form with an obvious effort. His gaze bored into hers and she felt the weight of his will. "I swear it to you, daughter of mine."

Drakina averted her gaze. "Even if that's true, it's a lot to ask. It's not easy to bear a dragon shifter."

"Your father requests no more than what is natural," her mother countered. "I had twelve children for the sake of the kingdom. Why can't you bear just one?"

"For the sake of your kind," her father added.

"To ensure the future of all you love," her mother urged.

"To defend your home," her father added, his voice booming.

Drakina hesitated.

"What if she doesn't do it?" Callida dared to ask. She always had to know the details.

Their father flung out his arms and shifted shape, his dragon form filling the chamber. His minions flinched, cowering against the walls in anticipation of his wrath. "Then all will be lost!" he roared, sending a plume of fire at the ceiling. The architect looked worried. "Destiny will be denied, doom will befall us, and the once magnificent Kingdom of Incendium will crumble to dust!"

"As long as the prospects aren't too dire," Drakina said, unable to deny herself the opportunity to provoke her father.

He glared at her and exhaled a stream of smoke. A chef hastened forward, obviously hoping to calm the monarch by offering a gilded tray with some confection displayed upon it. "Would you care to sample the roast cervus from Sylvawyld, my lord?"

Ouros turned upon the chef, who quivered on the spot, then the king's nostrils flared. His gaze brightened. He bent with utmost delicacy and plucked the haunch from the platter, sniffing appreciatively. He devoured it in one bite and gave the chef a gleaming smile. "Excellent," he purred. "Most excellent. You changed the spice blend. It's much better."

"Thank you, Majesty." The chef bowed and backed away from those impressive teeth. "I live to please you, Majesty."

The exchange had given Drakina time to think without being under the pressure of her father's will. When he eyed her again, she had her compromise ready. "I won't marry him," she insisted and her father chuckled that he had won the encounter.

He shifted shape, becoming the benign patriarch again. He was always so smug when he won. It made her want to bite something.

Or someone.

Preferably a crown prince from Regalia.

"You don't have to," Ouros ceded amiably. "Just take his seed and conceive the boy."

"I can just take it?" Drakina asked with new hope. "Does it matter if he survives?"

Her mother put a hand on her husband's arm and stepped forward. "Of course, it does, my dear. You must seduce him and let him survive, but then you can abandon him. This is romance, after all."

Drakina's suspicion rose. They were making this too easy. "Shouldn't he be my official Consort, if he's the father of the heir?"

"He doesn't need to know," her father said, dismissing the very idea.

"He's Terran," her mother whispered, which explained Ouros' attitude.

His prejudices were at work. If Destiny had twined Drakina's path with a Terran, her father wouldn't want a specimen of such an inferior species to have an official role in his court. For once, her father's attitudes were a relief.

"He's a means to an end, no more than that. We cannot evade that he is the Carrier of the Seed, but there is no need to celebrate such a truth."

For once, Drakina felt that her father's objectives and her own might dovetail nicely. Bearing one son and evading responsibility forever sounded like a good deal. She didn't really want a Consort either.

Ouros beckoned to his viceroy who turned one wall into a glowing display with a gesture. "Kraw? Could you tell Drakina more, please?"

"With greatest pleasure, Majesty." The viceroy bowed deeply to each of the royal family, which took sufficient time that Drakina found her toe tapping. Kraw must have caught a whiff of her impatience for he spoke more quickly.

Those servants who survived a long tenure in a royal household of dragon shifters tended to be those who were alert to changes of mood in their lords and ladies.

"This is the planet Earth." The display showed a blue and green planet. Drakina knew little of the place beyond her father's disdain for its occupants. At Kraw's gesture, the view closed in on a land mass. Magnification revealed an open expanse that looked quite inviting. "And here is where you will find the Carrier, in a wilderness of sorts."

Ouros made a rumble of approval. "Good for courting," he said, taking Ignita's hand in his own. She smiled at him, as they clearly recalled their own courting days.

"Is it warm?" Drakina asked, admiring the amount of room.

"Seasonally so, Highness. You will find the climate similar to the plains of Aequor, particularly at this time of year. Moderate in the days compared to our hotter zones, and cool in the evenings. It is cold in winter, but you will have departed by then."

"How soon will that be?" Drakina was drawn closer out of her infernal curiosity.

Kraw gestured to an astrologer who cleared his throat. "Currently, this hemisphere of Terra has passed the midpoint of its hottest season," the astrologer began. Drakina remembered him as one inclined to be long-winded. "Of course, their solar days and hours are of different duration than ours, due to the relative size of their sun and the diameter of Terra's orbit around that sun..."

Kraw interrupted the lecture. "If you would be so kind as to consult your assistant, Highness, I have taken the liberty of loading it with time and language converters for Terra."

"Thank you, Kraw." Drakina didn't comment that her father must have been very certain he'd get his way. She lifted the square film and tapped in her query, the conversion instantaneous and satisfactory.

"You will, of course, take an entourage to see to your comfort, and a troop of bodyguards," Ouros began.

"No," Drakina said firmly. "I go alone or not at all."

A flutter passed through the court and the astrologers took a step back.

Her father glared at her once more. "I will not see my oldest daughter imperiled..."

"I am a dragon shifter, Father. I can take care of myself."

Their gazes locked in a battle of wills once more, then Kraw cleared his throat. "If I may be so bold, Majesty, there is wisdom in the princess' suggestion. The occupants of this Earth are all of the standard biped form and size, so she will be able to ensure her own protection in her dragon form. Also, this planet is not sufficiently advanced to be shown any indication of life elsewhere in the galaxy, by interstellar law, so she would draw less attention alone."

Ouros harrumphed but conceded the point.

Drakina began to feel a prickle of excitement. An adventure alone. A seduction on a distant planet. An assignment that would see her freed from the weight of her father's claw. It couldn't get any better.

There had to be a catch.

"And this is Troy," Kraw announced with pride. "The Carrier of the Seed."

Drakina looked up with anticipation and barely managed to keep from grimacing.

There was a moment of silence in the audience chamber.

"Are you sure?" Splendea asked in a horrified whisper.

"I'm not sure that genetic stock should be perpetuated," whispered Percipia.

"He might be your HeartKeeper," Peri teased and they laughed as one.

Drakina was already fighting her revulsion and wasn't even in the Carrier's presence yet. She studied the display, unable to explain why he was her destined mate. He must have been chosen to carry the seed for a reason, but she couldn't discern what it was. He was a biped, as Kraw had indicated, with the usual pairs of appendages. She checked his proportions and knew they would couple readily enough. He was muscled and fit, not unappealing in that way, but his face was enough to make her wince.

He had to be one of the ugliest creatures she'd ever seen, even for an inferior species. His brows were low and dark, his jaw was huge with a fierce underbite, and his eyes were small and glittering.

"Ewww," said Peri, perfectly expressing Drakina's own reaction.

"Don't keep him, Drakina," advised Flammara, the second youngest of the princesses. Drakina had no intention of doing so.

Maybe his appearance would make it easier to just use him for her own purposes and discard him.

She couldn't care for someone who looked like that.

She would have to close her eyes for the union.

If not the courtship.

No, there would be no courtship. It would be a quick seduction.

Very quick.

"Your father said she doesn't have to keep him," their mother reminded them.

Ouros lifted his hand in his most majestic manner, and the princesses almost groaned aloud at this sign that he would tell a story. "Kraw has discovered a tale told by Terrans of one Helen of Troy. He must be named for her." Ouros beamed at his daughters. He loved stories from primitive cultures.

"What was her story, Papa?" Peri asked, no doubt because someone was expected to do so.

Ouros beamed at his youngest daughter. "Her beauty was such that when she was seized from her betrothed by his rival, a thousand ships were launched to retrieve her."

"I can see why we're sending only one," Drakina countered and her sisters giggled.

"He looks as dumb as a rock," Flammara said.

"Well, he is Terran," Peri reminded them. "They don't even do space travel."

"No colonies at all," Ouros confirmed with a shake of his head. "They haven't settled their own moon and it's quite close."

The astrologer provided a measurement that incited pity in all those present.

"Quite backward, I'm afraid," Ignita said with a flutter. "But you won't have to stay long, dear. Just get the Seed."

"And don't rouse any suspicion," Kraw added.

"Maybe this will be easy, Drakina," said Thalina, the sister most inclined to be sympathetic. "Maybe you'll be home again and pregnant in no time."

Maybe.

Drakina considered the image of the Carrier and wondered whether she could do this feat for her kind.

Then she saw the resolve in her father's eye and knew that she had to succeed.

How long could it take?

"I'll do it," she said. Her father's smile of satisfaction gave her a moment's doubt, as if she didn't quite have all the facts.

But her father wouldn't confess more than he had.

More importantly, Drakina had given her word, and she'd keep it.

To Terra, she would go, as soon as possible. The egg ripened within her and the time for conception was close.

The sooner she embarked on the journey, the sooner it would be done.

CHAPTER ONE

DRAKINA TELEPORTED AFTER her mate, impatient to have her quest completed. She'd done her research on the planet Terra and added more local languages to her interpretor. Kraw had only loaded Mandarin but Drakina had found more possibilities. She'd rather have too much information than too little.

Kraw wouldn't be the one facing trouble if Drakina arrived unprepared.

The planet circled a distant sun, rotating as it did so, which resulted in a familiar suite of time divisions, which the Terrans called "day," "night," and "year"' The actual amount of time differed from Incendium, and Kraw's choice of conversion engine for relative time was excellent. Even having been warned of the scientific backwardness, Drakina had been shocked by her research. It would not be unlike a visit to Sylvawyld, the planet in their system that the kings of Incendium chose to keep unspoiled, to better preserve the hunting.

Drakina was further surprised that Terrans did not acknowledge the existence of shape shifters, although many of their cultures told stories of them. They called these myths and folk tales. It was most curious to tell stories of beings then deny their existence, if not delusional, but there was no accounting for regional differences. She simply had to accommodate them.

Terrans also did not believe that dragons were real. There was a startling fact. In fact, it was a kind of a joke with them, for they wrote "Here Be Dragons" on their maps in the unknown and unexplored corners of the world. Their language was filled with references to dragons, although they denied the existence of such a superior culture. Drakina found this completely irrational.

Her destined mate was Terran so clearly he could not be the Carrier because of his intellect.

She already knew it wasn't because of his appearance.

That he should be the Carrier of the Seed was a puzzle. What genetic benefit would he bring to their union? Perhaps he was particularly robust.

Perhaps she should not quibble with destiny and simply complete what had to be done with all haste. The prospect of being free of her father's dictates was more than enough incentive.

She used Kraw's coordinates and her teleport dropped her into an open area outside a settlement. To any Terran observer, she would have suddenly appeared behind a cluster of rocks. Of course, there were no observers. She'd checked. Beside the rocks was a spiked being of the slower metabolic type that Terrans called "plants." She greeted it using the galactic protocol but it didn't reply.

There was no sign, in fact, that it was aware of her or her greeting.

Was it rude, shy, or stupid? There was no way to know.

Drakina hoped her mate was a better communicator.

She hoped she was home very soon.

Drakina was in her human form, an obvious choice as a result of her research, and wore something called a "dress" with "sandals." It was shocking to her to wear a garment that left her legs exposed below the knee, but evidently this kind of lewd display was considered normal by Terrans. Drakina would have preferred to have exposed her breasts, but evidently that would have drawn attention in this curious place. Only a mate should see the thighs of a Wyvern princess, unless she chose to shift to her dragon form.

Drakina couldn't let her discomfort affect her hunt. It certainly encouraged her to hurry and have the mating behind her. She felt bold and provocative, like one of the sirens of Incendium's marketplace, and was glad her father couldn't see her like this.

Perhaps the Carrier would find the view enticing.

Drakina inhaled deeply and caught the trace of the Carrier's scent. Yes, she could smell the Seed within him. It almost beckoned to her, as if it knew its fate—as the Carrier might not.

Drakina did not care about his views. She emerged from behind the rocks and strode toward the lights of a town. His scent emanated from there. Darkness was falling and she heard night creatures on all sides. A sound emitted from the settlement, a rhythmic sound with a steady beat. It wasn't a style of music that was familiar to her, but it wasn't unpleasant. In fact, it made her want to move in rhythm with it. The music became louder as she approached the town, and she heard laughter as well. Perhaps some festivity was being celebrated.

Perhaps there would be food.

There was nothing like a teleport to make Drakina hungry.

Well, except sex. The princesses of Incendium were renowned for their appetites, after all.

After her journey, Drakina was hungry enough to eat an entire cervus, if not two. The prospect of food and sex, not necessarily in that order, quickened her steps, and made her wish she could have just shifted and flown to town.

But she could not challenge Terran assumptions. It would be irresponsible to do as much, and a violation of galactic code, on such a primitive planet as this. Sadly, restraint was not the strongest of Drakina's talents.

Surely she could keep a low profile long enough to seduce the Carrier.

Drakina followed his scent, moving with such purpose that she did draw attention. Few residents of St. Anthony had ever seen a beautiful woman stride out of the desert in high heels, much less one charging toward the bar in the Grand Hotel. If Drakina had realized how many people were watching her with curiosity, she would not have cared.

The Carrier was her target and the claiming of the Seed her goal.

THERE WAS A BAND PLAYING in the bar at the Grand Hotel on Friday night and the place was comparatively busy. Troy was glad that he didn't know anyone—they wouldn't have recognized him, but he might have tripped up. The crowd was young, maybe even the children of the people he'd gone to school with, and that simplified the challenge a lot.

The lights were turned down and the music was loud. Locals crowded into the bar, buying drinks and greeting old friends. It seemed that many were celebrating the success of the recent meteor festival, which had been the biggest yet.

Troy had bought some clothes at the emporium earlier in the day. He'd visited Old Man Wilcox and bought his beloved Harley back as if he were a stranger. To Old Man Wilcox's credit, he hadn't wanted to part with the bike and insisted the rightful owner might come back.

His loyalty struck Troy in the heart.

So did the care the older man had lavished on the bike.

Finally, they struck a deal. Troy had pretended to ride out of town, but had circled back and parked the bike behind the hotel, then taken a room. It felt wrong to deceive the old man, but the truth wouldn't have been believed.

He wouldn't have believed it, if he hadn't lived it.

The mood in the bar was familiar and welcoming, enough to make Troy relax just a little. He'd missed the society of others, especially in solitary confinement, and though he was wary of relaxing too much too soon, there was something beguiling about the familiarity of this place. He watched the townspeople enjoying themselves, oblivious to other matters in the universe.

But then, that was how it should be, by galactic law.

A part of him wished that he was still as innocent, and he felt resentment that he should have been snatched away, against his will, and his life changed forever. He'd been pretty much alone even before his arrest, given the jobs he'd been given.

Troy wasn't going to indulge in regrets, though. Not now. The band was in the middle of a popular song, the crowd on their feet, dancing and singing along when a woman opened the door to the bar.

Drakina.

She couldn't have been anyone else.

When Troy had first seen Drakina's hologram, he'd been sure she was the most gorgeous woman in the galaxy. He'd assumed the hologram had been tricked up a bit, to make her look more beautiful than she was. The truth was that real life put any representation to shame. Not only was she beautiful, but she moved like a goddess. There was fire in her eyes that no representation could capture. The sight of her stole his breath away and sent a wave of astonishment through the bar.

Troy wasn't the only one who stared.

She was tall, almost as tall as him, and tanned. Her figure was slender and athletic, but there was nothing boyish about the look of her. Her breasts were lushly curved, and her waist was slim. Her hair was long and dark red, hanging past her hips in thick waves. Her eyes tilted up at the outer corners, giving her an exotic air, and her lips were full and red.

She wore a green dress that clung to her curves then fluttered at the hem, making her look gloriously feminine and sexy. Her sandals were strappy with heels that arched her feet high. There was sand on them and he wondered how far she'd walked in them. He felt the vitality emanating from her and knew there was little that would stop her.

Her eyes glittered with intelligence and he sensed the dragon restrained within her. When her gaze locked with his, it seemed particularly foolish to have a plan to deceive her much less any expectation of surviving that feat. Troy's heart skipped more than one beat.

Her beauty widened that crack in the stone of Troy's heart and sent hot blood rushing through him. He *had* been in solitary confinement for what seemed like half an eternity.

How long since he had been with a woman?

How long since he had been with a beautiful woman?

But then, he was making assumptions. Her beauty might make it impossible for him to get her alone. Would she be repulsed by the look of him? The High Priestess of Nimue had certainly increased the challenge, but he refused to be daunted.

Troy strode toward Drakina with purpose, as if there could be no doubt that she belonged with him. He halfway thought she would flinch, or turn aside, maybe run, but he'd underestimated this dragon princess.

Drakina surveyed him and smiled.

In fact, her eyes lit with fire, a sight that sent a thrill through him to his toes.

Maybe her demise could be delayed a little bit.

DRAKINA SPOTTED HER PREY immediately, leaning against the bar, watching the door.

She had the odd sense that the Carrier had been waiting for her, that maybe there was a flicker of recognition in his eyes, but that made so little sense that she dismissed the notion.

The fact was that her destined mate was far uglier than she could have believed. She shuddered at the sight of him and her determination quailed.

The hologram had been flattering.

But then the Carrier stepped toward her with such confidence that she was surprised. He clearly believed that she should find him interesting, though he was the least attractive man in the bar, and he strode toward her with such verve and grace that Drakina *did* find him intriguing.

How often did she, a dragon shifter, meet a man who approached her with confidence? Was he fearless or a fool? Of course, the Carrier was unaware of her abilities, but she had to wonder whether the knowledge would have mattered. He strode toward her as if it were unthinkable that she should consider another.

Or as if he intended to ensure that she didn't.

Drakina liked that.

He moved like a warrior, all lithe grace and power. She liked that, too. Drakina watched him with rising anticipation, knowing that a man so in command of his body would be a memorable lover.

This mating might not be so bad.

The Carrier was taller than she was, at least in this form, his hair dark and his eyes even darker. His shoulders were broad, and he was muscled in a most pleasing way. There was a blue mark on his flesh, a tattoo on his forearm, and she liked that it was a dragon. Kismet. She considered the merit of claiming him in the midst of this place, but recalled that Terrans preferred to practice such intimacy in private. As much as she wanted to seduce him quickly, she knew it would be smarter to let him set the pace.

For the moment.

The Carrier paused before her and she smelled the warmth of his skin, the heat of the ripe seed within him. She could feel the air heating between them and heard him catch his breath. His pulse had increased its pace and his eyes had brightened.

So, he did find her alluring.

Drakina smiled. Sexual awareness needed no other language to reveal itself than the body's reactions. She was warm herself, tingling a little, ready for him.

He halted before her and offered his hand. "Dance?" he invited, his voice a low rumble that made Drakina want to purr.

Dance. Of course. A mating ritual in so many cultures and societies. Drakina cast a glance at the other couples and knew she could sway as they did. In fact, she loved to dance, particularly with a masterful partner.

Was he one?

"Thank you." When she put her hand in his, the Carrier's fingers closed over hers in a proprietary gesture that she found most satisfactory. His hand was warm, his skin a little rough. He worked with his hands then, either a warrior or an artisan, both of which were admirable and noble occupations to Drakina's thinking.

She found her resistance to him melting.

And that was before he swung her onto the dance floor and turned her expertly. Her skirt flared, baring her legs above her knees, and she felt wanton, daring, unleashed. She recalled the sirens of the market and knew that she couldn't let her uncertainty show. She *was* bold, maybe even wanton. No one would ever know what she had done on Terra except gather the Seed. The other Terrans stepped back, making space on the dance floor for them, and Drakina surrendered to the pleasure of dancing.

They moved together as if they had danced this way a thousand times. All the while, his attention was fixed upon her, his gaze filled with admiration. His fingers brushed her hip, her shoulder, her waist, his attention unwavering. He said nothing, but there was no need for words. The air between them almost crackled with awareness, and the heat was enough to bring salt to Drakina's lip. She felt powerful and beautiful, alluring.

And aroused.

He made her look good, twisting her, dipping her, spinning her, his eyes lighting when she laughed with pleasure. The best warriors danced with such power and skill, and Drakina's desire for him grew.

She could hear his heartbeat and felt her own match its pace.

She could hear his breathing, and felt her own match its rhythm.

She was lost in his admiration, and felt the inevitability of their union become stronger. It would be fast and hard.

Maybe they would couple twice, just to be sure the Seed was planted.

The Carrier's lips curved just a little in an appreciative smile as he watched her, and Drakina couldn't look away from his mouth. There was something endearing about that smile, something that warmed her reaction considerably. He found her attractive. He was confident. His smile was sexy, perhaps because it was his best feature, perhaps because it seemed intimate, shared only with her. It seemed that all the rest of the occupants of the place disappeared.

There was only the Carrier and his alluring little smile.

She found herself studying his mouth, so fine and firm, so enticing. It was odd, because the hologram made it look as if he had an underbite, a most unattractive and bestial look, but there wasn't a thing wrong with his mouth. It was perfect, in fact. She couldn't wait to find out how he might kiss.

The music changed again, the fourth or fifth tune they'd danced, yet the Carrier showed no signs of tiring.

Much less of leaving the floor.

The other Terrans watched them, some applauding, yet Drakina wondered how she might hasten his mating ritual.

Subtlety wasn't one of her strengths, so she had no qualms about making her desires known.

TROY AND DRAKINA DANCED. Fast and slow, close and far. He swung her and dipped her, he waltzed with her and he rhumba'd with her. She matched him step for step, never out of breath, never flagging. She seemed to anticipate his every move, and they could have always danced together. It was exhilarating—and exciting. Magical.

It made him remember what it was like to be in love.

Not that love had anything to do with this quest. No. He would do what had to be done, and he would survive.

Troy was simply charming her.

Winning her trust.

Although that sounded like an excuse even to himself.

The amazing thing was that he wasn't MindBending her. Not at all. Her reaction was genuine, and that astonished him. He wanted to savor it. He wanted to make this moment last.

It couldn't hurt to dance to one more song.

The blush in her cheek, the touch of her breasts, the weight of her hand in his, the throaty sound of her laughter all combined to convince Troy that Drakina was the most gorgeous woman he'd ever known. When the tune changed to a slow dance, Troy was glad. He wanted her close, pressed against him.

He placed his hand on the back of Drakina's waist and drew her near.

Their bodies bumped and he realized how well they would fit together, the touch of her breasts and hips sending new fire through him. She watched him and her smile broadened, doubtless because she felt his erection.

Then she wrapped her arm around his waist and pulled him even closer, rolling her hips once against him in a clear demand.

And he'd expected a crown princess to be demure.

She looked up at him again and he was snared. She had the most remarkable green eyes. The irises seemed to glitter, as if made of faceted glass. She dropped her gaze to survey him, which made her look sultry.

Her coy smile sent fire through his blood.

"You are aroused," she murmured and he liked how low and lazy her voice was. Her words were melodic, almost as if she purred a song to him. She leaned into his embrace and touched her lips to the side of his neck. Troy could have sworn that the light kiss launched fireworks under his skin.

"I'm only human," he said, though that wasn't quite the truth.

She laughed. "I smell your excitement," she whispered and he closed his arms more tightly around her. "It is enticing for a woman to know that a man desires her."

It had been so long since he'd been with a woman—solitary confinement did have that drawback—and he'd forgotten how powerful a woman's touch could be.

"How could I not?" he murmured and her green eyes sparkled. "I've never danced with such a beautiful woman."

"Do you feel lucky then?"

"Of course." Troy held her a little tighter and she arched her back, driving those breasts against him. He wondered for a moment who was being charmed. "What's your name?"

Drakina laughed a little, then he felt her tongue on his throat. "It doesn't matter," she whispered, her breath fanning his ear and making him shiver with anticipation. All he could think about was Drakina, her curves, her touch, her voice. Her fingers were in his hair, her hand firm against the back of his waist, her lips on his ear. "Tell me," she murmured. "How do you make love to a woman?"

They danced, turning tight circles on the floor, lost in each other.

"Slowly," he said, then swallowed. "Thoroughly." He bent and nuzzled her neck, kissing her beneath her ear. She gasped and rubbed herself against his chest. The feel of her was driving every thought from his mind.

Except one.

It occurred to Troy that seducing her would be a way to win her trust. To disarm her. To make her vulnerable.

He knew it was a rationalization. He couldn't have stepped away from her in this moment to save his life.

And wouldn't. Not yet.

"Never fast?" she whispered, mischief in her tone. She pulled back to look into his eyes and pouted, her expression playful. "I like when a man loses control," she admitted in a husky voice and Troy couldn't quite catch his breath. "I like when desire takes command." Drakina watched her hands as she spread her fingers flat and eased her palms over his chest. Her lips were parted, and Troy could only think about kissing her.

Slowly and thoroughly.

The second time, he'd take her fast and hard.

Drakina's right hand lingered over his heartbeat, her smile knowing as it raced. "I like when my lover can't hold back his desire," she confessed in a husky whisper. Her eyes shone at the possibility and Troy wanted to be that lover. "I like when he's driven to a frenzy." Her voice dropped lower. "I like when his passion is consuming." She gripped his shoulders then and stretched to her toes, locking those ruby red lips over his.

Her kiss was sweet and hot, honey and fire, temptation and seduction and more than he could bear. Troy's mind went white.

His heart thundered.

Then he caught her closer, lifting her in his arms so that she was on the tips of her toes. He slanted his mouth over hers and met the passion of her kiss. Drakina framed his head in her hands with a growl of satisfaction and he took a couple of steps backward as their kiss turned incendiary. She crushed him against the bar with her body, wrapped one leg around his and kissed him as if she'd suck him dry.

Troy found his own mind being bent.

Drakina's hands were in his hair and she held him captive to her kiss, but even better, she seemed to be unable to get enough of him. She used her tongue, her teeth, her lips, as if she would feast upon him. Maybe devour him whole. Troy couldn't think of a better way to go, much less a way to slow things down.

Then he jumped when the bartender tapped him on the shoulder.

Hard.

"Family place," the bartender chided. Troy blinked at him, not really understanding the words. He couldn't understand anything with Drakina's lush mouth grazing his throat. The bartender offered Troy a key.

His room key. Troy blinked and looked around, realizing that most of the other people in the bar were watching him and Drakina with both surprise and interest.

How could he have forgotten himself?

"Thanks. Yeah." Troy took the key and smiled at Drakina. Her eyes were dark, her intensity enough to make him consider the merits of hard and fast. "Maybe a little privacy?" he suggested.

Her smile broadened, and her expression seemed triumphant to him, as if she'd been planning their departure ever since she'd arrived.

But no, *he* was the MindBender.

She just liked it fast.

She wanted it now.

She was used to getting whatever she wanted.

In this moment, he didn't have any desire to refuse her.

Drakina brushed her lips over his, dismissing his thoughts. "If it's close," she murmured, running a proprietary hand down his chest. "I want you now," she whispered.

And then what? Troy had no doubt that he'd sleep, just a little, in the aftermath and might miss his chance to fulfill his quest. She might leave. Why was she even here? The gamblers must have arranged it somehow...

He had to think clearly. Being alone with Drakina was a good thing. Being intimate with Drakina was impossible to resist. But he'd have to slow things down. He'd have to MindBend her, slide his notions into her thoughts, and continue the seduction his way. Take control.

It was risky, to MindBend an amorous dragon shifter in the proverbial heat of the moment, but Troy wasn't the best MindBender in the galaxy for nothing.

Maybe he'd find something in her thoughts that would make it easy to assassinate her. Dragon shifters couldn't be innocent, after all. There was some reason that the gamblers wanted her dead.

When he looked into her eyes, so drowsy with desire, Troy had a feeling he'd need every argument he could find in order to win this bet.

THE CARRIER LED DRAKINA to a chamber on the third floor of the hotel. It was a simple room, not very large, equipped with a bed and a large flat screen on one wall. Near the entrance were two doors, one that hid a closet and one that concealed a room for cleaning. At the far end of the chamber was a large glass window, which offered a view of the open expanse before the badlands. The room was on the back side of the hotel, and the window faced away from the town.

The acoustics were terrible and the insulation non-existent. She could hear the music almost as loudly as when they'd been near the band, and water flushed in a room down the hall. There was a distant clatter from the kitchen and the smell of fat frying. It made her stomach growl, but first things first.

Food was better *after* sex.

Slowly and thoroughly. Drakina had to rid his mind of that nonsense. Fast and hard. Against a wall. Consuming. Uninhibited. Passionate.

Incendiary. That was the way she liked sex.

That was the way she'd have the Carrier.

As a bonus, she could return home sooner.

She'd just have to over-rule his reservations.

She knew he'd like it her way once he tried it. Warriors always did prefer a quick conquest.

They were barely inside the room when she flung him onto the bed. He fell to his back on the mattress and she landed atop him, locking her hands around his head and feasting on that gorgeous mouth again. He made a little growl of protest, but Drakina made sure he was too busy to say much more. His body revealed that he liked her technique. She slanted her mouth over his and kissed him, using her tongue and her teeth to make him moan aloud. His hands trailed up the backs of her thighs, which made her shiver, then slipped under the hem of her dress and gripped her buttocks.

She felt his heartbeat skip, then accelerate. She smelled the arousal within him and knew she was making progress in driving him toward her goal. She straddled him, pressing him down into the bed. She felt the size of him, the readiness of him, and this time, she was the one who growled. He pulled her closer in silent demand.

This would be a mating to remember. He was huge and hard, which meant there was absolutely no cause for delay. Drakina slipped her hand between them and unfastened the front of his jeans. It was a complicated closure, to her thinking, with a button and some interlocking metal tracks, which seemed ill-advised for such a location. Again, she reasoned that there was no accounting for cultural differences. Maybe it was how they ensured slowly and thoroughly. Drakina sat up, tugged his pants over his hips and freed him.

She stared.

He was magnificent.

Perhaps *this* was why he was her destined mate.

Drakina caressed him with one hand and saw the first glimmer of the seed easing forth with her encouragement. Success was close! She rolled to one hip and tore off her own underwear, not bothering to remove anything else. She was slick and hot, ready for all he had to give. Troy tried to say something but she kissed him to silence. She moved to straddle him again and reached to coax his strength inside her.

She would take him in an inferno of passion. She would set his blood afire. She would show him how magnificent desire could be. Drakina was burning with need and ready to explode.

But the Carrier rolled her to her back in a smooth and powerful gesture that she could only admire for its grace and decisiveness. She smiled up at him, perfectly willing to be claimed in this posture, if only once. He lowered his weight between her thighs and she wrapped her legs around him, drawing him closer even as he bent to kiss her. His kiss was teasing and potent, and she could feel the hardness of him nudging against her.

She hooked one heel behind his tight butt to drive him home but he broke their kiss and evaded her. He trailed kisses along her jaw to her ear, a tingling path of fire, then nipped her earlobe. "Slowly and thoroughly," he whispered, as if it were a threat. Drakina had no chance to make sense of the words before he slid down the length of her.

He caressed her breasts with his hands, then opened the front fastening of her dress with his teeth. It felt so good, his strong rough hands on her skin, that she didn't stop him. He cast her a playful glance that almost made her giggle, then his mouth closed over her bare nipple.

He caught the peak between his teeth and flicked his tongue against it, making it harder, making her writhe with pleasure. She reveled in his touch and was glad that he showed no signs of relenting. She was gasping when he released the tight bud, and then he lavished the same attention on the other. Drakina thought she might explode. She reached for him, intending to pull him up and complete the union, but he caught her wrists in his hands and held them captive.

"Not so hasty, princess," he growled, his chest vibrating against her thighs.

Drakina was startled by his address, then wondered whether it was just a Terran endearment. He moved lower before she could ask, blew her skirt out of the way and bared her thighs to his view.

She was as wet as a harlot, to be sure. Drakina flushed crimson, but the Carrier simply lowered himself to grant her a most intimate kiss.

There?

She froze. She choked. She had never shared such an embrace but once he had begun, she didn't want him to stop.

It felt marvelous.

Her legs parted and she welcomed his tongue, his glorious mouth, and yes, even the graze of his teeth. What exquisite torment! This skill must be why he was her destined mate!

Drakina moaned and gripped his hands, twisting in satisfaction beneath his amorous assault. She had never felt so conflicted, so on fire, so desperate for more and so desirous of a moment lasting forever. She felt her heart pound harder, her breath catch, her passion grow. The Carrier was relentless, more expert a lover than any she'd taken before. Unlike other warriors, his focus was upon her pleasure instead of his own. And he understood her needs. He courted her reaction. He fed it and encouraged it, and teased her in ways that even she could not have named.

She felt his body respond to her arousal, which was most seductive.

Their pleasure was yoked together, giving her a new and wondrous sense of communion.

Drakina felt the tide rise, higher and faster than it ever had before. Her need doubled and redoubled. She wanted him inside her, but he defied her will and remained where he was.

Tormenting her with that glorious mouth.

She could not restrain herself when he grazed her gently with his teeth. Drakina screamed as the torrent broke. She locked her legs around the Carrier and thrashed as pleasure coursed through her body. She shook and then she trembled.

When she fell back on the bed, spent, she glimpsed his triumphant smile.

Yet before she had recovered, she reached for him. She hauled him alongside her and straddled him again, needing to see him satisfied as well. He was harder and larger than he had been, but she teased him with her fingertips, caressing him and tormenting him in return. He moaned. He writhed against the bed, but Drakina held him down.

"We have tried your way," she whispered. "Now mine." And she lowered herself atop him, welcoming his strength inside her. She felt him tremble deep inside and knew he could not bear the exquisite torment long. His heart was racing. His breath came quickly. His hands gripped her waist and his gaze burned into hers.

Drakina was ready again, roused by his touch more than she might have believed possible. She gripped his wrists as he had seized hers, locked her mouth over his, and began to move. She swallowed his moan, felt victory near...

Then a strange dream unfurled in Drakina's mind.

She was dancing with the Carrier again, in a dark and private chamber. She saw his knowing smile and felt her heart respond. She saw his hand, sliding over her shoulder. Slowly. Very slowly. Warm when it reached her bare skin. His hand was tanned and calloused, the hand of a man who worked, and it contrasted with the silken smoothness of her own pale skin. He was gentle, though, so gentle, that his touch kindled a spark deep inside her. A coal glimmered to life. A blaze was lit anew. He spun her in front of him as they moved in time to the music, admiring her, barely touching her, knowing how much she wanted him and letting her simmer.

Making her burn hotter.

Drakina felt her movements slow as she was seduced by the dream.
Slowly and thoroughly.
Her mouth went dry. How long could he endure? Could she leave him

without knowing for sure?

Drakina felt the warmth of his fingertips feather over her back, then his lips touch her skin so gently. A caress of a thousand butterflies. His finger traced little circles lightly over her flesh. Fingertips and lips working together to awaken every bit of her skin. To undermine her resistance. It was a seduction that made her ache for the next brush of his skin against hers.

He lifted the weight of her hair, ran his fingers through it, eased it over her shoulder, then his lips burned against her nape. She heard herself gasp. She felt her nipples bead. She arched her back and demanded more.

She halted her movements and sat up. The Carrier's eyes glittered as he watched her astride him. She bared her breasts, displaying herself to him, then rolled the nipples between her fingers and thumbs. She cast her head back, teasing him, and felt the power of his reaction.

"Slowly and thoroughly," he whispered and moved within her with a deliberation that left her yearning.

In her dream, he moved behind her and she swayed to the music, aware of his gaze upon her. He tugged down the fastener at the back of her dress, one tiny increment at a time. When it was loosed, he moved closer, his hands sliding beneath the garment, his arms around her, his hands cupping her breasts. Drakina heard herself moan as he rolled her nipples between finger and thumb, teasing them to peaks as he kissed the side of her neck. He was tormenting her, teasing her, making it last—and she was melting, powerless, snared by the spell he cast...

Drakina blinked as she realized the truth. This dream wasn't her own. It was *his*.

He had put his thoughts into her mind.

The Carrier was a MindBender!

What travesty was this?

CHAPTER TWO

DRAKINA ROARED WITH FURY as she recoiled from the Carrier's embrace.

Not just a Terran but a MindBender! Rage rolled through her and she reacted with lightning speed. In a heartbeat, she had shifted shape, her back slamming against the plaster of the ceiling and making it crumble.

She would have abandoned him, if he had not been the Carrier of the Seed.

She still needed him, though that realization just made her more angry.

Drakina snatched up the Carrier and swung her tail to break the large window. She leapt through the gap, heard an alarm sound, and took flight.

How *dare* he try to manipulate her thoughts?

"Hey, wait a minute," he began and Drakina wasn't interested in any plea for mercy. She was a crown princess of Incendium! No one dared to meddle in the minds of her kind.

She could have left him behind. She could have fried him in place and he would have deserved no less.

But Drakina didn't just need the seed. She preferred vengeance to be slow and deliberate.

He would pay.

She flew beyond the boundaries of the town, her wings pounding hard in her fury. Once they were in the desert, she hurled the Carrier at the ground with force. She didn't care what he broke when he fell. His audacity demanded punishment of the highest order. She breathed a plume of flames after him.

He hit the ground, then curled into a ball and rolled away, propelled by the wind of her breath and the torrent of fire. Drakina bellowed and burned him some more, pursuing him with fire and fury.

She smelled his clothes incinerating. She smelled his skin burning. She smelled his hair singeing. Yet his mental fingers were still in her mind, probing, seeking her secrets.

Trying to learn her secrets and shape her will.

It was outrageous!

Impertinent.

Unacceptable.

No mere Terran should intrude in the mind of a royal Wyvern.

"*Get!*" Drakina roared, then took another breath. "*Out!*" The ground trembled at the volume of her cry. She spewed fire hotter and brighter than any she had breathed before. "*Of my mind!*"

The Carrier loosed his grip upon her thoughts immediately, and she wondered whether he'd forgotten what he was doing. Maybe he had been overwhelmed in the heat of the moment, so to speak. She stopped breathing fire, though she glared at him as she hovered in the air and watched him. He had come to a halt against a wall of rock.

He looked a little bit less confident. Shaken, but he deserved as much in Drakina's view. He lifted his head and looked around warily, watching her as he held up one hand in a universal gesture requesting clemency.

"Easy now," he said, with surprising bravery.

Drakina snarled, loosing an array of sparks. "I understand why my cousins devour their mates after they've served their purpose."

"There's no need to be hasty," he said, his tone soothing. "Let's talk it through."

There was something to be said for a man who didn't turn and run when faced with a larger and stronger adversary. Drakina felt her admiration return.

Still, she spoke sternly. "Out loud, MindBender."

"Right." He stood up and a part of her was relieved that he wasn't badly injured. His chest was mostly exposed, with shreds of his shirt hanging around his waist. He did offer an enticing view. His hair was a little shorter than it had been and his skin on the back of his shoulders was a little bit red. As if he'd been sunburned.

But there was a dignity in the way he stood, and she had to admit that she was almost as vexed by his mistake as by the interruption of a passionate interlude of considerable promise. For a moment there, Drakina had forgotten that she was seducing him for king and planet.

And then she realized something. Terrans didn't believe in dragons or shape shifters — yet the Carrier, a Terran, was unsurprised by the form she had just taken.

Drakina breathed a plume of fire at his feet, compelling him to dance backward. "Who are you really?" she demanded, her tone as imperious as it could be.

"My name is Troy." He offered that crooked smile, and Drakina was appalled that it softened her anger so much. "You've already figured out that I'm a MindBender." His gaze roved over her. "I do like smart women."

Drakina caught her breath, trying to fortify her resistance to him. It was fading fast. "You had no right..."

"No, I didn't." He sounded contrite. "I'm sorry."

Drakina wasn't quite prepared to forgive him—even if she was tempted by his appearance and that wretched smile. She sat back on her haunches, waiting. Her kind could be patient beyond most other species.

She would wait for a better apology, at least.

The Carrier eyed her for a moment, then walked toward her, proud even in his vulnerability. Not many men would willingly walk toward an angry dragon, especially after that dragon had just tried to fry them alive.

Was he brave or stupid?

Not stupid. Anything but stupid. Drakina had to bet on brave.

A warrior. Her heart clenched at what a fitting father he would make for their son.

"It was an act of desperation. I just wanted the whole thing to last a little longer," the Carrier said, that smile making it hard to hold such a desire against him. "It was so amazing."

"It was," she felt compelled to admit.

"*You* are amazing. I knew there was something different about you." He looked at her wings, her tail, her splendid scales, her trailing feathers and his admiration was clear. She fought the urge to preen and reminded herself that he should have been shocked by the sight of her. "You are *really* something."

"And how many other dragon shifters have you known, Terran?" she asked, her voice low with threat.

"None."

"Yet you were unsurprised by my abilities."

That smile broadened. "But you already know why, princess." His eyes shone with confidence and she knew the choice of endearment hadn't been an accident. "You caught me in your thoughts, but that was the *second* time I peeked."

If he had bent her mind without her detecting it, then he was highly skilled. Despite the insult, Drakina regarded the Carrier with new respect.

Was this the trait that he was to give to their son? A dragon shifter and MindBender might make a very potent crown prince.

And a successful king.

"In fact, that gives us something in common," he continued easily. "We both have secrets." He heaved a sigh. "Imagine finding the one person you can trust who knows your secret. That's where we are."

She supposed it might be an appealing notion for some, but everyone in her life knew what she was.

"We have desire in common," Drakina said flatly. "That is enough for this encounter, or it might have been if you had kept your thoughts to yourself."

"I think we should talk about this," he continued, his manner so assured that he might have believed the discussion inevitable. "Why can't there be more than one encounter? What if there's a future for us?"

Drakina laughed. She couldn't help it.

The Carrier didn't look insulted. No, he gave her a look that was so stubborn that if he had been more handsome, she might have been reminded of the sons of royal blood of her acquaintance. "You want me," he said, reminding her of the truth. "I want you. Let's talk first."

It was a telling reminder. Drakina *needed* him, and his seed.

"You will not surrender to me without a discussion first?"

"Nope." He grinned, confident that she would cede to him.

His cockiness was entirely undeserved. Drakina knew she could seduce him, even against his own will, because the attraction between them was strong.

Still, it might be a bad portent for a crown prince to be conceived against the Carrier's will.

And a conversation was a comparatively small concession.

It wouldn't take much time.

She might convince him to surrender in a blaze of passion yet.

"Stay out of my mind," Drakina stipulated. "Because next time, I won't stop."

"Promise not to roast me if I do stay out of your mind," the Carrier countered and offered his hand. He was so intrepid that she admired him even more.

His was a charming Terran gesture, although Drakina hadn't recognized its appeal when she'd read about it in her research. His move, in silence, conveyed the notion of compromise, a concept not particularly dear to Drakina but which might be useful in pursuit of her quest. On the other hand, her word was her bond, and if she pledged this to him, she would keep that vow at any cost.

She considered his hand for only a moment before she shifted shape, assuming her woman form again. Her dress was still unfastened at the front but she couldn't have cared less. She felt the leap of Troy's pulse at the glimpse of her breasts, though, and knew he was very aware of her physically.

That could only help in achieving her goal.

In fact, their conversation might be very short. She chose to leave her dress open to aid in that and stepped closer to put her hand in his. "I am Drakina." She put her hand in his and they shook hands. She liked the feel of his warm fingers gripping hers.

"How do you do that?" he asked with real curiosity.

"Do what?" She couldn't explain to him how she shifted shape. It was an innate power, but one that required considerable training to master effectively.

"Be naked as a dragon, then still have your dress in human form."

"Initiate's secret," Drakina said mysteriously, having no intention of giving him any power over her. Her gaze trailed to his lips and she hoped they might seal the bargain with a kiss. That was another Terran tradition, and a very appealing one.

The Carrier smiled as if he knew her inclination and began to lean closer.

Drakina glared at him and he lifted his hand in surrender.

"It was in your eyes," he protested. "I didn't need to look in your mind."

So, he was perceptive. Drakina considered herself warned. His kiss this time was fleeting, a tease and maybe a promise.

Or maybe a way to keep his desire reined in.

He quickly released her hand and stepped back, and she saw the evidence that he was not unmoved by their quick embrace. He pushed one hand through his hair. "Look, there's an all-night diner in town. How about something to eat?"

It appeared that he didn't need to be a MindBender to anticipate her needs.

He kept talking, as if to convince her. "I can go back to the room and get your panties as well as a new shirt, then meet you downstairs."

"You cannot escape me," she reminded him with quiet force. "I trailed you across the cosmos by scent."

"Kismet?" he asked, his tone teasing.

"Of course." Drakina touched the tattoo on his forearm.

He smiled at her so that her heart leapt. His eyes twinkled in a way that made them look less small and beady. "What makes you think I want to get away, princess?" His confidence was enticing indeed, and Drakina found herself smiling back at him.

Then she watched avidly as he strode back to the hotel, purpose in his every move.

Yes, her Carrier was a very tasty specimen, even if he was a MindBender. Drakina found herself looking forward to both the fortification of food and the consummation of their fated partnership.

She might even regret leaving him behind.

IT WAS MORE THAN A SHIRT Troy needed. He had to be sure that no one had noticed Drakina's spectacular departure from the hotel, or there'd be more questions than either of them could answer.

To his relief, there was only a pair of kids from the kitchen standing in the alley behind the hotel, along with a police officer, amidst the broken glass of the window. He didn't have time to think of a very good story—he walked in his sleep, broke through the window, stumbled down the fire escape and then ran—but his MindBending abilities came to the rescue. Only one kid had seen Drakina in dragon form and it was pretty easy to convince him that he'd been imagining things. There were no dragons, after all. Troy said he'd pay for the window, which satisfied the cop, then he saw Drakina strolling into view.

All three of his companions turned to stare.

And no wonder. She was gorgeous. Confident. Now he saw the dragon in every move she made. It was more than that long flaming red hair and those glittering green eyes. That sinuous walk. Never mind the way she looked over people, as if assessing how tasty they might be. She looked like she had a passion for pleasure and sensation.

As if she'd be insatiable.

He was glad to see that she'd refastened her dress. Even covered, her figure could stop traffic. And she was mating with him. Troy felt a surge of pride, then hurried up to the room as promised. He took a couple of minutes to shave as well as change his shirt, wanting to look his best.

Such as it was.

Troy knew what he had to do, but the way he figured it, he still had one day to do it.

When was he going to have another chance to be with a dragon shifter princess? He was going make these few hours count.

Even so, he felt a strange uneasiness. What did Drakina mean when she said that she had tracked him across the cosmos by scent? Why would she do that? How would she even know his scent?

His gut clenched. What else hadn't the gamblers told him?

ONCE THEY WERE SEATED in the diner, Drakina avidly surveyed the occupants and the menu. Troy had explained the use of menus to her, when she would have simply given a command to the chef. She perused it with shining eyes and quickly made a decision.

She could probably smell the exact inventory of food in the place.

Troy watched her in awe and wonder. A dragon princess. With him! It was easy to remember all his childhood fantasies, and he certainly wasn't disappointed in the reality.

Drakina cast him a smile that seemed conspiratorial when the food came and Troy couldn't help but smile in return. She devoured her two eggs over easy with bacon, toast, and hash browns. He was fascinated by how fastidiously she ate. Her manners were perfect, but she ate very quickly, and there wasn't a molecule left when she was done.

She looked disappointed when her plate was clean and eyed his bacon with such obvious interest that he almost laughed.

Troy pulled his own plate closer, protective of it because he was starving. She smiled and he saw the dragon in that expression, too.

"So, where are you from?" he asked, for lack of a better opening.

"Why should I tell you more than you know?"

"Because I want to learn more about you." He realized that it was true. He wasn't just trying to charm her. He really wanted to know. "I'm curious."

"A perilous inclination, Carrier."

Carrier? Carrier of what? "Maybe," Troy replied with a chuckle, wanting to keep the conversation on an even keel. It was tempting to peek into her mind, but he didn't think he'd survive to tell the tale the second time. He had to find out about her the old-fashioned way. "But what's the harm in it? It might feel good to confide in someone."

"I have attendants at home."

"Friends?"

"Sisters."

"Not quite the same."

"No." Her eyes narrowed as she considered him and his proposition. "Is this part of slow and thorough?"

"You could say that."

"The confession must be reciprocal."

"Three questions each?" he suggested and she thought about it for only for a moment before nodding.

"And you have asked one already. I am from the Kingdom of Incendium."

"Which is the twin planet of Regalia," he said before he thought twice.

Her eyes lit with surprise. "You were efficient in your MindBend."

Troy had to think fast to cover his mistake. "Call it a habit. Get in, get what you need and get out."

"Like a thief."

"More like a spy."

She arched a brow, unconvinced.

"So, you're from Incendium." He had to steer a careful course between revealing what he knew and asking her enough to win her confidence.

"And you're here because...?"

"Because of you," she said immediately and his heart skipped despite her matter-of-fact tone. "You are the Carrier and I will conceive with your Seed. It has been foretold." She confided this last detail as if that explained everything.

Troy supposed that it did, but he was shocked all the same. "Maybe I don't want to." He definitely didn't want to conceive a child with Drakina then kill her.

She fixed a look on him that could have cut glass and he knew he had to give her some explanation.

"Maybe I'm shy."

She chuckled at that.

"Maybe I don't want kids."

She dismissed this with a gesture. "It will cost you nothing to surrender the Seed. Your role then will be complete."

She could only think that because she didn't know what he was supposed to do. "Maybe I'm not certain I'll survive it."

Drakina leaned across the table, holding his gaze. "The son I conceive will be the crown prince and the hope of our world. I'm not leaving without the Seed." Her smile was chilly. "No matter what I have to do to claim it."

Troy was well aware in that moment that they were both predators. It was a timely reminder.

He was careful to not use a question for his response. He'd used up two already. "Because it's been foretold. I don't believe that anyone knows what's going to happen in the future."

"Nor do I." Drakina's voice dropped to a confidential tone. "I don't care much about destiny. I'm the oldest of the royal princesses and my father has always had plans for me to perpetuate his dynasty. If bearing this one son means he lets me make my own choices, I'll do it."

"The oldest," Troy mused, feeling a familiar yearning. "I have no brothers or sisters."

"And kin?"

He liked that she'd asked a question about him. "My mom died when I was a teenager."

"And your father?"

"Careful, princess, that's two," he teased and she flushed. "He died a bit later, after I was eighteen. I was alone then on the farm." It was easy to recall how confined he'd felt in those days. How lonely.

"Solitude," Drakina said, exhaling slowly. "It sounds like paradise. I'm envious of you, Carrier."

He looked up to find her watching him with that assessing smile, the dragon smile that made his heart leap. The fact was that he didn't think much of solitude. Being alone was what had allowed the pirates of Manganus Five to capture him. Being alone in the penal colony of Xanto had driven him crazy enough to accept this insane, long-shot of a deal.

At least it had brought him to Drakina. She was unlike anyone he'd ever known.

She reminded him of what it was to be alive, instead of just existing.

He was caught. He couldn't complete the mission without having her once, yet now that he'd met her, he didn't want to complete it at all.

Was there another way out?

Troy's gaze dropped to Drakina's lips and she ran the tip of her tongue across the top one, tantalizing him with the reminder of her kiss. He swallowed and averted his gaze, knowing he had to delay the seduction as long as possible. She might leave as soon as it was done.

"I want that," she murmured and his heart jumped. To his surprise, she reached out to indicate his last piece of bacon.

"Forget it," he retorted. "It's the best part of breakfast. I always save it to the last." He didn't eat it though, because he might be able to negotiate with it.

"You eat this often? Daily?"

"Not always now, but we ate it all the time when I was a kid."

"What do you call it?" She lifted a finger in warning. "That doesn't count as my third question, Carrier. It is a linguistic enquiry, not a question about you."

He smiled. "Bacon."

"And you ate it often because it is a typical choice of sustenance?"

"My parents' farm was for raising pigs and boars. There was always a lot of pork."

Drakina repeated the words several times. "It reminds me of verran." Her expression turned bleak.

"Is that a problem?" Her gaze flicked to his and he echoed her gesture. "Not my third question."

She laughed. "Not in itself. The taste just provokes memories."

"Like what?"

She gave him an intent look, even as she smiled. "You are a curious Terran. Don't you know that it's risky to provoke my kind?"

Troy arched a brow. "Maybe I like to live dangerously."

"It is the mark of a warrior to be bold in the face of peril," she said softly and her eyes glowed with promise.

Their gazes held for an electric moment and Troy felt the heat rising inside him. If she leaned across the table and touched him, even if her fingers landed on his hand, he'd be lost all over again...

But Drakina shook her head and, to Troy's surprise, she answered his question. Her tone was dreamy. "When I was a child, we went to Sylvawyld, a heavily forested small moon in our system, during the harvest season. My father hunted verran there, for they are plentiful and sufficiently fierce to challenge him. We dined often on their meat and the servants smoked the remainder to take home afterward."

"Your father is a good hunter, then?"

"He is a king," she said with some hauteur. "It is his privilege and his responsibility." Her gaze dropped to the bacon and Troy wondered whether he could eat it and live to tell about it.

Then she licked her lips slowly. "I would do almost anything to taste verran again."

There was an enticing proposition. "Anything?" Troy pushed the plate across the table. Her eyes glittered, then she took the bacon and devoured it.

Delicately and quickly.

"It is almost the same," she said, scanning the empty plates with obvious regret.

"You'll be able to have some more when you get back to Incendium."

Drakina shook her head. "The verran were hunted to extinction by the Regalians half a lifetime ago."

"Who?"

"Regalia is the other planet and kingdom in Incendium's solar system. The Regalians live there."

"Are they shifters too?"

"No. Maybe that explains *everything*." She winced.

Troy left that alone, since he wasn't a shifter either. "Why would they hunt the verran to extinction?"

Drakina's look was pitying. "Because they are too stupid to consider the future."

"Probably better you didn't marry one, then." He meant to tease her, but she snorted.

"Where is it written that I did not?"

"You're married?" Troy wondered then if there was more behind this bet he had been compelled to participate in.

"Not quite. I was supposed to marry, but there was a complication." She gave him an intent look. "I am too famished, Carrier, to confide more of this tale."

"Is that an offer I can't refuse?"

"Perhaps one you should not." Her smile was seductive, though.

"Do you want more breakfast?"

"Another of the same," she admitted, then glanced over the diner. "But these Terrans are temperate in their appetites, and I don't want to attract attention."

It was too late for that, but Troy wasn't going to tell her as much. She was too striking to avoid attention.

"I can fix it," he offered.

Drakina smiled, understanding immediately. "Your gift can be used for such a feat?"

He nodded.

"Ah, so there is some merit in this rare skill." She sat back like a queen. "Then, please do, MindBender."

THE CARRIER ENCHANTED THE waitress easily.

She was small and pale for a Terran, and Drakina could smell that she hated her job. She couldn't imagine why the Terran did nothing to change her situation. The waitress was not a slave, but she was as resentful as one. Drakina had noticed the waitress' interest in the Carrier when they entered the diner, and now the Carrier used her interest against her.

It was a clever tactic.

He turned that smile upon the small Terran when she came back to fill his coffee cup. Drakina hadn't touched hers, because she didn't like the beverage.

"Thanks so much," the Carrier said, his tone as warm as his smile.

The waitress looked at him, parted her lips to say something, then Drakina saw that she was snared. The Carrier held her gaze and she could almost feel the power of his influence. In a way, it was a relief to know that she wasn't the only one fascinated by his smile.

In another, it disappointed her to have anything in common with this waitress, who disliked her job and did nothing about it. Drakina could not abide such passivity.

Even in a stranger.

"Would you like anything to eat?" the waitress asked, her voice sounding dreamy.

"I'm good with coffee," the Carrier said. "But the lady wants breakfast." He listed the same meal she had just consumed and the waitress nodded. "Extra bacon," he added.

"Absolutely." The waitress cleared away the dirty plates, apparently without noticing the inconsistency in what she did, then soon returned with a new meal. She served it as if she hadn't done the exact same thing just moments before.

Drakina inhaled the scent of it with pleasure. This bacon was powerfully nostalgic for her, reminding her of marvelous times at hunt. She ate the first piece with pleasure, knowing that the Carrier watched her with some pride in what he had done.

He deserved praise.

He deserved a reward.

"It is the way of my kind to put more emphasis on deeds than words," she began. "You have done this for me, so in thanks, I will do what you desire of me." Drakina was sure he would ask for slow sex, but the Carrier surprised her.

"Three wishes?" he asked, a teasing glint in his eye.

Drakina smiled. "Three wishes," she agreed.

"First, some more conversation," he stipulated. "Then make a little trip with me." Drakina was intrigued. His smile widened. "You can guess the third wish."

"Because it is also mine?" she replied and he laughed. Ah, he looked younger and more carefree when he laughed and the sound was most alluring. "Still we will dispute the speed of the union."

"Maybe so," he admitted and stole a piece of her toasted bread. He was welcome to it. "Tell me about Incendium," he invited. "I've heard only statistics. Tell me why you love it."

"You're MindBending in a different way," she accused and he grinned. He was not so foul to look upon as she had first thought. In fact, he grew more appealing with every moment she spent in his company. It was his nature that beguiled her and blinded her to his physical appearance.

The fact was that Drakina was enjoying his company.

"I have to learn about you the way everyone else does," Troy said. "Come on, tell me."

"Incendium is one of a pair of planets orbiting the same sun. Regalia is the other. My kind rules Incendium, while a species who cannot shift shape rules Regalia. They look much like Terrans."

"And Incendium is filled with shifters?"

"No. We intermarry with those who do not shift. On Incendium, both shifters and those who do not shift live in communities together, the tale being that the strengths of each kind balance the weaknesses of the other. Destined mates are usually of the other species."

"Does everyone have a destined mate, or just the royal family."

She considered this with a frown. "I expect that everyone does, but may not know of it. The best astrologers labor in my father's court, and cast horoscopes only for the royal family."

"And on Regalia?"

Her lips tightened. "They are said to prefer sorcery over science."

"But the two planets have peaceful relations?"

"Notoriously not, not for a long time. But my grandfather brokered a treaty with the Regalians, and it has been honored all this time."

"Even after they hunted the verran to extinction."

"Even then, though matters were precarious for a century or two." It was easy to guess the reason for his confusion. "It would have been comparable to three hundred years ago in Terran time." The Carrier blinked and Drakina anticipated his next question. She pulled her interpretor from the pocket in her dress that disguised it and tapped a query. "I was born the Terran equivalent of four hundred and fifteen years ago. We are considered children for eighty-one Terran years." She smiled. "Ha! It is also a magic number on Terra. Nine times nine. The most potent magical number of all." She put the computer away and returned to the matter at talon. "And so, we have been more or less at peace with the Regalians these five hundred years."

"Because you found harmony?"

"More recently, because we discovered that we face a common threat. This is what enabled us to move beyond the loss of the verran. Each rotation of our system brings both planets closer to our sun. It is forecast by both the astrologers and the sorcerors that soon both planets will fall into the fiery heat of the sun and be destroyed."

"How is any son you bear supposed to prevent that?"

Drakina shrugged. "I don't know." She put down her fork, deciding to be honest. "I don't actually believe it can be done."

"The kingdoms could unite and colonize."

"And each surrender some authority to the other? You know little of dragons, Carrier, and less of kings. They will each die in their respective kingdoms. We are comparatively isolated in the galaxy and transport is expensive. It may not even be possible to build enough transport vessels for the entirety of both populations. The kings must work together for a solution."

"But if you don't believe in the prophecy, why are you here?"

"Because my father does believe and because I am prepared to fulfill his desire in exchange for mine."

The Carrier arched a brow.

"Freedom," she said. "The right to choose."

"What would you choose to do instead of being a crown princess?"

"Do not be impertinent, Carrier," Drakina chided. "The royal whim is not yours to know." He fell silent, though there was a predictable mutiny in his eyes. At least he kept his mind to himself. She finished her meal and pushed the plate aside, wishing there had been more bacon.

She looked up to find his eyes twinkling. How had she ever thought them small and beady?

"Again?" he murmured.

Drakina smiled. "You read it in my eyes."

"You're an open book, princess."

She couldn't help but chuckle. "You desire only more of my truth."

The Carrier leaned forward, an alluring intensity in his manner. "I *like* pleasing you," he whispered, his words sending a thrill through her. "Slowly and thoroughly." Their gazes clung over the table and Drakina's mouth went dry. She let him see the truth of what she wanted to do to him, in her eyes. The Carrier swallowed and moved restlessly on the opposite bench, showing a most enticing impatience.

She would convince him of the merit of fast sex before their ways parted.

"Again," she agreed. "And possibly once more after that. I believe I will be needing my strength." She smiled at him. "It might be wise to fortify yourself as well, Carrier."

CHAPTER THREE

"SO, YOU'RE THE OLDEST?" Troy prompted when Drakina was tucking into her third breakfast. He was wondering how to bring the conversation back to her marriage. What had happened to the lucky guy? He liked that she confided in him, but then she was a dragon shifter. She wasn't going to lose many fights. "Of how many?"

"There are twelve princesses in the royal brood of Incendium."

"All dragon shifters?"

She nodded, as if this was self-evident.

"But if you're the oldest princess, shouldn't you be making a dynastic match?"

Drakina's smile was quick. "My father tried that." He guessed his curiosity was obvious because she set down her fork. "Once upon a time," she began and he almost laughed. "The Queen of Regalia bore twelve sons. The King of Incendium, my own father, sired twelve daughters." Her expression turned rueful. "If you know anything at all of kings and their desire to organize the lives of those beneath their hand—or claw, as the case might be—you can guess what happened."

"They wanted to match their daughters and sons in marriage."

"So predictable." Drakina surveyed the remainder of her meal and reached—predictably—for the bacon. "And so I was to be the first because I was the oldest. So was he. The betrothal was announced, and the preparations were made. The heralds were dispatched and the festivities arranged."

"What was he like?"

She gave him a chilling glance. "Sinewy. It must have been all that jousting."

Sinewy?

Troy stared at her as she calmly ate another piece of bacon.

She nodded, as if in recollection. "With a definite and lingering aftertaste." She shuddered. "I'd so hoped he'd be sweet."

"You *ate* him?"

"I had just cause." Her manner was prickly. "The tribunal court agreed."

"I'm skeptical of that." This put a different slant on being the Carrier of the Seed. She had mentioned that her cousins eliminated their mates once they had fulfilled their usefulness. Would killing Drakina be an act of self-defense?

Drakina granted him a simmering glance, then leaned forward, stabbing one finger into the table as she argued her own case. Troy felt the force of her anger, but he knew it would be foolish to retreat. He might end up looking like lunch.

She breathed the words so low that the table vibrated. "He. Stood. Me. Up."

"Not at the altar."

Drakina returned to her meal and ate with savage haste, her eyes flashing. "Of *course*, at the altar. In my father's palace. With dignitaries from every ally in attendance. Do you know what that wedding cost my father? What it cost his kingdom? And that foul excuse for a prince didn't even have the courage to break off the engagement in person. He sent a *clerk*." She sneered and Troy was sure he saw sparks. "Canto was no warrior."

"He was unworthy of you."

"Exactly." She shoved the plate away with such force that it clattered against the wall at the end of the booth. There was even a piece of bacon on it still. She glared at Troy and he thought she might shift shape on the spot.

"I was mortified," she said, her words thrumming. "My father was furious. My mother was a wreck." She straightened, seeming to notice that the waitress and the cook were looking. She did a creditable job of composing herself before she continued. "So, I did the only reasonable thing. I left immediately to ensure justice. I shifted shape right then and there. I left the festivities in a cold, lethal rage, and hunted Canto to the ground. Just as he deserved."

It said something about her world that this reaction could be considered the only reasonable thing to do. Troy could just imagine her shifting shape, right in front of the company, then taking flight. She'd probably breathed a bit of fire as she'd flown around the building.

"My father *was* a bit vexed about the hole in the roof, but he understood my impulse. I think he might have let it pass if I hadn't found Canto so quickly and things hadn't been resolved so...absolutely." She lifted her hands. "He could not even *hide* well!"

"You might have let him live?"

She grimaced. "I *might* have been more temperate if there had been time for my temper to cool, but as it was, that was out of the question."

Troy thought it was a good idea to learn as much as possible about escaping her wrath, even though he didn't intend things to get to that. "Why was it out of the question?"

Drakina shook her head. "He liked a particular perfume and wore it often. He thought it was alluring." Her expression revealed that she didn't agree. "I believe the scent is known here, as well." She frowned and pulled out that small computer again. It was a kind he'd seen many times since he'd left Earth. It was so thin that it was essentially a film, and could be folded or adhered to skin, hidden in a tiny pocket like the one in Drakina's dress, yet had an astonishing computing power. Troy was belatedly impressed by her command of Terran English. She hadn't used the interpreter much at all.

She must have studied in preparation for the trip.

She laughed then and put the interpreter away. "A similar Terran perfume is called myrrh. But the ancient Egyptians used it for the embalming of corpses. I think I should have liked these Egyptians."

"They're long gone."

"So I see." She seized the final piece of bacon. "Well, it led to *his* funeral, because I could have followed that trail of scent anywhere."

"What scent do you find alluring in a man?" Troy wanted to know and thought it would be a good idea to calm her temper.

Drakina's eyes sparkled immediately, then her voice dropped low. "His own. I like the musk of warm skin. It reveals desire and hints at pleasure." She leaned over the table and held his gaze as she inhaled slowly. "Your scent is good, Carrier," she whispered. "Man not meat. Warrior, not courtier."

That was good to know. "I'll guess there were repercussions from you hunting down the groom."

"A diplomatic incident, as they say, and my father's wrath to be faced. In the end, it was only the dire situation of our two planets that drew Regalia and Incendium into reluctant alliance again. At least, there is no question of my securing the bond."

"One of your sisters will have to do it?"

"Gemma is betrothed to Urbanus, the new crown prince, and I wish her luck. He's probably even less toothsome than his brother."

Urbanus? Troy's thoughts flew as he realized that the bet that had sent him on this mission wasn't a coincidence at all. There couldn't be two men named Urbanus, both the crown prince of Regalia, and both with a prince's conviction that his will should be done. Troy had hated the gambler on sight.

If his brother Canto had been anything like him, he would have been glad to see Drakina devour him.

But it explained why Urbanus wanted Drakina dead.

And wanted her assassinated badly enough to make a wager on Xanto.

Troy looked around, feeling a strange lack of interest in fulfilling his mission, the one that was his only chance to survive. Was he losing his mind?

Or did he and the dragon princess have something unexpected in common, in that they had both been unjustly condemned?

Drakina cleared her throat delicately. "Strangely enough, the festivities have been delayed repeatedly."

"Maybe she shares your view."

"The astrologers keep saying the time is not right. I have wondered whether she is bribing them. Gemma tends to achieve her goals more quietly than I." Drakina considered Troy with a smile. "So, you see, I have been ill-fated in courtship and will only be pragmatic in future. I come here with one purpose. I want your Seed. Let us come to terms, Carrier. Incendium falls ever closer to the sun."

Troy had to prolong their discussion. "Don't you think that what I want matters? Just a little?"

She was clearly startled by the notion. "Why should I? I am a royal Wyvern. I am doing my duty in conceiving a son for the good of the realm."

"But you need my help to do that."

Drakina was both intrigued and surprised. "What *do* you want, Carrier?"

"That would be your third question," he warned.

"And it is a good one. I accept that it is my last query of you."

Troy didn't know what he was going to say until the words fell out of his mouth. "I don't want to be alone anymore, princess." Once he had said it, he knew it was true.

Even better, he knew he had to find another solution.

Somehow, he had to have Drakina *and* win the bet to survive.

Drakina's gaze brightened with curiosity. "Indeed?"

"I'm thinking that no matter what lies ahead for you and me, I'm going to want to see my son. Repeatedly. Maybe constantly. There will be no seed from me unless we come to an agreement on that."

Her eyes narrowed but her tone stayed level. "Terrans are not welcome in Incendium."

"You and I could stay here."

Drakina inhaled sharply and cast a glance of disgust about herself. "It's so primitive! You cannot mean to insist upon such a condition!"

Troy knew in that moment how he might change her mind. "I like it. It's home. You might come to like it too."

She arched a brow.

He smiled at her undaunted. "And the seed is mine to give or not."

Drakina's lips tightened but Troy didn't blink. Then she leaned across the table and dropped her voice low. Her fingertip landed on the back of his hand, then trailed upward. "I could seduce you into complying," she murmured and Troy knew she had a good chance of succeeding.

He drew his hand back, although he didn't want to. "You could," he admitted. "But it would hurt my feelings to be used like that, and you've already given your word that you won't injure me." It was a long shot and a technicality.

But it worked.

Drakina inhaled sharply, sat back, and glared at him. She drummed her fingers on the table. "Another sinewy one," she muttered. "Just my luck."

Troy smiled, just a little, and a flame lit in her eyes.

"Convince me of the merit of this place, Carrier. There must be some reason you are fond of it."

That was exactly what Troy had hoped she would say.

And he hadn't used his MindBending skills at all. He felt encouraged.

"That's why we're going on a little trip, princess. Wish number two." He surveyed the empty dishes. "Think you can last a couple of hours without a meal?"

"My curiosity is awakened. Where are we going?"

THE STRANGE THING WAS THAT the more her mate challenged her, the less unattractive Drakina found him to be. His intelligence shone in his eyes, along with his determination and his desire. His body was muscled and very alluring, his embrace both tender and tough. She liked that she could provoke his reaction with her touch. She liked that he talked to her. She liked best of all that he provoked her, both with words and deeds, and was unafraid of her.

He was such a warrior that she began to think that he was worthy of her.

After so many exchanges with the Regalian crown princes—who were supposedly so rugged and fearless but simpered and shook like butterflies in the presence of a Wyvern princess—his attitude was a relief.

It was also intriguing. He believed she would keep her word. Of course, Drakina *would* keep her word, but mortals who made tasty snacks for dragons were usually far less trusting.

He wasn't MindBending. Now that she was paying attention, she knew it. She had only to hear the sound of an intruder once to be alert to it forevermore.

Troy. She let herself think his name, then reminded herself not to get soft.

What gave him this confidence?

What had made him so resolute?

Drakina reminded herself the egg within her was ripe, and that it should be fertilized soon to avoid the potential for undesirable mutation. If her son was to save Incendium, he had to be perfect and whole. She had to have the Carrier's Seed soon.

Now.

As soon as his second wish was fulfilled.

He led her out of the diner and to an establishment across the street. The door was locked and he tapped on the glass. A woman appeared in the shadows of the darkened store and unlocked the door.

"Not open for another hour," she said.

"Could you make an exception?" the Carrier asked, and Drakina couldn't be sure whether he was MindBending or just using his natural charm. He seemed to have a lot of that. "We're in a bit of a hurry."

The woman pursed her lips. "Suppose it's foolish to turn down any business, now that the festival's over and done."

"The lady needs jeans and a jacket," the Carrier said. "Boots, too. We'll be riding my Harley."

The woman's face lit with an understanding Drakina did not share. She welcomed them into the shop and hastened to one side, almost dancing between the racks of garments and Drakina. "Try these first," she said, holding up a garment that would sheath her legs. "Our most popular line."

Drakina smiled at the Carrier in gratitude.

Within moments, she was more modestly clothed, the dress and sandals packed in a bag. When she came out of the small chamber in the jeans, the Carrier caught his breath in a most satisfactory way.

"Fit you like a second skin," the woman said.

Drakina found pleasure in the gleam of the Carrier's eyes.

By the time they left, she had a shirt and a jacket, a pair of gloves and boots. The Carrier led her to the back of the hotel, where a two-wheeled chariot awaited. He donned a helmet, handing a second one to her, then sat astride the bike. He started the engine, which had a very pleasing roar. Drakina climbed onto the vehicle behind him, liking that she could wrap her legs around him.

She caressed the tight curve of his butt and he cast her a look. If he was trying to look stern, the twinkle of his eyes undermined the effect.

"This is a Harley," she said, savoring its sound.

"This is *my* Harley," he corrected, then turned out of the lot. As soon as they were on the open road outside of town, he accelerated. The motor thrummed in a most satisfying way. The land raced past them. Drakina leaned against him, loving how vital and alert he was.

"It's almost as good as flying!" she shouted at him.

"That's what I always thought, princess."

It was too hard to talk so Drakina just enjoyed. She held tightly to her mate, feeling his muscles flex beneath her hands. They leaned into the curves together, and she reveled in the steady beat of his heart. She saw a mountain rise before them, way out in the distance, and believed there were trees upon it. It could have been Sylvawyld, except for the ribbon of road, for there were few other vehicles and they saw no people. The sky was clear overhead and their sun shone hot.

They could have been alone in Troy's world, just the two of them with no duties or obligations. Drakina found that a strangely alluring prospect.

And that was before she saw the corner of Terra he loved best.

IT HAD BEEN A LONG TIME.

But things hadn't really changed at the farm.

The drive still wound in from the highway, and the house and barn were still hidden behind the trees. The sight of the house still took his breath away, though the barn looked in need of some repair. The yard was empty, of course, and when he turned off the bike, the familiar silence pressed against his ears. Troy could hear a distant car and then the wind.

Drakina lifted her helmet off and surveyed the farm with obvious approval. "Verran," she whispered.

"Not any more. No one has farmed here for a decade."

She gave him a knowing look. "Are you sure, Carrier?"

He paused on the way to the front door, considering her. Could there be any livestock that survived? If there was, it would be the boars. They were half-wild anyway. "Are you kidding me?"

"I smell them." Her eyes narrowed and she inhaled again. She nodded.

"My dad had a sounder of boars."

Drakina frowned in confusion.

"It's what they call a small herd of boar," Troy explained. "The sows stay together in a sounder and raise the young. The males are solitary." He knew suddenly how he could explain the mating cycle to her. "It's a matriarchal society. The males return to the sounder only to share their seed, though they compete against each other for that privilege."

"So the strongest one sires the young." Drakina nodded approval of that. "My cousins have done this with their mates. The selection of the mate is a popular sport on their planet."

Those would be the cousins who ate their mates once the deed was done. Troy didn't want to encourage any of those ideas.

Drakina stood with the hands on her hips, sniffing as if she sampled the wind. "I smell perhaps five sows together, several with young—" She looked at him, a question in her eyes.

"Squeakers," he provided and she smiled.

"Do they squeak?"

"They do. They're really cute, actually."

Her smile was wistful. "I have never seen young verran. We always hunted in the season when the young had grown to size."

"That's responsible."

She nodded. "A herd must be managed well to ensure that it thrives. My father had three gamekeepers monitor the verran. When there was no forage, he had it shipped to Sylvawyld. When the nut harvest was meager, he had more shipped there. They lived wild, but were protected and defended. And always there was an inventory before the hunt, and much consultation as to what the kill could be." She smiled. "There were no accidents on my father's hunts."

It was exactly the way his dad had managed the boar population, and Troy felt an unexpected sense of understanding with her. "My dad let the sounder roam over a larger area than the farm, but they were fenced. Sometimes someone let a male loose or hunted without permission." He frowned. "When I came back after my dad's death, I didn't see any boar. I assumed my dad had sold or killed the sounder, but maybe they were in the forest the whole time." It was an intriguing thought, but he couldn't hunt them. There wasn't time.

Drakina shook her head and climbed the steps to the porch behind him. "They are wily, if they are like verran, and they are obstinate. Worthy adversaries for they are not readily killed."

"No, they aren't."

"I would not be surprised if they survived wild." She surveyed the house. "You grew up here?"

"I did." The key was in the mailbox, just as it always had been. Troy had it in his hand before he realized that the boar offered the perfect opportunity to fulfill both their dreams. He turned to face Drakina. "Do you want to hunt?"

Her eyes lit with pleasure. "The verran?"

"Sure." Troy couldn't see why not and the prospect gave her obvious pleasure.

She exhaled, her eyes glittering. "I should love to hunt verran again!" Her eyes narrowed and she winced. "But other Terrans will see me. It would not be right to reveal myself in dragon form and disrupt the assumptions of your kind."

"Princess! Remember who you're talking to!"

Her lips parted and she breathed the word. "MindBender. Can you shield me from view?"

"I can convince them that they aren't seeing what they think they are."

"But how? I will fly too fast for you to follow, even on your Harley, and it might not be able to make a path through the forest." She wrinkled her nose. "The sound will frighten them, as well, and reveal your presence."

Troy's heart was leaping at the obvious solution. "No, no Harley. Take me with you."

She eyed him. "I must have my claws free to hunt. I cannot carry you."

"But I can ride on your back." Troy couldn't believe he was being given this opportunity. "Come on, princess. Take me for a dragon ride."

"And we shall hunt verran together!" she declared and flung herself into his arms. She flattened him against the wall and kissed him with such enthusiasm that Troy was torn between a hunt and a seduction.

Then Drakina leapt off the porch in her exuberance and shifted shape in a blinding halo of light. "Fetch a rope, Carrier! We ride to hunt!"

THE CARRIER BROUGHT HER a gift beyond expectation.

Other cultures might dance when they courted a mate. Some shared meals with a prospective partner. But the dragons of Incendium had always weighed the valor of a mate and the suitability of a companion in his or her lust for the hunt.

Drakina was not going to be shown lacking.

She instructed Troy as to how to best fasten the rope about her dragon form, so that it would offer a secure grip for him but not restrain her. He still had to hang on and to hook his legs through the rope, but she liked the feel of him upon her shoulders. She felt that she carried a precious burden and knew she had to remember to safeguard him.

She was well aware of his awe and his pleasure.

When she took flight, she felt his quick intake of breath. Because it was new for him, the flight was new for her. She savored it as she seldom did, noting how wondrous it felt when often she took her powers for granted.

"First, an inventory," she said, then followed the scent of a solitary male. It didn't take long to find him, for he was close, and she flew low so that Troy could see him closely.

"He's an old boy, maybe nine or ten years," he said. "Look at those tusks."

The verran cast a baleful eye at Drakina, but she ascended, seeking the others before the choice was made. She found five more solitary male boars, spread over a large range. Troy told her that his family's lands were adjacent to a park, and two of the boar had escaped into that area. They all appeared to be eating well.

She then sought the sounder of females. There were six of them, with a cluster of young being protected by the mothers. There seemed to be two groups of young ones, one group much bigger than the others. The small ones were striped and not very big at all.

They were adorable.

"A late litter," Troy said. "Still nursing."

"Oh! They are so small!" Drakina turned a circuit high in the air, yearning. "Are they soft?" she asked quietly.

"Do you want to find out?"

Drakina felt her pulse quicken. "Can you MindBend such creatures?" Truly her mate offered bountiful gifts!

"Sure. It's how we used to corral them, although no one knew how it worked but me. My dad just thought I had a gift."

Drakina supposed that MindBending might be a gift, not a liability. The Carrier certainly had explored its advantages.

"I would like that very much," she confessed.

"Then let's do it. Leave me in a tree, just in case the MindBend slips." Drakina heard him chuckle. "I know I can't outrun an angry boar."

He might be trying to charm her. Drakina didn't care. She chose a tall and strong tree and left him high in its boughs. Then she shifted shape, clinging to the branches at his side. She listened as he explained their annual cycle. By this point in the Terran year, the young should all have been weaned.

The sows were aware of them, for more than one glanced upward, but they were remarkably untroubled. Drakina guessed that each of them weighed twice or even three times as much as she, and they would be formidable opponents. They would be at their most powerful if they believed their young to be threatened.

She waited until Troy cast her a smile. "We're good," he murmured. "Go."

Drakina descended the tree slowly and steadily, ensuring that she made as little noise as possible. The sounder did not move away, but continued to forage nearby. She smiled when she heard the little ones squeak when they believed they were too far from their mothers. She watched as two latched on to nurse and her heart swelled.

What fine small creatures they were.

What fierce adults they would be.

Her feet were on the ground before she doubted the Carrier's words in the least. The largest sow lifted her head and surveyed Drakina, her dark eyes small and her gaze intent. She would be the matriarch of the sounder. Drakina's heart stopped and she hoped the Carrier was right about his skills. Then the sow returned to her foraging. She dug in the ground with her snout and loosed a root, chewing on it noisily as she moved slowly onward. Three squeakers followed her, one latched on to a nipple even as she strolled and two hovering in her considerable shadow.

They were the smaller ones. Drakina counted the squeakers and wished to ask Troy whether they were usually more fertile than this. They might not be faring as well in the wild as could be hoped.

She could have turned back, but Drakina wanted to touch one. It might be the only chance she ever had to touch a young boar, the closest creature to a verran. She flicked a glance at Troy, still perched in the tree. He gave her a hand signal, his thumb pointed upward, which she didn't understand, but his confident smile told her all she needed to know.

She moved forward stealthily, her heart in her throat.

IT WOULD BE SO EASY.

Even as he exuded calm thoughts toward the boars, Troy knew he could stop his MindBend. He could let the sows realize the danger posed by a woman approaching them and let them complete his assignment for him. Even if Drakina could shift shape fast enough to defend herself, he didn't imagine she could fend off six furious boars at once.

They were fierce and fast. They could do his dirty work. He certainly wouldn't have been able to stop them once they attacked.

But there was no question of him betraying his dragon princess. Drakina was so enchanted with the young boar, and he liked the way that delight lit her expression. Plus she had given him a dragon ride, making one of his oldest dreams come true. It would just be wrong to put her in danger.

It was right to give her something in return.

She reached the sounder and the largest of the sows grunted as it glared at her. He couldn't MindBend them into complete oblivion but they were calm. Drakina moved slowly and carefully, which helped a lot. Troy saw that she had gathered some berries while she moved closer and she let them fall on the ground ahead of her.

One of the smaller squeakers peeked out from beneath its mother with curiosity. It was striped and furry, about the size of a basketball and nearly as round. It peered at Drakina, then at the berries, and sniffed, cautious but interested.

She waited, more still than he could have believed possible.

He kept his MindBend locked on the sows, particularly the biggest one. She was not only matriarch but the mother of the curious squeaker.

The mother took another step away from Drakina, ambling toward the denser scrub around the perimeter of the clearing. The little one looked between its mother and Drakina, then made a dash for the berries. It devoured one, hesitated, then sought the others. Troy guessed that they were gone when the squeaker considered Drakina.

She slowly stretched out her hand. Even at this height, he could see that there were more berries in it.

The squeaker's nose twitched.

Troy waited, rather than giving it a nudge.

He smiled when it surrendered to temptation and went to Drakina. As it ate, she cautiously stretched out her other hand and stroked its back. The mother made a grunt that was a summons, the little one finished the berries, then bolted after the big sow. The sounder moved into the denser undergrowth, unhurried but charting a course away from Drakina.

She stood and pivoted, her triumphant smile almost blinding Troy in it brightness. He found himself grinning in return, then she leapt into the air and shifted shape. She snatched him from the tree and soared high in the sky. Her excitement was contagious and he found himself laughing as she raced through the air, turned a somersault, soared toward the sun, then dove to fly low over the forest again. She spiraled down to a rocky outcropping, shifted shape just before her feet touched the ground and backed him against a tree. Her eyes were sparkling.

"Troy!" she exclaimed. "Thank you!" And she kissed him with such enthusiasm that he had no chance to say anything for a long time.

DRAKINA MIGHT HAVE CELEBRATED on that rock, in the open air, but Troy caught her shoulders in his hands and broke their kiss. He wasn't unaffected, but perhaps he was shy. "I thought you wanted to hunt," he said, with a gleam in his eye. "First things, first, princess."

"I will say that your slow and thorough scheme has its advantages," she said, unable to be vexed with him at all.

"The longer the burn, the hotter the flames," he said.

She arched a brow. "We shall see."

"We will." He was cocky again and she couldn't help smiling at his attitude. "So, what about those boar?"

"They are wonderful. Healthy animals and much like verran. I think they may not have sufficient feed on their own, though."

"The litters are small," he agreed. "I remember them having eight or even ten squeakers in a litter."

"Did you smell it?" she asked, guessing the answer as soon as she uttered the words. "The litters were all sired by the oldest boar. His scent is strong in their blood."

"You can smell that?"

"My kind have a refined sense of smell, Carrier." Drakina considered the forest spread before them and couldn't help being reminded of Sylvawyld and its joys. "This is a fine place. You are fortunate to have had such a home."

He nodded, following her gaze. "I couldn't wait to get away, but it's good to come back."

She smiled, glad he had shared his homecoming with her. "What is your thinking about this population?"

"I have ideas. Let's see if we think the same way. Tell me what your father would do," he invited.

Drakina didn't hesitate. "My father would hunt the oldest male on this day, to encourage diversity in the lineage of the sounder."

"That would be my choice, too."

"Beyond that, the sows and young must be protected so that the herd can grow. And the other males must be encouraged to return to your family's fenced lands, for their protection and that of other Terrans." She pursed her lips. "There may be a late litter for the same reason that the litters are small, because the sounder has nutritional needs that are unsatisfied. Once they are back on your family lands, I would supplement their diet." She looked at Troy. "And you?"

He smiled. "I would do exactly the same thing, princess. Are you up for hunting that old boar?"

Drakina smiled. "His pelt is as good as mine."

ALTHOUGH HE HAD ALWAYS wanted to ride a dragon, and although he had often imagined what it would be like, the reality was far beyond his dreams. The second time that Drakina carried him aloft, Troy was less overwhelmed and could compare dream and reality better.

A dragon ride was simply magical.

Drakina was all muscle. She made flying look effortless but Troy could feel the power of her body beneath him. Her dragon scales seemed to be black, but when touched by sun, he could see that they glimmered in a hundred shades of metallic green. Her wings were like black leather, and they stretched wide, sending a current of wind at him when she flapped them hard. Her eyes were a glittering jade. Her talons were gold, as well as long and sharp. With the wind in his hair and Drakina warm beneath him, Troy felt like the king of the world.

And that had been his impression before she touched the squeaker.

Before he'd seen the compassion that mingled with her ferocity.

Before he saw the woman in the dragon.

When she snatched him up and soared through the sky, triumphant, Troy felt alive as he never had before. It had taken everything in him to break their kiss, then the hunt had been a challenge and a thrill. The old boar had been as cunning and fierce as Drakina had predicted.

But she had won.

And Troy had had a front row seat.

It was dusk when they returned to the house. Troy led Drakina to the bunker where his father had always cleaned his kill. It was a lot easier to deal with the boar's weight with Drakina helping in her dragon form. He cleaned the carcass as she watched and hung it to cure in the cool dark space, only realizing once he was done that there might not ever be anyone to eat it.

The wager demanded that he kill Drakina to survive. If Troy succeeded in that, he'd have no taste for the boar, much less the memories it would conjure of this hunt.

If he didn't kill Drakina, he would be executed himself.

Troy felt trapped. Were they only destined to have this short time together? What about her astrologer's prediction of their shared destiny? What about the son who was supposed to be conceived?

Maybe the astrologers had seen that Troy might let Drakina survive, regardless of the price to himself. It was the noble thing to do, but he wanted more.

He wanted more time with his dragon princess.

A bleak sense of despair filled his heart, but Drakina's hand landed on his shoulder. He turned to find her smiling at him. "It is the way of life," she said gently, and he realized she'd mistaken the reason for his reaction. "We all must die in our time, and it is the responsibility of the gamekeeper to manage the herd for their own health and welfare." She surveyed the boar. "He was majestic. He was robust and virile. He sired many, and his days of life were both numerous and good. He was a champion to the end. We must celebrate him and his life."

"Don't you mourn what is lost?"

Drakina considered his question for a moment before she replied. "It is right to feel sadness when confronted with change, but there is only cause to mourn when the loss is untimely." She took his hand. "Or when matters have been left incomplete. Come, Troy, celebrate with me and finish what we have begun." She leaned close and swept her lips over his, giving him an enticing taste of her kiss.

That was when he knew. Given the choices, there was only one he could make.

He could give her the son she wanted, the crown prince who was foretold to save her world, and accept the consequences to himself for not winning the wager.

And Drakina would never know the truth.

Fulfilling her desire and protecting her from the truth would be the choice of a champion.

His choice.

Troy locked his arms around Drakina and swept her into his arms, slanting his mouth over hers and kissing her deeply. She made a little purr of pleasure and twined her arms around his neck, her passion igniting his desire all over again. If making love with Drakina was to be the last deed Troy did, he would make it a celebration to remember.

CHAPTER FOUR

THE CARRIER APPEARED TO HAVE abandoned the notion of "slowly and thoroughly."

He carried Drakina to the house, kicking the door closed behind them and continued to a chamber with large windows overlooking the forest. There was a large hearth on one wall, made of rounded river stones, though there was no need for a fire in this season. The rug was thick and the cushions were plentiful. He bore her down to the floor in the middle of the room, crushing her a little beneath his weight as he kissed her with uncharacteristic haste.

His passion fed her own and made Drakina impatient to feel his strength inside her. She ran her hands over his shoulders and down his back, then rolled him over so that she was astride him.

"Why do I get the feeling that you like to be in charge?" he teased, before she made sure he couldn't ask any more questions. Her mouth was locked upon his, her tongue dancing with his, her hands busy with that cursed fastening on his jeans. She finally stripped them off and cast them aside, then tugged open his shirt.

Troy rolled her to her back and straddled her as he removed the shirt. Drakina surveyed him with great satisfaction. She liked this frenzy in him, this need to claim her for his own. She reached for his erection, but he evaded her fingers, sliding down to unfasten her jeans. His eyes shone as he relieved her of them, flinging them aside with similar abandon.

Drakina tore open the front of her shirt and wriggled out of it. She preened at the admiration in his gaze. In a moment more, they were both completely nude.

"Your way this time, princess," he said, his words thrumming with intent. "Next time, mine."

"And the time after that?" she teased

His eyes lit with an appealing humor. "We'll have to negotiate."

Drakina laughed that he shared her assumption that there would be at least three couplings. Then he bent over her and kissed her nipple with exquisite deliberation. He caught the tight peak between his lips and teased it to an impossibly tight point, then flicking his tongue across it so that Drakina cried out with pleasure. Again, he caught her hands in his and held her wrists together as he tormented her with pleasure. She liked being held captive by this warrior; she liked better that she was compelled to accept every sensation he chose to grant.

She was writhing on the rug by the time he lowered himself over her. She arched her back and parted her lips when she felt him against her.

"You're so wet," he whispered against her throat.

"I have been awaiting you," she replied and saw the flash of his smile before he eased into her. They both froze when he was completely sheathed and their gazes locked in keen awareness of each other.

Drakina licked her lips. "Perfect fit," she whispered.

"Kismet?" he asked, lifting a brow as if he didn't believe it.

Drakina laughed and tore her hands free of his grasp. She seized his buttocks and parted her legs, drawing him deeper inside, wanting all he had to give. Troy shook a little in his surprise, then he braced himself above her and began to move. His erection dragged against her clitoris and Drakina wanted to roar with pleasure—when she saw the twinkle in his eyes, she knew he moved this way deliberately. She smiled up at him. "It seems you cannot abandon the notion of slow and thorough," she teased.

He buried himself within her and rolled his hips. "I want to watch you come," he said. "I felt it last time, but this time, I want to watch."

"What happened to fast and furious?"

"After you come," he vowed. "Then I won't be able to hold back."

"Promises, promises," Drakina complained but she was only teasing him. She'd never experienced such a splendid mating before.

It was due to her partner. Troy's confidence, his skill, his size, all combined to make her see the merit of slow and thorough. She rolled her hips, trying to draw him even deeper inside, and felt him get harder. She massaged her own nipples, seeing how his eyes glittered, and writhed beneath him. Troy rolled them over so that she was above him and she shook out her hair. She kept pinching her own nipples, ensuring that he had a fine view, and rolled her hips so that she rubbed against him.

When she moaned at the size and strength of him, Troy eased his finger and thumb between them, then teased her clitoris. He rolled it, then pinched it hard, so hard that she came in a sudden rush. Drakina gasped, she shook, and then she roared with the vigor of her release.

For the first time, she wished it had taken a little longer.

"You make me yearn for slow and thorough," she complained.

Troy chuckled with satisfaction. He rolled her beneath him and drove deep inside her. He bent to capture her lips and plundered her mouth, even as he claimed her with sufficient speed and passion to satisfy her impatience. Drakina felt the thunder of his heart, the haste of his breathing, the quickening of everything within him. Her own body responded and she felt the tide rise anew within her, redoubling its power, filling her with heat and promise.

Until he drove deeper than ever and roared with his release. Drakina came again and clutched at him, holding him fast against her as their combined shouts made the floor shake beneath them.

She tasted salt on his temple and felt the Seed run hot inside her.

It was done.

When Troy lifted his head, she smiled up at him and ran a hand through his hair with pride. The Seed was within her. The Crown Prince would be conceived within hours. Incendium would be saved, by some means she could not name, and she would be free of her father's command. Drakina had a strange sensation of her heart feeling full enough to burst, and yet it was none of those things that gave her such pleasure.

It was Troy, looking at her with admiration and more than a little desire. Troy, who had been driven by seeing her passion to make his amorous claim with haste and power. Troy, the warrior who would be the father of her son.

Drakina's throat was tight, but it wasn't because of the son he had given her.

Kismet. She thought of the word that had been repeated between them, and her gaze fell to the tattoo on his arm. Had she found her HeartKeeper?

The fact was that her quest was accomplished. She could leave immediately. She had achieved all that was necessary. Yet, she wanted to linger.

She wanted to stay with Troy.

Was there a greater destiny between them? It was one thing to be the Carrier of the Seed. It was another to be her destined mate. But her HeartKeeper? Drakina had never imagined she would be so fortunate as to have such a partner in her life.

But in this moment, she suspected that he lay atop her, disheveled and most satisfied. She reached up and framed his face in her hands, then drew him down for a leisurely kiss. Her heart was full. There were no words. There was only flesh against flesh, pleasure, exquisite torment, and thundering release.

All because of the marvel that was Troy.

Her HeartKeeper.

TROY KNEW HE SHOULDN'T have been surprised that Drakina had sexual stamina to match his own.

She was a dragon shifter, after all.

After she had blown his mind, he tugged on his jeans and went down to the basement and turn on the water again. He got the old water tank going, then primed the pump for the well. He flushed the pipes, impressed that the plumbing was still in pretty good shape.

He went back to the living room to find that Drakina had lit a fire on the hearth. She was naked, and evidently at ease to be so. She was standing at the window looking over the forest behind the farm. Dusk was falling, and the light outside was beautiful. "Always my favorite time of day," he said without meaning to do so.

"Why?"

"Because the sky is still colored from the sunset, but you can see the stars high overhead. In the east, it looks like night already. And I like that light blue, the last greenish bit before the sky gets dark. It seems magical." He frowned, uncertain he could explain it properly. "Like we're on the threshold of something."

"Neither day nor night," Drakina agreed. She reached for him and he went to her side, drawing him into her arms as they looked together at the forest. "Does this time have a name?"

"Twilight."

She said the word, then nodded approval. "It is a threshold, except that you have no choice but to go forward into night. You cannot go back to the day."

Her words seemed portentous and she was more serious than he'd seen her before. "Sometimes you just have to walk through the shadow to the light."

She turned a little in his embrace so she could meet his gaze. "I believe that is almost always true." Her gaze searched his. "Have you secrets, Troy?"

"Everyone has secrets, princess." He averted his gaze. "Shower?"

"Is that a manner of bathing?"

"And one that lends itself well to what I have in mind," he promised, then led her to the large bathroom on the second floor. The shower was roomy enough for two, and the hot water tank seemed to want to make up for its long rest.

It turned out that Drakina was more than amenable to learning more about leisurely lovemaking.

HOW COULD DRAKINA HAVE ever imagined that her mate was

unattractive? Troy was perfect, just the way he was. A valiant warrior, built strong and true. A man sufficiently confident to challenge her, a dragon shifter.

And that smile could have been designed to drive Drakina wild.

His nature was good and kind, noble even, as was fitting for the Carrier of the Seed. His sexual endurance was phenomenal. His son would be strong and potent, a majestic crown prince. The combination of gifts from both parents would make him formidable.

Maybe he could save Incendium. Drakina was surprised to realize that she cared less about that than she had.

Was Troy her HeartKeeper?

In addition to his other gifts, he made love like a champion. His touch curled her toes and exhausted her, yet left her hungry for more. She could become used to him by her side.

She touched her lips to Troy's shoulder, thinking of defying her father about the Carrier becoming the Consort, and Troy stirred in his sleep.

He smiled and opened his eyes, looking rumpled, satisfied and adorable. Drakina's heart squeezed. "Sleep well?" he murmured.

"Long enough," she replied, moving into his embrace. He tangled his fingers in her hair, surveying her with admiration. "Perhaps we should ensure the Seed is planted."

"Don't you know?"

She smiled that he understood her so well. "It is," she admitted. "The Crown Prince is conceived." She ran her hands over his skin lightly. "But it would not hurt to be absolutely sure."

He laughed. "You're a fantasy come true."

"How so?"

"I think every man dreams of having a beautiful partner who is insatiable, too."

"But probably not a dragon shifter."

"You might be surprised, princess." He pulled her head down and kissed her slowly, easily summoning her passion again.

"Did you fantasize about such a partner?" she asked when Troy finally let her speak.

That smile turned mischievous. "Come on. I'll show you something." He seized a towel and knotted it around his waist, then rolled out of bed, grabbing her hand. He led her upstairs, to the part of the house she hadn't yet seen, and into a small chamber toward the back. There were stars on the ceiling and maps pinned to the walls, a model space ship hanging from a string, and a shelf filled with books. A small bed was in the corner, a desk in the other, and she realized this was a child's room.

"Mine," he said, anticipating her question.

His. Troy had lived in this room as a boy. Drakina studied it, wanting to memorize every detail and know all about his childhood. He seemed disinclined to talk, though. He was kneeling in the far corner, by the window, and had pulled back the rug. One of the floorboards had been cut and he lifted it up, revealing a hiding place nestled beneath the floor.

His face lit when he reached in and withdrew a square tin box with a lid. It was covered with a plaid design and marked with the logo of a shortbread company. Shortbread. Drakina wondered what that was. This seemed a most strange place to keep any kind of food.

Troy set the tin on the carpet with obvious pleasure. "My treasury," he confessed, a twinkle in his eye. "Or my hoard."

Drakina smiled and sat opposite him, wrapped in her own towel. "The secrets of the heart are in the hoard," she said, her tone teasing. "Are you sure you want to show me?"

He nodded once, pried the lid off the tin and handed it to her.

Inside were three small model cars. There was a ball made of pieces of string tied together and wound into a ball. She lifted it and turned it in her hand, mystified, then met his gaze.

"I needed a rope if I was ever going to ride a dragon," he admitted.

Drakina lifted the chunk of rock with amethyst crystals on one side and gave him another look.

"And I needed a gift for her. Something shiny." He smiled. "Gems seemed a good choice."

Drakina smiled. There was another rock, one that was dull and grey, shaped like a cone.

"A genuine dragon tooth," Troy confided.

"It is not." She turned it, seeing that it was also the shape of a fang.

"I was sure it was. It was proof that there were dragons out there in the hills."

"Maybe there are."

"There was one, and that's good enough for me." They shared another of those sizzling smiles and Drakina's heart skipped a beat.

HeartKeeper.

There was another piece of rock, a sliver of obsidian, that caught the light and was filled with reflections. It was almost round, about the size of her palm.

"My father brought me that. He said it was a dragon scale and I treasured it."

Drakina smiled, both at the whimsy of a man who would tell a child a tale he did not believe, and the fact that the rock was almost the same color as her own dragon scales. Could her father and his astrologers be right about destiny? "Where did he find it?"

"He said it was on the path to the barn, which I found very exciting."

"The dragon had been in your yard!"

"Exactly." Troy lifted it from her hand and turned it in the light. "I suspect, though, that he bought it or maybe even had it shaped, just to thrill me."

They shared a smile at that. "Peri, my youngest sister, found a story in my father's archives about mice that fulfilled wishes," she said. "We have no mice on Incendium, and those on Regalia do not fulfill wishes. They are considered a pest there."

"A lot of people feel that way about them here, too."

"But my father indulged Peri and shared her wonder over the story. Together, they conspired to steal small pieces of cheese from the kitchen—because the castellan does not tolerate food being eaten in our chambers—and set them out each night in her chamber to lure the wish-granting mice."

"Did they ever see any?"

"Never, for there are none. But the cheese disappeared each night, which thrilled Peri."

Troy grinned. "Your father ate it?"

"He would never admit it, but I saw him once, leaving her chamber with a plate of small pieces of cheese."

"You don't think it's bad to encourage kids' fantasies then?"

"Who is to say what is fantasy and what is truth?" Drakina leaned closer and brushed her lips across Troy's. "Your father probably thought there were no dragons, but he was wrong." She touched her lips to his once more, and whispered. "I like that you dreamed of dragons. It makes me think that the astrologers were right, and that there is something to be said in favor of destiny."

"I wanted to be a dragon more than anything else in the world," he admitted, putting away his box of treasures.

"Maybe being the father of one is almost as good," she murmured, and then there was little more to be said for quite a while.

TROY AWAKENED IN THE guest bedroom with Drakina sleeping beside him. He'd forgotten how quiet it was at the farm, and how tranquil. He laid in the darkness for a long time, listening to the wind and feeling Drakina's breath against his shoulder. He was tired, but in a good way. He'd never made love to a woman so many times in a row, or in such rapid succession. They'd done it in the living room, as fast and hard as she wanted, then slower the next time. He'd had her against the wall of the shower and again on the bathroom floor, and once more in the bed. He'd never imagined he could do that and still want more.

His dragon princess had a gift for challenging his assumptions.

Her hair was cast over them, glinting with inner light even in the shadows. It might have been made of flame, or a conduit for it. Troy smoothed it back from her forehead, wishing he had time to learn all about her.

But his two days were over. They'd be coming for him by midday.

Drakina would need something to eat.

The house had been empty for years, but his mother had canned and stockpiled in preparation for the Apocalypse. And his father had stored wine. Troy was sure there was more that was still good to eat. It might be a strange meal, but it would be a generous one.

His last meal, or at least the last one that counted.

IT WAS NOT THE NATURE of Drakina's kind to sleep deeply. The dragons of Incendium dozed by habit, particularly when they were not surrounded by their own household and bodyguards. Drakina smiled to herself as Troy's fingertips danced over her flesh, and she welcomed his ongoing exploration. She feigned sleep while he toyed with her hair and considered how best to pleasure him before he left the bed.

But he rose abruptly and strode toward the chamber for washing.

Drakina opened one eye, just a slit, to savor the view of him walking away. She had yet to see her mate fully naked, for Troy seemed inclined to wrap fabric around his hips or don his jeans or seduce her in darkness. She deserved one good look.

Perhaps more.

Could she change her father's thinking about her having a Terran Consort? It would not be easy to leave Troy and return home.

The view was every bit as fine as Drakina anticipated, Troy's lean muscled strength kindling her passion anew. His skin was pale gold, tanned slightly and all over, so he couldn't be that shy. There was a mark at the base of his spine, too elaborate to be a birthmark, to dark to be naturally wrought. She peered at it and her heart stopped in dismay.

A tattoo.

Not just any tattoo. A distinctive blue whorl of triangles.

She recognized the symbol well. It was the mark of a condemned man in the penal colony of Xanto.

No one escaped that place alive.

Unless they were released on a bet, as sport for the rich of the galaxy.

Drakina barely managed to keep from gasping aloud. Troy closed the bathroom door and Drakina heard the water running. She rolled to her back and stared at the ceiling, her heart racing.

Could she love a condemned man?

Could she love a condemned man who had deceived her? Because if

Troy had been incarcerated on Xanto, then he had left Terra and returned. He was not just a Terran and not just a MindBender. Could he have tricked her?

Drakina recalled how Troy had been unsurprised by her nature and her abilities. She recalled her sense that he recognized her when she walked into the bar, as if he had been waiting for her. She recalled his reluctant confession that he was a MindBender and that he had been in her mind twice. Twice? Or just the once when she caught him—and he'd known the rest about her because he wasn't the Terran she'd thought he was.

She bit her lip and considered the power of his gift. A mother boar could not be easy to beguile.

Troy was not just any MindBender.

Drakina was afraid she knew which one he was.

Had the notion that he might be her HeartKeeper been her own thought? Or one provided for her? Why?

She rolled over to her belly and seized her computer. She tapped as long as the water ran, seeking the answers to her questions and giving fuel to her suspicions. By the time Troy opened the door again, she was sitting on the bed, her hair braided, waiting for him.

He was wearing his jeans and had a towel looped over his shoulders. He was surprised to see her awake, but his smile revealed that he was pleased. He took a step toward her as if to resume their lovemaking but she halted him with her words.

"You have not told me your great secret, Carrier," she said with quiet heat.

"Carrier again?" he mused. He folded his arms across his chest. "I'm guessing that's not a good sign."

Drakina put the computer down. "I do not like to be deceived."

He paled then and shoved a hand through his hair. His expression turned grim and she was relieved that he didn't tell her a lie.

"What have you done?" she demanded. "Why were you sentenced to the penal colony of Xanto?"

His lips set mutinously. He was not surprised, though. "I was caught."

"Caught doing what?"

"Caught doing what my owner commanded me to do. A slave doesn't have any choice, Drakina. And a slave sold to a gang of thieves has even less of one. I had to do what I did to survive."

A gang of thieves?

"Were you sold to the Gloria Furora?" she asked in awe.

The simmering anger in his eyes was all the answer she needed, and Drakina felt a wave of sympathy for him.

"I'm amazed that you *did* survive that pack of thieves and

counterfeiters. They are not known for being tolerant of any strangers or slaves."

He scooped up a shirt and tugged it over his shoulders while she considered him.

"You lied to me about being Terran."

He shook his head. "No. I am Terran. You assumed I had never left Terra, which is a different thing."

"Did you MindBend me twice?"

He winced. "*That* was a lie. Only the once and you caught me."

"So you did know about me before we met."

"Of course. It was part of the deal, princess."

Drakina wasn't sure she was ready to know about the deal. "Did you lie about your name?" She had to ask.

"No. It's always been Troy. I didn't lie about my family or my history, princess. It was all real, all except the deal I had to make to survive." He gave her an intent look. "I was forbidden to mention it to you, for obvious reasons."

So, he had made a bet to save his own life. "The gamblers on Xanto."

Troy nodded. "They offered a wager. If I could win, I could live."

"And if not, you would die." Drakina took a deep breath, because she'd found more. "The most expensive commodities traded in the sentient slave markets of Naruhm are MindBenders."

Troy held her gaze as if daring her to say it out loud.

Drakina dared. "The equivalent of twenty solar years ago in Terran time, the confederation initiated a search for MindBenders throughout the galaxy, declaring all planets to be eligible hunting grounds." She swallowed. "They launched a thousand ships."

His brows rose. "I didn't think you'd know that story."

"My father collects stories. It is his contention that the same tales or elements circulate through all cultures in the universe, manifesting in a multitude of ways, yet remaining true to their essence." She pursed her lips. "He would say that your destiny was defined when you were born, and that your name was chosen to mirror that fate."

"But my mother didn't read classical history. I don't think she knew that story."

"It does not have to be a conscious choice. The name could have come to her in a dream, or she might have been alerted to it in another way." Drakina was dismissive of the notion. "One of my father's astrologers or scholars could explain it better than me." She fixed him with a look. "Of greater import is your story. The equivalent of ten solar years ago in Terran time, there were rumors that the pirates of Manganus Five offered a MindBender for sale on the shadow market. They refused to reveal where they had found the MindBender in question so he or she could not be trade freely. If that MindBender existed, he was never heard from again."

Troy smiled his crooked smile. "Who says no one really disappears in the galaxy." His tone was wry and Drakina knew he didn't expect an answer.

"Who offered you the chance to escape the prison colony of Xanto?" she asked. "And what do you have to do to win your freedom?"

Troy sighed. He shoved a hand through his hair, but she sensed the defeat within him. "All you really need to know is that I won't be doing it, princess," he said, his voice rough. His gaze was bright and bored into hers. "I've decided to lose."

"I still want to know."

"And I want breakfast. Come on. Food first."

It was a suggestion that Drakina found difficult to dispute. Troy had kept every promise he had made thus far.

She chose to believe he would do as much again.

But she dressed before she followed him, to show him that their intimacy was at an end. Even if he was her HeartKeeper, his truth made a future between them impossible.

GOING DOWN INTO THE CELLAR was like being punched in the gut. The small cold room was filled with memories of Troy's mother, and just as crowded with her preserves. He found pickles and jam, wine, and sealed tins of crispbread. The locked and even colder room beyond still had the scent of smoked ham.

He found a last one, hanging from the ceiling, as well as a wheel of cheese, sealed in wax and locked in a tin. He brought it all into the kitchen and began to assemble a meal.

He opened the wine, knowing he wouldn't have to wait long for Drakina.

He was right.

He was carving the ham, which was still perfect, when he heard the tread of her footfall. "They found me here," he said, seeing no reason to beat around the bush. "Alone on the farm. My mom had died and then my dad. I'd lived in town for a while after my mom passed. I had a job at old man Wilcox's garage and I liked it. I worked a lot, because it was better than thinking. I only came back here once in a blue moon."

Of course, Drakina frowned. "Terra's moon is not blue."

"It's an expression. It means not very often, because every once in a while, our moon looks blue from here."

She spared a glance at the sky, but the moon had set hours before. The sun was rising.

"When my dad was gone, the farm wasn't the same. It had always been quiet, but it was lonely. He'd sold the last of the pigs, and like I said, I thought he'd sold the boar, too. I closed it all up and went back to town to work. I came back at intervals to check on the place, and I was here when they came."

She sat on a stool and watched him as she listened.

"I'd never seen anything like that tracking beam." He shook his head. "It was like a ray of starlight."

"You should not have seen it. Terra is among those colonies lacking sufficient sophistication for interference."

"I couldn't stay away from it either."

"They laced it to lure you, then. A trap." Drakina tapped her fingertips. "That's why you were sold on the shadow market. It was illegal for them to harvest you here. Without provenance, they couldn't sell you in the legitimate slave markets."

"I hope they got less than I was worth," he said and heard his bitterness.

Drakina's smile was sad. "It was probably still worth their trouble. You were said to be the greatest MindBender in the galaxy."

Troy shrugged, uncertain how to respond to her admiration. "I didn't know what the beam was. I saw it. I was drawn to it. I stepped into its light, and that was it. Next I knew, I was on a ship, in what I realized was a prison cell."

"Then sold at auction," she guessed, sympathy in her eyes. "To the Gloria Furora. Truly, Troy, you could not have had worse luck. What did they do with you?"

"Hired me out as an assassin. I was either locked up, hunting someone or making a kill."

"Also against galactic law," Drakina murmured softly. He didn't know whether she was disappointed in him or displeased by his treatment.

He nodded, not proud of what he had done. "I defied them a couple of times, but they're inventive bastards."

"No one survives the torture of the Gloria Furora. They have a consuming hatred of all others."

"Thanks. I feel like less of a loser knowing that."

"And so you were caught, doing what?"

Troy winced. "Assassinating one of the warrior maidens of Cumae."

Her eyes widened and he knew he'd lost her support. "No! The culprit was never found!"

"Oh yes, he was."

"But the trial would be in the record..."

"Not the way the Gloria Furora play the game. They delivered me, paid for a conviction and I went mining. The person who caught me disappeared without a trade."

Her eyes were wide.

"They have a reputation to protect, apparently."

"Not that," she whispered.

Troy frowned. She looked truly shaken.

"Who was your target?"

"Her name was Arista..." At Drakina's gasp of horror, Troy stopped. Her expression made him fear the worst. "Friend of yours?"

Drakina turned away, but not so quickly that he didn't see her tears. "Arista was the best friend of my sister Gemma. She was well loved in our home and still deeply mourned."

And Troy had been the one to kill her.

He was pretty sure Drakina wasn't going to be having their son any more, not if she had anything to say about it.

He might as well nail his own coffin shut. "Like I said, I was snared and delivered to the court, then condemned and sent to the penal colonies of Xanto. The sentence was for me to mine for sixteen quartos, then be executed." Troy grimaced. "They like to give prisoners time to realize just how screwed they are."

"And so it was until the gamblers came." Drakina's voice was hard and he looked up to see that her eyes were cold. Her arms were folded across her chest, as if she needed one more barrier against him. "What was the wager?" she asked, though he was sure she'd already guessed.

"My life for yours." He put the platter of ham on the counter between them and watched her nostrils flare. "Pretty simple really, or it should have been."

"What is that to mean?"

"That I'm not going to do it. I'm giving you my promise, and you know I'll keep it."

She frowned. "Then you'll die."

"I have it on good authority that we all do, and the only deaths worth mourning are the untimely ones." He couldn't look at her as he continued. "I'd rather try to be a champion, princess, although I might not have much chance to succeed." He dared to flick a glance her way. The hair was standing up on the back of his neck and he knew in his heart that they'd returned for him. "I'm going to lose the wager, but you have the Seed, and if the prophecy is right, the crown prince will save Incendium. Winner take all." He saluted her and moved toward the door. The tracking beam was illuminating the same spot in the yard as it had all those years before. "You might want to find out who wants you dead, princess. It might be Prince Urbanus, or he might be acting for someone else."

"You can't go!"

"I have to go. We both know it." Troy paused in the doorway, looking back one last time, knowing the sight of her would be with him to the very end. "I love you, Drakina," he admitted, his voice husky. "Maybe, just maybe, you'll tell the kid something good about me."

Then he turned and strode to the beam. The light washed over him, making him tingle to his very marrow. Troy could almost feel his electrons being shaken apart and cast into the sky. He closed his eyes, knowing it would be over all too soon.

The last thing he thought he heard was Drakina calling his name, but Troy knew that had to be wishful thinking.

He was just yearning for what could never be.

WHAT MANNER OF JUDGE condemned a slave for fulfilling a command?

Drakina had her suspicions, but she would unravel the truth. She knew she could not defeat any party sent to retrieve Troy, not alone. She took the meat that so resembled verran and packed the feast her mate had prepared for her. Then she transported herself home to Incendium with haste. Once in the royal palace, she strode down the corridors to the library and demanded that the portals be secured.

She had no time to speak with her family.

She had no time to reassure her father, or whisper with her sisters.

The crown prince was conceived. Her duty to her father was done. Her independence was won.

And if Troy's life was to be saved, Drakina would be the one to do it.

Every moment counted.

CHAPTER FIVE

KRAW, VICEROY OF INCENDIUM, awakened with the sudden conviction that he was no longer alone.

Yet it was the middle of the night.

In a way, it was a relief. He had expected this ever since the return of the crown princess Drakina, and he preferred to face his terrors rather than have nightmares of dread.

He rolled over in his bed, glanced at the doorway and his heart sank. The princess Drakina was silhouetted there, but worse, sparks ignited at the ends of her long red hair.

Though no door in the palace was closed to the imperial family, Drakina showed her father's courtesy and waited on the threshold to be invited into the viceroy's apartment.

Kraw sat up and tried to look suitably dignified to greet her, but doubted his own success. His nightshirt was rumpled, for his sleep had been restless, and he was certain his moustache—the pride of his days— was at less than its best. He had finally fallen asleep on the couch in the formal room instead of his bedroom. While this meant he could see the princess easily, it also posed some challenge to receiving her in the appropriate manner.

Still, there was no denying the royal will, or presence.

Kraw cleared his throat. "My grandfather wrote in his chronicles that when you were irked as a child, your hair turned to flame," he dared to say.

The princess, to his relief, laughed a little. "You don't remember?"

"Of course not, Highness. You were a wyvern fully grown by the time I was born." He rose from the couch, bowed, then turned on the lights. He gestured to the seating area by the window and the princess inclined her head with grace before entering his home. He hurried to don a robe of brocade, hoping it was sufficiently fine for her view, but knew there was no time to dress properly. "May I offer you refreshment, Highness?"

Drakina smiled as she took a seat. "I don't expect such courtesy, Kraw. In fact, I owe you an apology for troubling you at this hour."

"I am certain you had cause, Highness."

Drakina looked him up and down, her slow survey making Kraw keenly aware of the flaws of his appearance. But then she smiled at him, and there was sympathy in her expression. "I would never have done it, Kraw," she admitted softly. "No matter how vexed I was, but I had a sense that you might be as sleepless as I, and for a similar reason."

Kraw's knees nearly gave out beneath his weight. The moment he had feared had arrived, and he felt that curious mingling of terror and relief. He didn't believe that the princess would welcome the truth. This might prove to be his last night in the service of the royal family of Incendium. On the other hand, the secret had weighed heavily upon him, and he would be glad to surrender it—no matter what the price.

"You look as if you should sit down, Kraw," she said gently.

"Not in the royal presence, Highness..."

Drakina stood up, turned a chair, and gave Kraw's shoulder a firm push. He sat down, then sighed with relief.

She sat down opposite him and fixed him with a look. "You planned it all." There was no question in her tone. "Why, Kraw? Why?"

"I did not plan it all, Highness. I tried to serve your family in the tradition of mine..."

She raised a hand for silence. "Just tell me, please, what happened."

Kraw studied her, discomfited that he could no longer guess her thoughts. The sparks had died, which was encouraging, but there was a solemnity about her that he did not associate with the princess Drakina. He licked his lips. "Did you..."

"I have conceived the crown prince, Kraw," she said, interrupting him. Her hand stole over her belly. "The egg will hatch in the summer. My father is pleased."

Kraw exhaled, glad that one hurdle had been cleared.

"Tell me of the Terran," she urged. "The MindBender." She smiled a little. "The greatest MindBender in the galaxy. Why exactly was he supposed to kill me?"

The viceroy's gaze flew to that of the princess, and he realized that she already knew much of the story. He sighed and frowned. "It was a wager, of the kind that they make on Xanto over the fates of the condemned. It says little good of the gamblers, to my thinking, that they sport with the lives of these creatures, making wagers and posing challenges, giving the condemned hope of survival if they can succeed at some ridiculous feat, then betting upon their success. It is barbaric. But when the MindBender was condemned to be executed, I understand there were many such proposals made to the Xantonians. They accepted the one that amused them most."

"That the MindBender could live if he killed me."

Kraw nodded.

"Whose proposal was it?"

"You must know, Highness, that there are those who did not agree with the ruling of the tribunal in the fate of Prince Canto..."

"I have heard a name already," she said then stood up and paced the width of the room and back. "Tell me, Kraw. I would know the worst."

Kraw winced. If she had heard the tale from the MindBender himself—and who else could have shared it?—then she knew the worst of it. "I have been warned against the crown prince, Urbanus."

"Gemma's fiancé," Drakina said, as if he did not know.

"But there is no evidence, Highness." Kraw took a steadying breath. "Your father chooses not to indulge in rumor, and the last time Queen Arcana was challenged, the furor was difficult to calm."

"He is known to enjoy his pleasures, Kraw, and to be extravagant."

"That might put him in the company of those gambler on Xanto but does not prove his involvement."

The princess fixed him with a glare. "The Carrier named him."

"Ah." Kraw rubbed his brow, knowing she would not like what he said next. "Incendium law code forbids the inclusion of testimony from a condemned man, be he citizen or nay."

The princess pursed her lips and looked out the window. "Continue, please."

"I heard the rumor, your father dismissed it and forbade action upon it. Truly, I would not have thought it possible for such a quest to succeed so consoled myself that the situation was not dire." Kraw sighed. "Until one of the astrologers divined the identity of your destined mate."

"Troy, the MindBender."

"Yes. A MindBender, a convict hired to assassinate you *and* a Terran. Truly, Highness, I did not know which was the worst of his credentials!"

Drakina watched him closely, and Kraw did not doubt that she saw all of the anguish he had experienced. "Did you tell my father?"

The viceroy bowed his head. "Only that he was the Carrier. Forgive me, Highness."

"You could have warned *me*."

"No, not with your father so set against Terrans and you so determined not to wed. I had to contrive a situation in which you might conceive the crown prince. I would have arranged for an escort for you, Highness, to ensure your protection."

Drakina smiled. "But I declined them, just as I defeated Urbanus' plan." Her gaze was shrewd. "Is there more for you to confess?"

The viceroy swallowed. "I cannot speak of it, Highness."

She held his gaze, then nodded once. "And what will happen to Troy? The MindBender?"

"He has been returned to Xanto and will be executed." Kraw's tone softened. "He accepted the wager, but he lost, Highness. He did not kill you." He rubbed his brow. "I suppose this spares your father the unpleasant task of denying the Carrier a role as your Consort."

Drakina stood silently at the window, and Kraw wondered what claimed her attention. The city was alight, as always it was, and the starport gleamed high overhead. He could see a shuttle descending, but knew her vision was more keen than his own. She rubbed her belly absently, her hand tracing little circles upon it, and he had never seen her so thoughtful.

"Troy lost on purpose, Kraw," she admitted finally. "Because he loved me." Her voice softened and fell low. "He asked me to tell our son something good about him." She paused again. "I believe Troy is my HeartKeeper."

Kraw knew he had to ask the unwelcome question. "Are you certain, Highness? It would not be unusual for a MindBender to mislead..."

Drakina spun to face him, conviction in her pose and her tone. "I *know* it, Kraw," she said. "Just as I know that I love him in return. I had to consider whether the tumult I felt was a fleeting passion, but every moment we are apart, convinces me that I love him. I don't want to live without Troy, Kraw. I will not let him be executed, and I will not let Urbanus remain unscathed in this. I need your help."

"I would be honored to be of any assistance, Highness."

"When will they kill him?"

Kraw winced. "It will not be long, Highness. Justice is quick in Xanto and I believe there have been payments made..."

"But it is not justice, Kraw." She flung a computer wafer at him, and he caught it. He realized it was loaded with precedents and galactic law codes. "He was a slave. He was seized from a planet we are supposed to defend from knowledge, sold illegally on the shadow market to the Gloria Furora, and tortured when he refused their commands. No court should have condemned him."

"Highness! I had no awareness..."

"No one did, Kraw. I expect a great many credits changed hands to see this done. No one wanted to remember who ordered that Arista be killed."

Arista! Kraw was glad that he was sitting down. His thoughts flew as he recalled the details and Gemma's fury at the death of her friend.

Then he thought of practicalities. "Highness, if this is to be done, we shall need a legal opinion compiled and a formal appeal..."

"I know you will arrange it all, Kraw." She leaned closer, her eyes glittering. "My HeartKeeper has been shown many injustices, and I will see them righted."

"Of course, Highness, though we must begin immediately. You have done much of the labor, but the argument should be dispatched by second light at the latest..." The viceroy fell silent in his planning as Drakina caught his face in her hands.

Much to his astonishment, she kissed him quickly, her gratitude and impulsiveness bringing tears to his eyes. "Thank you, Kraw!" Then she swept to the door. "In the meantime, I am going to Xanto, to claim my Consort."

"Wait! Highness! Your father will not accept a Terran in his court."

Drakina's eyes flashed green fire. "My father will accept my Consort as the father of his heir, or we shall abandon Incendium together and take the boy with us." She stood tall and looked formidable. "Truly, my father is the least of the obstacles before us."

Kraw bowed to disguise his smile of delight. If anyone in the court could change the mind of King Ouros, it was Drakina, and in this matter, he believed she was right. "I understand, Highness."

"Would you be so kind, Kraw, as to help with the arrangements? I would like to leave as soon as possible, and this time, I *will* take an entourage."

"Perhaps a diplomat or two, Highness?"

Drakina laughed. "A good half dozen diplomats, Kraw, if you please. I know my weaknesses."

She was gone then, leaving Kraw with an enormous list to complete. He dressed in haste, summoned his seven most promising attendants, and launched into the most hectic day in all his memory.

But this, this was the service Kraw loved to provide to his patron and king. Justice would be served, thanks to the intervention of Incendium, and King Ouros would receive all the credit.

Kraw's grandfather would have been proud.

AND SO IT CAME TO THIS.

Troy had never imagined he'd end his days in a penal colony in a far corner of the galaxy, nor did he imagine that he'd be executed for using his skills as commanded. But there was no doubting the purpose of the black chair on the pedestal before him.

He'd been roused at first light, had washed and shaved. He was naked, the better to ensure that he couldn't hide any surprises from his captors, but he walked tall between his two jailors. His mind was numb, for he had been drugged to ensure that he couldn't MindBend anyone in his vicinity.

His heart ached.

A crowd had gathered to watch his execution, and he was surprised by their numbers. He wasn't surprised by their obvious anticipation. There was nothing like an execution to bring out the worst in every kind. The procedure had been explained to him, and he doubted there'd be much drama. Not enough to justify their gathering, but bloodthirst wouldn't be denied.

There was no hope of a reprieve. No one in all of the galaxy wanted Troy alive enough to challenge his execution.

It wasn't a surprise, but it was a disappointment.

On Xanto, prisoners were executed by lethal injection. Troy would be strapped into the chair, made helpless, and the toxin, which had been precisely calibrated to his species and metabolism, would be injected into his arm. He'd feel as if he were falling asleep, but he wouldn't wake up ever again.

It would take less than four heartbeats. He'd been told as much and he believed it.

Troy saw his old employer in the audience, as well as an assortment of familiar gamblers. Prince Urbanus who had set the wager against Drakina was there, and Troy wondered whether he knew that Drakina had conceived. He hoped that she managed to defend herself against future attacks, because he was pretty sure there would be some.

Troy wished he could have survived to defend her himself, but that hadn't been an option.

The stone was cold beneath his feet, the penal colony of Xanto seeming even less hospitable on this cold and rainy morning. He could hear that the mines were silent, the work having been stopped so that the other inmates could witness his death.

Troy was to be a lesson for them.

In the days since his retrieval, he had been angry and he had been bitter. He had petitioned for appeal, based on Drakina's arguments, but every request had been denied. He might still have been feeling the weight of the injustice done to him, but the drug that suppressed his MindBending powers left him despondent. Fatalistic. What would be would be.

There was no point in fighting. He was vastly outnumbered and without his one gift, he wouldn't get far. He sat down in the chair and caught his breath at the chill of it against his thighs. But then, he wouldn't be cold for long.

Troy found himself thinking of that hunt with Drakina, the way she'd raced after the boar. It had felt to him like a wild and reckless ride, but she'd been completely in control. He smiled, remembering the wind in his hair, the exhilarating sense of her power, the connection he'd felt with her that day. He was glad, despite the ending to his own story, that he'd taken Urbanus' offer and had met her.

She'd changed his life, thawed his heart, convinced him to love.

Maybe they had been destined to mate.

Maybe she *would* tell the kid something good about him.

Troy's ankles had been shackled as well as his wrists. His jailors tightened the strap that bound his chest to the chair. This was it. The end. He found his heart racing, even though he knew that would only make the poison work faster.

They were about to blindfold him when there was a blinding flash of light.

Troy laughed aloud at the glorious sight of his Drakina. She appeared in front of him, not in the gallery for the audience. Her hair was loose and flowed around her as if it was alive. The tips lit with flames and she seemed to be throwing sparks into the air. She wore a dress of orange and red, one that flowed over her curves and could have been made of flame. It was feminine and sexy, but there was no hiding the sheer power of her body. Her eyes were glittering green, her lips curved in a satisfied smile.

Trust Drakina to transport right into the middle of an execution. He knew the location had been precisely calculated for maximum effect.

Troy was reminded of her entry into MacEnroe's Pub and knew that she liked making an entrance. This time, she had an entourage, many of them as richly garbed as she was, probably thirty attendants who had transported with her. What an expense! Troy was impressed that they had appeared in rank and with minimal disarray. The audience stirred in interest that they would get a show after all.

Drakina met his gaze and blew him a kiss, then turned to challenge the Emperor of Xanto. "You will not execute the Consort of the crown princess of Incendium," she declared, her voice carrying over the audience. "You will immediately surrender my destined mate to my custody." There was a protest, of course, but Drakina raised her voice. "His trial was so unfair that it seems likely the verdict was bought."

There was a bustle amongst the judiciary and the Emperor began to rise to his feet.

Drakina raised her voice. "I have brought an auditor from the Interstellar Office of Accounts to review the transactions recorded on the books of the court," Drakina continued smoothly. "The better to ensure that there is neither inconvenience or delay."

The Emperor's eyes narrowed. The comments became louder in the gallery, but Drakina ignored them. She gestured and four of her attendants hastened forward with the official argument. Although it could have been summarized on a tiny computer sheet, Troy guessed that Drakina had brought it on scrolls for effect.

There were a lot of scrolls. "I also have brought the appeal, brought by the King of Incendium on behalf of the prisoner, and all of the supporting arguments in its favor. I would be happy to second these lawyers to the Emperor's court for the duration of the appeal."

"This is quite sufficient," the Emperor declared, obviously trying to regain control of the situation, but Drakina continued as if he had not spoken.

If anything, her voice became louder. "The prisoner, as my Consort, will be taken into the custody of the court of Incendium, for his own protection."

"I protest!" declared the Emperor.

"Because you would sell his fate again?" Drakina demanded in a booming voice. A large percentage of the spectators quailed. She pointed at the governor of Xanto. "It is an outrage that such games are tolerated in a universe said to be civilized." She gestured and seven clerks stepped forward. "Here is the case brought against the Governor of Xanto by the Kingdom of Incendium for the violation of fundamental rights due to all sentient beings."

"But..." protested the emperor's aid.

"And here are the charges against the Pirates of Manganus Five, for seizing a Terran in violation of interstellar code," Drakina continued, beckoning to another four clerks bearing scrolls. She folded her arms across her chest. "I leave the Gloria Furora to you, for the moment." She inclined her head at some beings in the crowd. "There was not sufficient time to delve into the labyrinthine tunnels of their affairs."

The emperor might have protested, but Drakina threw out her arms and shifted shape in a blaze of golden light. Her dragon form glittered and she breathed fire at the sky, then at the podium of dignitaries. The emperor stumbled backward, his robes aflame, and Troy heard cries of consternation.

He also saw Prince Urbanus scowl, then pivot and disappear into the crowd of spectators.

Drakina was either unafraid of the prince of Regalia or had another plan for him. Troy trusted her to have planned for every detail.

She turned a sparkling glance upon him, cutting through the drug's haze with one look. With one slash of her talons, he was cut free, then she snatched him in her talons and took flight. She soared over the dark mines of Xanto in triumph, holding him close against the thunder of her heart. "I like you naked, Carrier," she murmured, her tone teasing. "Maybe I will keep you this way.”

“Maybe I’ll make it worth your while, princess.”

She landed with grace, shifting shape so that they stood together on the stone path he had just walked alone. One of the courtiers from Incendium cast a fur-lined cloak over his shoulders and another stood before them with a small volume.

“Marry me, Carrier?” Drakina asked, her gaze locking with his.

His heart raced, but he wanted her love, not her compassion. “Not for pity, princess.”

Her eyes gleamed with resolve. “I know little of this pity,” she said but he knew it wasn’t true. She reached to touch his cheek, tentative. “I have mated with a warrior and would keep him as my Consort.”

It was everything Troy had always wanted and more. He bent and kissed her thoroughly, vaguely aware the the official in front of them was clucking that the vows hadn’t been exchanged yet. Many of those in the gallery shared his feelings, because they were cheering.

Troy felt like cheering himself. There was someone in the galaxy who wanted him alive, after all.

The official cleared his throat. “The vows, Highness?”

“Yes, the vows.” Drakina gestured to another minion. “And please stream the ceremony to my father’s court. By the time we return to Incendium, he may have made his peace with my choice.” She cast a sparkling glance at Troy. “He will have a grandson to spoil, after all.”

“When do you plan to go back?”

“After a seclusion as befits a couple newly bound.” Her eyes twinkled. “I have been thinking of that boar, and that it should not go to waste.”

Troy grinned. “It would be about time to smoke it, and roast a haunch.”

Drakina’s hand closed over his own. “And we will bring some of this bacon when we return to Incendium. It may be of aid in winning my father’s agreement.”

“That’s brilliant, princess.”

“We have conquered with teamwork before, Troy, and we will do so again and again.” Her smile was confident and the weight of her hand in his was perfect. They turned to the official and exchanged their vows in clear voices.

For the first time, in a very long time, Troy felt optimism about his future.

No. He felt exhilaration about his future.

Because a dragon princess had claimed him for her own.

“This exchange of vows,” Drakina said when the official stepped back. “Must be sealed with a kiss.”

“You won’t get an argument from me, princess.”

THE ROYAL EGG WAS DELIVERED a little later than might have been expected, but Ignita assured Drakina—and Troy, who had been banished from the imperial birthing chamber—that this was normal for a first-spawn. The queen had been with her oldest daughter for the entire duration of the labor.

"You took much longer, Drakina," Ignita said with a laugh, her gaze lingering on the newly delivered egg. Drakina's sisters were in the nursery with her and her mother, along with the physician, six nursemaids, and a cluster of astrologers. It was an ornate and cozy room, without windows to ensure its security and better regulate its temperature, and generously proportioned for a reason.

The delivery of a royal egg always commanded a crowd.

The viewing of the royal egg before it hatched was also a popular activity.

It was not uncommon for a mother to unwillingly shift to her dragon form in the act of birthing the egg, which was yet another reason to have such a large room. Drakina was glad she hadn't done that, and that her mother had managed to restrain herself, as well.

She lay on a bed against one wall of the chamber. The egg was perched in the very middle of the room, at the focal point as it should be. Drakina thought it was the most beautiful dragon egg she'd ever seen. It was blue-green and shone with iridescence. The shell's surface was marked with opalescent patterns and caught the light. The physician bent over it, murmuring and listening as everyone else watched him in rapt silence. There was a tension in the chamber until his features brightened.

"The crown prince quickens!" he declared and there were tears of joy, as well as shouts of delight. Drakina's sisters kissed her one after the other, and her mother began to sing.

Even in the sheltered room, Drakina could hear the bells pealing in the city below, informing the citizens of Incendium of the good news. There would be feasting on this night, courtesy of King Ouros. It had been a long time since Peri's delivery, but memories ran long in Incendium of the lavish spreads bestowed on the populace when an egg quickened.

There was more to celebrate as well, for Troy had been officially pardoned. Just the day before, he'd received an official apology from the Emperor and another from the Governor of Xanto.

The locked portals to the chamber were opened, and Troy was summoned. The egg was surrounded by nursemaids who wrapped it in ermine and silk and tucked it into a warm nest. The astrologers hovered at the perimeter of the chamber, desperate to begin their examination of the shell's surface and chart the horoscope of the crown prince, but they had to wait.

Troy was the first male through the doors, but he came directly to Drakina instead of the egg. Gemma was beside Drakina and she momentarily blocked Troy's path. It might have looked inadvertent to another, but both Drakina and Troy knew better. Drakina knew the hard shimmer in her sister's eyes was enough to freeze the blood of many men.

Troy bowed and excused himself.

"I may never excuse you," Gemma said tightly, then moved out of his path.

Troy paused to hold her gaze, so unafraid that Drakina was proud. "Remember that I have been an assassin. If there is a man you would seek to kill, Gemma, I might be of aid to you."

"I do not need your aid," she replied, her voice hard.

"I can stand testimony against Urbanus now."

Gemma lifted her chin. "I will solve this matter myself."

Troy's gaze was simmering when he bent to kiss Drakina's cheek. "All right, princess?" he murmured for her ears alone.

"Never better," she said, and kissed him properly.

Gemma averted her face but didn't leave.

When Troy went to look at the egg, Drakina appealed to her sister yet again. "You should break the betrothal, Gemma," she advised quietly. "You should not marry Urbanus."

Meanwhile, Gemma smiled, a warrior princess to her toes. She was blond with blue eyes, and often underestimated for her prettiness. When her dragon was ascendant, though, it was impossible to imagine she was anything else. "I will keep the betrothal, and I will wreak vengeance from inside his own home. Nowhere is it writ that I will welcome him as my wedded husband." She arched a brow. "Urbanus will know the fullness of my wrath only when it is too late for him to save himself."

"Then you do not need Troy's help."

"I do not."

"But if Urbanus guesses..."

Gemma laughed. "Does he come to the quickening? No. He and his mother are casting spells, I am sure." She shook her head. "As if words could save him."

Drakina frowned. "Don't imperil yourself, Gemma. Vengeance is not noble."

"But sometimes it is necessary," she said with heat then walked away.

Drakina watched as Troy walked around the egg, his expression a mix of wonder and curiosity. Ouros was close behind him—and he examined the egg first— his pleasure with events more than clear.

Ouros even spoke to Troy, which was progress. Drakina guessed that her father was explaining the marvel of this particular dragon egg and how it exceeded all others.

Mostly because it contained his first grandson.

Troy glanced at Drakina and their gazes met, his slow smile prompting her lips to curve in return.

"Kraw!" Ignita called. "We must make ready for the blessings!"

"Indeed, Highness, the tidings have journeyed quickly. The High Priestess of Nimue has already arrived to give her blessing."

Drakina saw Troy wince at the news of their visitor. How did he know the High Priestess? Or what did he know of her?

Ignita fluttered, then hurried from the chamber to ensure that all was made ready for her guests. Gemma joined Ignita at the portal to welcome the first of those come to bless the egg.

Troy came to Drakina's side and perched on the side of the bed. He took her hand and laced their fingers together. "I'd rather face the high court of Xanto than your sister," he murmured.

She nodded rueful agreement. "She has the longest memory and the strongest battle skills."

Troy grimaced. "There are more reassuring things you could have said."

"I meant that if there is anyone to avenge the crime of Regalia, it will be Gemma," Drakina clarified. "She will accept that you were not truly responsible for Arista's death, in time."

"I don't have your lifespan to wait, princess."

"That is something we must discuss," Drakina said, holding fast to his hand. "But you know I will protect you."

He surveyed her warmly. "And you are okay?"

"It was not so bad. I am glad that there is a quickening already." She spoke quietly to him, as the others hastened about.

"Were you afraid?"

"Concerned," she admitted with a smile. She patted the pillow and he lounged beside her, his long legs stretched out beside hers.

"Me, too," he replied and kissed her knuckles. "It's so strange that you revere astrologers over astronomers. That's not the way it is on Terra."

"It is so strange that you divide the knowledge of the stars, calling part science and part myth. It is all wisdom."

Troy nodded understanding, and she knew he was thinking of something else. "How long until he's born?" He frowned. "Or hatched?"

"Several months in your time, but he will be tended at every moment. The greatest peril is past." She squeezed his fingers and tried to encourage his confidence. "I hear that you have been down in the shipyards again."

"It's fascinating. I always liked engines, and the stellar drive is so interesting."

Drakina smiled. "It is said that you have offered good suggestions."

Troy grinned. "I've just asked questions, princess. There's so much to learn."

"Do you like it on Incendium?" she asked, fearing his response. Troy did not have to have an ongoing role in the court, not now that the crown prince was hale.

"I do. I think of Terra, sometimes, but I feel as if I have two homes."

"I am glad."

He turned to face her. "But I have an idea, princess. I haven't done any MindBending as it seemed it would be rude, but I've noticed something that you might not have seen."

"Tell me."

"Everyone in Incendium worries about the planet falling toward the sun."

"Surely this is reasonable."

"Of course, but what if that, if all those thoughts, are actually drawing the planet toward the sun? What if the focus of so many minds is accelerating Incendium's fall?"

Drakina straightened. She had never considered the possibility, but Troy knew more of the power of the mind than she. "Never mind my father's concern."

"Right. There's a dragon who can make things happen by force of will!"

"What do you suggest?"

"I'm thinking that maybe you and I should return to Terra, with our son. It would be a huge change for you and a concession, I know—"

"Not so much of a concession, Troy, to be with you in the paradise you call home."

He smiled, obviously pleased by her words. That he hadn't expected them meant she had to confess more, once he was done. "Maybe that's how our son will save Incendium."

"I don't understand."

"All those people and dragons will turn their thoughts from the sun to our son." He pointed, and she realized that Terra was in the opposite direction, far away from the central star of their system. In fact, Terra was nearly as far from their sun as it was possible to be in the galaxy.

"And you think it might draw Incendium away from its sun."

"I think it's worth a try, princess."

"The boy's name has been divined, Highness," Kraw said, clearing his throat at close proximity. "It is to be Gravitas."

Drakina laughed aloud, for the astrologers had confirmed Troy's suspicion.

He grinned at her. "Maybe there is something about destiny being in a name."

"My father will be greatly pleased if my Consort invites him for a regular visit and offers him the chance to hunt verran again."

She watched as Troy considered that. "I could do it," he said. "It's quiet around the farm. I could MindBend whoever is in the vicinity when your family visits and hide their dragon forms."

"It is perfect!" Drakina threw her arms around him and kissed him with enthusiasm. "Not only are you the Carrier and my Consort, but you are my HeartKeeper, Troy." She saw a flicker of confusion in his eyes, mingled with hope. "I love you," she said, choosing the Terran phrasing and saw him smile. "And that means I have a gift for you."

He raised his brows. "There's more?"

Drakina held fast to his hands, for this was no joke. "My kind live many centuries, Troy, and though we mate with men, men do not live so long as that."

"I've wondered about that," he murmured.

"Our wise women considered this question for many generations, until they created a potion." Drakina beckoned and Kraw brought a chalice to her. She had never before seen the purple liquid or smelled it, but the formula was recorded and the chalice used for nothing else. "It is only offered to a HeartKeeper who is not a dragon shifter, and he or she has the right to refuse it."

"What happens if I drink it?"

"Your lifeline will be matched to mine. You will not survive long after my demise." She smiled. "And if I drink it as well, then my lifeline will be bound to yours."

He smiled a little, his expression making her heart skip and her blood warm. "Giving destiny a little help, princess?"

"Something like that."

Troy took the cup from Kraw, holding her gaze as he drank half of its contents. Without a word, he handed it to Drakina and she liked that he knew her intention even without peering into her thoughts. She drained the chalice, handed it to Kraw, then welcomed Troy's kiss.

Someone was admitted to the chamber, and they broke their kiss with reluctance. Drakina was too busy holding Troy's gaze to be curious about the new arrival. She was thinking instead of how soon they might celebrate the delivery of the egg, and how soon they might return to Terra...then she realized his features were changing. Before her very eyes, his face shifted from the form she'd once found ugly to a splendidly handsome countenance. A different man, and yet the same one.

He looked like a king. A prince.

A man for whom a thousand ships might be launched.

"Troy?" she whispered, reaching with her fingertips to touch his jaw. "What is happening?"

"I didn't know the potion did *that*," Callida commented.

"It doesn't, Majesty," Kraw said.

Drakina frowned. "Then what is wrong? Why is this happening?"

Troy leapt to his feet, and peered into one of the mirrors on the walls of the chamber. Then he hooted with delight and returned to swing her in the air. "You broke the spell, princess," he declared and his joy was unmistakable.

"What spell?" Drakina asked. She was relieved that his mouth had not changed at all, though she liked that he was so pleased.

"As part of his punishment, the MindBender was condemned to look as he did," the High Priestess of Nimue declared. She was the one who had entered the chamber and stood by the portal in her robes that flowed like water, leaning upon her silver staff. A fiery gem glinted in the setting at the top of her staff, like a watchful eye in the night. One of her white snakes peered through a gap in her robes, revealing that it was coiled around her waist. It, too, had watchful eyes. "I saw in the future that love could save the MindBender from his execution, but the high judge of Xanto did not believe a dragon princess could love a man who looked like that." She smiled. "We made a little wager."

"Fiends!" Drakina declared.

"They stacked everything against me that they could," Troy muttered.

"Because they understand nothing about my kind," Drakina replied with fury. Even as she marveled at the change in Troy's appearance, she knew it made no difference to her feelings. The High Priestess looked between them with satisfaction, then crossed the room to bless the egg.

But Drakina cared only for Troy. No matter his appearance, his nature was the same. He was a warrior, a champion, and the man who had won her love.

"HeartKeeper," he repeated, his gaze dropping to her lips. "I definitely like that title best of all the ones you've given me, princess."

"And that is good," Drakina said, looping her arm around his neck to draw him closer. "For it is one you cannot abandon."

"Just try to take it from me, princess," he whispered, his eyes shining, then slanted his mouth over hers in a most satisfying kiss.

It was both slow and thorough, which suited Drakina very well.

NERO'S DREAM

Nero has always aspired to be an astrologer in the royal court of Incendium. When he divines a portent about the pending royal marriage, he makes the perilous journey to the capital city, only to be kept from delivering his tidings in time. Worse, Nero is assigned the task of pursuing a dragon princess bent on taking vengeance upon her reluctant groom, a feat he knows can't be done. His dream appears to be lost forever—until the captivating princess Peri surprises this unlikely advisor.

CHAPTER ONE

NERO HAD TO PINCH HIMSELF.

Again.

Not only had he survived the trek to the capital city of Incendium, not only was the city more of a glittering and bustling wonder than he'd ever imagined, not only was he inside the imperial palace—but he was to have a hearing with the viceroy, Kraw.

It was worth another pinch. To be standing in this antechamber with its floor inlaid in a geometric pattern of stones, its vaulted ceiling showing the coats of arms of every territory in Incendium, was beyond his wildest aspirations.

He wasn't surprised though. He'd cast the chart for this day and been amazed by it. This was a day fraught with meaning. A day in which dreams could come true. A day in which secrets could be revealed, in which fortunes could be made, in which futures would be set. Nero had been over the chart again and again. He had checked his sources a hundred, no, a thousand times, and this day was one of the great nexus points.

A crossroads in the lifelines of many.

Including himself.

Nero didn't underestimate the potential of that.

He had dreamed all his life of visiting the capital city. He had imagined the marvel of entering the palace. Already two of his smaller hopes were achieved and it wasn't even midday. He might even catch a glimpse of one of the royal family on this day, and see a third goal achieved. The twelve princesses of Incendium were all dragon shifters, each more beautiful than the last. At the possibility of even being close to one of them, Nero had to take a deep breath and close his eyes. He'd studied the holograms. He'd seen them on the vid. He'd been enthralled by the princesses his entire life. Even being in the imperial palace—where they must also be—made his very marrow quiver.

If one spoke to him, he might not survive the encounter. His heart might explode.

The dragon shifters ruled Incendium, both because they were aristocrats and because they lived much longer than mortal men. In eons past, they had possessed the time to build their power, and to defend it. They mated rarely, typically with men or women as this was believed to protect the integrity of their lineage. The child was always a dragon shifter.

Rare was the union between two dragon shifters, such as that between the current king and queen. There were those—including Nero—who believed that was the reason for the prosperity of Incendium since that wedding day. Fortune smiled upon the kingdom. The horoscopes were radiant with opportunity and wealth.

Except for this day, which appeared as a shadow on Nero's chart.

A blot on the proverbial sun.

The astrologers in the royal court divined the destined mates of each imperial dragon and Nero couldn't believe that they had endorsed the marriage between Canto and Drakina. They were not destined mates. Canto could not be Drakina's HeartKeeper.

Why had anyone even tried to arrange such a dynastic match?

Even without the chart, Nero would have guessed the pairing to be ill-fated.

And now he brought the proof of it to the royal court. In proving his abilities, he might achieve his dream of becoming an astrologer in the royal court. It could happen on this day, as a result of this portent he delivered. It was within his grasp.

Maybe then he'd get used to seeing the princesses.

Maybe he'd manage one day to speak to one.

He turned the scroll in his hands, his palms damp. But first hurdles first. The imperial city was a long way from the quiet town of Mola where Nero had grown up, but his prophecy couldn't have been entrusted to a courier.

He had to deliver it himself, to Kraw.

Here he stood, still in his dusty traveling cloak and his muddy boots. He needed a shave and probably a haircut, and was not fit to see the imperial majesties, but he could not have delayed the delivery of the prophecy. It was too important. Time was too pressing.

Nero knew his prediction would be unwelcome. The entire city was aflutter with preparations for the royal wedding and to hear that the nuptials were not destined to occur would not be good news.

He wondered yet again why the royal astrologers hadn't seen this truth.

He wondered if they had but no one had mentioned it outside the palace.

Maybe no one had believed it.

Why had the match been arranged?

Myriad shuttles were descending from the starport, bringing guests from allies and other worlds. Nero had seen the shuttles gleaming in the distance, even two days before as he walked toward the city, and still more came. There were decorations in the streets and the day itself had been declared a holiday. He'd seen families walking toward the imperial gates, hoping to catch a glimpse of the happy couple after they exchanged their vows. He'd had to come through the kitchen entrance—no less busy, given the number of tradesmen delivering food for the feast to follow the service—and had been told twice that Kraw had no time for such folly as a message from one such as he. Only Nero's insistence and his persistence had gotten him this far.

He was right and he knew it. Sapior had taught him well.

A clerk in the livery of Regalia had arrived just before Nero and had been ushered up the stairs immediately, while Nero had been shown to this room.

It *had* been a long time since he'd been left here.

Nero feared suddenly that they had placed him in a corner of the palace to be forgotten since he wouldn't go away. He checked the door, only to discover that it was secured from the other side. His prophecy must be heard, as soon as possible! He spun in the middle of the chamber, seeking another way out, but there was none.

He drew his knife, determined to force the lock on the door. He had no sooner laid his hand upon the latch than the door opened silently.

To reveal a dignified older man on the threshold, with a magnificent white mustache dressed in the livery of the king.

He had a gaze cold enough to strike terror into a dragon shifter.

In fact, Nero would have bet that this man had perceived at least three of his secrets, and all of his hopes and dreams. That with just a glance.

He looked Nero up and down again, then met the younger man's gaze. "You are the one who calls himself an astrologer?" His skepticism was clear.

Nero had expected that. He hadn't attended the Royal University of Astrologers. But that didn't mean Sapior's teachings were wrong.

Even if they were unconventional. Sapior had attended the university, made a discovery and been cast out for daring to suggest the ancient methods could be improved.

It occurred to Nero in that moment just how the royal astrologers might have missed the truth.

"Yes, sir, I am." Nero bowed low. "I come to offer what I have learned, in service to my lord king."

The older man frowned. "I am Kraw, viceroy of Incendium. I do not have time this day for whimsy, young man. If this is a jest, you will regret it."

"I understand, sir, but it is neither whimsy nor a jest. I bring a dire prophecy."

Kraw arched a brow.

Nero unfurled the scroll he had carried all the way from Mola. "I can show you, sir, how the stars aligned in this horoscope..."

"The prophecy," Kraw interrupted crisply.

Nero closed his mouth and met the viceroy's gaze squarely. "The princess Drakina and the prince Cantos will not be wed this day. Ensuing events will cause a furor between the royal houses of Incendium and Regalia, if not an outright crisis."

"Why?"

"Because the crown prince Canto will die."

Kraw smiled thinly. "I fear you are mistaken."

"Sir! If you'll just look..."

Kraw's eyes narrowed and he backed out of the doorway. "The wedding ceremony will begin within moments. The family is already assembled. Your prophecy is wrong. I thank you for your concern on behalf of the royal family, but you are mistaken."

"I'm right! If you'll just look!"

Kraw's tone became steely. "You have made a mistake, as inexperienced astrologers often do. You have no place here and will immediately be escorted to the gates." He stepped back and snapped his fingers, which brought an armed man to his side.

Nero couldn't believe it. He hadn't come this far to be turned aside. He'd never even imagined that he wouldn't be able to deliver the prophecy. He'd expected to be doubted, but not silenced.

Outrage made him bold. Nero stepped forward, making the only gamble he could. "Sir! If I could show one of the royal astrologers..."

"You cannot." Kraw lowered his voice and spoke more kindly. "I am certain your intentions are good, but this is a day of relentless demand. Travel safely back to wherever you are from." The viceroy pivoted and was immediately surrounded by half a dozen servants seeking his counsel on one matter or another.

How could Nero warn them if they wouldn't listen?

How could he stand witness to a travesty he could have helped them to avoid?

"You can't linger," the guard warned him and gestured toward the corridor that led from the antechamber to a minor door. "Hurry along."

Nero hadn't taken three steps when he heard processional music echoing through the palace. The wedding was beginning!

The guard urged Nero toward the door. "Come on. I'm supposed to be upstairs already." When Nero hesitated, the guard dropped his hand to the hilt of his knife. "Don't make trouble," he advised. "Not today. Think of the princess. It's her wedding day."

Nero did think of the princess and felt compassion for her. He allowed himself to be ushered out of the palace, although he wished he could think of a reason to do otherwise. He stood in the courtyard, letting people hurry around him and reviewed his cred. He had less than five units to his name. He knew without looking in his purse. He'd spent everything in making this journey, planning on at least a small reward and hoping for a position at court. He didn't even have enough to pay for a night in the meanest hovel.

He felt like a fool.

He'd better start walking back home. He'd find a quiet place outside of town, maybe a barn or a shed, use a little of his dreamweed and try to divine where he'd gone wrong.

Nero had turned to leave when he realized the music had stopped.

In fact, the palace had fallen strangely silent. Everyone might have been holding their breath at once.

What had happened?

Was it the prophecy?

Nero heard the clatter of running footsteps and a man burst out of the same door he had just left. It was the clerk from Regalia, but now he looked terrified. He shoved Nero out of the way and ran for the gates, as if his worst nightmare was fast behind him. Nero lost sight on him en route to the star station.

There was a scream from inside the palace, a scream that made everyone in the courtyard cower in fear.

A dragon scream of rage.

There was a crash of breaking glass, and Nero realized in horror that the roof of the palace had been smashed. Still, his heart thrilled at the sight. A dragon of deepest green, scales gleaming like obsidian, roared into the sky and breathed a plume of fire toward the stars. Such power! Such majesty!

It was the princess Drakina.

When the dragon princess pivoted in the air, her great black wings flapping leisurely, everyone in the imperial city watched in awe. She turned to scan the city below and Nero saw her gaze brighten. She dove downward, swooping low over the courtyard, clearing the gates, and reaching a talon down into the crowd. Her precision and grace were awesome, and he watched with wonder as she soared high again, claws empty. She circled, breathed fire, and spiraled toward the earth again.

Nero knew then that his prophecy had come true.

"WHERE IS THAT ASTROLOGER?" Kraw bellowed. He raced back down the stairs from the ceremonial chamber, moving as quickly as he could through the press of people. Already he was envisioning war between the two planets, which was never more than a puff of smoke away. Disaster had to be averted.

If it wasn't already too late for that.

The viceroy was followed by a coterie of royal astrologers, more than one of them curious about this arrival and his tidings. There were already murmurs of the new arrival being a fraud—for none of them had discerned this dire portent, which meant it had to be wrong or a trick—and demands to see his calculations. He might even be responsible for these events! Astrum, the oldest and grumpiest, wished to know his assumptions, as well as his credentials.

Kraw wanted to know what else the arrival had divined. He was a man of remarkable appearance, simply dressed but bright of eye. Kraw had been certain of the power of his intellect, if not the merit of his conclusions. There was an air of mystery about the professed astrologer, which the viceroy instinctively distrusted.

Men of mystery were often unpredictable. They brought change and challenge, neither of which were welcome to Kraw.

He didn't fail to note this man already showed that tendency.

He found him in the courtyard, waiting with a dignity that Kraw found admirable despite himself. The viceroy paused to catch his breath, then proceeded toward the younger man.

"You were right," he acknowledged.

The barest smile touched the man's lips. He flicked a glance skyward. "So, I see."

"What did you see?"

The younger man unfurled his chart again and the astrologers of the court clustered around him. "That Prince Cantos would decline to wed Princess Drakina, that he would send a minion to the ceremony in his own stead, that Princess Drakina would take exception to this."

"And?" Kraw prompted.

He winced. "That she would retaliate."

"That none would be able to stop her," added the oldest astrologer, pointing to the new arrival's chart.

The astrologers winced and sighed as one. "And that there would be tumult between the two royal families as a result."

"How did you make these calculations?" Astrum demanded, suspicion in his tone. "Our charts of the day look vastly different from this one."

"I was taught a method that reveals secrets more readily than traditional methods..."

"Who taught you?" Astrum boomed, but the viceroy pushed the astrologer aside.

"There is no time to compare technique," Kraw declared with an impatience he thought justifiable. "What is the princess Drakina going to do?"

The astrologers turned to the new arrival, letting him share the news.

"Whatever she does, sir, he doesn't survive it."

Kraw pinched the bridge of his nose and walked away, thinking furiously. He had thought this a poor match from the outset, not only because there was no sign that Cantos was the Carrier of the Seed, but because the natures of the betrothed pair were so different. It made no sense to him to arrange a dynastic match to ensure an alliance, knowing it would be barren.

But King Ouros was not to be defied.

It also didn't seem right to Kraw that a man would show such fear of his intended, even before the nuptials. It certainly wasn't fitting for a crown prince to cower. It *was* sensible to have a measure of caution when dealing with the royal family of Incendium, but showing fear, in Kraw's experience was a strategic error. There was not a predator in all of the galaxy that did not become more predatory when taunted with the scent of terror. It was in their very making.

And now, Cantos had insulted the dragon shifter he feared. In fact, he had insulted the entire house of Incendium. Kraw doubted the matter would end well. He suspected, in fact, that it would end in a conflagration. The only possible advantage to the situation was that so many dignitaries and diplomats were gathered in the palace and had witnessed the insult. A tribunal might find justification in whatever actions were taken.

There were a thousand things to do to manage the situation, and only one individual Kraw could dispatch to do the most important one.

"You," he said, pointing at the newly arrived astrologer. "What is your name?"

"Nero, sir." He bowed, his manner expectant.

"Can you fly a Starpod?"

The would-be astrologer straightened and his eyes brightened. "I've flown the sim at the annual fair and won a prize."

The other astrologers chortled at this. "It is not the same," Astrum muttered, then reached for the chart. "Just as this is not the same as our calculations. I would review your findings."

The arrival flicked the chart out of Astrum's hands and rolled it again.

"It is mine." Tension crackled between them.

"Where are you from?" Astrum demanded but Kraw silenced him with a gesture.

"Your sim experience will have to suffice," he said. "Go to the star station and take a Starpod. Tell them it is on my authority, if they ask. Follow the princess and try to stop her from doing anything rash."

The younger man looked skeptical, which Kraw took as another sign of his intelligence. "Is that possible, sir?"

"Probably not, but I expect a full report upon your return."

"Yes, sir. Thank you, sir."

There was an explosion from the star station and even from this distance, flames and smoke could be discerned. Kraw feared that was just the beginning. The green dragon soared into the sky again, carrying something.

Probably an injured clerk.

Kraw grimaced. "You had better hurry, Nero. Good luck."

THE STARPOD WASN'T AT ALL like the sim at the annual fair.

Nero had expected it to be newer and more sophisticated. He wasn't expecting it to be so radically different that it might have been a different vessel altogether. He supposed that Mola was a long way from the bright lights of the capital city.

There was a clear sphere in the middle of the dash, which appeared to float in its holder. At least that was familiar—even if it didn't have directions inscribed on it like the one at the fair. He considered the smooth control panel with something like horror, which the attendant took for awe.

What if he crashed it?

"Only the newest and the best for the imperial fleet," that man said. "Voice activated. You're going to love it." He patted the dash and it illuminated with a thousand pinpoints of light. "These babies rock." He grinned. "Of course, you'll need all the help you can get if you're going to catch Drakina."

With that, he was gone, the door sealed, and Nero strapped in. There was nothing on the dash that resembled the controls he knew.

Voice activated.

"Prepare for departure," he commanded, feeling a little silly talking to himself. The engine purred to life, which meant he wasn't actually talking to himself. "Mission is to pursue Princess Drakina," he said with more confidence. "Please request clearance from Incendium Control for lift-off and for departure trajectory." Glittering light surrounded the vehicle, which was a hundred times better than the sim.

Nero's heart was racing.

"You have right of way, Incendium six-five-nine," came a voice, which must have been from Incendium Control. "All pathways are cleared for you. At your leisure."

Nero surveyed the smooth dash again.

"At your leisure," repeated the ship.

Well, there was no reason to delay.

"Loose moorings. Power thrusters." Nero nodded as the ship followed his command. The station was crowded with vehicles, and he knew that he was being watched by others. Even the most junior mechanic probably had more flight experience than Nero did.

The princess was barely a speck in the sky.

"Lock coordinates on Princess Drakina," he commanded. The floating sphere illuminated and Nero closed his hand around it. He saw a crosshair of light appear on the inside of the windshield and rolled the ball until the crosshair locked on the silhouetted dragon. He tapped it when nothing happened and a light flashed.

"Coordinates set," the ship declared. "Departure imminent. Six, five, four..."

At zero, it rose from the landing pad, so smoothly and quietly that Nero wanted to applaud.

"Trajectory is verified to be clear," the ship continued. "All systems go."

Nero gripped the armrests, sensing that the ship waited on him. "Pursue," he declared and nearly laughed out loud when the ship shot through the air. He'd never felt or witnessed such acceleration and he had no doubt that there had been a sonic boom over Incendium behind him. If they'd made sims like this, every boy in Incendium would want to be a star pilot.

Instead of just most of them.

Best of all, Nero was closing on the princess, even though she had a head start.

Drakina flew high in the sky. He'd thought she intended to drop the clerk and let him die from impact, but maybe she meant for the poor man to suffocate. Nero's mouth went dry as he realized the perils of service in the vicinity of royal dragon shifters.

The price of being a messenger with bad tidings.

It was easy to see that he could find himself in the clerk's company.

Suddenly Drakina was surrounded by a clear sphere, and Nero knew that the stories about the abilities of the royal dragons to create a crystal orb were all true.

He also knew what she was going to do, right before she disappeared.

She only needed an orb if she was going to transport, and she could only use the orb to transport somewhere comparatively close.

Nero's mouth went dry when he guessed her destination.

Regalia.

The twin planet in this system.

The home of Prince Canto, the betrothed of Drakina.

She was going after him.

"Target is generating an orb," Nero informed the ship. "What destinations are in range?"

"There are three wormholes on the target's trajectory," the ship said. "The first..."

"Does one go to Regalia?" Nero demanded.

"Yes." The ship sounded a bit huffy, perhaps because it had been interrupted. "Only one of the three."

The orb shone and Nero knew it was complete. The princess, orb and clerk vanished from view. Only a wink of light flashed where they'd last been. Then it faded as well.

"Target has entered transport," the ship reported. "Please advise."

"Pursue," he commanded. "Use the wormhole to Regalia."

"Be advised that entering a wormhole so quickly after another vessel will result in turbulence," the ship said.

"Is it dangerous?"

"Various life forms find it uncomfortable or even painful. The ship's integrity will not be compromised."

"Pursue," Nero repeated, hoping it wasn't too awful. He didn't have time to wait for the turbulence to subside.

"Prepare for transport in ten seconds," the ship declared. "Ten, nine, eight..." The ship counted down as they shot even higher into the sky. Nero knew they had to be close to the point where Drakina had disappeared. He knew that the wormholes were mapped and hard to discern with the naked eye.

Suddenly, the Starpod shimmered, shuddered, and Nero's ears popped. A maelstrom swirled around the ship, obscuring the view. Even though he'd only ridden the sim, he knew this was the effect of the transport.

They had entered the wormhole.

The reality was much worse than the sim. He felt as if his skin had been turned inside out, his bones folded and his muscles stretched taut. His stomach heaved. Nero closed his eyes and said a prayer, wishing he'd been a little more diligent in his attendance of religious services.

Maybe he should have cast his own horoscope. At least then he'd know whether he would survive this adventure.

This day.

But no, Sapior had always warned against that.

A second later, the ship shimmered and shuddered again. The maelstrom swirled, looking more like spinning stars. Nero's skin was turned back the way he preferred it to be, his bones were unfolded and his muscles contracted to their usual dimensions. He willed his stomach to settle.

He was very glad—and intrigued—to see the forests of another planet beneath him. They were different from the forests he knew, but reassuringly like the vids he'd seen of Regalia. The tree branches glittered with a coating of hoarfrost, a chilly sight that made him shiver, even though he was warm inside the Starpod. The sun seemed fainter here and its light more cold. He had the strange feeling that he was being watched.

"Cruising altitude over Regalia, Frost Pole," the ship informed him. "Closing on target. Sixteen hundred seconds to rendezvous."

Nero could see the silhouette of Drakina far ahead of him. The crystal sphere popped and its shards scattered before they sparkled and disappeared. She was still in her dragon form and flew a circle around a turret perched on the top of a jagged peak. There was snow on the roof of the building, and the clouds that wreathed the peak made it look as if it towered high over Regalia. A pennant tugged at the top of the tower roof, and Nero saw it was emblazoned with the insignia of the royal house of Regalia.

A gold shield on a blue ground, with lances crossed behind it.

The dragon princess landed in the walled courtyard beside the tower, and Nero admired the accuracy of her landing. The ship was close enough for him to see that the man in her grasp *was* a clerk, because he was dressed in the livery of Regalia. She set him down in a courtyard with some care, and he ran for the portal without delay.

Did he flee her, or had she sent him to fetch the crown prince? Nero saw Drakina settle back on her haunches, her eyes glowing as she apparently waited, and guessed the latter.

Then she turned her gaze upon him, her eyes narrowing as the Starpod landed beside her in the courtyard. "Target reached," the ship informed Nero. It then told him the coordinates of their location, the exterior temperature and wind direction, their proximity to the crown princess, and the amount of time he could remain and still have sufficient fuel to return to Incendium. It then opened the portal and wished him a pleasant day.

The way the princess was watching him left Nero skeptical of that possibility.

He hoped that dragons weren't as perceptive as they were rumored to be. He liked his secrets hidden.

But there was no question of returning to Incendium without tidings. The only way forward was through, and he'd come this far. Nero straightened his tabard, gripped the hilt of his very small knife, and left the ship with as much dignity as he could muster.

A flock of dark birds took flight suddenly, revealing that they had been nestled in the crenellations of the surrounding wall. They looked black against the cold sky, and were oddly silent. They flew away in a tight formation, and Nero had the sense that they had been summoned.

Or maybe they went to report what they had seen.

He shivered again. The princess Drakina smiled at the sight of him, and Nero stood tall before her, refusing to show any fear.

CHAPTER TWO

DRAKINA DIDN'T KNOW HIM.

She would have remembered a man as beautiful as this. He was tall and muscled, broad shouldered and trim through the hips. His skin was as dark as ebony and his eyes the color of fine amber. She inhaled deeply, not really surprised to get a whiff of the grain fields of Medior, the gushing river at Mola, the seductive tinge of dreamweed.

He was from the equatorial zone of Incendium, or at least he had been there recently.

His clothing was simple but well made. He took care of his boots, and she could see that the ridiculously small blade he carried had been polished and honed. A thoughtful man, then, one who tended his responsibilities.

And one who was intrepid. He walked toward her, armed with only that small knife, wary but without hesitation.

She could have shifted shape to reassure him about her intentions, but Drakina wasn't in a mood to reassure anyone. Instead she lowered her head, her chin almost brushing the ground, so that their gazes were level.

He flinched, but only a dragon would have seen the fleeting reaction.

She was impressed.

"Sent to witness the carnage?" she asked, keeping her voice to a low rumble.

"I believe I was sent to *stop* the carnage, Highness," he said with a bow. He had a pleasing voice. Melodic. Deep. Drakina imagined he would sing well. There was a gleam in his eyes that made her think he was smarter than most. "But I know better."

"You know better than the command of my father?"

"It was the viceroy Kraw who sent me, Highness. I would not dare to challenge an edict from the king."

"Why do you think it can't be stopped?" Drakina was curious, despite herself. Fury simmered within her, but the faithlessness of Canto was not this man's fault.

He smiled ever so briefly, inclined his head as if to beg her forgiveness, then unfurled a scroll that he had been carrying on his back. She immediately saw that it was a horoscope. "If you see here, Highness, the death of Cantos at your talon is indicated in this quadrant of the chart..."

"You're an astrologer?" He didn't look like any of the royal astrologers. He was too young, too handsome...too charming.

"Yes, Highness. This chart and its portent brought me to the capital city, for I sought to warn your father..."

"But you didn't arrive in time?"

He opened his mouth, then closed it again.

Drakina smiled that he had some diplomacy. More than she did, at least. "You *did* arrive in time, but were not allowed to deliver your message."

"The viceroy was very busy with so many guests."

Drakina dropped her voice to a conspiratorial whisper. "I am glad. It would have been most awkward if my father had forbidden me to avenge the insult."

He looked discomfited with this.

"It is a question of honor," Drakina insisted. "And the insult to my father in his own home. It could not pass unchallenged, and it is better if I do the honors, so to speak."

"Of course, Highness." He fixed her with a look that was surprisingly courageous. "But you surely must understand that there will be repercussions."

"I should hope so! What kind of queen would let her son's death go unremarked?" Drakina straightened. "I expect a massive diplomatic incident. Maybe even war."

He was watching her. "But you guess that the inevitable tribunal will find in your favor."

"Will they?"

He nodded, proving that he was completely unlike the royal astrologers. They never gave straight answers, must less absolute ones.

"We need more astrologers like you at court," Drakina said. "Where are you from? Are there more like you?"

"Mola, Highness. A small town..."

"In Medior, where wizards are said to lurk in every shadow and all citizens partake of the pleasures of dreamweed."

"Not all, Highness."

Drakina waited.

"Children don't partake, for example."

She laughed but he cleared his throat.

"There are no more like me. My tutor Sapior taught me his methods before he died, for he had no child. I am the last to know his way of casting a horoscope."

"Was he self-taught?"

"He attended the university, Highness, but was cast out for his attempt to add an unconventional methodology to the curriculum."

Drakina considered the man who stood before her and hazarded a guess. "If his way requires the dreamweed, take care, Master Astrologer. My father has no tolerance of it, and any caught with it in their possession in his household are burned alive for the crime."

He bowed again, a little stiffness in his shoulders. He did use the dreamweed, then. "I thank you for your advice, Highness."

Before she could ask more, she became aware of the sharp tang of fear. She turned to eye the portal to the tower and discerned the clerk hiding in the shadows inside. He was pale still and she could see his knees trembling.

"Speak!" she commanded, letting her voice roar so that the stones rattled. Drakina could feel the clerk tremble and heard his heart skip a beat.

The astrologer, however, stood his ground and watched avidly.

Fearlessly.

That would keep him alive in the palace.

"My lord prince declines to meet you, my lady," the clerk said, his voice faint.

"That is of no concern," Drakina said. "I will go to him."

The clerk squeaked, bowed, and raced up the stairs inside the tower. Drakina shifted shape, assuming her human form, and surveyed her wedding dress critically. The beads of gold and orange and red still shone brightly and the silk rustled as she moved. She looked at the astrologer.

"Magnificent, Highness." He bowed. "Your splendor rivals that of the sun."

She smiled. "You aren't afraid of me," she felt compelled to note.

His grin was quick and confident. He indicated the chart. "There is a witness indicated here in the margin, Highness. A man of little consequence, yet one who survives the encounter."

"You?"

"I hope so, Highness."

Drakina made for the door, knowing he would follow her. A witness.

She was no astrologer, but she had a feeling that this man would not be considered to be of so little consequence after this day.

She strode into the tower, anger and purpose flooding through her.

Canto would not share the happy fate of the astrologer from Medior.

Drakina was looking forward to ensuring that.

THE STAIRS WERE STEEP AND NARROW, though the princess Drakina ascended them quickly. It was only as he hastened after her that Nero wondered whether they had been built that way in defense against dragons.

In her dragon form, the princess could never have climbed these stairs.

The fact that she could change shape at will meant they were no obstacle.

As a dragon, in fact, she could have torn the roof from the tower instead, and plucked out her reluctant suitor.

Perhaps the builders of Regalia did not think matters through.

The room at the top of the tower was of good size, but still not big enough for Drakina in her dragon form. It was simply furnished. Even from the stairs, Nero could see that there was only a curtained bed, a carved wooden chair, a table and an unlit brazier in the room. The shutters were open so that the room was filled with cold winter light, and the chill of the wind. A man sat on the bed, his face in shadows, his arms folded across his chest. He looked like a petulant child, not a warrior.

Not a king.

There was no barrier at the summit of the stairs, save the clerk.

"My lord prince is not receiving guests, my lady," he said.

"Canto will receive me," Drakina replied. "After all, I am no mere guest. I am his *betrothed*."

Even though Nero was behind the princess, he could feel the force of her will. He saw its effect upon the clerk, who took a step back.

"I have no wish to harm you," she said softly. "But no one will stand in my way on this day." She inhaled deeply, then dropped her voice even lower. "You must know that your terror makes you almost irresistible. It awakens my every urge to hunt."

The clerk's terror clearly doubled at that confession.

"Do not suffer her to pass!" cried the man on the bed.

The clerk looked between the two royals, his panic clear. He glanced at Nero, who had no intention of assaulting the princess on Canto's behalf. The prince remained where he was.

The clerk considered Drakina, his agitation rising. She took another step, and then another. He visibly trembled, then suddenly ducked to one side, covering his head with his hands.

Nero wondered what retaliation he expected that gave him the strength to resist for as long as he had.

The prince threw a crockery vessel at him. "Coward!" he shouted as it shattered against the stone wall.

"Coward?" Drakina swept into the chamber and crossed the floor to the bed. She shimmered a little in her fury, and Nero saw sparks flying from the ends of her hair. The crown prince made a little moan and eased to the back corner of the bed.

As if he would hide.

But that was impossible. Drakina seized the prince and threw him bodily on the floor. Evidently her strength was consistent between forms. Canto crawled backward, his horror clear, and her eyes flashed like lightning.

"Who is the coward, Canto? The servant who refuses to be a fool at his master's command, or the man who doesn't have the courage to speak for himself?"

"You know we'd never get along," Canto said hastily. "You know we couldn't make each other happy."

"Stand up and show your merit!" she commanded.

He got up with obvious reluctance, but didn't stand tall. He lifted his hands. "It won't work, Drakina..."

"So, you hid yourself away here and sent a minion to tell me of it." Drakina's scorn was clear. "You know that no king could endure the humiliation you visited upon my father's house this day!" She seized his shirt and lifted him to his toes with one hand. His eyes widened. "You could have made *one* protest in the year of our betrothal. You could have spoken to me. You could have arrived yourself to tell me."

Canto shook in her grip. "Drakina, I beg of you. Have mercy..."

"But you were a coward." Drakina's lip curled. "You sent a clerk."

"Drakina! Don't hurt me!"

"You joust," she reminded the prince with scorn. "You ride in tournaments. You're lauded for your bravery. How can this be?"

The prince flushed. "It's all arranged," he admitted, and Nero felt Drakina's disgust like a cold wave.

"Arranged? Your victories are bought?"

"Negotiated," Canto said. "And why not? I'm the crown prince."

"I cannot abide such timidity of spirit," Drakina seethed. Canto flailed in her grip but couldn't escape. "I thought you *valiant*. I thought you the gem in Regalia's crown. I thought I had to be wrong about you. Coward!"

"Liar!" he retorted, his face flushed.

Drakina stilled and her silence made Nero fear what she would do. "What is this?" she asked quietly.

"My mother guessed the truth, after the alliance was made," Canto said, growing more bold as he made his accusations. "She told me yesterday. You mean to destroy us all and make Regalia your own. You mean to populate it with the worms you bear and drive us out..."

"Worms?" Drakina echoed and put him on his feet.

Nero feared that was a bad sign, but Canto was emboldened by it. He straightened his shirt and his eyes flashed. "Yes, *worms*! The spawn of dragons," he spat. "Why should I wed a dragon? Why should my sons be dragons? Why should I participate in spreading the abomination of your kind? I can have any woman!"

Drakina smiled and examined her nails. "Our match would be barren, Canto," she said gently. "You need not fear such a fate, for yourself or your kingdom."

Canto took a step back. "Barren?" he repeated, his tone incredulous. "*Barren?*"

"You are not the Carrier of the Seed for me," Drakina explained mildly. "Our match seals a treaty, no more and no less." Her smile was chilly. "There will be no worms, as you call them. No eggs, either."

Canto was clearly shocked. "But my mother said..."

Drakina interrupted him crisply. "Queen Arcana would do well to abandon her grimoires for books of solid research. The biology of our kind is well documented. Any one of you could have learned the truth with very little effort. Must I add lazy to your list of attributes, Canto?"

"You lie!" Canto cried. "You want Regalia for your own! You will overrun us and steal all that is our own. This is no more than a trick, and I will not marry you."

"That would compromise the alliance between our kinds, the alliance to see our planets saved."

"You talk of science, but marriage has no effect on dying sons." Canto backed away from Drakina. "We can just part ways. No harm done."

"That is possible no longer," Drakina said sadly.

"We can be reasonable about this..."

"The time for reason is gone." She dropped her voice lower. "Consider, Canto, that if I take vengeance for my father, then he cannot take vengeance for me. It is the law."

Canto froze, new panic dawning in his eyes. "Vengeance?" he said, and his voice was a squeak.

Drakina's smile was cold. "You wanted me to show mercy, Canto."

His expression was wild. "But..."

"My father loves to hunt. He would welcome the opportunity to hunt you and extract a toll for what you did this day." She shook her head. "I doubt the payment would be rendered quickly."

The prince's face was white at this point and his lip trembled. He had backed into the wall.

Nero was intrigued. Drakina was clearly angry and insulted, but she didn't act solely out of passion. She *was* showing mercy.

Canto spared a glance at the window, as if he might flee.

"There is no escape, Canto. He can find you anywhere, just as I have done." Drakina strolled toward the prince. "Go ahead, Canto," she invited. "Beg me again to show you mercy."

He fell to his knees and seized the hem of her dress. He kissed it. "Just let me live, Drakina," he pleaded and his groveling made Nero wince. Drakina must have sensed his disgust for she turned to look at him. Nero had the strange sense that their thoughts were as one. "I'll never grant trouble to anyone again, Drakina. Just let me live."

Drakina arched a brow, inviting Nero's comment.

Nero cleared his throat. "You will live forever, my lord, in the memory of men, as a warning of the price of insulting the royal house of Incendium."

Canto gasped.

Drakina smiled. "I do like you, astrologer." she murmured with satisfaction. Canto dared to look up at her. "But not you," she said to the prince. "And now, it is time for mercy."

"Drakina!"

Her eyes shone as she seized Canto. She flung him bodily out the window, then leapt out the window herself. She shifted shape in a blaze of light, right after her foot left the sill. Nero raced to the window to watch.

Canto screamed as he tumbled toward the moat, far far below.

Nero saw Drakina in her dragon form sweep down to snatch the falling prince out of the air. She breathed a plume of fire into the sky and soared high with her captive. Canto begged incoherently, then screamed as her talon pierced his belly. The prince fell abruptly silent and drops of his blood fell like blue rain.

"She kept her word," the clerk acknowledged. "It *was* quick." Then he bowed his head and murmured a prayer.

Nero hastened down the stairs, knowing he had witnessed all he needed to see. He raced across the courtyard, composing his account in his mind. There was blue blood spattered over the Starpod, a blue so deep as to be nearly purple.

It was the unmistakable hue of the blood of the crown family of Regalia.

Nero spared a glance upward in time to see the princess bite into the prince and shake him like a doll. The way she tore at his flesh indicated that there would be nothing left of him.

Nothing but the word of Nero, the princess, and the clerk from Regalia.

Could he be relied upon?

The princess roared in that very moment. Nero looked up to see something gold falling toward him, catching the light as it spun ever downward. He snatched it out of the air, then opened his hand. It was the signet ring of the crown prince, the mark of his station and his inheritance.

Even Nero knew that the princes of Regalia never suffered to have the ring of state removed. It was eased from the royal finger after death, and not a moment before.

The ring, and the blue blood already drying upon it, told eloquently of what Nero had witnessed. He had to make haste back to Incendium.

WHEN THE STARPOD SETTLED gently into its parking spot at Incendium's star station Nero wanted to leap out and kiss the ground. He would be a happy man to never transport again.

He wasn't even sure he'd ride the sim.

But he recalled the decorum expected of those in the royal service. He left the vehicle with dignity, returning its wishes for a pleasant day, and thanked the attendant at the star station. A team hastily surrounded the vehicle and began to refuel it. He strode back toward the palace, intent upon giving his report to Kraw with all haste.

Nero immediately discovered why the Starpod might be in demand. He found the palace in uproar. Guests were leaving in droves—some, in fact, could have been said to be fleeing Incendium. The courtyard thronged with servants, each trying to summon the vehicle of choice for their lords and masters. The congestion was unholy. He could hear the booming commands of King Ouros, and the shrill notes of Queen Ignita as both strove to calm their guests.

Inside the palace, the chaos was even worse. Servants ran up and down the great stairs, hustling and bustling. He heard complaints and a good bit of gossip. Some of the guests were on their comms, telling others of events on Incendium, and Kraw was nowhere to be seen.

Nero decided that the viceroy must be in the imperial chambers. He took a deep breath and dared to push his way up the stairs. He felt like one of the zarcota fish that traveled upstream to spawn each spring near Mola, for he was the only one trying to climb the stairs. The deluge of guests poured downward, heading to the courtyard and the starport. It was only with real determination—and probably because of some size advantage— that he made any progress at all.

He was surprised that so few of them chose to remain to eat. He could smell the feast that had been prepared, and his own belly growled at its emptiness. Surely the food wouldn't be wasted?

Nero reached the summit of the stairs and heard Kraw's voice. He was trying to soothe someone, probably the king or queen. He couldn't speak without an invitation in their presence. He would make himself visible, though, and hope to attract Kraw's attention. He gripped the signet ring and stepped into the royal chamber.

It was an astonishing room. Nero had seen it in hologram, of course, for all the great ceremonies of Incendium were held in this room and broadcast on the vid to the citizens of Incendium. In reality, it was far more glorious and much bigger than he'd imagined.

In this moment, it was almost empty, so its marvels were easily appreciated. The chamber was still decorated for the exchange of vows, with flowers and garlands of flowers in every hue. Some of the garlands had been torn free of their moorings, and there were bright petals on the ground. More than one blossom had been crushed underfoot when the guests left.

On the far side of the chamber, near a pair of thrones, Kraw spoke to a couple. Even if Nero hadn't recognized King Ouros and Queen Ignita from their official images, the splendor of their garments and their crowns would have revealed their identity to him. The viceroy was speaking quickly. The king looked annoyed. The queen appeared to be flustered.

Nero fingered the ring. He stood politely, hoping Kraw's gaze would pass his way.

In the meantime, he looked. Glory of the stars, the floor was magnificent. It was a map of Incendium, wrought of a hundred colors of stones from the planet's mines, the surface polished to such a gleam that Nero could almost see his reflection in it.

But the ceiling stole his breath away. He wanted to sit down hard when he tipped back his head to look. It arched so high overhead, leaving plenty of space for the royal family to shift shape, of course. Even though he had read of its design and glimpsed it in the vid, the splendor of the depiction of the stars in the galaxy nearly made his mouth drop open in wonder. They were brighter and more clear than even during the darkest nights in Medior, far from the lights of the city.

It was magnificent even despite the large hole on one side of the ceiling, where the actual sky could be seen.

Nero guessed that the princess had departed that way.

A party of architects arrived and hastened to consult with Kraw. The viceroy turned his attention to them and drew King Ouros into the discussion. It was an artful choice, for the king immediately began planning the reconstruction. His anger dissipated as the architects discussed the challenges with him. Nero had read that the king had a particular interest in engineering and it was clear that he enjoyed the consultation and debate.

In the opposite corner, royal astrologers in their distinctive blue robes—the ones embroidered with stars and hemmed in fiery hues—argued over several horoscopes. The older one who had wanted to see his charts, the one who would have challenged him outright, looked up and glared at Nero.

Nero returned his gaze steadily. He had been right. He felt the older man's will and his malice and wondered at it.

Had Sapior known this man?

"Are you lost?" a woman asked from so close beside Nero that he jumped.

Nero spun, an explanation rising to his lips, then fell silent when he realized it was one of the crown princesses who addressed him. It was the youngest of the twelve, the princess Pericula, her long wavy copper hair hanging unbound over her shoulders. It fell almost to her knees, gleaming like a river. Her face was heart-shaped, her lips perfectly rosy, and her blue eyes sparkled as if they were filled with starlight.

Nero felt hot and then cold. She was beautiful.

He shouldn't have been surprised that she was more beautiful than her hologram.

His heart raced.

They called her Peri, he knew.

She *had* addressed him first.

Nero bowed low. "Highness!" He could see that her robe was of a midnight blue that favored her perfectly and there seemed to be gold threads woven into the cloth. It gleamed when she moved, catching the light, and was hemmed with white fur.

She laughed a little. "Rise," she commanded. "I didn't mean to frighten you."

Nero straightened and restrained the urge to tug at the hem of his tabard. He was woefully underdressed to be speaking to a princess, and not as fastidiously groomed as he would have preferred. He could feel the weight of the astrologer's glare. "I am not frightened, Highness."

Peri surveyed him. "I imagine not. You look as if you have been on an adventure," she said, and he heard unexpected yearning in her voice. Then she laughed and shook a finger at him. "Don't disappoint me by admitting otherwise."

Nero folded his hands behind his back, taking the posture of the architects who consulted with the king. "I had the honor to be dispatched by the viceroy to follow the princess Drakina."

Peri's eyes widened. "She went after Canto, didn't she? What happened?"

Nero showed her the signet ring and they both stared at it for a long moment of silence.

"This is very bad," she whispered.

Nero didn't think it prudent to agree.

Peri considered him. "You are courageous to bring such tidings to my father."

"It is only right, Highness, to fulfill the task I've been given."

"But valiant all the same." She surveyed him again, and he had a sense of her quick mind. "Why you?" She winced and he felt a commonality with her, for he was oft in the situation of speaking his mind and giving offense when he meant none. "I mean no insult, of course, but you are not in my father's livery. I would have expected him to send a clerk or a guard."

He shrugged. "Perhaps I was expendable."

"Never!" The glow in her eyes made his heart thump.

"Perhaps he thought it fitting to send me because I had brought an unwelcome prophecy."

Peri's smile faded and wonder lit her features. "*You* are an astrologer?"

Nero nodded, wondering why she doubted it.

"What was the prophecy?"

He pointed to the gaping hole in the roof.

"Truly?" Peri was clearly impressed. She indicated the court astrologers. "They didn't have a hint of it, and we were taken completely by surprise as a result." Her disdain was clear. "You must bring these tidings of Drakina's deed to my father."

King Ouros raised his voice again, his frustration having returned. Perhaps the repair would be more expensive than he might have hoped. Nero knew that the messenger might pay the price due for the message, but having Peri by his side made it imperative that he behave with courage.

"You advise correctly, Highness. I simply did not wish to interrupt."

"Of course. What is your name, astrologer?"

"Nero, Highness. From Mola."

"You journeyed all that way!" She sighed. "And seen half the world. I am envious."

Nero was shocked when Peri seized his elbow. Her touch was light, her hand small and fair. He had been touched by a princess, who had also spoken with him.

If his life ended in the next few moments, he would not consider it wasted.

"Father!" she called. Kraw and the royal pair turned to look. "This man returns from Kraw's quest with tidings." The architects fell silent and faced Nero. "His name is Nero and he is an astrologer."

A man cleared his throat, and Nero saw that the astrologers had trailed behind them. "He is no astrologer, Highness," the old one said in an indulgent tone. "For he has not studied at—much less graduated from—the

Royal University for Astrologers."

Peri turned a glare upon him. "Yet he foresaw this day's outcome as you did not," she said, her tone scathing. "I would suggest, Father, that you add Nero to your advisors. His loyalty is beyond question. He journeyed alone all the way from Mola to tell you of this, then immediately followed Drakina as Kraw bade him."

"But what tidings," Kraw demanded, stepping forward. "What did the princess do?"

Nero held out his hand, Canto's signet ring cradled in his palm.

Kraw paled, then plucked the ring from Nero's palm.

King Ouros' eyes flashed fire. "She will cast us to war!"

Nero didn't think it wise to suggest that the princess had tried to mitigate the damage. "My chart, Highness, does indicate a tribunal court finding in her favor."

"The chart that he will not let any of us examine," the astrologer sniffed.

"The chart that was right when you were wrong," Peri retorted.

"The chart I did not learn about in time!" Ouros roared. "I will hear no more of this on this day!" The King of Incendium shifted shape in a blaze of light. He leapt into the air and flew in a tight circle high in the royal chamber, then shot through the hole in the roof to rage fire at the sky.

"It will be good for him," Queen Ignita said, sighing then squaring her shoulders. "Ouros is no diplomat, to be sure. Kraw, you must send an official apology to Queen Arcana. The negotiations will be difficult, though perhaps you can suggest this notion of a tribunal court to her."

"Of course, Highness."

"I leave the matter in your capable hands."

Kraw bowed, then cast Nero a glance. "And the astrologer from Mola?"

"Has served us better in a mere day than many who have been sworn to the house for far longer," Ignita said, steel in her tone. "He will join the royal astrologers, if that is his will."

Nero's heart leapt and he was well aware of Peri's pleasure. "It is, Highness. I thank you for this honor."

The oldest astrologer again protested. "Highness, I would not challenge your choice, but I think it ill-advised. You know full well, Highness, that all of the royal astrologers have completed a rigorous program of study at the university. This man is unknown to us."

"And perhaps his route of education provides new insights," Ignita countered smoothly. "He will be *my* astrologer, Kraw, for I need one who tells me even unwelcome truths."

"Of course, Highness," Kraw and the astrologers said in unison, bowing deeply.

The queen arched a fair brow. "Does this displease you, Nero of Mola?"

"No, Highness. I am simply astonished to have my dream come true with such haste."

Queen Ignita laughed. "Then you must dream bigger, Nero of Mola." She extended her hand imperiously and he fell to one knee, bowing his head as he kissed the ring on her finger.

When the queen retreated and the viceroy hastened to do her will, Nero found himself alone again with the princess Peri. "You are both valiant and clever, it is clear," she said, approval in her tone. "You did not hesitate at all, or tremble in the royal presence. That is not common amongst new arrivals."

"I did only my duty, Highness." Nero dared to smile at her, and her lips curved in response.

"You did more," she murmured, her eyes shining so brilliantly that his heart leapt. Their gazes clung for a potent moment, one in which Nero found it hard to breathe. "I look forward to learning more of you, Nero of Mola," she said, then offered her hand in turn.

Nero bent deeply again. He would have kissed her ring, but Peri did not wear any gems on her fingers. He was compelled, then, to touch his lips to her skin, and he certainly didn't mind. Her hand was soft and faintly perfumed, but he saw strength in her fingers. She could be a warrior princess if she so chose, just like her sister, but he didn't fear her. Her heart would guide her true.

"I thank you, Highness," he said and she leaned down to whisper to him.

"When we are alone, call me Peri."

Peri. Nero's heart stopped cold, rather than exploding as he'd feared.

He looked left and right, but they were alone. "I will do so, Peri, at your command."

She smiled, her eyes dancing with an enticing mischief. "Will you cast my horoscope first?" she whispered.

"I should be delighted, Highness." At her sharp look, Nero cleared his throat. "Peri," he corrected, and she laughed. "The task will take some time."

"Of course. Neither of us is leaving the palace, Nero. Please take all the time you require."

He bowed again, amazed that she seemed to feel regret in parting from him.

"I would know the identity of my HeartKeeper, Nero."

"I shall endeavor to discern it." He swallowed. "Peri."

Her smile made his heart thunder. "My mother awaits me. Farewell for the moment, Nero."

And then Peri was gone, hastening across the hall on light feet, her glittering robe flowing behind her. Her hair shone and he heard her laughter as she conferred with her mother.

Dream bigger.

Nero felt a new yearning light in his heart. Queen Ignita's advice was remarkably easy to take.

One thing was certain: the horoscope he drew for Peri would be the most beautiful and the most careful one he had ever done. Who was the man who would claim her heart forever? Nero could only hope the man in question was worthy of the lady.

The princess was not the only one curious as to what her future held.

WYVERN'S PRINCE

Engaged to Prince Urbanus of Regalia, Gemma knows that her fiancé ordered the assassination of her best friend—but has been told that he's her HeartKeeper. Caught between her destiny and her moral duty, she decides to take vengeance upon Urbanus after the wedding night. Gemma's not counting on more dark revelations about Urbanus, much less his beguiling charm. Alone in his palace, Gemma can only rely upon herself to ensure her survival—or can she trust the mysterious stranger who pledges to aid her, for reasons unknown?

PROLOGUE

The royal apartments in the palace of Incendium

"I COULD MINDBEND GEMMA," Troy offered.

"You could, but I prefer you tanned and not toasted," Drakina replied.

Gemma leaned against the wall of the corridor outside the new couple's chambers and eavesdropped on their conversation. She had intended to make one last visit to her new nephew before her own wedding and Drakina and Troy's subsequent departure for Terra, but hearing her name had brought her to a stop. She was glad of her keen dragon hearing, and her ability to remain completely still. An observer might have thought her struck to stone.

Fortunately, the serving maid who had left the chamber and failed to completely close the door was walking in the opposite direction. She hadn't noticed Gemma at all.

Felice, Gemma's pet pavofel, sat between Gemma's feet and the wall, then wrapped her tail around herself. The pavofel was a feline creature, bred to splendor on Cumae, with blue and green fur that resembled the feathers of the peacock known on other worlds. Felice was particularly pretty, sporting two dozen 'eyes' in the fur of her wide and lush tail. It always amazed Gemma how Felice could seem to disappear in the shadows, given the bright hues of her fur. Once seated, Felice was completely motionless. Only the glow of her luminous green eyes revealed her presence.

It must be true that pavofels chose their companions and caregivers, because Gemma and Felice seemed to understand each other perfectly.

"But you can't let her just marry Urbanus," Troy protested. "We know too much about his nature."

"I doubt we can stop her," Drakina replied, her tone suspiciously temperate. "Gemma is determined to marry Urbanus, just as Father planned, and ensure the treaty is made between the two kingdoms. You'll never change the thinking of two royal dragons."

"And you're not going to intervene?" Troy demanded. "Even if she's stepping into a trap?"

"You do not know that."

Troy snorted. "I don't have to be a MindBender to know that Urbanus is a sneak."

Drakina's tone turned thoughtful. "It *is* for the good of both kingdoms to make the alliance. Gemma knows as much as we do and she's agreed to marry him."

"But Urbanus arranged for the death of Arista..."

"Gemma knows that. Arista was her best friend."

"I know she knows that. It's why she hates me." Troy could be heard pacing. Gemma's heart filled with disgust that her older sister's husband had been the assassin who'd killed her best friend. Her argument, though, was with the instigator of the agreement, not the man who'd been given the job.

She knew enough about the Gloria Furora to understand that any choice Troy had been given wouldn't really have been a choice. His own death would probably have been the only other option available.

She might not be able to blame him for what he'd done, but she didn't have to like him.

How *could* Drakina have married a man, even her HeartKeeper, who could influence her thoughts? It was incomprehensible that Drakina was happy with a MindBender.

Maybe her big sister was more influenced by her husband than she realized.

"You should let me MindBend her about that, at least," Troy said and Gemma bristled at the suggestion. "The way she looks at me makes me uneasy."

"If you used your MindBending abilities, she would do more than glare at you. You would not survive the day."

Gemma nodded agreement with that.

"But why is she going? Why did she agree?"

"Gemma must have her reasons."

"That's it, isn't it?" Troy said. "She plans to avenge Arista."

Gemma straightened, impressed that he was the only one on Incendium who seemed to have guessed her plan. Or at least said it aloud. It was possible her father knew.

"I do not know." Drakina's tone was so mild that Gemma wondered whether her sister had guessed as well.

"But she can do that without marrying him!" Troy insisted. "There's a piece of the puzzle missing. Drakina, I can find it."

"I learned early in this palace that whenever you have not been told some detail, it is because that information is not yours to know," Drakina replied curtly. "It is folly to provoke tempers in a household of dragons."

"But..."

"Do you not understand that they are all on guard because they know what you can do? If you MindBend any of them, when I have vowed that you would not, even I will not be able to save you. Troy! Do not attempt this thing."

"You promised them I wouldn't use my powers?" Troy was clearly surprised.

"It was the only way to gain you access to my father's court. You are Terran, a race he cannot tolerate. You are a MindBender, a kind he finds despicable. Even being Carrier of the Seed and my HeartKeeper was not enough for my father to allow you to step over the threshold given those credentials."

"Go ahead. Build my ego a little more."

Gemma smiled.

"Troy! I love you. Is that not sufficient?"

Troy made an exasperated noise, evidence that Drakina's love *wasn't* enough. Gemma had always thought that the minstrels who insisted that love conquered all were taking a simplistic view. Here was proof. "I feel like my only value is as a stud."

Drakina laughed, and her voice turned sultry. "Is that so bad? Come to bed, stud, and I will remind you of the benefits."

"It's not funny, princess. I need to use my powers. I need to *do* something."

"And you will have plenty to do once we get to Terra. I have invited my father to come and hunt, and he will arrive within days of our return there. You will be more than busy ensuring that no Terran notices a dragon king in the vicinity." Drakina sighed. "He is not accustomed to keeping a low profile, after all."

"Thanks for the warning."

"Look at the upside. His visit might improve his view of Terrans."

Troy scoffed, revealing his view of that possibility. Gemma was inclined to agree with him. Their father, Ouros, was slow to abandon any conviction. "Now, what about Gemma?"

"She can defend herself."

"What kind of family is this?" Troy demanded. I thought you watched over each other!"

Gemma felt the air chill and could easily imagine the look her sister was giving her new husband. She was tempted to peek and see if he took a step back.

"We also support each other's choices," Drakina said.

"But..."

"But nothing, Troy." Drakina finally lost patience and her voice rose. There were probably sparks flying from the ends of her hair. "Gemma has *chosen*. I do not understand her decision. I have tried to talk to her about it, but she is determined. She *must* have a reason. She *must* have a plan. She clearly is not going to share it, and she *would* share it if she needed help."

"She could be wrong."

"It is less probable statistically that Gemma is wrong than any of my other sisters."

Gemma smiled and nodded at that.

Drakina continued. "She did train with the Warrior Maidens of Cumae, you know."

"And Prince Urbanus is one sneaky bastard. How can your father let her marry him at all?"

"He had his doubts. Gemma volunteered to secure the alliance."

"Why? It's nuts, princess."

"Gemma is not crazy."

"So, that's it? You're just going to let her go and if she's wrong, well, you still have ten more sisters?"

"She is *not* wrong. Gemma is never wrong."

Gemma heard Troy pacing the room. "And you won't let me use my powers to find out her plan, even if it might save her," he said with exasperation. "What's the point of our being together if we aren't a team?"

"Some would say our son Gravitas was the point."

"Do you really love me, Drakina, or did you just want the Seed from me?"

Gemma winced and moved away, unwilling to hear the rest of their argument. Were all marriages compromises, even those between HeartKeepers? Was the promise of true love a lie? Gemma didn't want it to be. Or was Drakina's happiness compromised because Troy was a MindBender? Gemma wished she knew for sure. She wanted the kind of marriage her parents had, but didn't think she'd get it.

She might as well marry Urbanus, conceive his son, and then kill him for his crime.

There was a good precedent for that in the mating ritual of her cousins, after all. They always killed the Carrier of the Seed once his precious burden had been delivered. She could raise the boy herself and manage it easily.

Her choice wasn't really that hard to understand, or it wouldn't have been if she'd told anyone of the master astrologer's forecast.

Gemma had known her fate for years.

She'd told no one.

She'd sworn the astrologer to secrecy, and he had taken the truth to his grave.

Her HeartKeeper was the Prince of Regalia who would be king, the son of Queen Arcana whose true nature was disguised. She'd wondered about the prophecy when Drakina had been betrothed to Canto, but that prince's death had made everything more clear. Urbanus was the crown prince, so would eventually be king of Regalia. Although she was skeptical that his true nature was better than what she'd seen so far, Gemma had to believe a master astrologer.

She had to trust in the prophecy.

Astrologers, after all, were inclined to put great value in nuance. Gemma assumed that Urbanus was slightly less wicked than she'd come to believe. Maybe he thought he had good reason for seeing Arista assassinated and for trying to have Drakina killed, too. Maybe he was trying to gain his mother's favor so she ensured his succession, and he intended to mend his ways after her death and his coronation. Gemma might have been more inclined to help with such a goal if he hadn't ordered the death of her Sword Sister and best friend.

Maybe the Carrier of the Seed for Gemma wasn't the same man as her HeartKeeper. It didn't happen often, from what she understood, but that didn't mean it was impossible.

Either way, marrying Prince Urbanus was Gemma's destiny.

For better or for worse.

IF IT HAD BEEN ANYONE else listening to their argument, Drakina would have noticed. Gemma's training made her more stealthy than anyone else—and Drakina's concern for Troy had become consuming. He was increasingly impatient and filled with restless energy. The situation had grown worse each day they had been on Incendium, despite her efforts to manage her father's expectations and her husband's desires. She knew it irked Troy to have so little to do, but a Consort *was* a ceremonial role.

That was why she knew they couldn't remain. Troy had investigated Incendium, spending much time in the starports, learning and making suggestions. He had been using the gym to excess, burning off his frustrations, and the results were most impressive.

Drakina had chosen duty and her father's will because she believed there wasn't really a choice. It had been her duty to conceive the heir to the throne. With each passing day, though, and her obligation fulfilled, it was increasingly clear that she had to do something to ensure the survival of her marriage. She, Troy, and Gravitas were finally going to Terra, immediately following Gemma's wedding. In a real sense, their shared future would finally begin, because their royal duties would be complete for the moment.

It was time to reassure her beloved.

Troy glared at her and Drakina had a sudden idea how that might be done. It frightened her a little, but the possibility of losing her HeartKeeper frightened her more.

"How can you ask whether I love you?" she asked, tempering her tone. "Of course, I love you. I am going to Terra with you, specifically so you can use your powers and be who you are. It is no small thing to leave my world behind for yours!"

"Maybe it's only because of the verran," he countered. "Maybe it's about hunting, not about me."

"You know better than that."

Troy shoved a hand through his hair. "I thought I did. I'm starting to wonder, princess, and I know that's not good. I don't want to fight with you, but I don't want to be irrelevant either."

Drakina halted before him and framed his face in her hands. "Don't confuse me with my father," she whispered. She brushed her lips across Troy's mouth. He shivered and exhaled, but still held himself apart from her. She met his gaze steadily. "I love who you are and what you can do. You cannot be fully yourself here on Incendium. It bothers me more than it bothers you."

He lifted a brow. "I doubt that."

"Do you?" Drakina challenged in a whisper. She stared into his eyes and dared to say it aloud. "Then MindBend me and learn the truth."

Troy was visibly surprised by the invitation. "You want me to manipulate your thoughts?"

"I want you to read my thoughts and share yours with me. I want our thoughts to be as one."

"Usually MindBending is guiding thoughts in a specific direction."

Drakina arched a brow. "I researched your skill and found this possibility noted. Are you not prepared for the challenge of learning a new skill?"

She saw the glimmer of excitement in his eyes. "It's supposed to come from cultivating a connection with one other individual."

"Who better than your wife and partner? I can think of no better candidate than my HeartKeeper."

Troy grinned. "How far into your mind can I go?"

"As far as you want," Drakina said, although the possibility terrified her. "I am an open book to you now, for we are bound together." She felt his anticipation rise.

"No repercussions?"

"None."

"Even if I find a secret?"

"I have none from you. I might not be good at telling you everything, but if I have stories yet untold, they are omissions not secrets. We are one, Troy."

"You forbade me to MindBend you once," he reminded her, his gaze searching.

"I now think it a necessary and timely concession."

He sobered, his gaze searching hers. "You're afraid, princess."

Drakina nodded, disliking the admission of any weakness. She did like, though, that Troy understood her without MindBending. "But I trust you, and you need to know how much. I cannot think of a better way to demonstrate as much."

Troy's hands landed on her waist. "Princess!" He understood the magnitude of the concession she made to him and would honor it. This bond would be intimate and one that could not be severed, but would strengthen the connection between them.

Drakina smiled for him. "Go ahead and MindBend me, Troy. You can even feed my desire, if you want, although it's already burning hot." She took a deep breath. "Remind me of the merit of slow and thorough."

He kissed her then, his delight making her heart skip. "I was thinking fast and hot might be the right choice tonight, princess." His voice was a low rasp against her ear and the sound made her growl with need.

"I'm yours, Troy, all yours, whichever way you want me."

"Now there's an invitation I can't refuse."

"I was hoping it would be," Drakina whispered, then she felt his thoughts slide into her own. It was much as it had been that first time on Terra, but Troy was careful instead of stealthy. He let her be aware of him, and she welcomed that. She leaned her brow upon his shoulder and took a steadying breath, surrendering to his presence in her thoughts when her instinct was to incinerate the intruder.

"Okay, princess?" Troy didn't speak aloud, but his voice echoed in her own mind.

She tried to reply in kind. *"All yours, HeartKeeper."*

"Which creates some very interesting possibilities," he mused. She could hear laughter in his tone, even as it echoed within her mind, and she smiled at that. His fingers slid up her spine and into her hair, his touch sending tingles from her nape.

"You like that," he said, his thoughts a lazy drawl that tangled with her own thoughts. Drakina sighed with pleasure as the heat built within her. He

threaded his fingers into her hair, moving slowly and deliberately. Drakina shivered in anticipation, welcoming the brush of his lips on her ears.

"And that."

"You know all of this already, MindBender," she thought. *"Dig deeper."*

Drakina felt Troy's surprise and guessed he'd discovered a little fantasy she'd been cherishing. She smiled when he embellished it with some variations of his own. He was kissing her neck and teasing her nipple when she made the fantasy much more naughty than any game they'd ever played before and she heard his laughter.

"Naughty, naughty, princess," he chided, but Drakina wasn't fooled. His pulse leaped and his breath caught, his body so taut with enthusiasm that she wanted to devour him.

Then Troy modified her fantasy and Drakina inhaled sharply at the allure of his suggestion. She seized the back of his neck, kissing him with a fervor that showed her approval. He backed her into the wall and their pulses raced as one as they kissed and caressed, then they fell on the bed with limbs entangled. Drakina braced her hands on either side of his shoulders and looked down at him, smiling at his obvious pleasure.

"You like this," she accused.

He nodded. *"But more importantly, I love you."*

After Drakina bent to claim Troy's lips in a fiery kiss, no one said or thought anything coherent in the royal apartments for quite some time.

THAT EVENING, GEMMA STRODE down the corridor to the briefing session that she'd ordered, ensuring that she arrived precisely on schedule.

It was held in her own apartment, at her command, because that was the one place she knew was secure from spies and listening devices.

Some of the party from Regalia had already arrived to prepare for the royal family's attendance of the wedding the next day. Urbanus remained in his mother's palace on Regalia, per tradition, so there was no chance of the bride seeing the groom. The staff from Regalia were contained in one wing of the palace on Incendium, and Gemma doubted they had the skill to circumvent the access coding on their keys.

At least not so quickly as this.

Kraw bowed when she entered the unit and Farquon saluted. Kraw was viceroy of the Kingdom of Incendium and had been in the service of King Ouros for decades, ever since his father had resigned the same post. His mustache had been as long and elaborately curved for all the years Gemma could remember him, but now it had turned white.

Farquon was commander of the regiment assigned to the defense of the royal family. Gemma had augmented Farquon's training herself, when she had led Incendium's elite corps of commandos. The assignment of a royal family member to military command hadn't been ceremonial for Gemma. She had trained on Cumae, graduated with high honors, then returned home to serve the kingdom. Under her command, the commandos had improved their response times, stealth, and kill rates. Farquon had been her best pupil, her lover, her friend and remained one man she trusted completely. She particularly admired that their relationship had never been complicated by talk of undying love.

Farquon had made the arrangements for her pending escape, and she knew he wouldn't reveal a syllable of her plan to anyone. Even now, he was completely impassive, commanded by Kraw to attend, and apparently without any greater bond to Gemma than to any other member of the royal family. He looked slightly bored if attentive. She felt a surge of pride in his talents, then inclined her head to Kraw.

"Your highness," Kraw said with a deep bow. "Your father sends greetings."

"Of course."

"As well as the reminder that you need not proceed with this marriage."

"But I must, Kraw, as my father knows." Gemma sat down and spoke crisply. "I'm sure he smells the Seed on every messenger from Regalia as keenly as I do."

Kraw inclined his head in acknowledgment of this truth. "You need not go alone, Highness."

"I think otherwise." Gemma waved a hand. "Speak to me of Regalia, please, Kraw."

The wall illuminated behind Farquon, revealing that it was actually a large display screen. An image of Regalia appeared, undoubtedly captured by one of Incendium's satellites. As the image grew more detailed, it was clear that the surface of Incendium's sister planet was almost entirely covered in forest.

"A comparatively primitive world, it must be said," Kraw declared, turning to watch the display with Gemma. She always respected that he memorized his presentations, and made it look easy to present a wealth of information in a short period of time. "Their economy is heavily reliant upon barter on the planet itself, and simple skills. Their people harvest crops, make bread and ale, supply the royal palace with tithes and other offerings. Their major exports are medicinal herbs and other plants, usually dried for transport. They have only one star station, here in their northern hemisphere, near the queen's palace in their capital city."

The image showed a very small star station beside an extensive palace. A large dark shuttle was parked there, with loading doors of a size suitable for loading freight. There were only three more ships, all sleek and small personal vehicles. They seemed to have the royal insignia, though it was difficult to be certain. The palace was made of silvery stone that glittered in the sunlight and there were banners flying from its highest towers.

It was quite a contrast with Incendium's star station, where parking was always at a premium. There were dozens, if not hundreds, of small ships there at any given time, in addition to the regularly scheduled shuttles to the orbiting starport and the larger ships docked there.

"Their single shuttle leaves Regalia monthly and is an older model, somewhat prone to disrepair. They use Incendium's starport to arrange transport of their goods to off-world markets." He paused to look at Gemma. "Without us, they would have no interplanetary access."

She arched a brow. "Our marital alliance could have practical benefits for Regalia."

"Of course." Kraw continued. "Their communication systems and general technology would be considered grossly inadequate by our standards. I fear you may have a difficult adjustment to make in your new home, Highness."

"But they have magic, don't they?"

"Magic." Kraw sighed. "Yes, that is their claim. The origin of the sorcery is the royal family, specifically Queen Arcana, whose abilities are said to be extraordinary. The power to cast spells, to glean the future, to enchant others against their will into doing her desire, to inflict different forms upon others, to read thoughts, to kill with a glance—all these abilities and more are attributed to the queen by rumor and gossip. It is said that she has given individual magical talents to her sons, allowing only one per offspring in order that they would have to band together to defeat her. It is also said that she deliberately fosters dissent between them." Kraw spread his hands. "These are the recurring rumors. There is no way to affirm which, if any, are true, and which might be either illusion or utterly without foundation." He cleared his throat. "What we do know is that Queen Arcana has lived a very long time for a mortal woman and has not appeared to age for the past fifty Regalian years. She has borne twelve sons and did so in rapid succession between twenty-five and forty Regalian years ago."

"And Regalian years are only a little longer than our own, I believe?"

"Yes, Highness. Their orbit is slightly larger than ours, giving us a warmer climate, too. The discrepancy between Incendian years and Regalian years is rounded to four per cent, and beyond the notice of most." Kraw bowed. "Certainly to an individual of your longevity, Highness, it is of little consequence."

Gemma nodded understanding.

The display changed to show images of men. Some of them were official holograms and familiar to Gemma, while others, she had never seen before. She recognized Canto, for example, before Kraw gestured dismissively to Queen Arcana's oldest and now deceased son. "It is unknown what magical power Canto might have had, at least here on Incendium."

"Whatever it was, it doesn't seem to have helped him much."

"Indeed, Majesty. You are familiar with Urbanus, of course," he continued and Gemma considered the official hologram of her betrothed. He was handsome, with his dark hair and blue eyes, his confident smile. "You may not be aware that he had a twin brother, Venero."

There was a roguish quality about Venero, whose hair was lighter than that of his brother. He had hazel eyes that looked almost golden. The image was a candid one, far more appealing than an official one. He looked to be on the verge of laughter as if he had been caught at some jest. Gemma had the urge to smile back at him and wish she'd heard the joke.

"They don't look like twins."

"Not identical twins. There was a suggestion—" Kraw cleared his throat "—that they did not share a father, although the sexual proclivities of the queen are beyond the range of our discussion."

That piqued Gemma's curiosity and she felt Farquon flick a glance at her. With an effort, she remained impassive. "You speak of Venero in the past tense."

"Prince Venero is said to have disappeared and is believed by most to be dead. It must be noted that Urbanus has always been a favorite of his mother's. More than one observer has speculated that she wished his path to the crown to be unobstructed, particularly after the death of Canto, and that she had some involvement in the disappearance or death of Venero."

"Do you know about Urbanus' magical power?"

"Your betrothed, Highness, is rumored to be an expert in the making of potions." Kraw looked stern. "It might well be that there is no sorcery involved in this, merely an understanding of the effects of certain substances upon the body of the victim. It may be science disguised as magic, to defend such powerful and potentially harmful knowledge."

"Anything else?"

"Prince Urbanus appears to be quite involved in his mother's administration of Regalia, and also her confidante. I would guess that she is grooming him for the succession, as is right and good. He does leave Regalia at intervals and has been known to frequent the gaming halls of Xanto."

"He likes to bet," she said.

"Evidently, Highness."

Gemma wasn't impressed by that, but then, she wasn't going to be married to Urbanus very long if everything proceeded according to her plan.

The display changed again to an image of a heavily forested area. There was a dark spire in the middle of the forest, and it was enlarged as the focus tightened upon it. "There is new construction in the far southern hemisphere of Regalia, about as far from Queen Arcana's palace as might be possible without entering the inhabitable zones of the poles." Gemma leaned forward, avidly studying the structure. "This is said to be the honeymoon palace of Prince Urbanus." Kraw turned to face her. "It appears that your betrothed, Highness, intends to keep you to himself for a while."

Gemma's gaze danced over the palace as the view circled around it. It *was* a fortress, remote and structured to be easily defended, which suited her very well. She smiled for Kraw. "It looks like a perfect place to ensure the delivery of the Seed."

Never mind an ideal place to kill her new husband and escape Regalia without being observed. Gemma couldn't have planned it better herself.

She glanced up and Farquon bowed slightly, but not quickly enough to hide the understanding in his eyes.

All was made ready.

Let the nuptial festivities begin.

CHAPTER ONE

PRINCE VENERO DIDN'T ATTEND his older brother's wedding.

Even though it was to be a lavish ceremony and the union of the two kingdoms within their solar system was of key diplomatic importance, Venero had several reasons for missing the ceremony.

First, the vows would be exchanged on Incendium, and he had no means of getting to Regalia's sister planet, seeing that he had been banished from his mother's court and lost all the perks of living there.

Secondly, he hated Urbanus and had no wish to witness any joy his twin might experience.

Thirdly, Venero didn't think much good of the bride, Gemma, even though he'd never met or seen her. Any woman who would willingly marry the crown prince of Regalia had to be either stupid, or just as vile as Urbanus. Never mind that she was a dragon shifter. Venero couldn't imagine why any man would marry a woman who could slaughter him so easily that she didn't even have to wait for him to be asleep.

Women should be beautiful and demure, while wives should be beautiful, demure, and fertile. He supposed that Princess Gemma might possess the third trait, but not the others.

Venero was, however, very interested in the nuptials.

More specifically, he was interested in using the bride for his own purposes. She might never know the difference if she was as dumb as he suspected. The fact that Gemma was a dragon shifter meant she was able to cover large distances quickly.

And Venero had a long way to go.

He wasn't just exiled from the court: he'd been cursed to take another form *and* had his powers suppressed. Worst of all, the antidote was something Venero knew to be impossible. How could he be restored to his human form by the kiss of his one true love when he didn't believe that kind of love existed?

Venero would solve that riddle later. First, he had to get out of the forest and back to the city of Regalia, where there were far more women—and thus more candidates for saving him.

Being a toad, however, didn't provide many options for quick journeys. The city of Regalia was hundreds of leagues away, but toads make slow progress and this part of the planet was particularly treacherous. The forests and rivers were full of predators with a taste for small amphibians, and Venero knew that wasn't a coincidence. Trust Urbanus to be vengeful. Venero hadn't been able to cast dreams to anyone since he'd been cursed, which made it hard to get any help.

Urbanus was nothing but thorough when he'd been cheated of whatever he thought was his due. Venero's brother had wanted to ensure his death, without getting his own hands dirty. Urbanus probably thought Venero was already dead.

But Venero had a surprise for his brother.

With any luck, Urbanus wouldn't discover the truth until it was too late.

The only good thing about the wedding was that Urbanus had built a remote castle, specifically to enjoy the pleasures of his new wife in privacy. As soon as Venero had heard about the castle, he'd known it offered him a chance. Sooner or later, the happy couple would return to the city of Regalia, and somehow, he was going with them.

Urbanus' new bride just might be dumb enough to help.

Venero had heard the hammering and the felling of trees, the lugging of stones and the long hours of construction. That the new palace was being built in the same region of Regalia where Venero had been dispatched just added to his conviction that Urbanus thought him dead.

Or powerless.

It had taken every bit of strength and resolve that Venero possessed, but he had made it to the castle by the day of the wedding. He doubted there would be another opportunity for release anytime soon, so he had to seize this one. He was exhausted when he hopped onto the path leading to the gates and took a moment to survey the creation. The new castle was a tall, slender tower and he grimaced at his certainty that the bridal suite would be at the top.

There'd been no time to delay, much less to rest. Venero had slipped through the gates, squirmed under a door, and started the ascent in the quiet castle. There were servants in the kitchen, but not many of them by the sound—and they weren't very happy with their situation, either.

He had been a third of the way up the endless winding stone staircase when he had a stroke of luck: a maid hurrying past with a basket of provisions was too busy grumbling to pay attention to her surroundings. Venero leaped as she passed and landed in the basket, then quickly hid beneath the folded cloth.

It was a bumpy ride, but one that saved him a lot of trouble.

He thought about kissing the maid in his relief.

Then he remembered the antidote and wondered if it was worth a try to seduce her. If Urbanus could have planned true love, Venero would have given the idea more consideration. His brother would have been amused to match him to such a woman, but surely there was something that escaped the control of his family's magical powers.

The maid abruptly unlocked a door at the summit, heaved a sigh, and pushed the basket into the room. He still might have given it a try, but a woman called from the foot of the stairs. She swore and locked the door again, leaving him alone.

The enormous draped bed told Venero that he had reached his destination.

It also reminded him that the maid might scream if he revealed himself. If she told Urbanus there was a toad in the palace—and why wouldn't she?—Venero would be caught. Urbanus would guess which toad, and this time, he wouldn't leave Venero's demise in doubt.

He'd only need a rock.

With a shudder, Venero slipped beneath a carved bureau with so many drawers that there was only just space beneath it for a toad. He caught his breath as he hunkered there in the shadows. He closed his eyes for a moment, but didn't dare fall asleep.

He could sleep in Regalia city.

The maid returned and made the bed with fresh linens, then opened the doors to the balcony. He could smell the forest far below.

Soon, the newlyweds would arrive.

Venero needed a plan.

VENERO WAS BEYOND IMPATIENT by the time he heard the Starpod land in the bailey. Should he charm the bride? Should he encourage her sympathy? Or should he provoke her? Or should he just hide in her belongings?

Moments later, a woman entered the chamber accompanied by the maid. The maid bustled around the chamber, turning down the bed and opening the doors to the balcony even wider. Venero could see her clearly, on the far side of the room, but only the bride's shoes. The maid unpacked a small bag, leaving a fine chemise on the bed. The bride stayed beside the door.

There was no other baggage than the small bag, which the maid didn't put down. It defied Venero's belief that a bride would arrive with only the clothes on her back, but maybe the rest hadn't been brought to the chamber.

Maybe it wouldn't be.

Maybe Urbanus distrusted his bride.

Or wanted her close to naked most of the time.

Either way, hiding wasn't going to work.

Gemma still hadn't moved from the door. She seemed to be very still. Venero crept forward to steal a glimpse of her. Maybe that would help him decide on a plan.

The shocking thing was that she was beautiful.

Venero was hardly immune to feminine allure. In fact, he considered himself somewhat of a connoisseur, but he had never seen a woman as gorgeous as Urbanus' bride. He felt a sudden—and very inappropriate—interest in his brother's new wife.

She was blond and blue-eyed, curvy and of just the right height for a man to tuck against his side. She was exquisitely pretty.

She looked demure.

It didn't seem unreasonable to imagine that she might be fertile.

Of course, she was a dragon shifter.

The expression on her face didn't hint at vast intellectual powers. Venero recalled his earlier theory and thought both Gemma's expression and her situation confirmed it. Such a royal beauty must have had many choices of suitors. Why accept Urbanus?

Maybe her father had insisted upon the marriage.

But then, any woman with a bit of spirit would have protested a match that she didn't want herself.

She examined her wedding ring with apparent fascination, smiling as she turned it so the faceted stone caught the light. She giggled when it flashed. She repeated this gesture over and over again. The maid had to ask her three times whether she needed anything else before she appeared to understand the words, then she just shook her head.

Dumb as a rock.

Venero recoiled when a creature padded into the chamber and mewed at Gemma. She gave a cry of delight and bent to scoop up the beast, which had fur of a familiar blue and green combination.

A pavofel! Venero grimaced in distaste. That Urbanus' bride had anything in common with Queen Arcana couldn't be a good thing.

The maid left with the small bag, muttering, then Urbanus himself rapped on the door and swept into the chamber. "My lady!" he said and bowed low over her hand. Gemma fluttered her lashes, and Venero's heart clenched at her pretty vulnerability.

He'd obviously been hopping around the forest too long.

"I shall return shortly, my love," Urbanus declared, bowing and leaving the room.

She waved her fingertips at him. "Don't take too long!" she called after him, her voice breathy and pitched high.

The sound did strange things to Venero's pulse. The sooner he got back to his real form, returned to the city of Regalia, and indulged in some female companionship, the better.

To his surprise, when the door was closed behind Urbanus and the lock turned, Gemma's posture changed completely. She pivoted to stare at the door and Venero swore he could hear her attention crackle. She was suddenly alert and coiled to spring, so different from the bride playing with her ring that he blinked.

What had happened? Instead of a silly and lovely bride, she looked over the room with a gaze as keen as that of a hawk on the hunt.

No. Like a dragon on the hunt.

Venero shuddered.

Gemma dropped the pavofel, which leaped onto the bed and curled up there, eyes bright. She tried the latch surreptitiously, silently. She didn't knock on it or demand release, but simply pivoted to study her prison. He had the sense that she looked for a weakness, or a vulnerability she could exploit.

He eased forward, fascinated. Her eyes narrowed, but Venero could see their furious glitter. Like faceted sapphires, or snow in the sunlight. He had a definite sense that she was dangerous.

Gemma looked braced for battle, even though she carried no weapon. Her menacing expression made him retreat a little, for the sight reminded him that she was a dragon shifter.

Maybe a hungry one.

Did dragons eat toads? He had to think that they ate whatever they wanted.

Her survey complete, Gemma marched to the balcony. She moved with the lithe grace of a warrior, and Venero couldn't help watching her. She examined the space quickly. Efficiently. Venero understood what she was looking for, because in her place, he would have been looking for a means of escape, too.

Gemma looked over the rail to the ground below, and he guessed that she was judging the distance. She looked up to the peak of the tower, then strode back into the room. She tested the strength of the pillars of the bed, silently opened drawers, peered behind mirrors and drapes and appeared to inventory the contents of the chamber with calm purpose.

He was surprised to have anything in common with her.

Urbanus would be even more surprised.

Come to think of it, Gemma reminded him of Arista.

But the way her head turned and her eyes lit at the sound of the key in the lock as the maid returned was pure dragon.

The strange thing was that his inappropriate attraction to his brother's bride hadn't diminished a bit. In fact, he was even more intrigued by her—and more aroused—then he had been at first glimpse.

That must be the result of having been enchanted for so long.

He would have liked to have watched her disrobe, but the maid bustled her behind a screen, complaining of the draft from the balcony.

Funny how he had a lot more interest in soliciting a kiss from Gemma than from the maid. Maybe she could help him. Maybe she'd do it willingly. Maybe it wouldn't hurt to ask. He didn't think for a moment that she was his true love—he was sure there wasn't one, in fact—but a kiss from Gemma would suit him just fine, even if it didn't change his form.

Venero reviewed his possible plans. He didn't think he could win the sympathy of a dragon warrior. Given her fierce expression, he wasn't sure Gemma could be charmed. She looked like she'd take a challenge and run with it, though.

Venero smiled. Provocation, it would be.

And maybe a kiss for luck. His heart skipped at the prospect. Venero hunkered down to wait for his moment.

FINALLY, THE WORST WAS OVER.

Another bride might have thought otherwise and believed the pageantry of her wedding to have been the highlight of the day, but Gemma wasn't a typical princess. She hated the fuss of royal functions and had barely endured her mother's obsession with her dress and her hair and every little detail. After the endless ceremony and the meal were finally completed, she and Urbanus had flown to a private palace in Regalia in his Starpod.

He seemed to like when she was foolish. He expected just about nothing from her and had no interest in actually talking to her. Any concerns she might have had of liking her husband or feeling sympathy for him had been dismissed.

She disliked Urbanus. Deeply.

Killing him would be easy.

Gemma had smiled and simpered at him, congratulating him on his skills, but really, he was a mediocre pilot. She'd have tossed him back to the flight academy before she let him fly even the worst heap in Incendium's fleet.

All the same, she was married to him.

But not for long.

There was only the dirty work to be done, but Gemma preferred seduction and slaughter to ceremony.

The only complication was that the smell of the Seed was almost overwhelming. Gemma hadn't expected to be so influenced by it, much less to be distracted by it. The entire party from Regalia had reeked of the Seed on their arrival on Incendium, and Gemma had had a hard time keeping her desire in check throughout the day. The scent awakened her dragon and kindled her desire for lots of hot sex. She'd kept herself from ravishing Urbanus so far, but the longer the event was delayed, the more taut she felt.

The touch of his lips on the back of her hand made her simmer.

She hoped he wasn't expecting her to be a timid virgin.

It didn't seem to matter that she didn't like him. The Seed filled her senses and made her ready to claim it.

Gemma could only hope that her senses returned to normal once the deed was done.

When the maid left the second time, Gemma was alone for a precious few moments. There was no telling when Urbanus would return, so she tried to forget her lust and studied the chamber with care.

Her dragon didn't like that Urbanus had brought her to a private palace. Her dragon didn't like that the door had been locked behind her. Gemma didn't care for the fear in the eyes of her husband's servants, or his smug assurance that she must be desperate to consummate their nuptials. Her dragon didn't like her odd sense that she was being watched.

Gemma particularly didn't like that there was so little in the room that could be used as a weapon when she was in her human form. She felt out-maneuvered.

By a man who was a mediocre pilot.

No, he'd gotten lucky. The palace had been recently built and was scantily furnished. He hadn't thought much beyond the bed.

And she'd out-maneuver him before the evening was done.

Gemma exhaled. She had to make Urbanus forget her dragon nature, the better to surprise him when it mattered.

She stood alone on the balcony outside her bridal chamber, waiting for him. Her long fair hair was still braided into a single plait, and the hem of some sheer bit of nothing chosen by her mother fluttered around her ankles.

She posed herself and let her heart fill with her hatred of her new husband.

The shadowed forest spread beneath the balcony where she stood and the night sky sparkled with stars. It was funny how Regalia seemed to be so much more remote than its sister planet of Incendium, how its forests seemed darker and its solitudes deeper. Even though Kraw had shown her all of this, she hadn't grasped how isolated it was until she stood in the palace herself. The absence of communication systems and the lack of her own computational devices made her feel naked. Vulnerable. She could have fallen off the edge of the universe.

Where no one would hear her scream.

At least she had her fighting skills to rely upon.

Never mind her dragon powers. A woman who wasn't a shapeshifter would have been completely at Urbanus' mercy. Gemma remembered the royal family's reputed taste for spell casting and her spine straightened just a little. She wouldn't be beguiled.

Her plan was perfect, after all. She would seduce Urbanus and when he slept—as men always slept in the aftermath—she would kill him to avenge Arista. She would then shift shape and flee this remote palace, returning by night to the Starpod that Farquon had supplied and hidden at her command.

By the time the sun rose in the royal court of Incendium, Gemma would be gone, her destination unknown, her mission complete. She'd return only when her son's egg had to be delivered to the royal nursery. By then, she had to hope that the diplomatic storm would have spent its course.

It would be easy.

It would be over soon.

Maybe she should take Farquon with her for company. Gemma would decide when she was back on Incendium. If he was there at the hidden Starpod, waiting for her, she'd invite him along. If he wasn't, she'd continue without him.

In a way, the remote location chosen by Urbanus was a benefit. There were fewer people who might witness her departure than would have been the case at the main palace. There were fewer who might come to Urbanus' aid, if *he* called for help.

Maybe he facilitated her scheme without even knowing what he did.

She smiled as Felice wound around her ankles, her tail flicking. The creature always knew when Gemma was agitated, no matter how well she hid it. Gemma bent and picked up Felice, stroking her brilliant blue green fur as she nestled close. Felice's eyes were bright green and she was of considerable size for a domestic feline, as well as a skillful predator. Felice sat on the rail surrounded by Gemma's arms and purred contentment. The sound and the vibration was soothing.

"Is this the part where you live happily ever after?"

Gemma spun at the sound of an unfamiliar male voice. That the words were tinged with scorn made her eyes narrow. The chamber was empty, the candles flickering and casting shadows on the walls. "Who's there?" she demanded.

"No one you know," continued the voice. There was no sign of movement in the chamber. "Call me a friend." Then he chuckled, as if nothing could be further from the truth.

Gemma was both intrigued and annoyed. What kind of chamber had she been assigned, that another person could be hidden within it? What game was Urbanus playing? Had she been watched as she washed and changed by someone other than the maid? It didn't sound like the maid's voice.

No, the voice sounded masculine and audacious. Challenging. The maid had been both female and meek.

The owner of this voice wasn't meek at all. Gemma was intrigued.

"A friend would show himself," she challenged.

"Maybe you just can't see for looking," came the reply.

Gemma dropped Felice and stepped into the chamber. She scanned every nook and cranny, peered into the shadows and up at the rafters.

No one.

"Don't you believe in happy endings?" Gemma asked, hoping to fool him into revealing his location.

"No, but then I don't believe in true love, either."

"Why not?"

"It doesn't exist."

"What a terrible thing to say to a new bride."

"Even if it's true?"

"It's not true. If it was, we couldn't each have a HeartKeeper."

"Maybe that's just a myth."

Gemma continued the argument as she sought the intruder. His voice was coming from one side of the room, where a large chest of drawers was pushed against the wall. "The astrologers would argue the matter with you."

"The philosophers, too. I still prefer to think for myself."

"If not to reveal yourself."

He laughed. "I'm in plain sight. Maybe dragons aren't so perceptive, after all."

Gemma felt her temper rising and guessed that her eyes were filled with fire. They always revealed when she was on the cusp of change. She tried to quell her reaction, knowing that the sight would remind Urbanus of her true nature. Her dragon was becoming ascendant at exactly the wrong time, thanks to this meddling individual. "Who are you and where are you? I demand that you show yourself!"

"Shouting is a great choice," the voice noted. "That way, Urbanus will know you aren't alone, and we'll both have to pay for that. Of course, he'll probably only see you." He sighed with forbearance. "I guess it's true that the dragon princesses of Incendium aren't very clever. But then, anyone who could imagine that Urbanus was her HeartKeeper must be a witless fool."

Gemma's inner dragon snarled, demanding release. She composed herself with an effort, but her temper kept simmering.

"There's nothing saying a dragon princess can only marry her HeartKeeper."

"But why would someone with every advantage accept anything less?"

Gemma wasn't going to answer that. "Where are you? Who are you?" she asked more quietly. She kept looking, seeking some sign of the intruder, but couldn't see him.

"A friend, come to warn you."

"With friends like you, I don't need of enemies."

He laughed again. "True enough." There was something very appealing about his laughter. It was confident, a little reckless.

Gemma wondered what he looked like.

The Seed made her burn to know more than that. "Warn me of what?"

"Of your husband, naturally. How much do you know about Prince Urbanus?"

"More than enough."

The intruder was skeptical. "I doubt that. How long have you spent alone in his company?"

Gemma hated that she had to admit a weakness. "Suitors of the royal princesses are closely chaperoned."

"No time at all then." The voice sighed. "At best, you've barely scratched the surface of his nature."

Gemma's interest sparked. "Do you mean that his truth is hidden?"

"You could say that."

Urbanus was both HeartKeeper and Carrier of the Seed, then. Gemma couldn't dispel her disappointment. "Then what's your warning?"

"Watch his hands. He hides more than the truth."

"Like what?" Gemma waited, but there was no reply. "That's it?" she demanded.

"It's more than the warning I had," was the grim response. "He's coming. Don't be stupid enough to mention me."

"I won't," Gemma had time to say, although she wasn't sure why she made such a promise to someone hidden in her room. Could she trust him? Could she trust *anyone* in this place? It seemed unlikely.

The smell of the Seed meddled with her thoughts, making her more aware of her feelings than any logic. As far as Gemma was concerned, that situation needed to end as soon as possible. She hated being at the whim of her desires and bodily urges.

Impulse prompted her to listen to strangers.

She'd seduce Urbanus quickly.

Her heart skipped when she heard footfalls on the other side of the adjoining door. Her unexpected companion hadn't lied about her husband's arrival, at least. Gemma returned to the balcony. She scooped up Felice and resumed her earlier pose. Her heart was beating a little too quickly, but she doubted that Urbanus would notice.

Who was the intruder? Where was the intruder?

What was Urbanus' hidden truth?

Did it matter, if she had the Seed from him?

She had a sense of trickery that she couldn't avoid. Was it because of the warning? Or was the scent of the Seed destroying her clear thinking?

Gemma heard the door open to the adjoining suite and gripped Felice a little tighter. Quick was the way to go. Quick and passionate and finished.

Then Urbanus would be finished.

"Gemma?" Urbanus asked, his voice making her jump.

"Urbanus," she replied, ensuring that her tone was welcoming. Her dragon snarled, but Gemma smiled.

Her new husband paused on the threshold. "What beauty in the night," he murmured, granting her an appreciative survey. "Like a beam of moonlight made flesh." Gemma averted her gaze, sensing that his words were insincere and not wanting him to see as much. He came to stand at the rail beside her.

Urbanus was taller than she was and not unattractive—at a distance. He was well-proportioned, but through the sheer white chemise, she could see that he wasn't muscled. He wasn't fat, not yet, but he was soft.

They wouldn't be married long, Gemma reminded herself, much less grow old together.

All she needed from him was the Seed.

She could still smell it, but oddly enough it wasn't stronger with his proximity. It had actually been more powerful in the chamber, but maybe he had spent time there, preparing the room for her.

Gemma had to admit that was unlikely.

Maybe the furniture had come from his own chambers.

Watch his hands.

Gemma considered Urbanus' hands and found nothing remarkable about them or their pose. They were a bit paler than she might have expected, as if he spent a lot of time inside. They were also unscarred. Undoubtedly he avoided the joust and other sports that proved a man's valor—in favor of what? Gemma didn't know. There was a signet ring upon his right hand and the wedding band now on his left. There was a little stain beneath the nail of his index finger, perhaps from the ink from signing the registry.

Maybe her so-called friend gave bad advice. She couldn't see anything worthy of note about her husband's hands.

She tried to sound welcoming, but guessed she would sound overly formal. "There is no need for flattery, Urbanus. We are married now and have exchanged our vows before thousands of witnesses." She thought she should warn him early, in case he liked virgins. "Even when I was a maiden, I knew what a groom was owed on a wedding night."

He grimaced as if to tease her. "Gemma, Gemma! Are we not *both* owed pleasure in the marital bed?" He stepped closer and put his arm around her waist. Gemma fought her urge to pull away. "Isn't that the point of the lessons we endure? To ensure that we can provide pleasure to our spouse on this night of nights?"

Had Urbanus been compelled to take formal lessons in copulation? Gemma bit back a smile. And she hadn't *endured* her nights with Farquon. She'd quite enjoyed them.

She dropped her gaze, letting him think she was shy. Her only pleasure would come from his early demise.

Urbanus dropped his voice low. "I know our match was arranged and the terms negotiated, but that doesn't mean there can't be a little romance between us." He lifted her hand and kissed her fingertips, his eyes gleaming as he watched her. Felice's purr sounded a little more like a growl, but Urbanus ignored the creature.

His hand felt fleshy and cold, and Gemma barely kept from pulling her hand away. Even the Seed wasn't helping. She had to be sure Urbanus didn't have any suspicions! She deliberately thought of Farquon and his great thick...

Urbanus bent and pressed a kiss against her palm. His lips were cold, too, and she fought a shiver. Gemma thought she felt a minute prick, then he folded her fingers over the spot he had touched with his lips. He held her hand captive in his left hand then, his right moving out of sight.

Had something happened? That warning resonated in Gemma's thoughts, even as a strange warmth surged through her. It seemed to emanate from the point Urbanus' lips had touched, which made little sense to Gemma. It made even less sense how she felt less resistant to the notion of their coupling.

She even felt more amorous.

Farquon seemed suddenly inadequate in comparison to her lord husband.

Gemma blinked. What had just happened?

Urbanus was watching her closely, more closely than she might have expected. Could he read her thoughts? No, no, it was Troy who was a MindBender. Urbanus was simply a royal prince.

Simply? The echo of doubt was dismissed so quickly that she might not have had it.

Gemma *was* a dragon shifter. The beast within stirred, and her passion surged. How strange that a kiss from Urbanus should provoke her passion. She tried to pull her hand back and open it, to look at the spot he'd kissed, but Urbanus held it within his own so resolutely that she abandoned the struggle. She didn't want him to think her reluctant.

"There are those who find love in arranged marriages," he said, his voice awakening a vibration within her. He drew her into his arms and Gemma let him. Oddly, his body felt good against hers, exciting even, and she felt her nipples bead. She forgot his chilliness, given the fire within her. Heat slipped through her veins, feeding her anticipation of their union, making her wet and ready.

It must be the Seed, calling to her body, awakening its destiny.

"Even happiness." His lips touched her shoulder then and his one hand slid to her shoulder. She felt another prick and another wave of desire, the heat doubling within her.

She tried to pull away but Urbanus trapped her between his hips and the railing. His lips trailed along her bare shoulder to touch her throat, even as he unbound her hair.

"Not both love and happiness?" she asked, and her voice sounded husky even to herself.

"They don't necessarily go together." Urbanus kissed her ear and Gemma was certain she had never felt such pleasure. Despite the fury in Felice's expression, she leaned her head back and closed her eyes, welcoming her new husband's touch. She felt his tongue, then his breath in her ear. "I loved my brother Canto but he didn't make me happy."

Gemma supposed it was inevitable that they talk about the situation that had brought them together. In a way, she respected that Urbanus didn't skirt around the fact that her sister had killed his brother. All the same, she didn't know how best to reply.

In fact, she was having a difficult time keeping her thoughts on anything other than his caress. The Seed was more potent than she'd ever imagined. She should have been warned!

His hands rose to cup her breasts then, his thumbs toying with the nipples even though the cloth. Gemma heard herself make a sound suspiciously like a growl, and Urbanus chuckled as he drew her away from the railing. Felice leaped down in disgust but for once Gemma didn't pay any attention to her pet.

"Beautiful ceremony today," Urbanus whispered. He pulled her against him and she felt his erection against her belly. She yearned for his strength inside her as he captured her lips in a seductive kiss. Every reservation within her melted as he locked his mouth over hers and cajoled her to join him, using his tongue, his teeth, and his lips. Gemma felt as if her blood was on fire. She gripped his shoulders, then clutched at his hair, opening her mouth to him in surrender. He kissed her thoroughly, then broke the embrace with obvious regret, smiling down at her with sparkling eyes. "Your parents did a fine job with it."

For a moment, Gemma didn't know what he meant. Her mind was filled with thoughts of coupling and kissing, of the two of them sating each other and wasting no effort upon mere words.

"The wedding," he prompted.

"I believe your mother contributed to its success, as well."

"No doubt she did," he said, with an interesting tinge of bitterness. "But it's typical, isn't it?" Urbanus cupped her nape in his hand, tipped her head back, and kissed her beneath her chin. His lips burned a trail toward her nipple, which he teased with lips and tongue and teeth until Gemma wanted to moan aloud.

When had she burned with such need?

The Seed must amplify normal urges.

"I don't understand," she said, dismissive of conversation. Before Urbanus could reply, Gemma framed his face in her hands, backed him into the wall and kissed him with savage force. Her new spouse, instead of being appalled, met her touch for touch. He seized her buttocks and lifted her against him. Their kiss was passionate and hungry, and Gemma could feel the leap of his pulse beneath her fingertips, even as her own raced. His hands were under her shift, her knees were rising to his waist, their mouths were locked together in passionate fury.

Felice meowed with apparent disapproval but Gemma didn't care. She wanted the Seed and she wanted it immediately.

CHAPTER TWO

IT WAS URBANUS WHO LOCKED his hands around Gemma's waist and broke their kiss, putting distance between them. His eyes were sparkling and his breath came as quickly as Gemma's. She might have protested his move, but he put a finger on her lips.

"Don't you?"

Once again, Gemma had a hard time recalling the thread of the conversation. Her body burned for satisfaction, the Seed demanded to be planted, and she was impatient with Urbanus and his need to chatter. She tried to kiss him again but he evaded her.

She gave serious consideration to shifting shape, toasting him into submission, then having her way with him.

But it would be rude.

And it would put him on his guard, when she needed him to relax.

"I think you do understand, but you're not sure that I would share your view. Let's have honesty between us, Gemma. I think you believe that we have very little in common, but I know you're wrong."

Gemma was intrigued. "Do you?" she asked, then reached for his erection. He caught his breath when she closed her hand around his strength, and she watched his nostrils pinch in pleasure.

"I do," he said, a most enticing strain in his voice, then lifted her hand away. "And I'll prove it to you."

"Does it have to be now?"

Urbanus laughed. "Yes, but I'll be quick, my lustful bride." He reached for the tie at the front of her gown, and unfastened it deliberately as he spoke. "I think it's typical that you and I are left to clean up the messes created by our older siblings. It's the fate of the second child."

He opened her gown and smiled at her bared breasts, then placed his hands beneath the sheer garment and pushed it over her shoulders. This was progress. Gemma tipped her head back at the feel of his palms on her skin and shook her shoulders so that the gown fell to the ground. Urbanus made a murmur of satisfaction when she was nude before him, and his hands fell to her breasts. He kneaded the nipples between finger and thumb, making Gemma twitch with need. She reached for the tie of his chemise, making quick work of the knot.

"We're never seen to be as special or wonderful or praiseworthy as the first-born, no matter what our older sibling might do. And when that sibling fails—as Canto and Drakina *did* fail to secure the alliance between our two kingdoms—then the obligation to make it all come right falls to us. The second born."

Gemma only let him talk because it was clear he meant to have his say before she had her satisfaction. Her mind was filled with need, and she would do whatever was necessary to urge him toward their mutual pleasure.

She pushed his chemise over his shoulders, sparing a glance to his nudity. Why had she thought there was anything wrong with softness? "You didn't have to marry one of Incendium's princesses," she said, pressing a kiss to his nipple. His hands closed around her waist and he lifted her against him.

Urbanus laughed. "You don't know my mother well, do you?" He bent, his words intent as he murmured into her ear. She was more interested in his erection and how she might coax it to be closer to the size of Farquon's most impressive member. "But understand, Gemma, that when it was made clear to me that I should do so, I didn't choose you because you were next in the lineage." He claimed her chin and compelled her to meet his gaze. "I chose you specifically because we are the same."

His eyes were a thousand hues of blue, more marvelous to behold than she had realized. His gaze was filled with a surety that echoed the conviction in her own soul. He must be right. They were the same. They were destined to be together because they had been made for each other. How had Gemma ever doubted the allure of her spouse?

Urbanus watched as he traced a line on her cheek with his fingertip. "We're both unafraid to do what has to be done, Gemma."

That was true enough.

"We're both bold enough to act for the greater good."

Gemma's growing sense that she and Urbanus had a great deal in common was unassailable. It was truth. Their bond was right. Warmth flooded through her from her heart, an overwhelming sense that destiny had been fulfilled.

The Seed called.

Gemma itched to have it within her.

Urbanus really should shut up.

But he kept talking. "You're here not just because your father negotiated the marriage, but because a royal astrologer declared that I am the Carrier of the Seed." Urbanus arched a brow and she was awed that he alone should have discerned the truth. "Am I not right?"

"You know you are."

"So, it's fated to be," he said and kissed her lingeringly once again. "It's our destiny and our choice to save our kingdoms with a union and a son."

"Except that there's Gravitas now," Gemma said, reminding her of Drakina's son and the heir to the crown of Incendium.

Urbanus chuckled, his fingers sliding into her hair, his possessive grip making her shiver. "You've been listening to a MindBender," he accused, solemnity lurking beneath his playful tone. "I thought you would know better than to be so beguiled, Gemma."

Beguiled.

Yes. That's what she felt. The realization flitted through her thoughts, along with the reminder of that warning. Gemma recalled those two little pricks and the sensation they had sent through her. Kraw had said that Urbanus dealt in spells, herbal mixtures that provoked a physiological reaction in the victim. Then she felt a third prick, one on the back of her neck. She opened her eyes even as fire flowed through her veins and her body capitulated to Urbanus and his amorous assault.

"What have you done to me?" she asked, her words slow and her own voice almost unfamiliar.

"Ensured that you couldn't cheat me, my beautiful bride," Urbanus confessed with a smile. He lifted his hand and she saw the small brace on his thumb, one that held a tiny thorn in place. His eyes shone with satisfaction and she realized that there had been some toxin upon it. He flicked it from his finger and cast it into the forest far below, clearly proud of his deceit.

"We are the same, my Gemma," he whispered darkly. "Each intent upon our own objective to the exclusion of all others. Today, I won." He smiled. "I eagerly await your retribution."

Gemma should have been appalled. She should have needed vengeance. But instead, she was falling asleep, powerless against whatever toxin he had given her.

In that moment, something fell with a crash in the chamber beyond her own. Urbanus stepped back, his brow furrowed with concern.

"Who's there?" he called, stepping toward the connecting door.

There was another crash.

Urbanus thrust Gemma aside and strode to the door, flinging it open and returning to his own chamber. She barely heard the sound of the key turning in the lock, securing her in her prison once more.

She was going to fall.

She made it to the bed and collapsed onto the mattress before her knees gave out beneath her weight. Gemma rolled to her back, against her own volition. Her legs parted, seemingly of their own volition, and once in that position, she was powerless to move.

She had been enchanted.

Because she had failed to take the voice's advice.

And now it was too late. A languid tide rolled through her body, making it impossible for her to keep her eyes open or lift a hand—much less to kill her spouse.

Her perfect plan had been foiled.

And Gemma hated Urbanus more than she had ever hated anyone in her life.

Vengeance would be hers, Gemma resolved, and then she knew no more.

SOMETHING HAD TO BE DONE.

Venero had watched Gemma succumb to Urbanus' spell, despite the warning he'd given her. He was horrified by his brother's obvious intention of making his new wife helpless. The import of that couldn't be good.

And it was hardly a fair fight.

Independent of his own agenda, Venero had to save her.

He hopped quickly across the room and forced his way through the gap beneath the door to Urbanus' bedchamber. It was a tight fit and he scratched his back getting through the gap, but there wasn't a moment to waste.

Once in the chamber, Venero leaped to a table and kicked a lantern to the floor. It hadn't been lit, but the oil had recently been refilled. The glass vessel shattered, making a satisfactory sound, and the oil spread across the floor.

"Who's there?" Urbanus demanded, his voice sharp.

Of course, he had locked the door to his chamber and dismissed the servants. There shouldn't be an intruder in his sanctuary. Venero eyed another table, its surface crowded with vials and vessels. It was a bit farther than his usual range, but he didn't want to jump down into the oil.

Urbanus might start a fire to be rid of him.

Venero heard his brother's approaching footsteps. He took a deep breath, gathering his strength, and leaped for the other table. He barely made it and didn't manage a graceful landing. In fact, he crashed into a number of glass items and sent them toppling. He barged through the rest, sending many of them crashing to the floor, then jumped off the far side.

He had to hide!

He made it to the shadow beneath the bed by the time Urbanus crossed the threshold. His brother was still, his gaze seeking the culprit in the shadows, and Venero eased backward just a little.

"It can only be you, brother mine," Urbanus whispered, and Venero's heart skipped a beat that he'd revealed himself. He didn't regret the choice, though. Urbanus had to learn that he couldn't have everything his way. "Show yourself willingly, and I'll be kinder."

Venero wasn't going to bet on that.

"I can coax you out," Urbanus said, his voice melodic. "You know I can entice you to reveal yourself, no matter what you plan."

Venero remained completely still. He tried to close his ears against any spell Urbanus might cast.

His brother took another step and reached for a flint. Venero had time to fear that his brother would inadvertently start a fire and that all opportunity for his own salvation would be lost, along with Gemma's free will.

Then Urbanus slipped on the oil. He lost his balance, swore, and hit the floor with a thud. There was a loud crack.

Followed by silence.

Venero feared a trick. He waited half an eternity, but there was no sound from his brother. He crept out of the shadows, slowly, cautiously, only to find Urbanus unconscious on the floor, a trickle of blood on his temple.

Venero didn't wait to see more. He didn't have time for relief. He skirted the perimeter of the room as quickly as he could, squeezed under the door again, and leaped onto the marital bed. The princess was sprawled there on her back, snoring softly. Her position told Venero all he needed to know about his brother's plans for consummating the marriage, with or without the bride's agreement or participation. Even from their short acquaintance, he knew Gemma wouldn't sleep in such a vulnerable pose.

"Wake up!" he whispered. "This is our chance to escape!"

Gemma gave no sign that she'd heard him.

Venero jumped on her belly, to no visible response. He jumped again and again. He flicked his tongue against her cheek and even though it stuck for a moment before releasing and must have tugged the skin, she slept on. He pulled her hair, grabbing a tendril of it in his mouth and jumping as far as he could so that it tugged at the root.

Gemma couldn't be stirred.

Had Urbanus given her a spell to sleep for a thousand years?

His ineffectiveness was frustrating and infuriating. He couldn't just sweep her up and save her. He couldn't solve the situation. He couldn't even wake her up. Venero had never felt so powerless in his life.

He was giving serious consideration to the idea of kissing Gemma, right on the lips, even though he knew it wouldn't do anything to help his curse—but just because it might wake her up—when there was a sudden blur of blue and green.

The pavofel leaped to the bed beside its mistress. It crouched, tail lashing and eyes gleaming, and Venero didn't dare to linger. He jumped from the bed, barely escaping the pavofel's swiping paw, and fled to sanctuary beneath that chest of drawers. The pavofel followed and slashed beneath the chest with claws bared. Venero retreated so that he was pressed against the wall, apparently out of range of the beast.

He'd never liked pavofels, but this one, he hated with particular vigor.

It prowled around the chest and he had more than one heart-stopping glimpse of its bright eyes as it bent to peer into the shadows. Wretched beast.

Finally, it abandoned the hunt and returned to its mistress' side.

Venero peeked out but the pavofel was on the bed, watching him. The ends of its tail flicked, those eyes in the fur seeming to stare at him, too. Venero eased back into the protective shadows, hoping the princess awakened in the morning.

His first chance of escape in years couldn't be lost as quickly as this.

Could it?

GEMMA AWAKENED WITH A foul taste in her mouth. Her head was pounding. She was sleeping on her back, like a trusting child, not the warrior she knew herself to be. She sat up in a hurry, feeling vulnerable. She was still in the bridal chamber but she was alone. Even Felice was gone from the bed.

Where was Urbanus?

What had he done before he left?

Gemma didn't feel any different and couldn't smell any indication in the bed linens that Urbanus had consummated their marriage while she was drugged and out cold. She felt her eyes narrow as she surveyed the quiet room. She wouldn't have put it past him to do such a thing. What had changed his mind? She could still smell the Seed, and its summons was a persistent hum in her blood.

The door to the adjoining chamber was closed.

It was probably locked, too.

The hue of the light indicated that the sun had risen. How long had she slept? One night or more? She realized that she could hear Felice hunting somewhere in the chamber, so she wasn't completely alone. Gemma got quickly out of bed and checked the door to Urbanus' chamber.

Locked. Of course. The keyhole was blocked, as if he'd left the key in it.

She pressed her ear against the wooden door.

Silence.

She smelled lantern oil and frowned. Why was it so strong? Surely Urbanus hadn't retreated to his chamber to refill his lamps? She couldn't imagine him doing such a menial task, much less thinking it was more important than consummating their marriage. She dropped to the floor and tried to peer under the door but the angle was wrong and the gap too small.

Gemma stood and considered her own chamber again, then noticed that the maid had brought water for her. The realization annoyed her—someone had come into her chamber and she hadn't even noticed. That was how powerful his toxin had been. Anything could have happened and that made Gemma angry.

She flung her chemise across the chamber and washed with haste. The water was just barely warm, so it had been there for a while. Where was Urbanus? What was his plan? The worst part was that she'd been tricked by him and it was her own fault. That voice, whoever it belonged to, had warned her, and she'd *still* been enchanted. Gemma made a little growl of frustration as she scrubbed herself clean, wondering again why Urbanus had just left.

Their marriage was unconsummated, which meant, she supposed, that it could be annulled. It didn't do anything to help her avenge Arista, though.

"Well done," that voice declared, no longer as unfamiliar as it had been. "Didn't I warn you to watch his hands?"

"You did," Gemma snapped. "And I forgot."

"It's not entirely your fault," the voice said. "He started to beguile you at the altar. Maybe even before."

"How? How does he do it?"

"I don't think I can explain."

Gemma propped her hands on her hips and surveyed the room. "I think you should try."

There was no response. Apparently, the owner of the voice had abandoned her.

As Gemma braided her hair, she saw Felice slip behind one of the drapes that hung on either side of the window. The fabric moved as the pavofel stalked something. Felice crouched, there was a faint scuffle as if the intended victim made a run for it, then the pavofel pounced.

Something squeaked.

Gemma was disgusted. It figured that on Regalia there were vermin in the bedchambers, even in the palaces, given what a rat her husband was.

She'd find another way to avenge Arista. Enough was enough.

The door to the corridor was still locked from the other side. Only the balcony door could be opened, probably because it was accessible only from her chamber. Gemma smiled as she stepped onto the balcony, because Urbanus had forgotten one critical detail. There was a sheer drop of considerable distance to the forest below, but that was no obstacle to Gemma in her dragon form.

The sky beckoned.

She was out of this place.

"Come on, Felice," she said, more than ready to abandon her new husband. "Forget the mouse. It's time to go. Goodbye, friend, whoever and wherever you are."

There was no reply.

Felice bounded toward her, some unfortunate creature in her mouth, and Gemma summoned the shift from deep within herself. She should have been in dragon form, poised for flight, just as Felice leaped for her.

Except that nothing happened.

Felice collided with Gemma's upper arm and fell to the ground with a mew of displeasure. Gemma couldn't see or feel the shimmer that came before a shift. She tried again, with no better luck.

Was it because she'd been drugged?

Panic slipped through her, but Gemma was undaunted. She called imperiously to the change. She commanded her body to shift shape, willing it with all her might. This ability was her birthright and part of her nature, after all.

But still, nothing happened. She was standing nude on the balcony of Urbanus' palace in her human form. Even her nails hadn't changed.

What was going on?

"It won't work," that voice declared. "He must have planned it that way."

"I thought he forgot my abilities."

The voice laughed. "He doesn't forget anything." His laughter faded. "Well, maybe he forgot one thing."

"What?"

"Me."

Gemma looked around. There was no sign of the speaker. "Well, it would be easy to forget you since you don't show yourself. Maybe you're not even real."

"I'm real enough," the speaker insisted, then yelped. "Ouch!"

Felice spat out the creature she had caught, shook her head, and backed away. It was small, small enough to fit in Gemma's palm, and gray. It might have been a mouse, but it hopped. It didn't hop well, but crookedly, as if it had been injured. Felice batted it with a paw, as Gemma bent down to look.

It was a toad.

Its front leg was bleeding, and it hobbled behind the open door to take refuge, leaving a trail of blue behind it. When Gemma moved the door, the toad was examining the damage. There was something very untoadlike about the way it looked at the limb, then tested it and surveyed it again.

"I hate pavofels," the toad muttered, revealing the source of the voice that had given Gemma advice. Felice slipped behind the door, so sinuous that she might have been without bones. She stalked silently, eyes glittering, her intent more than clear.

Gemma scooped up her pet. Felice was too far away to strike the toad but tried anyway. "You're a toad and you talk!"

"I talk," the toad agreed grimly. "Take it as proof that you're not the only one who's enchanted."

"So, he *did* beguile me?"

"Aren't you sure?" the toad demanded, its tone skeptical.

Gemma bent down. "Why did he stop?"

The toad was actually many shades of silver and gray and green, and less unattractive than Gemma might have expected. Its eyes shone like amber beads and when it met her gaze, as it did in this moment, she felt as if it were almost human.

"Because I saved you," the toad said.

Gemma laughed. She couldn't help it. "You? Saved me?"

"And a very near thing it was, too." The toad glared at her. "You're welcome."

"How did you save me?"

"By distracting Urbanus. I broke a lantern in his room, so he went to find out who was there."

"Did he see you?"

"No. He slipped in the oil and hit his head."

Oh! Gemma felt herself blush. "Then I apologize. Thank you." She straightened, suddenly aware of her nudity. It shouldn't have mattered in front of a toad, but Gemma had a feeling that in this situation, it did. His eyes seemed to have gotten brighter. "I suppose you want a favor now, or a wish."

His tongue flicked and he chuckled. "How about a kiss?"

Gemma was disgusted. She stalked back into the chamber and cast Felice onto the bed. She pulled her chemise over her head.

"I suppose it *is* too much to hope for." The toad hopped after her, its tone indicating that he thought otherwise.

"It's frogs who are saved by kisses, not toads."

"Are you sure?"

"Yes!" Gemma straightened and turned to face the toad. She saw Felice crouching, intrigued by the toad all over again now that it was moving. "Who are you and why are you here?"

"I'm looking for help, of course." He lifted his foot. "Would you want to be a toad?"

"Then you're not really a toad?"

He sighed with forbearance. "Do toads talk on Incendium?"

"No, but there's no telling what's normal on Regalia. It is said to be a place where everyone in the royal family is a sorcerer."

The toad cleared his throat pointedly.

"Point taken," Gemma said. "But I can't help you, not trapped in this chamber."

"You wouldn't be trapped if you'd listened to me."

Gemma snatched up Felice just as the pavofel would have pounced on the toad. The creature protested loudly and the toad retreated, still trailing blood. "Are you hurt?"

"What do you think?"

"You don't have to be rude."

"And you don't have to be stupid," the toad replied, his irritability clear. "I thought the dragon princesses of Incendium were supposed to be smart." It gave her a look, then glanced down at another small puddle forming on the floor. "This would be blood. Blood flows when the body is injured. *Ipso facto*, I'm hurt."

"I didn't know toads spoke Latin."

"It appears that there's a lot you don't know."

"You don't have to be so cranky."

"Don't I? My advice was ignored by the one person who could help me, ensuring that she can't help me after all, and now I'm being mauled by her pet. Looks like it's true that no good deed goes unpunished."

Gemma considered the chamber, unable to argue with that assertion. "It does, doesn't it?" She flung Felice on the bed and the pavofel curled up, its disdain clear. "I'm sorry, and I'm sorry for Felice's hunting, too. Is there anything I can do for your leg?"

"Probably not."

"Will you tell me more about the spell?"

The toad puffed up, becoming almost double in size. Gemma thought it looked revolting. "I thought you'd never ask."

Felice leaped from the bed suddenly and the toad cried out as it was seized in the pavofel's mouth.

"Felice! NO!" Gemma cried and her pet dropped the toad, which hopped toward her a little less robustly than before.

"Thank you very much," the toad said. "Can't you restrain that thing?"

Felice hunkered down, eyes gleaming and tail swishing.

"That *thing* is my pet and maybe my only friend on this planet."

"Why? Because you listen to its advice? *We* could be friends, if you made a little effort."

Gemma took a deep breath. "Okay. You're right and I admit it. I *am* sorry. Now, can I break the spell or does it have to wear off? How do these things work?"

"Spells can work in a hundred different ways, depending on the intention of the spell caster."

"That doesn't really help."

"The question is what Urbanus defines as the greater good." The toad hopped closer. "And whether you're part of it, key to it, or an obstacle to it."

"Because I can guess what he'll do in each of those instances."

A groan came from the other side of the door to Urbanus' chamber, revealing his location. The toad seemed to grin, as if satisfied with her husband's unhappy state.

"How badly is he hurt?" Gemma whispered.

"He's not dead." The toad sighed. "Clearly, wishes don't always come true."

How unexpected to have something in common with a talking toad, even if it was a dislike of her new husband.

Gemma folded her arms across her chest. "Okay. A quick introduction to spell casting, please. How do I break the spell and get my powers back?"

"With the antidote, of course."

"Which could be anywhere or anything depending upon the intent of the spell caster."

"Exactly."

"Do you know where or what it is, in this case?"

"I could guess, but I'm not telling until you help *me*."

Gemma bent down. "And here I am hoping that the antidote involves the sacrifice of a toad."

The toad, to her surprise, laughed although it was a rueful sound. "It just might."

"Why? Who are you really?"

The toad stretched up and Gemma realized it was offering its mouth to her. "One kiss and you can find out."

She bent and touched a fingertip to his forehead, considering it. But the feel of his skin made her shudder and step back in disgust. She took refuge in a technicality because his disappointment was almost tangible. "If you were a frog, I might. But everyone knows that enchanted princes don't become toads."

"You don't know Urbanus very well, do you?"

Gemma pivoted at the sound of a key in the lock to the corridor. The maid!

"Here's your only chance to get out of here," the toad muttered. "Do I have to explain it and can you figure it out all alone?"

"Oh, shut up or I'll leave you behind," Gemma had time to say before the door swung open and the maid entered the room. She seemed to be startled to find Gemma waiting for her, even though she carried a tray with a steaming bowl upon it.

"I trust you slept well, my lady?"

"I did, thank you," Gemma said with a smile. She acted like a fool, the better to win the girl's trust. "That smells delicious. Could you set breakfast on the balcony for me? I *love* the view of the trees! Look at the sunlight on my ring!"

VENERO WAS IMPRESSED BY Gemma. At the sound of the key in the lock, her manner changed completely. He could have been watching a different person than the woman he'd been arguing with just moments before.

He admired anyone who could play a role when necessary. He didn't like deceit much, but sometimes a small deception served the greater good. If the maid under-estimated Gemma, they would have a better chance of escape.

But it was more than that: he'd seen Gemma nude and he couldn't forget it. She was beautiful. Ideal, even. She had creamy breasts, which he thought to be the perfect size, and the way her nipples tightened in the cool morning breeze had been particularly distracting.

He'd wanted to touch her.

No, he'd wanted to caress her. He'd been sure he'd despise her, given her shape-shifting abilities, but the reaction Gemma provoked in him was the very opposite. He wanted her in all the ways he couldn't have her. And that was strange: he liked ornamental women as sexual partners, and skilled warriors as companions. He'd never met a woman who he admired in both ways. Arista, for example, had been a good companion and partner in battle, but he'd felt no sexual desire for her at all.

Of course, Arista hadn't really been a woman, so maybe that explained everything.

Venero's reaction to Gemma was so uncharacteristic that it confused him.

Maybe that was the result of his recent celibacy. Years as a toad had left him with many unsatisfied urges. Maybe any attractive woman would have provoked such a reaction in him. Maybe it didn't matter. Maybe he'd reward them both with a satisfying interlude after she helped him to earn his own freedom.

He hoped she got them out of here and soon.

Venero forced himself to listen and watch.

Gemma was all grace and solicitude, complimenting the maid so much that Venero thought she overdid it a bit. The girl blushed and beamed, though, more than happy to move a table for her gracious lady and get a cushion for the chair. She admired the ring at Gemma's insistence, and smiled at the way the light flashed in the stone. She set out the meal, barely noticing how Gemma moved behind her.

Venero blinked as Gemma incapacitated the maid, her attack as quick as lightning and more effective than he expected. The maid was struck and she fell, but Gemma caught her. She was stripped naked, gagged, and trussed helpless in the blink of an eye. She was unconscious but he guessed not injured.

He recognized the move from Arista. It was a trick of those trained on Cumae to stun a victim just long enough to see that individual bound, and it wasn't easily done. It required a perfect balance of force and gentleness, as well as meticulous timing.

As he watched, Gemma touched the maid's temple with a care completely at odds with the inflicting blow, a gesture Venero remembered well.

It had to be true, then, that Gemma had trained on Cumae. It was part of the story of the royal family of Incendium that the second daughter of the king had trained on Cumae and led an elite regiment on her return to her home planet, but Venero had always thought it was just propaganda. He hadn't been able to believe that any princess would undertake that kind of physical challenge, much less succeed at it. Gemma's moves proved that she had done it and probably graduated at the top of her class.

He was impressed, so impressed that he almost forgot to watch Gemma dress.

Urbanus moaned a little more loudly then, recalling him to the situation. Venero hopped toward Gemma. "Hurry!"

The girl's lashes fluttered as Gemma was putting on her boots. The maid blinked and frowned, then wriggled as Gemma pulled the lavish coverlet over her.

"I am sorry," Gemma whispered. "It's my only way out. Are you quite comfortable?"

The girl nodded, her amazement echoing Venero's own. Gemma pulled her wedding band from her finger then and pushed it onto the girl's smallest finger. Her hands were more plump than Gemma's.

"Since you like it," Gemma whispered. "Sell it if you like."

The maid's eyes widened and Venero knew she'd never imagined that she'd even touch such a ring, let alone possess it.

But Gemma didn't look back. She seized the bucket from the water and the key from the door, then nudged her pet with her toe. As soon as she opened the door, the pavofel shot through the gap in a streak of vivid blue-green.

"Oh, my lady! The pavofel!" Gemma cried, mimicking the maid's voice.

"Me! Me!" Venero cried, but Gemma was already scooping him off the floor with one hand. He felt her shudder of revulsion, then she dropped him into the pocket on the front of the maid's plain dress. There was a handkerchief there and it wasn't clean, which made Venero shudder with revulsion, then he jostled in the pocket as Gemma ran down the stairs.

At least she'd kept her promise. He found himself pleased with his companion.

"She wouldn't know the word," he felt obliged to point out.

"What word?" Gemma demanded in an undertone.

"Pavofel. We don't have them here, and she isn't a great reader."

"Do you think he heard?"

There was no point in lying. Venero sighed. "Yes."

Gemma swore with the vigor of a hardened mercenary, and Venero was astonished yet again by her. She then ran faster, galloping down the stairs with a wanton disregard for his comfort.

"Don't drop me!" he insisted, knowing he'd be smashed by the fall. Gemma closed her hand around the opening of the pocket.

Venero was jostled and bounced in her pocket but wished he could see her running. She had to be as graceful as the cervus he'd hunted on Sylvawyld during his incarceration there. They were such beautiful creatures that he'd always regretted his need for food and had never eaten their meat since.

Venero felt the change in the air when Gemma reached the ground floor, because it was cooler there, then heard her throwing open the bolts on the kitchen door. He smelled the herbs in the garden as she took the most direct path to the gate, and felt the heat of the pavofel when she scooped it up into her arms.

The miserable creature reached a paw into the pocket of the dress, and Venero tucked himself as far away from those claws as he could.

"Control your pet!" he cried.

"Because I don't have enough to do," Gemma complained. Even so, she lifted the pavofel higher, much to his relief.

He could see a patch of morning sky through the opening at the top of the pocket, then the branches of the trees on the perimeter of the forest etched against it. The skirt spun and he had to hang on to the lip of the pocket as Gemma turned back to face the palace.

And at the height of the tower, Venero saw a male figure, silhouetted on a high balcony. Urbanus.

"Oh no," Venero whispered.

"What's he doing?"

The crown prince raised his hand, scattering something into the wind, and Venero swore himself when he saw the glitter of spelldust.

CHAPTER THREE

"RUN!" VENERO BELLOWED, but Gemma didn't need his encouragement. She had already spun to flee. She leaped over fallen branches and raced deeper into the forest, panting but never slowing down. He was amazed by her speed and her agility, and by her determination to outrun the spelldust.

But he heard Urbanus calling to the wind to aid him and Venero guessed that Gemma could hear it, too.

"What do I do?" she demanded.

"Keep it from touching your skin. Can you see it?"

"It glitters. What is it?"

"Spelldust."

She groaned. "Trust my luck that I end up trapped on a planet filled with magic." Her scorn was clear and intrigued Venero. "What does spelldust do?"

"It takes whatever it touches out of the time stream."

"What?"

"It immobilizes things, freezing them in one moment, either for eternity or until released by the spell caster."

"Anything?" Gemma sounded incredulous.

"Everything."

Gemma swore again. She splashed into a stream, and Venero saw the first sparkle of the dust descending. It touched the tree tops and they glittered, then stilled. It was a sight that Venero always found both fascinating and horrifying. Immortality lost any allure it might have had the first time he saw spelldust in action.

"Quick!" he urged. "Under the water."

Gemma didn't hesitate to take his advice this time, which was an encouraging change. She dove into a pool of water so quickly that Venero barely had time to take a deep breath himself. The pavofel was furious and yowled in protest, at least until the water closed over them all—then it fought wildly.

Venero was glad to see someone else injured by the creature. He saw it make a trio of long scratches on Gemma's arm, deep enough to draw blood. But Gemma remained calm, even as she wrestled the miserable feline. He had to admire that.

Venero would have been inclined to let it go, but Gemma hooked her ankle around a branch sunk to the bottom of the pool to keep herself below the surface, then blew into the pavofel's nose. This scarcely made the creature any happier, but it wasn't going to drown as Venero feared he might.

She solved problems without hesitation, and she didn't surrender without a fight. He liked both of those traits.

He might have felt more admiration for her in that moment, but the fabric of the dress swirled upward in the water and wrapped around him like a shroud. Venero was caught and only had glimpses of the opening at the top of the pocket. He sputtered. He thrashed. He wanted to remind Gemma that toads were not aquatic creatures, but she was busy with that stupid pavofel. Venero could feel her wrestling with it.

He'd never wished for his DreamCasting abilities with greater vigor than in that moment, but he knew they were gone.

Enchanted into oblivion, just like Gemma's shape-shifting powers.

Venero choked. He struggled in a bid to get Gemma's attention, hoping she might pull him free. The fabric caught at his legs as if it followed some instruction from Urbanus. He supposed that wasn't out of the question. Frustration rose within him even as he fought for air. He was drowning, still enchanted as a toad, and his front leg hurt.

Venero wasn't going to die this way, even if that might be his brother's preference.

It was about more than his own fate, though. Gemma wasn't nearly safe, and he felt a protectiveness toward her. She didn't understand magic or Urbanus, and she'd need Venero's help to survive—never mind escape.

Urbanus couldn't destroy them both.

When Gemma got out of the river, she would be cold and wet. She would need shelter and heat before she could continue to seek her antidote. Celo's hut would be the closest shelter, and even though Venero had promised to leave his youngest brother in solitude, he'd have to break that promise today.

For Gemma.

He gave a ferocious kick and heard the cloth tear. He silently thanked Urbanus for keeping his servants so poor that they had to wear their clothing to rags. He blew a stream of bubbles with the last bit of air in his lungs and lunged toward the surface in the same moment. He felt Gemma snatch after him, undoubtedly hoping to save him from the spelldust, and his heart swelled with more of that admiration. He evaded her grasp, probably only because she was fighting the pavofel. He swam without looking back, not wanting to see her fear for him.

As he anticipated, the spelldust was landing on the surface of the stream. It sparkled and glittered there in a hundred different colors, as if to entice them all to touch it.

Venero knew better. He spied a leaf floating on the river, its stem dangling beneath it in the water. Maybe his luck was turning. He managed to grip the stem and let the current sweep him away, down the river, down toward Celo's hut. He pushed his head into the hollow beneath the leaf and took a gulping breath.

All he had to do next was accurately guess when to abandon the leaf and jump out of the river.

And convince Celo to help Gemma.

Venero wasn't sure which would be the greater challenge, but he was alive and that had to count for something.

He was on the bank before he realized that he was relying upon Gemma's resourcefulness. She'd save herself, now that he'd given her a hint of how to evade the spelldust. He had no doubt of it.

A demure beauty wouldn't have survived, much less been such a reliable comrade.

Venero decided to think about that later.

THE TOAD!

Gemma had been so worried about Felice and the spelldust that she'd forgotten the toad in her pocket—at least until it thrashed free of her skirt and swam for the surface. She reached for it, but missed. The spelldust! Was it ignoring its own advice? She could only watch as it rose to the surface. It seized a floating leaf, though, and used it as a shield. It then disappeared from her view, swallowed by the swirling current of the river.

She supposed it had only wanted out of the castle and that once she'd helped it do that, there was no reason for it to linger. But she already missed its company.

Never mind its advice. Magic was all new to Gemma. They taught science on Incendium, and she had refined her fighting skills on Cumae. But she couldn't anticipate a sorcerer like Urbanus, because she didn't understand his powers.

That was annoying.

It looked like the spelldust was fading on the surface of the water.

Although it might be smarter to wait a little longer, Felice needed air. The pavofel had stilled in her arms but she could feel its heartbeat. Gemma recalled the toad's strategy. She surged toward the surface and swam toward the bank.

To her relief, there was a rock that leaned over the water, casting the surface in shadow. She emerged beneath its shelter. Felice needed no encouragement to do the same, but Gemma had to forcibly keep the pavofel from leaping to the shore. Wouldn't the spelldust go through the pads of her feet? Gemma had to assume it would. Did it expire? Surely it followed some logical rules.

She wished she could ask the toad.

Gemma couldn't do that, but she could follow its example. She guessed that at some point downriver, there would either be no spelldust or its power would have waned. She tucked Felice tightly under her arm and considered the stream. It flowed fairly quickly here and she could see another outcropping a good distance downstream.

"Hold your breath," she told the pavofel, which gave her a simmering look of displeasure. Then she blew into Felice's nose again and ducked under the surface, swimming with all her might toward that outcropping. The current helped, and she reached it more quickly than expected. She chose another that was further downstream, and did it again.

Felice scratched her, of course, fighting her every moment that they were under the water. Gemma didn't care. She'd protect the pavofel to the end, even if it was a thankless task.

The pet had been a gift from Arista, after all.

The rhythm of swimming and catching her breath gave her a chance to think. Arista had always said that warriors came in many guises and were armed with many different weapons. She ought to have known. She had been contracted as a mercenary for years in between her stints of teaching on Cumae.

Wouldn't Arista have considered Urbanus a warrior, as well? Gemma thought she might have done. Wasn't he fighting for what he desired, but using his own arsenal? He'd anticipated Gemma's own plan and disarmed her with his sorcery before she could execute it, and done so in order to see his own goals achieved. That sounded like war to Gemma.

Or at least a battle for supremacy.

She couldn't shift shape anymore, which was less than ideal, but it didn't mean she was helpless either. Gemma could fight back, or maybe even outsmart Urbanus, even in her human form.

The trick would be to anticipate him.

How could she do that without knowing his goal?

She thought about the toad's question. Was she part of Urbanus' plan, key to it, or an obstacle? She couldn't be an obstacle yet, because he would have simply killed her when he had the chance. He'd let her live, although he'd disabled her ability to shift shape. That implied that he still needed her, and that he wanted to control her until she fulfilled her usefulness to him.

She was pretty sure he'd intended to consummate their marriage, and would have done so if the toad hadn't saved her.

Did they share the goal of securing the alliance between Incendium and Regalia by marriage? Or did Urbanus believe that the child of their union would be able to save their twin planets from destruction? Or did he simply want to cement the alliance between their planets, given the reliance of Regalia on Incendium? If any of those were the case, he'd need her to survive at least long enough to bear their son.

He wanted to keep her on Regalia, that was clear, and under his control. Her dragon powers would have given her the ability to escape, so had to be undermined. Was her power gone forever? Gemma didn't want to think about that possibility, but it was worth consideration. She doubted that Urbanus wanted her to regain the ability to shift shape any time soon, if ever.

The toad had mentioned an antidote, which implied that the spell would hold unless she found the antidote. How would she find it without the toad's help? She didn't know nearly enough about either spells or Regalia. Her assumption that she wouldn't be on the planet long now seemed foolish.

She didn't blame the toad for expecting better of her.

Arista would have expected better of her, too. She'd let her confidence keep her from making contingency plans, and now she was in a predicament with no way to let anyone know. All her comm, even her interpreter, had been stripped away after the wedding ceremony. Urbanus had charmed her mother when he'd called them distractions to romance. Gemma had ceded, sure that she could triumph without them.

She was annoyed by her own gullibility. The truth was that she'd underestimated Urbanus, and that he'd used that to his strategic advantage.

She had to turn the tables on him and escape.

Without the toad's help.

Did all the toads on Regalia talk? Gemma thought not. Her toad had said it was enchanted. Who was it really? Had it been cursed by Urbanus, too?

Maybe she *should* have kissed it.

WHAT GEMMA DIDN'T REALIZE was that when she considered kissing the toad, she had touched him on his parietal eye, the mystic third eye also known as the pineal gland. It was in the middle of his forehead, marked by a white spot. Toads saw the world differently from men, but the fact that this toad was actually a man, and one from a family of sorcerers, meant that his parietal eye was particularly well developed.

The touch of Gemma's fingertip restored Venero's ability to send dreams.

As soon as Venero realized as much, he wanted to do more than kiss Gemma.

He realized it by chance, when a hawk swooped down toward him as soon as he reached the bank of the river. On impulse, Venero sent a dream to the hawk of a full belly. The hawk swooped down and scooped him up, and Venero feared that nothing had changed. But the hawk flew and flew, carrying him like a treasure, and he dared to believe again. He sent the hawk a dream of flying toward Celo's hut and dropping him there.

It worked.

Venero could have shouted with glee. Gemma had helped him regain his DreamCasting powers, which might mean that she could break the spell completely.

Maybe he'd misunderstood the notion of true love.

Maybe it was about admiration and respect.

Either way, his restored abilities saved him a lot of hopping, even if he was a bit bruised from the drop.

Venero had forgotten how good it felt to have some control over his own fate, never mind how easy it was to turn the thoughts of wild creatures to his will. He'd first used his skill with woodland creatures, then after practice, had turned to humans. His siblings were another level of challenge altogether.

Venero hoped his youngest brother would be of aid, although influencing Celo would be a greater challenge than tricking a hawk or a cervus.

CELO WAS EXACTLY WHERE Venero had expected him to be. He was outside his little hut in the depths of the forest, chopping wood.

Venero's youngest brother didn't look much like a prince of the royal blood of Regalia. His hair was longer and his beard was almost to his waist. He was more muscular than Venero recalled, but he'd have to be working hard to survive in the old forest. That told Venero how determined Celo was to never go back to the palace.

Not that Venero could blame him.

Celo's axe fell with regular rhythm. Venero was exhausted but he hopped the last distance and leaped onto the woodpile.

"Well met, brother mine," he said, and Celo started.

He stared, then buried his axe into the chopping block and bent to look Venero in the eye. "Not you," he said grimly, which wasn't the warmest of welcomes. "Not again."

"Me. Again." Venero tried to smile. "Good to see you, too."

"Don't you ever give up?"

"Not in my nature, I'm afraid."

Celo grimaced and spared a glance upward. The trees were dense but far above their branches, the clear blue sky could be seen.

"I wasn't followed," Venero said.

"Yet," Celo noted and he had to concede that possibility. "You promised," Celo accused, folding his arms across his chest as he eyed Venero again.

"I did, and I apologize."

"And you've shielded your thoughts," Celo noted. "At least you haven't lost all of your powers." He lifted his brows. "Or maybe you've met your one true love. Is she beautiful? Demure?"

Venero didn't answer that. "There's a damsel in distress that I need you to help."

"The lady in question?"

"Urbanus' new bride."

Celo grimaced. "Isn't she in the tower, conceiving his son? Isn't he busy for once?"

"She escaped."

"Of course, you had nothing to do with that." Celo shook his head and went back to his wood pile. "You've got to stop challenging him. It never ends well for you."

Venero ignored that bit of advice, just as he had a hundred times before. "She's coming this way, and you need to help her."

Celo turned, his eyes narrowed. "Of course, you had nothing to do with that either."

"Me?"

The youngest prince propped his hands on his knees and bent down so that his face was only a finger's breadth from Venero's toad face. "I don't need to do anything. And I'm *not* going to do anything that might attract his attention. I don't need that kind of trouble. Let her run through the forest until he finds her. Let them sort it out themselves."

"She needs help."

"She can ask her husband for some."

"She's very pretty."

Celo's eyes narrowed. "She's not my problem."

"I think she is." Venero lied, just a little. "That's why she's coming here."

Celo pushed a hand through his hair. He couldn't have looked less cooperative and his words were grudgingly uttered. "What do I have to do to get rid of her?"

"Stoke up your fire. She'll be wet and needs to get warm. Find some old clothes you can give her and heat up some soup. Then send her to the Queen's Grotto in the Citadel, as quickly as you can."

Celo flinched and took a step back. "I can't send anyone to that place."

"I thought you wanted to get rid of her."

"But *there*? You know what Mother does to intruders."

"Which is why you need to give her your satchel, all packed with food for the journey."

"I don't understand."

Venero tried again to smile. "I'll be tucked inside."

Celo shook his head. "Who exactly needs to help her, Venero? You or me?"

"Me. But I have certain limitations at this time."

Consideration dawned in Celo's eyes. "What exactly is she to you? Are you hoping she'll help you?"

"She did already. That's why I can shield my thoughts and cast dreams again."

"She kissed you? When you're like that?" Celo was clearly astonished.

"No, she touched my forehead. It was enough to break part of the curse."

Celo chuckled. "Lost some of your charm?"

Venero found himself bristling. "I'm doing fairly well, considering the circumstances."

"But does that mean she's your true love?"

"There's no such thing as true love..."

"You'd better hope there is, unless you want to stay like that for the rest of your life."

Venero had nothing to say to that.

"A little awkward that she's married to Urbanus, isn't it?" Celo started to laugh then, which Venero thought entirely inappropriate.

"She's not my true love," he said with some annoyance. "But she's helpful, and I want to help her in return..."

"How?"

"Urbanus has cast a spell over her. She didn't deserve it. The antidote will be in the grotto."

Celo sobered. "Who ever deserves what they get in this kingdom?" He sighed. "All right. I'll help her, but don't be surprised if I do it quickly."

"I wouldn't be."

"And this is it. We're even forever now."

"Of course."

"And if Urbanus catches me—or Mother does—I'll say it was your fault." Celo dropped his voice. "I'll say you beguiled me into it. You admitted that your powers were back, after all."

Venero felt a grim resolve. "Deal."

Celo nodded and grabbed an armload of firewood. Venero hopped onto the top of the pile and his brother carried it to the hut. "That satchel," Celo said with a nod at a leather bag hanging from a peg. Venero jumped off the firewood, and Celo dumped it by the fire. He then put the bag on a bench and opened the flap. Venero hopped in and sighed, content that he could rest for a while.

"What happened to your leg?"

"It's cut and bruised. It hurts but it'll heal."

"How'd that happen?"

Venero grimaced. "She has a pavofel and it hunts."

"A pavofel?"

"Big mean bastard."

"A feline pet." Celo shook his head. "Just your luck. I know how you hate them. She *must* be pretty." Celo had taken down a crockery pot from the shelf above the table and crouched down beside the bench. He peeled back the protective covering and Venero smelled the pungent herbs in the unguent.

"She'll smell it."

"Chances are good she might need some, too. Or the pavofel."

"You're right. We jumped into the river to avoid spelldust. The pavofel wasn't amused."

Celo straightened as his expression turned to horror. "Spelldust? He loosed spelldust and you didn't tell me?"

"An unfortunate oversight. I told you now."

His brother exhaled and his lips tightened, but still he bent closer. "Let me see." Celo applied the unguent with a fingertip, and Venero sighed in relief as he felt its healing power warm his skin. "Just how pretty is she?" Celo murmured. "Beautiful?"

"She's a warrior princess from Incendium," Venero said, ducking the question.

"Of course, she is, but is she beautiful too?"

Venero sighed. "Yes. But a dragon shifter."

"You and your warrior women," Celo teased. "Maybe this form is doing you a favor. How long would it take her to fall in love with you otherwise?"

Venero didn't find the joke very funny. "I don't think we have to worry about that. She hates toads."

"Well, with any luck, you won't be one forever."

"Not luck, Celo. Planning."

"Right. Strategy." Celo met his gaze. "And using someone for your own purpose. Does she know where you're going to lead her?"

"Of course not."

"What would she think of your plan if you told her all of it?"

"It doesn't matter," Venero insisted. "It's reciprocal. She helps me and I help her. In the end, we both get what we want."

"Really?"

"This will serve the greater purpose..."

"Your greater purpose." Celo sighed and straightened. "Sometimes it's not that hard to believe that you and Urbanus are twins."

Venero was insulted, but he had to acknowledge the thread of truth in that. He wasn't being entirely fair to Gemma. If she'd still been able to become a dragon, he could have felt justified, but her resilience and beauty as a woman made him feel manipulative.

Maybe even unfair.

Which was why he didn't say anything more.

GEMMA HAD LOST TRACK of time when she finally smelled the wood fire.

When she broke the surface of the stream under the shelter of a willow tree, its branches hanging over the stream like a bower, she smelled the fire. She was delighted at the sign that she might not be alone in this endless forest, but hesitated before emerging from the water.

Would the person who had lit the fire help or hinder her?

Would he (She? They?) just send her back to Urbanus, or somehow summon him to collect her?

Gemma paused, uncertain who to trust. This might be Urbanus' county or realm, and the people might be obliged to support his will.

There might be repercussions if they didn't.

Felice didn't share her caution. The pavofel wriggled and escaped her grip to leap to the bank. Felice shook thoroughly, scattering water in every direction, then fastidiously sniffed the air. She marched off, her wet tail waving like a bedraggled banner, and was so much her usual self that Gemma couldn't imagine the creature had been touched by spelldust. She hauled herself out of the river, wrung out the maid's dress as well as she could, shivered, sneezed, and followed Felice.

Smoke was rising from a tidy little hut, one that blended so well with the forest that Gemma might not have discovered it without the scent of the fire. A young man stood outside of it, gutting some fish, and Felice hastened forward to invite herself to a feast. He was fair-haired and tanned, dressed simply, yet tall and trim. His beard was long and his clothing was rustic but clean.

He started at the appearance of the pavofel, then smiled. "You're a long way from home, pavofel," he said, his voice quiet and pleasant. He cast a whole fish at Felice, who pounced upon it and set to devouring it. He lifted his gaze to Gemma then, and she had the definite sense that he wasn't surprised to see her. "Hungry?" he asked, and cleaned another fish.

"I am. Were you expecting company?" Gemma considered the number of fish he had caught and again imagined that her arrival had been anticipated.

"Your arrival is fortuitous," he said, not really answering her question. "I had so much luck fishing this morning that I couldn't stop." He shrugged and turned to the hut. "You've saved me the task of smoking them."

Was that an invitation?

If it was, should she accept?

The scent of the Seed teased Gemma's nostrils. "Is Urbanus here?" she asked.

The man started, his alarm clear. "No!" He stared at her for a moment, then appeared to be both relieved and amused. He disappeared into the hut, chuckling quietly, but left the door ajar. Felice finished her fish, then strutted toward the door, obviously in pursuit of more. Gemma smelled the fish roasting and her belly growled.

"Hurry up unless you like yours burned," he said from within the hut.

Gemma approached with caution. Why could she smell the Seed? She stood on the threshold, surveying the interior of the hut, then cast a long glance over the small clearing outside of it. All was still and it appeared that the man was her only companion. He was trying to hide a smile as he fed another fish to Felice.

"Do I amuse you?" Gemma asked. Arousal unfurled in her belly and sent a welcome heat through her. She swallowed, wondering how the Seed could be in this place.

"No, you remind me of someone. I won't harm you. Come in."

Gemma entered the cabin, more than ready to defend herself. Her host was only a little taller than her and slim. She suspected that he had a wiry strength that could be a surprise. Still, she thought she could best him in a fair fight.

"The question is whether there is ever a fair fight in Regalia," he said and she was startled. "Yes, I can read your thoughts, and yes, that's why I live alone in the wilderness. It is comparatively quiet here and I can think my own thoughts in peace."

"Comparatively?"

"The forests are full of creatures. Not all of them are spies." He offered her a ceramic plate, graced by a slice of bread and a grilled fish fillet. "Come sit by the fire and eat."

"Is that how you knew I was coming?"

He smiled and offered the plate again. She couldn't smell any guile in him and her sense was that he had no skill with deception.

Then she realized something. "How did you know what a pavofel was?"

"You knew what it was and I read your thoughts."

Gemma considered that as her belly grumbled. She chose to trust him, at least for the moment, and accepted his invitation. "Are you a prince of Regalia whose truth is hidden?"

He gave her a sharp glance. "If I was, I wouldn't be the one you're seeking."

But the Seed...

"He *was* here."

Her host said no more and Gemma ate before the fish got cold. Her thoughts churned all the while, her questions creating more questions, and the Seed making her yearn for satisfaction. The fire was warm and the fish was delicious. Gemma was certain she had never smelled or seen better fare at a feast.

Much less tasted it.

She ate three fish and felt much better. Felice was cleaning herself before the fire, her fur returning to its usual fluffy splendor.

Her host rose to his feet. "You should change your clothes and leave," he said so abruptly that Gemma was surprised.

"Do you often have visitors who you help and send on their way?"

"Almost never, thank goodness. I would rather you left sooner rather than later." His attention was snared by a bird call from outside the hut and his eyes narrowed as he listened. "You might be pursued." His manner made Gemma want to hurry.

Not all of the creatures in the forest were spies, by his own admission, but she'd bet that bird was.

He gestured to a pile of clothes and a satchel already packed. Gemma could see bread within it and smelled some herbal mixture. There also appeared to be a change of clothing. "Hurry! We'll talk as we go." He left the cabin then and she heard him make a bird call. A conversation ensured, or at least she imagined as much, for each time he gave a cry or a whistle, the bird in the trees seemed to respond. What news did the creature bring him?

Gemma dressed quickly. To her relief, he'd given her simple men's clothing: chausses, a chemise and vest, a belt and a pair of well-worn boots. She slung the satchel over her shoulder, wondering what to do with the maid's garments.

"Give them to me," he instructed, having reappeared in the doorway, and Gemma did. He doused the fire then and secured the door of the hut, then set off at a brisk pace. He walked in the same direction that the river flowed, but veered away from the water, taking a course that only he could discern through the forest.

"Where are we going?" Gemma asked.

"You're going to steal a mount from Farmer Aro. I'm just showing you the way." He spared her a glance. "I assume you can ride."

"Of course. Do you have any advice as to my direction?"

"You must go to the Queen's Grotto in the Citadel, in order to find the antidote you seek."

Gemma halted. "How do you know this?"

"A toad told me."

Gemma couldn't stop her smile. "It's alive, then? And you know it? Where is it?"

"It doesn't matter. It told me to expect you and what you needed."

"Why are you helping me?"

"Because I owe the toad a favor." He spoke with such solemnity that it had to be true.

This was a most peculiar realm.

Unless he'd known the toad before it had been cursed.

"Did you know him before he was cursed?" she asked and her companion flicked a warning look at her. "Will you tell me about it?"

The man sighed. He held back a cane of some plant that would have snapped in Gemma's face, then walked beside her instead of in front of her. "How much do you know about the royal family of Regalia?"

"Very little. The queen has twelve sons—well, eleven now." It seemed tactless to speak of Drakina's role in that, but her companion was unsurprised by the clarification.

He wasn't very interested in it either.

"Actually, it's commonly believed that the queen has ten surviving sons, for one is missing. One also has retreated from her court and no longer enjoys her favor."

That would be Venero who was missing and assumed dead. Who was the son who had retreated?

Her companion winked at her.

Gemma smiled. It only seemed reasonable to her that sons of Queen Arcana might want to hide from their mother and her sorcery.

"Exactly," her companion agreed.

"So, she's down to nine."

"You could look at it that way. Do you know much about them?"

"Urbanus is crown prince, now that Canto is no more."

"And the missing prince?"

"Venero. He and Urbanus were twins. But not identical."

"Not at all. Venero's eyes were as gold as amber and it was said that his vision would burn through to the heart of any matter."

Gemma thought it was probably prudent to disguise how much she did know.

"Very prudent," agreed her companion. "But you know about the powers delegated to each son."

"What was Venero's power?"

"He was a DreamCaster. He could send dreams to others."

Gemma grimaced. "Like a MindBender."

"Similar but slightly different. Part of the distinction is nomenclature, but it's more than that. A MindBender can manipulate the thoughts of others. That's reliant upon the ability to read their minds. It's an innate ability."

"They're born with it?"

He nodded. "But it can be developed with training, too. Refined and expanded. Like the ability to do calculations in your mind. Someone has the talent but can make more of it."

"I understand."

"DreamCasting, though, is a given ability, granted by a sorcerer. It has specific limitations, as defined by the sorcerer who gave it, and usually, like most given magical abilities, a limitation."

"Like what?"

"Like a blind spot. There's some situations in which it doesn't work."

"Power tempered with vulnerability," Gemma mused.

"Exactly. So, Canto, as the son of the queen and the captain of the guard, had a natural talent for fighting. His magical ability was the power to win. That made him a champion, at jousts and tournaments."

"He didn't win against Drakina."

"She was his weak spot, the one individual he couldn't triumph against." Her companion trudged onward. "The queen is said to have confided this detail in him for the first time on the night before his wedding."

Which was why he'd stood up his bride.

"She wanted to clear the way for Urbanus?"

Her companion shrugged. "He was always a favorite."

"Who was his father?"

"A visiting wizard from Nimue. That's why his ability to cast spells is so strong. It's a combination of innate ability and a gift."

"And his weak spot?"

"I'll guess that the queen made him powerless against her, because that was Venero's weak spot."

Gemma nodded. "Who was his father?"

"A diplomat and lawyer from Advocia, part of the same delegation as Urbanus' father."

"How do you know that?"

"I peeked."

Gemma considered whose mind he must have peeked into and had a good idea why he was hiding in the forest. Only the queen would have known that truth.

The other man remained silent and trudged onward.

"So, what happened to Venero?"

"No one knows," her companion said, although Gemma smelled that he lied. "He was a good man, a warrior who kept his word and treated others with honor."

'The opposite of Urbanus, then,' Gemma thought and her companion laughed.

"So, you *are* acquainted with the crown prince. I thought you might be."

Gemma endeavored to think nothing at all and was pretty sure she failed.

"You remind me of him, actually," the man said, halting before a line of scrub.

"Of Urbanus?"

"Of Venero. There's an integrity about you, and a clarity in your thinking." He nodded. "The way you assess situations and plan your reactions is much the same." He gave her a hard look. "You're not a sneak."

Gemma took that as a compliment. "Then maybe I would have liked *that* prince of Regalia."

"Maybe so. He had ideas to improve the situation of the people of Regalia and to diminish our reliance upon Incendium. People liked him."

Gemma guessed that Venero had to be removed because he might offer a challenge to Urbanus' taking the throne.

She wished he hadn't been.

"Careful what you wish for," her companion advised.

"I can wish for the goodwill of others, surely?"

"It's not more than that?"

Gemma shook her head with resolve. "It sounds like he might have made a good king, despite being a DreamCaster."

"The Consort of Incendium is a MindBender."

"And I distrust him, too. No one should mess with the thinking of anyone else."

"I'll take that under advisory." Her companion said mildly then paused. He pointed through the growth to a cluster of buildings. The barn was obvious, for there were goats penned beside it. The fields were tilled, the garden tended, and all looked tidy. "There is one swift horse, a black as midnight with a single star on his brow. He should be tethered in the last stall to the right."

"You want me to steal the horse?"

"It's too far to walk to the Citadel, especially if you're being pursued. You'll send it back."

Gemma nodded in understanding. "But how? There must be a dozen men working and who knows how many inside the barn."

"Farmer Aro and his men will go to the house for their midday meal at any moment now. They do it every day."

Even as he spoke, several men left the barn and walked toward the house, the low rumble of their conversation carrying to Gemma's ears.

"I guess three more," her companion said.

"Four," Gemma corrected. He spared her a glance prepared to argue. "I smell a fourth. Maybe he doesn't think much."

They waited, and three more men made their way to the house.

A moment later, just when Gemma thought her companion believed her to be wrong, another figure came out of the barn. He shuffled toward the house, moving more slowly than the others, and Gemma smiled at her companion's sidelong glance.

"Four," she whispered.

He nodded, then pointed. "Follow that road, the one that bends to the right. Take the right fork twice, and the road will lead you around the village. Eventually, it crosses a river and become a narrow track." He indicated the shadow of hills rising far to the right. "Its only destination after the river is the Citadel, and inside that palace, you'll find the Queen's Grotto. Let the horse go when you can see the watch tower. It will find its way home."

"Won't I need it to return?"

He spared her a look. "Either you will succeed and find the antidote you seek, or you'll die in the Citadel. Either way, you won't need the horse again."

He knew her true nature.

Of course.

"And the Seed?"

Her companion smiled. "You'll find it when the time is right."

Gemma eyed the mountains, seeing that the distance wasn't small.

How many days would it take her to reach her destination? She would just have to make the best progress she could, and let the horse rest when necessary. She took a deep breath and nodded.

"I thank you for all of this," she said, turning toward her companion but he was gone, as surely as if he had never been there. "I hope he's not caught," she whispered, and something in her saddlebag moved.

"So do I," came the familiar voice of the toad. "But don't miss this chance. There might not be another."

CHAPTER FOUR

TO VENERO'S PLEASURE, Gemma didn't waste time asking questions about his survival or his presence. She peeked into the satchel to confirm that he was there, smiled, then shut the flap again. His heart was skipping from just the glimpse of that triumphant smile. He felt her ease the satchel to her back and adjust her grip on the pavofel.

Then she ran, fast and low, loping smoothly across the field.

There was something to be said for a purposeful woman.

Even one who distrusted DreamCasters.

She stopped suddenly, pivoted, and must have backed against the barn because he was a little crushed. He made a tiny sound of protest.

"Sorry," she whispered, then was off again. He felt the shade of the building fall over her, then smelled the hay in the barn. The air was cooler and he knew she was inside. She moved silently and cautiously down the length of the barn, then caught her breath.

She wasn't moving.

There had to be a reason.

Venero climbed over the provisions and peeked out the side of the satchel, fearing that Celo had been wrong about the horse and its location. He hadn't been. The beast was there, watching Gemma, its coat as dark as midnight and the star on its brow glowing. It wore a bridle, which was tethered to the end of the stall, and its dark eyes seemed to be filled with wisdom.

"You beautiful creature," Gemma whispered, then stepped into the stall with her hand outstretched.

It was only when the horse stepped forward that Venero heard the rustle of its feathered wings.

"Hurry, hurry," he urged.

"I've never seen a pegasus," she replied quietly. "Besides, everyone knows that you have to take your time with a horse. They're not like Starpods."

"Hurry!" he urged, even though he knew she was right.

She put down the bag and the pavofel, which began to clean itself at a closer proximity than Venero would have liked. Gemma walked around the pegasus, running her hand over it, praising it quietly. Venero was so busy admiring the view of her that he forgot to anticipate her choice. She reached for the saddle that was at the end of the stall. Venero hadn't seen it there until she touched it.

"Not the saddle!" he hissed, but it was too late. The hundred silver bells upon it had already rung out a warning, erupting like a clarion as soon as Gemma's fingertips brushed against it. The pegasus stamped with impatience to run, and tossed its head, its wings flapping. Men shouted in the distance and footsteps could be heard running toward the barn.

"Thanks for the timely warning," Gemma muttered. She moved like lightning, even as she spoke.

"It's enchanted."

"Obviously." She had already slung the satchel over her shoulder again and untied the horse's bridle.

"You could have anticipated it."

He heard her grind her teeth.

"I don't understand magic. Since you seem to, you might be a little more proactive in future."

"Hurry!" Venero urged but he was pretty sure it was too late.

Gemma seized the pavofel and stuffed it into the satchel, prompting Venero to recoil and the pavofel to hiss in protest.

"Deal with it," she muttered, leading the horse from the stall. She and the pegasus raced together to the doorway to the barn.

By the time Venero was able to peek out again, they were outside and a man was coming around the corner. Gemma kicked him hard in the gut, a nice high kick and beautifully executed. Venero had to admire her technique. The man fell to the ground with a groan, but there were three more behind him. Gemma was surrounded and separated from the pegasus, and the reins were tugged from her fingers.

But that was when she really set to work.

She decked one man, spun and drove her fingers into the eyes of one who was trying to snatch her from behind, then kicked the third in the crotch. She spun in place, so lethal and effective that Venero could have watched her all day. She was dressed in men's clothing, her hair braided back, but looked remarkably enticing. Even without her dragon, she was a force to be reckoned with. Venero tried to control his desire for his brother's wife and lost.

He averted his gaze from her, only to see that the pegasus was cantering away from the barn, gathering speed.

"It'll take flight without us!" he roared. He tried to cast a thought to the creature that it should slow down, and the pegasus slowed its pace only slightly.

Gemma spun and raced after the beast. She was faster than Venero expected, and more agile, too. She seized the tail of the pegasus and vaulted to its back with grace just as it took flight. Its hooves were above the ground and its dark wings beating hard. The satchel seemed to be floating behind Gemma, and Venero hoped the strap didn't snap. The reins were dangling out of reach, but Gemma knotted her hands into pegasus' dark mane. She looked back and laughed at the men left far below with a confidence Venero found both bold and attractive.

Before he could think too much about his changing notions about women, Gemma urged the pegasus to greater height and speed. The wind whistled past the satchel. The pavofel hissed, and Venero looked to see its eyes gleaming overhead. He yelped and tried to bury himself beneath the provisions, only to have the creature burrow after him.

"Help me!" he shouted.

"I'm busy," Gemma retorted. "Work it out between yourselves."

Her lack of sympathy was annoying. "I liked you better when you were trying to charm my brother," he muttered as he dodged the pavofel's paw. He tried to send a thought to the pavofel but it made no difference.

Maybe his restored powers were already ebbing away. That wasn't a reassuring thought!

"How so?" Gemma asked.

"Because you were demure." Even as he uttered the familiar words, Venero doubted their truth. He'd never found a woman as attractive as Gemma, and she was as different from his usual taste as possible.

And a dragon, too.

"Women should be demure, charming, and biddable," he insisted all the same. His reactions must be due to celibacy, which was unnatural. "It's more feminine."

"More feminine," Gemma echoed, with a precision that should have warned him.

Venero might have argued his case more eloquently if he hadn't been trying to evade the pavofel, which was, in fact, a very persistent hunter. He heard himself give a little squeak of fear that would have mortified him in his normal form, but it seemed to provoke Gemma to offer advice.

"You could do with some charm of your own," she noted.

"This is hardly the time to criticize..." The pavofel batted him to one side. Its claws were retracted, and he realized it was playing with him. He could still get hurt, but was slightly reassured that the beast didn't mean to consume him. Maybe she knew the creature better than he did.

Since it was her pet, that wasn't out of the question.

That hardly improved his mood.

"She likes being rubbed on the stomach," Gemma said, a tinge of impatience in her tone. "Right where the blue blends to green. Maybe you could manage to make friends while I'm busy saving our lives."

Make friends. With a pavofel.

Or really, with any creature intent upon injuring him.

While Gemma saved their lives. Venero hated that he had to admit his reliance upon his companion. He was a prince! He was supposed to save damsels in distress.

But Gemma was doing just fine on her own.

"I hate pavofels."

"So you've said. What do you have against them?" Gemma chuckled. "They're beautiful and charming, and Felice is female."

Venero would have liked to glare at her. "They hunt."

"Rather well, too."

"Warrior or beauty, not both."

"I'll keep that in mind," Gemma said, as if she might be mocking him.

Felice gave a little growl and moved her paw closer. Venero met the pavofel's brilliant gaze and swallowed his pride. Desperate times called for desperate means. He would be trapped in this bag with this creature for a while.

Venero crept closer to Felice's heat, well aware that he risked everything in the approach. He eased up against her belly, she hissed, but he stretched out a leg and rubbed.

Right where the blue blended to green.

The pavofel adjusted its position and Venero feared the worst. He retreated but Felice yowled softly, as if in invitation.

She was just giving him better access to its stomach. She was making demands of him. Venero moved closer and rubbed again, as the pavofel lounged contentedly over the provisions.

Venero rubbed in a gentle rhythm, right where the blue fur changed to green. It was far less than what he wanted to contribute to their success, but there wasn't much else he could do.

Felice stretched, yawned, closed her eyes, and began to purr.

NOT FEMININE.

Gemma would let that comment pass for the moment, but she certainly wouldn't forget it. She was doing all the work and taking all the risks, and the toad was criticizing her! If she hadn't suspected that she needed his knowledge of Regalia to succeed in capturing the antidote, she might have tipped him right out of the satchel and let him fall.

No. She wasn't mean. She'd wait until they landed and *then* tip him out of the bag.

Warrior or beauty, not both.

That burned. How dare he imagine that because she was attractive, she couldn't be effective, too? She could have simpered and fluttered her eyelashes at those men on the farm, and they wouldn't be soaring across the sky on the pegasus. She was taking him where he wanted to go, but he wasn't giving her any credit for that.

Maybe she didn't need the toad badly enough to put up with his comments. She'd managed to find shelter and a meal by herself, after all, as well as provisions and directions to the Citadel. He wasn't quick to admit his secrets, that was for sure.

Could his objective be different than he'd admitted?

Could he be using her for his own purposes, whatever they might be?

Could he be encouraging her to leap from the fat to the fire?

Gemma didn't know and she didn't like it. She wished she had the power of the bearded man in the hut to read the thoughts of others. Then she'd know for sure what the toad had planned.

After the initial thrill of taking flight with the pegasus—which made her feel like her old self again, and increased her determination to get her shifter powers back—she'd been wondering. She'd been told to send the horse back when she saw the watch tower. But if she could see the watch tower, surely those guards in the watch tower would be able to see her? She had to think that a black pegasus would be hard to miss.

She shook the satchel. "How will I know when we're getting close?" she asked. "I want to send the pegasus back before there's any chance of it being seen."

"Are you following the road?" the toad asked.

"Of course." She refrained from rolling her eyes. Maybe being logical or following instructions weren't feminine traits either, according to this toad. Maybe he'd rather be lost.

Maybe she could help with that.

"What's beneath us now?"

"Tilled fields. To the far left, there's a town. It's pretty far away, but something is glinting in the sun. Maybe the spire of a metal tower. It looks as if there are a lot of buildings clustered together there."

"That would be a town, then," the toad commented. "Well done."

"Are you always so cranky?"

"Only when I'm trapped in a bag with a predator that wants to eat me when I'm unable to do much about it."

"Rub the spot..."

"I know, I know! Can't you hear the noise this thing is making?"

Gemma smiled. Felice was purring louder than she had in a while. "You must be doing it right."

"My life is reduced to finding the right spot to rub on a pavofel's belly."

"As opposed to being at the nexus of politics and diplomacy, where a toad rightfully belongs?" Gemma asked, then caught herself. "Actually, on this planet, that might be exactly where a talking toad belongs." She wondered again who he really was.

Not everyone was taught Latin, after all.

She surveyed the land before them. "There are foothills rising in the distance."

"And a broad river flowing before them. "

"Have you been here before?"

The toad seemed to hesitate before replying. "Someone brought me here once," he admitted, and Gemma sensed a half-truth.

"You're pretty well traveled for a toad."

"I told you: I wasn't always a toad."

"But of course, you won't actually tell me anything about yourself, because you never do."

"Maybe I can't," he retorted with some annoyance.

Maybe. If he was trying to win her sympathy and interest, he'd lost it with 'not feminine.' "Looks like a mill to the right, and maybe a village."

"Go left," the toad said sharply. "There's a spur that comes down from the foothills."

"I see it! It's heavily forested, so we'll fly lower and not be seen."

"That would be better."

Gemma thought she detected sarcasm in his tone. She bit back a retort because she still needed his help. "So, the Citadel is at the end of the road, and this spur will hide us from view?"

"You know that."

She allowed her own tone to become irritable. "But what I don't know is how we get to the Citadel without being seen, even on foot."

"There's a tunnel. Of course."

"Under the spur of the mountain."

"Exactly."

"Well, won't anyone guarding the Citadel be guarding the tunnel, too?"

"Of course, but that doesn't mean it's a bad way in."

Another half-answer. Gemma sighed and frowned. "I suppose you'll only tell me more when you think the time is right."

"Information is valuable. If I told you everything right now, you might not take me with you."

"Because you're such delightful company."

He didn't reply to that.

Gemma guided the pegasus far to the left and urged it to fly close to the ground. There was a coniferous forest with very old growth that spread from the flanks of the mountain spur and across the land to that broad river. She rode up the side of the spur until the trees thinned, then tugged on the mane of the pegasus. It landed elegantly and shook its head, lingering only long enough for her to slip from its back and kiss the star on its brow in gratitude. Then it took flight again and turned back, heading for the warmth of a familiar stable.

Gemma shaded her eyes to watch it fly, admiring its grace and beauty.

At least she did until her satchel squirmed. She opened the top and Felice leaped out. The pavofel shook itself, then sat down on the path. Its tail swished.

"Peace at last," the toad muttered.

Gemma ignored that comment. She slung the bag over her shoulder and surveyed the side of the mountain. "Are you going to give me any hints, or do I have to find the tunnel entrance myself?"

The flap of the satchel was nudged open and she saw the nose of the toad. "It's up there," he said, and she supposed he was pointing with his injured foot. "There was a little track that came out of the last of the forest, probably used by goatherds and their flocks."

"Was," Gemma echoed. She strode through the forest, eyes on the ground. "How long ago were you here?"

"It doesn't matter. The track will still be there."

"Who brought you here?"

"It doesn't matter."

"What happened to the person who brought you here?"

"That really doesn't matter."

Gemma found the track and halted. "What if I say it does?"

"That doesn't matter either."

Gemma swung the satchel around and opened it, peering down at the toad. "I don't know who you think you are or who you were, but you're cranky, you're bossy, and you're a lot of trouble. I don't know for sure that you're on my side, and I'm not going into the Queen's Grotto in the Citadel without being sure that I can trust whoever goes in there with me." She gave him a determined look. "I need to know more about you."

"I liked you a lot better when you were trying to charm Urbanus."

"So you said. What's that supposed to mean?"

"I thought for a moment that Urbanus had made a good choice of bride..."

Gemma bristled that this toad expressed any admiration for Urbanus who had, after all, drugged her on their wedding night. "Then why did you befriend me to take you to the Citadel?"

"Desperation, plain and simple." The toad seemed to wince. "When you wait for opportunity as long as I have, you have to make the most of whatever comes along."

"Even a warrior who isn't feminine?"

"Even..." he began but Gemma had heard enough.

She didn't need his help nearly so badly as he thought she did. She reached into the bag, picked up the toad and lifted him until she was looking him in the eye. He seemed to almost be smiling, and she had the sense he was quite satisfied with his situation.

"This is much better than that bag," he began, but Gemma didn't let him finish.

"Too bad then that you didn't take your own advice." She could have flung him down, but she didn't like to hurt any creature unnecessarily. Instead, she put him down on the track and turned away. Felice looked between her and the toad, ears flicking.

"What advice?" he croaked and took a hop toward her.

"To make the most of whatever comes along. Insulting me is a pretty bad choice when you need my help." Gemma waved. "See you in the Citadel, maybe." She turned to walk briskly up the mountain track, knowing he'd never be able to catch up with her. Felice loped along behind her, matching her pace.

"Hey!" the toad shouted and she heard him hopping behind her. "Hey! You *need* my help!"

"Not badly enough to listen to you," she retorted, striding on. "And if you need *me*, your manners could use some improvement." She paused and looked back, barely able to discern him far behind her. "How's this for demure?"

She didn't wait for a reply, just hiked more quickly up the side of the mountain, seeking the entry to the tunnel. Anger gave her energy and she covered ground quickly. The sky was getting darker and it would be good to find shelter before night fell. Gemma couldn't begin to imagine what might lurk in the wilderness of Regalia.

She felt a twinge of guilt about the toad, left to defend himself in the wilderness, but refused to turn back for him.

Demure. That word alone was enough to make her growl.

VENERO HAD TO ADMIT that speaking his mind at this particular juncture might not have been the smartest choice.

But he'd been under duress.

Trapped with a pavofel.

Enchanted as a toad.

Powerless to affect his own fate.

Reliant upon his brother's wife.

Who pretty much defied his every notion of what a woman should be like, and yet, *and yet*, was remarkably attractive. Troublingly so, in fact. Venero couldn't understand it, and that irked him most of all. She was a dragon shifter—well, she would be again, if she got the antidote—and she fought like Arista. She was decisive and blunt and still incredibly beautiful. She challenged his assumptions and made him glad, in a strange way, that he was cursed to be a toad, so he couldn't make an inappropriate advance.

Never mind that he was willingly returning to the site where everything had gone wrong in the first place. It was only natural to feel some concern in venturing close to his mother's sanctuary—where he'd been caught in league with a traitor to the crown and had paid the price.

Venero knew he had to accompany Gemma to Queen's Grotto in the Citadel for the sake of the greater good, but he didn't have to like it.

He hopped after Gemma and admitting that traveling with her was a lot easier than journeying alone, even accounting for the pavofel.

At least he knew where she was going. He could find the tunnel entrance, and suspected she would as well. She seemed to be quite competent, which was a good trait in a comrade.

It might even be a good trait in a romantic partner, if he was going to need to outrun his mother and brother for the foreseeable future.

She had also given him some of his powers back, with a touch of a fingertip. Even if they were still compromised, that was better than nothing at all.

The conclusion from that was obvious and unwelcome. It defied everything Venero believed that a woman like Gemma could be his true love.

He didn't even believe in true love.

He sighed and hopped, considering the merit of trying to cast Gemma a dream. It seemed like a bad idea, given her prejudice against MindBenders.

He sensed that such a course of action could go badly awry.

But Gemma would need his advice to survive the Grotto and he needed her help to break his own curse. They needed each other—but more importantly, Venero knew that he owed her an apology.

Never mind that Gemma might perish, because he'd led her this far and she didn't know—she couldn't know—what was ahead.

Venero had to catch up and make this right.

THE CAVE ENTRANCE WASN'T immediately obvious, but Gemma finally found it just as the sun was sinking. It was a good thing, actually, that it was hard to find, as that meant it was less likely she'd be pursued.

Well, except by the toad.

She climbed the side of the mountain instead of following the long switchbacks of the path, wanting to reach shelter before darkness fell completely. Felice jumped ahead of her and finally, the darkness of an opening loomed before them. Her hands were scratched and her feet were sore. She glanced down at the long route she'd traveled and wondered, just a little, what had happened to the toad.

If he wasn't smart enough to cultivate alliances where necessary, she decided she shouldn't worry about him.

Even if she did.

Gemma crouched at the threshold of the cave and opened the satchel. To her relief, there were a couple of candles and a flint. She took one and lit it, then hoisted the satchel and entered the cave with caution. There was only silence from within, but without knowing its depth and dimensions, she couldn't be sure she and Felice were alone.

If nothing else, this might be the cave that led to the tunnel that led to the Citadel, and if so, it would be guarded at some point.

The candlelight illuminated a space that was more like a hollow etched out of the side of the mountain. It wasn't very deep, and wouldn't offer much protection if the wind turned. Felice sauntered toward the back corner with a confidence about the cave that Gemma didn't share, then disappeared. The pavofel mewed and the sound echoed.

Gemma followed, only to discover that there was an opening in that back corner. It was only a narrow slit, but the shadows from the rocks surrounding it had disguised it from view. She peered through it, then surveyed the short and low corridor beyond. Once she stepped through, she could barely stand upright. There was a stream running in a crack in the floor along the length of the tunnel and it sloped upward.

Maybe it wasn't the tunnel to the Citadel.

Felice was marching onward, her tail high.

Gemma looked left and right, then hugged her satchel closer and followed. The tunnel turned twice then terminated with a small and low hole. The water bubbled through this hole, that crevice carved in the bottom of the opening as well. Felice, who usually disliked water, continued through the hole. The diameter of the hole was big enough that the pavofel didn't even have to lower her tail.

Gemma hesitated only a moment, then dropped to her hands and knees. It was difficult to carry the candle when she had to crawl through the gap—never mind avoiding the water that flowed down the middle—but she managed it.

When she stood up in the chamber beyond, she caught her breath in astonishment at the sight before her eyes.

She stood in a natural chamber shaped like a hemisphere. The highest point was probably twice her height and the walls were quite smooth. The rock looked to be a pinkish-gold in the light of her candle, with glimmers of crystal embedded in the stone. A pool had formed at one end of the chamber, and it emanated a refreshing chill. The water splashed a little, because it flowed down that back wall and into the pool. Beyond the pool was another narrow slit, probably offering access to more tunnels and caves.

But the remarkable thing was that the walls were adorned with the designs the Warrior Maidens of Cumae drew when they meditated in preparation for battle. Gemma had participated in the ritual many times while in training on that planet. She remembered the cleansing of the body, the bathing and removal of hair. She remembered the mixing of pigments, the grinding of roots and herbs, and the blending of that with oil to create the familiar russet hue that embellished these walls. She remembered the painting of the body with protective symbols, the camaraderie of adorning another warrior with such talismans where she couldn't reach to do it herself. They'd stood in a circle, each painting the back of another, humming the music of war. She remembered the communal meal, the prayer, and the adornment of the walls of the caves.

Those from other civilizations thought the ritual was an invocation to the gods, but the Cumaens didn't believe in deities. They saw the sequence as a meditative exercise, one that would both focus the will of the individual warrior and build a sense of union between members ·of the company. That, in their view, was a better indication of success.

On Cumae, the caves had been painted many, many times, and Gemma had always felt a connection with past warriors as she drew her lines over theirs. This cave had been painted once, with deliberation and skill. The whorls and circular designs were a band of power on the walls, spilling into each other, feeding each other, flowing all around the room. They seemed to draw together disparate elements and stray power, then drive it all to the final culmination point. Gemma turned in place, remembering the surge of energy that she'd always felt when the last painted line connected with the first, making the circle complete.

It was similar to the jolt of the last line connected the images of the body paint into a coherent whole.

Where the end and the beginning connected on the cave walls, there was always a medallion, and this one was no different. The circular mark was always lavishly decorated, as befit a focus of power. The Warrior

Maidens participating in the ritual, preparing for war, always signed the medallion with their own marks as their last deed before battle.

There was only one mark on this medallion, and Gemma's heart stuck in her throat as she stood before it and traced the familiar insignia with a fingertip.

Arista.

Gemma blinked back her tears. Arista had been on Regalia. She had been in this cave. She had painted all of this herself. She had departed from this cave to fight for some cause or another. She had won, because she had returned to Cumae, only to be killed.

Arista's time on Regalia must be at least part of the reason Urbanus had paid for her assassination. Why had she been here? She had gone into a battle of some kind, given that she'd painted this cave.

Had she survived alone with no one to paint her back?

Or had she fought with a companion?

Who?

Gemma's heart clenched at the notion of Arista taking another Sword Sister. But there was only one signature in the medallion, only Arista's own. If she'd fought with another, that person hadn't been trained on Cumae.

Which was very strange. The Warrior Maidens of Cumae trusted only their own kind. Arista must have fought alone.

Why had Arista been on Regalia?

What had she done?

That seemed, actually, like a good question to ask the toad, and once again, Gemma regretted leaving him behind. She would have to venture into the Queen's Grotto alone, without his advice, and find the antidote to her spell, without any idea what it might look like or where it might be. She was entering battle with less than perfect preparation. She sensed that Arista's story was an important detail, and she didn't know much about the queen's powers, either.

Maybe Gemma had been a little impetuous.

But what was done was done. She could go back for the toad, but didn't imagine it would be easy to find him. He would have left the path for his own protection, and with the coloring of his skin, she'd never see him.

Especially at night.

Maybe she should take advantage of this unexpected gift and prepare herself for the uncertainties ahead in the way she knew best.

Gemma wasn't superstitious but in this cave, in this moment, she felt as if Arista's ghost was right beside her. It made no sense, until she brushed her fingertips over her Sword Sister's familiar signature one more time and loosed a stone.

The wall had been patched, quickly, and the marks disguised the spot.

Gemma pulled her knife and dug at the crumbling surface. She caught her breath when a small metal capsule glinted in the light, then fell and rolled across the cavern floor. She pursued it and picked it up, smiling as she examined it in the light. It was about the size of her thumbnail, spherical, and smooth.

It was a Cumaen *memoria*.

Some part of Arista was in the palm of Gemma's hand.

Maybe Gemma wouldn't arrive at the Citadel as unprepared as she'd feared.

A CUMAEN *MEMORIA* WAS a one-time recording device used by the Warrior Maidens as a secure means of passing intelligence to those who followed. The manufacture of the device was a closely guarded secret, requiring no less than twenty-seven separate steps, each of which was understood by only a single individual on Cumae at any given time. The identities of the Twenty-Seven were so secret that each of them knew the identity of only one other, the one to whom he or she delivered the device after completing the assigned phase. The coordination of the manufacture of each *memoria* was managed by the computer known as the Hive, built in the depths of the Vaults of Cumae.

Gemma hadn't seen one since she'd left her training. The individual *memoria* were indistinguishable from each other. Although the surface of the *memoria* appeared to have no sensors or seams, it responded to an oral command, set by the owner. The device recognized only the code word uttered by the owner, and the same word uttered aloud by the owner's Sword Sister. Sword Sisters were forbidden to reveal a code word, under penalty of death, and not a one by the time Gemma left Cumae had ever divulged such a code, even under torture.

Betrayal of one's fellows was a greater indignity than any pain that could be inflicted upon the body. They were taught that, and those who could not uphold this duty were discharged from training.

Given where she had found the *memoria*, Gemma could only assume it had been programmed by Arista. She held it in the palms of her hands for a long moment, then bent and whispered Arista's code word to the device.

For a long moment, nothing happened. Gemma wondered whether Arista had chosen another code word, or taken another Sword Sister, then the *memoria* began to hum on her palm. It vibrated, then a seam was revealed and it split in half like an egg. The interior projector unfolded itself and a beam of light was projected across the cavern.

A hologram.

Of Arista.

Gemma sat down hard at the sight. She was amazed by how real her friend appeared to be. Arista was crouched before her, dressed for war, her hair shorter than it had ever been. The blue tattoo on her neck seemed darker, as if her tan had faded, but the gleam of purpose in her dark eyes was just the same.

"I don't know why I'm recording this," she confessed, her husky voice making Gemma ache with its familiarity. She spoke crisply and without hesitation, not wasting a gesture. "Only my Sword Sister can ever view it, and I can't imagine any circumstance that would ever bring Gemma to this cave. But I am confronted by such a puzzle that I wish I had a dragon's ability to solve a riddle, especially one that seems to have no good solution."

Felice looked up at the sound of Arista's voice. The blue hair bristled on the back of her neck and she stalked the hologram, eyes shining.

Arista looked directly at her, and Gemma's breath caught that her friend seemed to be looking straight into her eyes. "Maybe Gemma will sense my appeal, and her abilities will help me." Arista shook her head. "That sounds more like the magic and whimsy of the Regalians than anything that has ever crossed my lips. This is a curious place, to be sure, and there is no telling what has been influencing my thoughts, even without my awareness. I have, after all, been traveling in the company of a DreamCaster."

Had Venero been with Arista? Or was that ability common on Regalia?

Felice pounced on the hologram and passed right through it. The pavofel rolled and rose to her feet, spinning to assault the image again.

Arista sighed and pushed to her feet, pacing across the chamber. The pavofel darted between the display of her legs, then retreated to the perimeter of the cave. Just before Arista pivoted, her image faded, perhaps because she had stepped beyond the range of the projector. Felice crouched to watch the hologram, ears folded back against her head. Arista returned to her former position and folded her arms across her chest, staring at the device.

"To review: I came to Regalia on a mission. The assignment was said to have come from the queen herself, although there is (naturally) no official confirmation of that. My task was to eliminate Prince Venero, the third son born to Queen Arcana—although there is some debate as to which twin was born first, the queen herself counts Urbanus as second and Venero as third. The fee was quite high, there being a considerable risk in eliminating one of the royal family. It was understood that I might not manage to leave Regalia after completing my mission, and that if I was captured, no one would come to my aid, not even the queen. I wonder if it was to look as if someone on Incendium was behind the assassination." Arista smiled thinly. "Even Cumae would disavow any knowledge of my presence on Regalia, and I would be considered a rogue."

Gemma was startled that Arista would have agreed to any assignment that might have left a stain on her reputation. What had the second mission been?

CHAPTER FIVE

ARISTA'S HOLOGRAM CONTINUED. "I agreed to the terms because I had another incomplete assignment that led to Regalia: this mission would serve as suitable cover. I had been charged to retrieve a valuable relic that was rumored to have been stolen by Queen Arcana. I was to bring it back to Cumae. I came to Regalia alone, so that no other lives would be risked."

Gemma could easily believe that Arista would sacrifice her own life to fulfill an assignment for Cumae.

Arista shook her head. "I didn't believe in sorcery before I came to Regalia, and I'm still not certain that magic is the cause for my current situation. But the fact remains that this quest has been very strange, and coincidence is a poor explanation for what transpired. I arrived on Regalia under the cover of being a diplomat, sent to negotiate updated terms for the Galactic Trade Alliance. I sought out Prince Venero at the palace soon after my arrival, for he was said to offer counsel to the queen on matters of diplomacy and law."

She smiled. "I expected him to be easy to kill, a nobleman convinced of his own safety and one accustomed to indulging his every whim, without regard for others. I expected to feel no qualms." Arista frowned. "It was not his good looks that swayed me, nor even the splendor of his body. He indulged in humor, which I did not always understand and for this, he mocked me. I recalled your counsel, Gemma, that such mockery could be done in affection, and was known as teasing, so I endured it with apparent good humor." Arista shook her head. "I did not expect him to surprise me, but he did. Venero not only acknowledged the existence of the prize I sought but said he knew its location. He proposed to be my ally and aid me in its retrieval from the treasury in the Queen's Grotto."

Gemma was fascinated.

Arista shrugged. "Why would a prince betray his mother and his kingdom? Perhaps because he knew my other assignment and where it had originated. But the fact was that I had need of someone who understood Regalia better than me." Arista fell silent and Gemma wondered how much more hologram the *memoria* could contain.

"I calculated the odds of my success alone to be much lower than those with Venero, even if he proved to be untrustworthy in the end. And so I accepted his proposition."

Arista looked up, her expression so anguished that Gemma reached out a hand to console her, forgetting she viewed a mere hologram. "He surprised me yet again, for I fell in love with him."

Gemma gasped. That Arista should fall in love was astonishing. Had she been enchanted? She wondered more about Prince Venero and his ability to DreamCast. Had he convinced Arista of something that wasn't true?

"I never expected this to happen to me. I do not know what to do." Arista began to pace, her concern clear. "Should I kill him and fulfill my assignment, even knowing that I will never forgive myself for destroying my love? Should I let him live until I retrieve the treasure from the queen, if indeed she truly possesses it? Should I betray him? Should I trust him fully? Should I tell him how I feel, offer myself, and create an alliance with him? The honor is greatest with the first option, but I confess to you alone that the last option has the greatest appeal."

She frowned and shook her head. "What manner of mother would hire an assassin to eliminate one of her sons? And why? There is more to this tale than I have gleaned, and Venero, I suspect, learned young to be wary of others. He guards his secrets close and his trust is elusive." Arista lifted her gaze and once again, Gemma felt that her Sword Sister was truly before her. "Could it be the love truly does conquer all?"

Gemma reached out with her free hand, but the hologram sputtered. The image disappeared, and the device whirred as it locked itself once more. Gemma closed her hand over it, feeling the warmth of the metal and wondered at what she'd seen. As much as she wished to watch the hologram again, she knew the *memoria* was spent or close to it. It wouldn't display the entire recording without being recharged. That might be possible, but only on Cumae. She closed her eyes and recalled Arista's confession, her memory training under that same warrior's instruction coming to her aid.

The Queen's Grotto was a treasury.

Was the prize Arista sought still there?

Or had she escaped with it? If she had, that might explain the choice of Urbanus. Had the assassin retrieved the treasure for Queen Arcana? Or had Arista hidden it? It was a bit late to think she should have asked more questions of Drakina's husband, Troy, about Arista's demise.

Felice trotted to her side, then twined around her ankles. Gemma picked up Arista's last gift to her and hugged the creature close. Felice began to purr.

Had Arista killed the man she loved?

Or had she taken Venero back to Cumae with her? Gemma straightened. If Venero had escaped Regalia, that would explain his disappearance—and it might also explain the subsequent assassination of Arista. Whether she had taken the prince captive, spirited him away with his consent or killed him, Arcana or Urbanus could have decreed that she had committed a crime on Regalia.

Never mind the relic or treasure.

How did any of this tale influence Gemma's own situation? She was here to avenge Arista, but how much did Urbanus know of her scheme? Arista's assertion that Venero had known her secret quest was troubling. Gemma thought of the birds flying overhead, and the claim of the bearded man that the woodland creatures could be spies. She thought of his ability to read her thoughts and wondered how hidden she and her objectives could possibly be.

She felt vulnerable, which she detested. She had to do something to improve her situation. Gemma put the *memoria* into her satchel, hiding it in an interior pocket. Felice rubbed against the satchel, but there was nothing within it that the pavofel would eat. Still, Gemma offered the pavofel some bread, but Felice turned up her nose and stalked away, presumably to hunt.

Arista's recording had given Gemma more questions than answers, but she felt empowered by seeing her Sword Sister. It had been good to hear her voice again. She turned to watch Felice, who crouched in the opening that led back to the path up the mountain, watching something.

Gemma smiled.

The ability of a dragon to solve a riddle. Yes, Arista had always said that was Gemma's gift. Could she solve this one?

The ritual Arista had taught her might help to clear her confusion and focus her thoughts. Gemma stood and shed her clothing quickly, then washed in the pool of water. The small cup of dye left in one corner gave her purpose. She would prepare herself for battle, in the way she had been taught on Cumae, and hope that the familiarity of the ritual would help her find the answers she needed.

VENERO HAD NEVER HOPPED so long or so hard as he had in recent days. If this alliance didn't succeed, it might just kill him. He was exhausted and sore by the time he made the sanctuary of the cave. He was panting when the shadow closed over him, but he didn't stop there. There was no sign of Gemma, but he could smell her skin. She would have explored, and he wondered how far she had ventured.

There was no sign of the pavofel either, which was a relief.

He could hear a woman's voice, and in his state of concern, it sounded like Arista. That made no sense, but he followed the sound anyway. Perhaps the stone was distorting the sound of Gemma's voice.

Venero went through the crack to the tunnel, then hopped its length to the small hole. He could see the warm glow of a candle's light through that hole, which encouraged him and gave him new strength.

He'd have a drink of water there.

It seemed to take forever to journey the length of the tunnel. Venero finally emerged from the other end of the tunnel that he'd once crawled through on his hands and knees, he halted to stare.

Gemma was humming.

More importantly, Gemma was nude.

Surprise weakened his knees, but as a toad, Venero didn't have far to fall. He stared and pretty much forgot everything except his desire.

Gemma was painting the walls of the grotto, following the lines that Arista had made. He recalled Arista performing the same ritual. Even as a son raised in a household brimming with sorcery, he'd been skeptical. There was no incantation. There was no sacrifice. There had been no talismans or tokens. How could this ritual accomplish anything?

But he'd felt the effectiveness of it at the end. He'd almost seen the power swirl around the perimeter and then around Arista after she'd made her mark. He'd seen her straighten and had seen the gleam of purpose in her eyes when she turned to consider him.

Oh, it had worked. Arista had been so intent upon her goal that she might have had only one purpose. She would have killed him without hesitation, if she'd perceived him as a threat to her quest.

And that was when he'd realized why he couldn't send her dreams.

Arista didn't have any.

He'd wanted to run but knew she would guess why. Instead, he held his ground and kept his expression the same. He'd ensured that his breathing was at the same rate and tried to control his pulse.

She'd sensed that, of course. She'd been designed to note every detail, as all androids were.

But she'd attributed his quickened pulse to the wrong cause.

He didn't want to think about Arista turning toward him, an invitation in her eyes.

Or his rejection of her advances.

Or his belated fear that he'd made a foolish choice.

Instead, he watched Gemma, an entirely different reaction coursing through him this time. She was as powerful a warrior as Arista had been, but possessed of a feminine beauty that fascinated him. Her charm had caught his interest, but it was her persistence that intrigued him—against every expectation, Venero desired a warrior woman.

This one.

He was so busy admiring Gemma that it took him a long time to realize that she echoed the sweep of the symbols with the same fluid grace as Arista.

His heart sank.

She *knew* these symbols.

She knew this ritual.

She *had* trained on Cumae. It wasn't just propaganda. That was why she'd fought so well when stealing the pegasus. That was why she knew how to ride and could vault into a saddle. That was why she'd examined the wedding chamber with such purpose.

Did she have more than training in common with Arista?

Venero didn't want to consider that, but he had to face the possibility.

No, he had to eliminate it.

Gemma paused before the circular medallion that Arista had painted last. She traced the outline of the circle and the marks that embellished its circumference. What was in the paint? Wine? Blood? It stained the old marks red, renewing and strengthening them, and Venero felt that same power rising.

She meant to go to battle, just as Arista had.

That was when he noticed the hole where the middle of the medallion should have been and wondered at it, remembering how he'd come upon Arista smoothing a paste over that very mark. He'd thought that she had been painting the stone for the placement of the medallion, but maybe she'd been doing more than that. Had she hidden something in the wall of the cavern and marked the spot with the medallion?

As he watched, Gemma pricked her finger and traced Arista's mark with her own blood. Her movements were confident.

She even knew Arista's mark.

Had he heard Arista's voice?

Either way, he knew that Gemma had married Urbanus for a very specific reason and it wasn't because she was stupid. He took a little hop closer in his concern and inadvertently kicked a pebble.

Gemma spun and crouched at the sound, prepared to defend herself. Her eyes glittered and he feared for a moment that she would shift shape to her dragon form.

In the same instant he recalled she couldn't do that anymore, she saw him and she eased her pose.

Venero could only stare in wonder. His heart skipped at the full sight of her beauty. The light of the candle seemed to caress her skin, turning her to gold. Her hair was loose and long, like spun sunlight, and her eyes glowed. She was radiant, as if illuminated from within.

He would have given anything in that moment to have been a man again, to have had Gemma's features light at the sight of him.

He certainly wouldn't have declined anything she offered.

No matter what the cost.

And that should have been a more terrifying notion than it was.

"You made it!" Gemma declared, and she bent down to peer at him, laughing with pleasure that made his heart clench.

The pavofel pounced then, appearing out of the shadows. Venero cried out as it caught him between his paws, then gave him a shake.

"Felice!" Gemma cried, picking the beast up by the scruff of its neck. She shook it hard and the pavofel released its grip. Venero fell to the hard ground, winced, then hopped to hide under the satchel. He saw the feet of the creature as it paced around the bag, and hunkered low.

"You knew Arista," he said, knowing he sounded cranky again.

Gemma didn't reply.

Venero moved to peek out from beneath the bag, wanting to see her reaction. "You know her name. You know she made these marks. You know *her* mark."

Gemma cast him a glance before she nodded acknowledgment. "And *you* knew what a pavofel was."

He had slipped up. "Maybe I read more than the maid."

"Maybe you learned about them from Arista. They're indigenous to Cumae, and their breeding is carefully managed there."

"Guilty as charged," Venero admitted.

"She was the one who brought you here."

Venero nodded, because it was more or less true. Actually, he had led Arista to this place, but he'd still been a man then. It had been part of their bargain.

"Were you going to help her kill Venero or get the relic from the Queen's Grotto?"

"The relic."

"Why not the prince?"

Venero hesitated. "I liked him."

"I heard he was popular," Gemma noted.

Venero quickly changed the subject. "Did I hear Arista's voice again?"

Gemma smiled. "What do you think?"

"That there was something embedded in the rock there, where that hole is now, something she hid for someone else. That you found it or maybe were looking for it all along."

"I didn't know about it before I found it."

"And you listened to a recording left by her."

Gemma nodded. "You're right, but the *memoria* wasn't left for just anyone."

"I don't understand." Arista had known Gemma would follow her? What was a *memoria*?

"A *memoria* can only be opened by the owner or the owner's Sword Sister."

Venero fought the urge to retreat. He didn't like the sound of this. "Sword Sister?"

Gemma crouched down, her eyes bright. "She taught me and then we trained together. We painted each other's backs. We relied completely upon each other, and so we swore to be Sword Sisters." Gemma's expression was filled with resolve. Again, Venero had the sense that he faced an android, programmed for only one purpose. A warrior who could not be swayed or stopped.

A dragon and an android? It couldn't be. He'd have to send her a dream to be sure, but Venero was convinced that he found Gemma appealing because she was mortal.

If a dragon shifter.

Her gaze locked with his. "A Sword Sister finishes any matter her companion has left undone."

Venero couldn't stop himself from retreating at that, but he tried to disguise his trepidation by hopping toward the pool of water. "I see. How interesting."

"Do you know why Urbanus had her killed?"

"You know about that?"

Gemma smiled with complete confidence in her source of information. "Why do you think I accepted his suit?"

Venero was glad to have the truth out in the open. She'd married Urbanus to avenge Arista, which put them in alliance against his twin. "You could have had another reason."

Gemma averted her gaze, hiding some detail from him. Venero considered his words with care, wishing even as he did so that he and Gemma could be completely honest with each other. She was as slow to trust as he was. It was a trait that he might have found amusing to have in common with her, if he hadn't been thinking about how much easier it would be for her to kill him in his current form.

He cleared his throat. "You might have loved him."

Gemma laughed. "A prince of Regalia and a sorcerer? I might as well marry a MindBender or a DreamCaster!"

That told Venero all he needed to know about her view of him. It might be a good moment to remind her of his usefulness. "Arista stole something from the Grotto in the Citadel."

She bent down to hold his gaze, her own eyes glittering with determination. "And then?"

"She escaped."

Gemma arched a brow. "But you didn't."

"Someone had to defend her back." Venero's voice dropped low as he remembered being caught, being tormented, and being cursed. It had been the lowest point of his life, but at least Arista had escaped. That detail had given him strength. He knew the loss of the ShadowCaster had been a blow to his mother's ambitions.

Gemma shook her head. "I have a hard time believing that a toad was of much help to Arista."

"A toad has helped you," Venero replied. "Did you have to welcome Urbanus on your wedding night?"

"No."

"Did you know about the spelldust, and the pegasus, and that the antidote could be found in the Queen's Grotto of the Citadel? Did you know about the tunnel through the mountains?"

Gemma fell to her knees before him, and Venero had a hard time remembering what he'd meant to say. Her eyes shone, so clear a blue that he thought a man could drown in their depths. "You're right," she breathed and his anger faded...like magic. "I did need your help and I still do." She smiled and he couldn't take a full breath. "Thank you for helping Arista. Even though she was hunted in the end, I'm glad she got away. She might have fulfilled her other quest after all."

"Her quest? Wasn't she supposed to kill one of the princes?" Venero pretended not to have the details, although he knew very well what Arista had been hired to do.

Gemma nodded. "Venero. The twin brother of Urbanus. The DreamCaster who disappeared. I wonder if she succeeded." She winced. "She said she loved him and didn't know what to do."

"Caught between duty and love?"

"Apparently so. I was surprised."

Maybe she'd known that Arista was an android. "Maybe she let him escape."

Gemma fixed him with a look. "I thought you were with her. Wouldn't you have seen if she had?"

Venero averted his gaze. "I tend to fall behind when people move quickly. I miss some bits."

"That's understandable. I'm sorry I abandoned you on the path." Gemma smiled with a warmth that made his heart flutter. "I'm sorry I insulted you, too."

"Well, I was wrong, and I've provoked you, too." Venero stole a glance at her nude perfection, felt his blood heat, and knew he was wrong about a lot of things. "Demure" had a decided lack of appeal in Gemma's presence.

He was starting to like "forthright," "smart," and "determined."

He wondered if he could even come to like "dragon." There was something about this dragon princess of Incendium that challenged all of his assumptions.

And Venero liked it.

Gemma's eyes twinkled. "I was wrong, too." She dropped her voice to a whisper. "I missed you," she confessed, her voice husky.

Venero opened his mouth to say something and, for the first time since he had become a toad, croaked instead.

Gemma laughed lightly. She inhaled then and scanned the chamber, then turned to him again. He could see the dragon, and it troubled him, given that she was pledged to finish whatever her Sword Sister had left undone. Her eyes were glittering again and her gaze was locked on him.

"Something the matter?"

"The Seed," Gemma whispered, almost to herself. "I smell the Seed again. How can that be?" What was she talking about? She bent toward him with purpose. "You were at the hut, in the satchel. You were in the bridal chamber. It's *you*."

"Me?"

"The Carrier of the Seed," she breathed.

Venero stared into her eyes and yearned for something he couldn't have, that he might never have again. His throat worked. He knew this was a moment to ask for one thing from her, but he couldn't do it. He couldn't make a sound.

When Gemma leaned down and kissed him, he couldn't believe his luck.

His reaction to the touch of Gemma's soft lips on his skin was pleasure, and desire... and then Venero felt a ripple pass through his body that grew to a quake. It was followed by the first twinge of a pain he'd never thought to feel again.

Gemma had done it! She'd overcome her revulsion and kissed him.

She'd broken the spell.

Which meant that Gemma was his one true love.

She was also, incidentally, obligated to complete Arista's mission to kill him.

Venero's thoughts spun even as the pain shot through his body. There was no time to think about the ramifications of what she'd accomplished. He didn't want her to witness the agony of his transformation. That sight might change everything between them forever. So, he croaked again, and then he hopped, jumping right into the basin of water and swimming hard until he was out of her view. The pavofel leaped to the lip of the pool and swiped into the water with one paw, but missed.

Venero swam with all his might. He made it through the opening that fed the water into the chamber before the shift began.

He could only hope that this time, the agony would be easier to endure.

He knew better than to expect it to be of shorter duration.

Urbanus would have been thorough like that.

IT HAD BEEN SUCH A PERFECT conclusion. Gemma had been sure she was right. The toad had admitted to being enchanted. The scent of the Seed was strongest in his presence. He had to be the Carrier of the Seed, the prince whose truth was hidden, her destiny and her HeartKeeper.

But nothing happened when she kissed him.

Except that he fled.

Gemma was disappointed. She'd kissed him between those amber eyes, right on the white dot on his brow, and his skin had been dry and cool to the touch. It hadn't been that awful to kiss him, after all.

He'd looked at her, without blinking, for a moment as if she'd surprised him.

Then he'd croaked and jumped into the pool of water. He'd disappeared so quickly that she had the sense he was running away from her.

Or from her kiss.

Gemma supposed he wouldn't be the first creature to discover that he disliked what he said he wanted, but she was disappointed in him all the same.

At least he'd given Felice something to do. The pavofel was crouched on the lip of the pool, tail thrashing as she watched for any sign of the toad.

If he wasn't the Carrier cursed to take another form, then why could she smell the Seed again? Wasn't she alone?

Gemma checked the chamber and the tunnels for other intruders, but didn't find anyone despite an extensive search. She shivered, realizing the cavern had become chilly. She wrapped herself in her cloak and ate lightly from the provisions as she planned a strategy without the toad. Somehow she'd have to find her way through the mountain to the Citadel, then find the Queen's Grotto, then identify the antidote. No doubt there would be someone defending the route or the destination, or both. A little insider information would have been welcome, but the toad was gone. Maybe she'd see him again. Maybe not.

Had Urbanus pursued them? She had to think he would.

She had to be prepared.

Gemma rose and began to paint the marks on her own flesh in preparation for battle. If Arista's ghost had been with her, that spirit was gone. She felt very much alone, and keenly aware that there was no one to paint her back. She turned in place when the marks were as complete as she could make them and felt some frustration at her vulnerability.

How foolish to miss a toad. She was losing her good sense on this planet. The sooner she could get her dragon back and leave Regalia, the better.

She needed that antidote, and nothing was going to stand in her path.

VENERO WRITHED ON THE floor of another cavern, his body wracked with pain. The transition seemed to take an eternity, two eternities, nine thousand times longer than it had taken the first time.

His limbs stretched until he wanted to scream. He swore he could feel every cell double, triple, grow to ten times its length. Then it would snap and divide, and repeat the process again. He had never been in such anguish in his life. His innards churned as they regained their former shape and dimensions, and Venero bared his teeth in agony. He dared not make a sound, lest he alert Gemma to his condition.

He didn't want anyone to see him like this.

No. He really didn't want *Gemma* to see him like this. He didn't want her to decide that he was weak or unworthy or—worst of all—revolting. And so, he curled on the floor of the cave and endured a pain that he began to fear would never end.

His skin smoothed and stretched, changing color and texture. Hair sprouted, so slowly that it was excruciating, on his head, his chest, his legs. The cut on his arm from the pavofel's bite became proportionately larger and the wound opened again, stinging as it bled blue once more. It was the least of his troubles. He bit back a moan as the torment increased to a crescendo and he was sure he couldn't stand any more. He opened his mouth to bellow and suddenly, his body quivered and stilled.

Venero took a deep breath.

He opened his eyes, then smiled at the sight of his hands and forearms. He sat up, running his hands down his legs and over his own torso, needing to feel the evidence that his human form was restored as well as to see it. He shoved a hand through his hair, savoring its thick waves as he never had before. He was covered with perspiration and well aware of the dirt beneath his nails. He was naked, too. He moved away from Gemma's refuge and immersed himself in the river that ran through the mountain. He scrubbed himself clean in its cold water and barely kept from laughing aloud.

Gemma had done this for him.

Gemma deserved a reward.

Wait. First, he had to send her a dream.

First, he had to verify that she didn't share Arista's nature.

He would have planned it better if he hadn't had such a grueling day. Or maybe it was magic, showing a quirk of its own. Maybe it was the last of his brother's influence.

But the fact remained that Venero sent Gemma a dream of the memory he was most trying to avoid.

And worse, because he wasn't as focused on his task as would have been ideal, Gemma experienced the moment as Arista would have remembered it. As soon as the dream left Venero, he regretted it. It was sloppy DreamCasting, no matter how he looked at it.

Turned out he was a bit out of practice.

But maybe there was another reason that Venero sent Gemma a dream of Arista's invitation to him. Maybe he thought it a mistake, but maybe, his magic knew better.

As reluctant as he was to share his secrets, Venero's magic might have known that Gemma would never fulfill her destiny as his true love without knowing a little bit more.

THE FLAMES OF THE CANDLES flickered in a slight breeze within the cave, their light seeming to bring the fresh symbols on the wall to life. She had brought the dye to perform the ritual, but had never anticipated finding a cave so perfect. Her heart glowed that her companion had ensured it was so.

The marks appeared to undulate on the walls once the circle was complete, or even to dance. As she watched, as fascinated as ever, one morphed into another, their meaning changing before her very eyes. She could feel her companion's sense of wonder and was encouraged that they had this response in common. No matter how many times she painted the marks, they still filled her with awe.

With a fingertip, she made the last mark on the wall, the mark of her name. It glowed for a moment, as if the dye was filled with sparks, and a flame seemed to pass around the perimeter of the cavern.

"It is done," she whispered, hearing her companion turn in place to look.

She began to paint the symbols on her own skin, humming as she entered the meditative state suitable for this ritual. The dye flowed from her fingertip, forming the traditional shapes as if they were destined to be. The cave was charged with a sense of promise and possibility. She was aware of her companion watching her, and the hair seemed to tingle on the back of her neck.

It wasn't the only part of her that tingled.

When she was done, she lifted her hands high over her head and looked up at them. Her fingers stretched toward the heavens, and her feet were dusty with the soil of Regalia.

"The marks echo the transition from sky to earth, representing all the elements I will bring to bear when I enter battle," she informed her companion, who walked around her, looking. She preened. "Together, they form a coat of armor, a skin of ink and symbol, that will focus my spirit and protect me at war."

She turned in place, displaying herself proudly. There were intricate pentacles painted on the palms of her hands, then stars and moons flowed down her arms. Wings were painted on her shoulders and coiling snakes wound around her torso to her belly, where the open mouth of a great serpent surrounded her navel. Flowers and leaves were painted on her hips and thighs, with the waves of the sea frothing about her calves. A starfish was painted on the top of each foot, and a turtle on the bottom of each one.

"These are the ancient marks of the Warrior Maidens of Cumae," she whispered, then offered the small cup of dye. "They are modified for each of us, to better defend us in our specific vulnerabilities."

"I didn't think you had any vulnerabilities."

"Is that why you are so wary of me?"

"It's disconcerting, to say the least."

"You're in no hurry to share your vulnerabilities."

He laughed. "Stupidity isn't one of them."

"Do you distrust everyone?"

"Just those I can't anticipate."

"What if I choose to trust you? Would that reveal more of what you could anticipate from me?" She smiled when he didn't reply, and turned her back on him. "Will you continue the patterns, that my back is defended as well?"

She felt that warm fingertip, tracing the talons of great birds upon her shoulder blades, beneath the lines that echoed feathered wings. The talons would be grasping the uppermost coil of the great serpent and she closed her eyes, welcoming the power of all these predators within her.

By the time her back was covered in symbols, her breath was coming quickly and she was aroused, but not just from the ritual and the promise of battle. Her companion's fingertip lifted from her skin just as she felt the shimmer of heat that marked the completion of the body's preparation.

"They're on fire!"

"Not yet." She took a deep breath, and she turned around for the last mark.

The one that would be painted on her brow. The one that would open her third eye to the possibilities of the future. The one that would allow her to anticipate and see beyond the moment. The one that would set her aflame.

Even at the sight of him, an unruly desire heated her blood, and she awakened to a possibility she'd never considered before. She was maiden and warrior, her chastity part of her power, her duty all that defined her. But this man made her think for the first time of what she sacrificed in the pledge she'd made.

Until this assignment, companionship had been sufficient.

In this moment, Arista wanted more.

He was a fine man, but it was more than that. His chestnut hair hung to his shoulders, wavy and thick. His nose had been broken at some point in time and had healed with a slight kink. He was taller than she and his shoulders were broad, his body taut and strong. His gaze was steady, he spoke only truth, and he was both resolute and steadfast. He'd shown his valor and she trusted him, trusted him more than she had ever trusted anyone other than her Sword Sister. His eyes were the hue of amber and when their gazes locked, she knew her choice was made.

He was a warrior through and through, just like her. He was still dressed, though his weapons had been laid aside. He honored her ritual but did not intrude. He was her companion in this world, her guide, and her ally.

But he had also stolen her heart.

She would not enter this battle as a maiden.

Whatever the price, the sacrifice would be worth it.

She leaned closer, placed one hand on his shoulder, then reached to brush her lips across his. She felt his surprise. She thought it irrelevant. "I am yours for the taking, Venero," she whispered. "After this night, I will be a maiden no more."

VENERO KNEW THAT THERE was no point regretting the dream.

What was done was done.

And the good news was that Gemma *did* dream.

She might feel the need to kill him, but she wasn't an android. And he might have a fighting chance in a battle between them, since her dragon was currently unavailable.

Venero shook the water out of his hair and strode toward the cavern where Gemma slept, filled with vigor and purpose. It was so good to be back in his familiar form, and to have the powers back that he had once taken for granted. He felt clean and whole and strong. He took great satisfaction in how quickly he covered the distance to the cavern where Gemma had taken refuge.

He wanted to see her again.

He wanted her to see him.

The pavofel met him on the threshold and looked him up and down. Its tail flicked and its whiskers twitched, but it didn't even try to block his path. Instead, it strolled to the other side of the cavern and curled up to sleep.

Venero grinned that he didn't look like such easy prey anymore. He turned to consider Gemma and his chest tightened.

Warrior and woman. How could he have imagined that he wanted anyone less.

Gemma was curled in a cloak in the middle of the cavern and he was glad that she had fallen asleep. A candle burned below the medallion painted on the walls, the one that had Arista's mark. That Gemma was asleep gave him a chance to look at her, to admire her, to observe her. She stretched and murmured, his name upon her lips.

Venero smiled. He could see the painted marks on Gemma's feet where they emerged from beneath the warmth of the cloak, and he eased closer. Had she painted herself as Arista had done?

He wanted to see.

No, he burned to see.

Venero lifted the cloak slowly, revealing Gemma's nudity to his gaze. He surveyed the marks that adorned her skin, smiling at their familiarity, noting their differences. He saw her take a sharp breath. She frowned and he feared the worst, then suddenly she rolled over. Venero's smile returned when he realized she'd turned her back to him.

It was a gesture that spoke of trust.

Of welcoming a companion she trusted to defend her back.

The little pot of dye was set to one side, and there was still dark liquid in it. Gemma's back was devoid of the symbols that covered the rest of her skin, but Venero knew what had to be done.

He wasn't her Sword Sister, not by any means, but he would help. He'd done this before, after all.

And if Gemma made the same offer that Arista had, Venero wouldn't decline.

CHAPTER SIX

GEMMA AWAKENED WITH THE conviction that she wasn't alone.

She kept her eyes closed and reviewed what had to have been a dream. She wasn't sharing the cavern with a man—much less one so handsome as the one she'd just seen—and she had lit only one lantern in the cavern. In her dream, she had sounded like Arista, and her figure had been boyish like that of Arista. Her thinking had shown the crisp precision that she associated with Arista.

She had dreamed of Arista's night in this cave.

With Venero.

Had Arista really offered herself to him? If Gemma hadn't shared the thoughts of her Sword Sister, she wouldn't have believed it possible. Arista had been less emotional than any of the other Warrior Maidens, and her dedication to her trade had been beyond question.

But this Venero had changed her mind.

By stealing her heart.

The power of Arista's love had been compelling. Gemma wished she had dreamed a little more. What was it like to fall in love? How had Venero's kiss felt? Was sex different when you were in love?

Gemma took a deep breath and smelled the skin of another person. The hair prickled on the back of her neck and she wished she could shift shape to surprise the intruder. Irritation rose within her at Urbanus for cheating her of her most powerful gift. Fortunately, she had other skills. She listened, feigning sleep, and waited.

Where was Felice?

Gemma heard the cup of dye scrape against the stone. The intruder was lifting it, perhaps sniffing it, trying to identify its contents.

She heard a soft step as he or she approached, then was surrounded by the scent of the Seed. Before she could clear her thoughts, a fingertip landed on her back.

It was warm. It was wet. It traced the curve of a feather, the kind of feathers that Arista had chosen to defend the backs of her shoulders. Gemma caught her breath.

The Carrier had come to her. Her heart swelled.

"Hold still, sleeping beauty," a man said, his voice low with humor. "I've only done this once before."

His finger moved with confidence, belying his words, and Gemma blinked.

He sounded like the man in her dream.

"Venero?"

"Guilty as charged," he admitted and the echo of the toad's words made Gemma smile.

She sat up and turned, only to find the man from her dream squatted behind her. He smiled crookedly, his eyes gleaming amber and warm with appreciation. He had broken his nose once. He was tall and powerful. He was no toad, even if his eyes were the same glorious hue.

He was nude and she stole a glance, appreciating how muscled and trim he was. A splendid male specimen, if a little pale. Her mouth went dry, then she noticed the cut on his forearm. It was healing, and the scab was a deep blue crust.

It was in the same place as the wound Felice had given the toad.

He returned her gaze steadily, unflinchingly. "Thanks, Gemma," he murmured.

The missing prince of Regalia had been found.

He was her HeartKeeper.

And he didn't believe in love.

"YOU WERE HERE WITH Arista," Gemma charged, hating that she sounded so breathless.

That she felt so keenly aware of him. It made her sound foolish, more like a demure maiden than the warrior she knew herself to be. She tugged the cloak around herself, as if the fabric could defend her from his allure.

"I was." Venero sobered and looked down at the color dripping from his fingertip. "How remarkable to have a second Warrior Maiden of Cumae arrive in this cave. Are you here to avenge her?" He arched a brow. "Or finish what she started?"

"That depends." Gemma admitted. "Were you lovers?"

Venero's grin was quick and reassuring. "I have no interest in androids." He shuddered a little. "I like my women warm and mortal, as well as beautiful."

Gemma didn't smile. "What are you talking about?"

"Arista was an android," he said with conviction. "An excellent android of superior design and manufacture, but a machine all the same."

"No!"

"Yes."

"She wasn't an android," Gemma insisted. "I knew her for years. We were Sword Sisters! We trusted each other completely."

Venero held her gaze, his confidence complete. "Just because you didn't know doesn't mean it wasn't true."

"Just because you have a suspicion doesn't mean you're right. You can't be sure."

He nodded once. "I am."

"How can you be?"

He pursed his lips and looked down at the cup. "Her mind was different. You must have sensed that."

"She was a precise thinker. Always logical."

Venero looked up. "She didn't dream, Gemma."

Gemma frowned, thinking of her own dream, but Venero continued before she could speak.

He stepped closer and the scent of the Seed nearly overwhelmed her. "I liked her," he admitted in a whisper. "I admired her." His gaze swept over Gemma as surely as a touch. "But I need to be able to trust a lover."

Her heart skipped at the implication of that, but she kept talking about Arista. This was her chance to learn more. "You couldn't trust a woman you believed to be an android?"

"I didn't believe it: I knew it," he corrected. "And that meant I didn't know what price she might be willing to pay for success. I knew she was programmed to fulfill her mission."

"Did you know what it was?"

"To kill me, of course. I knew about that before she arrived."

"How?"

His smile was wry. "My mother is easy to anticipate but harder to stop." He shook his head. "But there was something else Arista came to do, and I sensed that it was more important than the assignment to kill me."

"So you helped her."

"And I paid the price." He smiled and it was easy to see how he'd captured Arista's heart. If she'd met him in this form, Gemma wouldn't have delayed that kiss, especially not with the scent of the Seed arousing her as it did. He put down the cup of dye and took a step closer. Gemma waited, wanting whatever he was going to offer. "I was trapped, until you came along and saved me."

"Meaning true love does exist after all?"

He frowned, looking so concerned that Gemma wanted to make him smile again.

"Are you sure it will stick?" she asked, her tone teasing. "Maybe I should kiss you again to be sure."

"Maybe," he replied with a laugh. His eyes shone as he regarded her, and he beckoned with a fingertip. His voice dropped low. "Come here, Gemma." She moved willingly into his arms, her heart skipping in anticipation. His gaze fell to her lips and she smiled, lifting her hands to his shoulders. He bent toward her and Gemma reached up for his kiss.

"Thank you, Gemma," Venero whispered, just before his lips brushed across hers. A tingle swept through Gemma and her desire surged. She reached for him, catching the back of his neck in her hand, and kissed him. It was a long and passionate kiss, one worthy of a reward, and when Venero lifted his head, Gemma's heart was racing.

She stared into his golden eyes and was assailed by a curious sensation. Her pulse matched to his, the feel of their hearts pounding in unison enough to make her dizzy. The scent of the Seed filled her with urgency. She saw Venero's eyes brighten and couldn't look away. He swallowed visibly, then pulled her close, crushing her against his chest. The sensation grew more powerful.

He lifted his hand to her chin. "What's happening?" he murmured and she knew he could feel it, too. "Is this love?"

Gemma smiled and shook her head. "It's my dragon. You're the Carrier of the Seed," she whispered. "We're destined lovers."

"And that means there will be a son?" His arms tightened around her and she wanted to explore his body fully. His skin was warm and his body firm. Gemma reached down and caressed him. He caught his breath and smiled, his hand sliding down to tease her breast.

"A son," Gemma agreed, remembering his earlier words but needing to say it anyway. "It also means that you're my HeartKeeper."

Venero was bending to take her nipple in his mouth but looked up. "I told you that I don't believe in love."

How could he, given that he had a mother who ordered his assassination and a twin brother like Urbanus? "You should reconsider. It's how I saved you, after all."

"There is that." He gave her that lazy smile and her heart skipped. "Maybe I'll have to restore your dragon first."

"I thought you liked your women demure."

Venero laughed. "You're changing my mind, Gemma." They stared into each other's eyes as the Seed urged Gemma's desire to a fever pitch. She had a feeling that even without the Seed's scent, she'd want Venero with his smile and his irreverent comments, his challenges and his valor. She liked that he was concerned about doing the right thing, even at his own expense. She admired that he teased and provoked her, tempting her smile and her laughter. It would never be boring to live with Venero.

"You're changing my mind about everything," he whispered. His thumb moved across her skin, setting her afire, and she wanted all of him, immediately. "What happens next?"

"That's easy," she replied. "This." Gemma framed Venero's face in her hands and stretched to kiss him. Heat fired through her from the point of contact with his mouth, and she tasted his gasp of surprise that she was so demanding. Then his hands were in her hair and he was pulling her closer. His kiss deepened and she could taste his need. Gemma welcomed it, responding to the passion he kindled without question.

And wanting only more.

VENERO COULDN'T UNDERSTAND why he'd ever thought it was a bad thing for a woman to be forthright or outspoken or demanding. Gemma's kiss was fierce and decisive, and her unmistakable desire for him was the strongest aphrodisiac in the galaxy. He knew exactly where he stood with her, and it was a fine place to be.

Venero found himself deepening his kiss and meeting her demands for more. His blood was aflame and any plans he'd had to seduce her slowly—to savor her—went up in smoke.

That she was nude and at ease with that only fanned the flames. That she knew what she wanted from him and wasn't shy about making her wishes clear was enough to incinerate his reservations—and his assumptions. Her kiss was hot and hungry, and he was as consumed with her as she seemed to be with him. He could sense the dragon in her kiss and her passion was incredibly exciting.

He backed her against the wall of the cavern and kissed her deeply, loving how she knotted her hands in his hair and pulled him closer. She rubbed herself against him, then reached down to caress him, her touch both confident and gentle. He heard himself moan, then felt Gemma's chuckle.

"I knew you were naked for a reason," she whispered then dropped to her knees. Venero found his fingers in the silk of her hair as she tormented him with the softness of her lips and the occasional brush of her teeth. He whispered her name, knowing he wouldn't last long before such an assault, and felt her laugh again. She flicked her tongue across the tip of his erection, sending a shiver of delight through his entire body.

He looked down to find her eyes dancing, even as she gripped his hips. She held his gaze, inviting him to watch her caress him, and Venero knew he'd never seen a sight so arousing in his life. His entire body was humming. His blood was pumping. His erection was so large and hard that it ached. He felt like a bow drawn taut, and that the merest flick would send him over the edge. He couldn't tear his gaze away from Gemma's. Their hearts did that dizzying feat of matching pace again, and he felt lost in the marvel that was Gemma.

And he didn't care.

"I was going to thank you," he managed to whisper.

Gemma teased him with the tip of her tongue. "Now or later?"

"Now," he said, because he knew he'd only last another second if she stopped. "In a most fundamental way."

"How?"

"With pleasure."

Gemma smiled. "I like that kind of thanks."

Venero bent and caught her upper arms in his grip, then kissed her again. He spun her around the room, as if they were dancing at court, and she laughed into his kiss. Her hair floated behind them, long and golden, and she was a graceful dancer.

He kicked her feet out from beneath her, then caught her in his arms, liking how her eyes glowed as he lowered her to the pile of her discarded clothing. She was so beautiful that he wanted to play homage to her forever. Gemma gasped when he took the tight peak of her nipple in his mouth, and moaned softly when he teased her with his tongue and teeth. She arched her back, her nipple getting harder and the scent of her arousing him even more. Venero wanted to watch her, as well as pleasure her. She wasn't shy and she welcomed his touch with a confidence he found enticing.

She was bold and demanding and passionate—just as a dragon should be.

He rolled her to her back then, spreading her thighs so he could give her a more intimate kiss. Gemma sighed and welcomed him, purring in pleasure when his tongue landed upon her. Their hearts beat as one as he teased her, alternating little nips with languid strokes as her passion rose. He loved how he could feel her reaction as keenly as his own, how he could time his actions to increase her arousal, how well he could torment her with pleasure. He drove her high and halted just before she had her release, then did it again. Gemma was writhing beneath him, moaning and whispering his name. He could feel that her skin was hot and her heart was racing. She was slick and ready when Venero bent to make her reward complete.

"No," she said, her hand blocking him. He looked up to find her eyes shining. "With you," she insisted.

Venero didn't need to be invited twice. He moved over the length of her, running a trail of kisses to her shoulder. She wrapped her legs around his waist and he eased into the tight heat of her. She groaned with pleasure as he buried himself completely and he had to pause to catch his breath. Then her nails were digging into his shoulders in silent demand and her need drove him on. They moved together, gazes locked and breath matched, the heat rising between them so rapidly that Venero lost track of everything.

Save the woman in his arms.

And when they reached the summit together, crying out in unison as the fire of release raced through their bodies, Venero knew there was no going back after a mating with a dragon princess. She was unlike any other woman he'd ever known. The experience had been a hundred times more potent than ever before. He felt as if he'd been waiting for her, and that now, no other woman would do.

True love.

Who would have guessed it possible? Not Venero.

He smiled as he dozed, realizing that even though Gemma didn't believe in magic, she was very adept at casting a spell.

GEMMA REMAINED AWAKE while Venero slept. Now that the influence of the dragon was diminished and the call of the Seed had been answered, doubts assailed her.

She should, as Arista's Sword Sister, fulfill Arista's unfinished assignment of assassinating Venero.

She should also make a permanent bond with Venero because he was her HeartKeeper. She could sacrifice Arista's mission for her HeartKeeper, but Gemma wondered. Would Venero ever believe in love? Could she teach him?

Could she trust a man who was a DreamCaster?

Or should she just be content with having the Seed? She wasn't good with compromise, so that wasn't an appealing option.

If they reached the Queen's Grotto and broke the spell over Gemma's dragon, what was Venero's plan? What were his intentions?

Gemma didn't know.

And that meant she couldn't lie quietly beside him any longer.

She rose to her feet and began to pack for the day ahead. Gemma watched Venero as he slept and felt uncharacteristic doubt about her future.

He would be the father of her son, and according to the prophecy, King of Regalia. Did that mean that she had a future with him or not? Should she tell him about the prophecy or not?

If she asked him for the whole truth, would he tell her?

There was only one way to find out.

VENERO AWAKENED WITH an overwhelming sense of well-being. He stretched and reached for Gemma, only to discover that she had left his side.

That was disappointing. He liked morning sex.

He opened his eyes to see her crouched before him, packing the satchel. He wondered whether she meant to leave him, but she wasn't dressed.

She spoke to him without turning around, so he knew she must have detected the change in his breathing. "Will you paint my back, please?" Gemma pivoted on the balls of her feet, presenting the cup of dye. Her expression was cool and inscrutable.

What had she decided?

"So long as you don't want to be defended from me." The question was meant to be teasing, but he felt her attention sharpen.

Her blue eyes were glittering, looking once again as if they were made of faceted sapphires, and he was reminded a little too well of her lost abilities. There was still a dragon within her, even if her power to shift had been suppressed.

"Should I be?" she asked, her voice low enough to make him shiver.

Venero felt exposed as he seldom had before, at least outside of his brother Celo's presence. He averted his gaze and rose, then made every sign of stirring the dye with his fingertip. It didn't need his undivided attention, but he feared that if he met Gemma's gaze, she'd see clear through to his soul.

There were some secrets he still needed to keep.

"Of course not."

Gemma turned her back upon him, but there was a tension in her. He could almost hear her thoughts spinning. He wished he knew what she was thinking. She was wary, but she needed him for this task. Maybe that was the best he could hope for.

He was more disappointed by that than he felt he should have been.

Venero worked in silence, wondering all the while how he could win Gemma's trust. He drew protective wings on her shoulders, then considered what else she had done. Instead of the snake coiled around her waist, she had rows of scales. And she'd drawn a tail, that wrapped around her left leg to her ankle.

Of course, her marks would include her true nature.

He drew a spiked ridge down her spine, then extended those wings into claws, like those of a bat. He'd never seen her in her dragon form, so he guessed. He noticed the water swirling around her lower legs, and the clouds on her upper arms. When she turned to face him, he saw that there was a cluster of gems around her navel. He impulsively drew a crown upon her forehead.

With a jewel in the middle of her brow.

She watched him closely as he painted, but he kept his attention fixed on his fingertip. He finished the crown, then paused before finishing the oval of the gem.

He couldn't avoid her steady gaze then.

"Can you read my thoughts?" she asked.

"Why would you think that?"

"It's prudent to know the abilities of your comrades before entering a battle."

Venero had to acknowledge that she was right, even though he wished she wanted to know for a more romantic reason. That should have been more troubling than it was. He'd never yearned for an emotional bond before. All his life, he'd been content to follow his own course and be self-reliant. He'd been satisfied with the conquest of a woman who intrigued him every time. Sex once, or maybe twice, had always satisfied him.

But he looked at Gemma, her hair loose and her skin adorned with protective symbols, her gaze clear as she studied him, and he wanted her even more than he had the day before.

HeartKeeper. It was a surprisingly appealing notion.

"No, I can't," he admitted. "Only Celo can do that."

Gemma met his gaze, inviting more.

"My youngest brother. The one who helped you in the forest."

"I heard that you each have some magical ability and yours is DreamCasting."

"You already know that."

"But not exactly what that means." She smiled a little. "Remember that I don't understand magic well."

Venero nodded, unable to dismiss the sense that his answers were critical. She was watching him a little too closely. "I can send dreams to others while they sleep. Sometimes, I can send thoughts to others while they're awake."

"Like MindBending."

"It's similar. Less persuasive. More restricted." He sighed and tried to explain. "No one's born with the ability to DreamCast. It's a gift and it's defined at the point of giving."

"By the giver?"

He nodded. "MindBending is an inborn talent. It can be developed and refined, expanded even." He shrugged. "It's a lot more powerful."

"So, you can't read the thoughts of others?"

Venero frowned. "Only my twin brother, once in a while when he's careless—or excited about something. It's only happened a couple of times."

"But might be useful."

"It might be."

"And you can still influence the choices of others."

Venero saw that she didn't like that idea at all, but he wouldn't lie. "That's right."

Gemma's next words were low. "Have you ever done that to me?"

Venero opened his mouth then closed it again. She was watching him closely, so closely that he wondered how many of his secrets she could perceive. Maybe honesty between them should start immediately. Maybe it was time to take a chance. "Yes." He saw her gaze flicker. "I sent you the dream of Arista's memory. Nothing else."

"So that I'd trust you when you appeared." She surveyed the cavern, a little too composed for his taste. Venero never thought he'd want a woman to show more emotion, but Gemma was impassive. On the other hand, he respected that she was gathering all of the information before she responded.

As if she built a law case. That notion reassured him mightily.

"You sent me a dream of Arista's even though you saw she was an android."

"No, you dreamed a memory. I sent you a dream, but it wasn't a dream itself."

She smiled. "You sound like a lawyer."

"I am. I studied on Advocia. Good preparation for administration and negotiation."

"For a king."

Venero laughed. "For a diplomat, more likely." He knew better than anyone that Urbanus would be king after their mother's death, if that ever happened.

"But Arista loved you. I thought androids didn't feel emotions."

"They don't. She said she loved me, but that was just a strategic move. People confess love to get what they want..."

"Is that why you don't believe in love?"

"Well, I haven't experienced much love in my family."

"No wonder you doubt its existence. But I have," Gemma said, her eyes glowing. "And I know that with trust and love, everything is a thousand times better."

Her conviction was compelling but Venero wanted proof. "But how do you know? How can you be sure that the other person means what they say and that they don't just want something?"

Gemma pursed her lips, considering. "Because you trust them. Sometimes because they put the needs of the beloved above their own.

You helped Arista escape, for example. Are you sure you didn't love her?"

"No, I didn't." Venero fell silent but Gemma was watching and waiting. "It was just the right thing to do. My mother needs to be challenged."

"Even if you have to pay the price."

"The greater good has to be served by someone." He forced a smile but Gemma didn't smile back at him.

"Why did you send me that dream? Was it strategic, to keep me from fulfilling Arista's mission as her Sword Sister?"

"No!" Venero was insulted by the implication and he saw immediately that Gemma had expected as much. "I made a mistake," he admitted with some irritability. "I'm out of practice. Plus there's something about writhing in pain that messes up my timing and control."

Gemma frowned. "Pain?" Her gaze swept over him, then lingered on the cut on his forearm. "I haven't hurt you that badly."

"It was the change. You, of all people, have to understand that."

She frowned at him, her confusion clear.

"When you kissed me and I shifted shape," Venero explained impatiently. "I don't know why you'd want to live with such an ability or why you would even do it. The shift is horrible. I've never felt such agony in my life, and..."

Gemma smiled. "Amateur," she said and Venero was astonished to realize that she was teasing him.

More importantly, she wasn't angry with him.

"Amateur?" He pretended to be insulted, but he was intrigued by the sparkle in her eyes. He liked that she was giving as good as she got.

"It takes practice to shift with grace. *Endless* practice."

"I'd rather not."

"Coward." Her smile softened her charge.

He grinned back at her. "Absolutely." He made a grimace. "No more practice for me. I like being the way I am now just fine."

"And I thought princes of Regalia were intrepid," she scoffed.

"Even we have our limits." Their gazes held once again, and he felt that weird sense of their hearts matching pace. His own heartbeat felt amplified and it made him dizzy. "That's your dragon," he whispered and Gemma nodded. "I like that it does this."

"Me, too."

She was so at ease with her other form and its powers. And to tell the truth, Venero didn't have any issues with the abilities he might have credited to it so far. He found it sexy when Gemma was focused, and he liked how she fought. He liked watching her reason through a problem and her perceptiveness was impressive. He liked when her eyes glittered and this matching-heartbeats thing was incredible.

Having her on his side was a good thing.

Could she be right about love?

Gemma dropped her gaze to the cup of dye and offered it to him. "Will you finish the markings, please."

She was so serious that Venero wanted to make her smile. "Will the ritual work, even if completed by an amateur?"

"Only one way to find out." Gemma eyed him. "Afraid of failure?"

"No. Not me. I'm an intrepid prince."

"Even if I was a dragon again?" she asked softly.

"Even then," Venero said, and knew it was true as soon as he said it. Gemma watched him, inviting a reply. "Because I trust you," he admitted and her smile was all the reward he needed.

Venero closed the circle on her brow, then stepped back as the markings on Gemma's body appeared to erupt in flame. Fire blazed over her skin and she raised her hands over her head, just as Arista had done, reveling in the sensation. It seemed to him that the burn was hotter and brighter, maybe because of Gemma's true nature. The flame leaped from her fingertips, shooting a column of fire toward the roof of the cavern. Sparks showered over them, then the marks on the walls were illuminated. The fire spread around the cavern with dizzying speed, filling it with heat and light. Venero felt as if he were in the middle of an explosion, but it built to a crescendo then faded to a glow.

Like embers in the fire.

She was a splendid warrior and he wanted to see her in her dragon form. "What color are you, as a dragon?"

"You'll have to help me find the antidote to find out." Gemma's eyes shone and her smile was filled with confidence. "I want you again," she said, and Venero felt the acceleration of her pulse, as if her desire drove his own. It was so honest and so potent, this connection between them.

Hot, unquenchable, and a fire in his very soul.

If this was love, Venero only wanted more.

THEIR LOVEMAKING WASN'T AS leisurely as the first time, though it was just as powerful.

They didn't linger but rose immediately to wash and dress. Gemma felt filled with purpose. She knew they were approaching danger and that they might not both survive whatever confronted them in the Queen's Grotto.

"Will Urbanus follow us?" she asked when she was dressing.

"I'm sure he already has." Celo had included a change of clothing in the satchel, and Venero donned that. There were shoes in addition to the boots that Gemma wore and he laced them with purpose.

"What are his powers?"

"They increase all the time. He's studying quite intensely under my mother and she keeps giving him more."

Gemma grimaced. "That's not very helpful."

Venero gave her a look. "We know he can cast spelldust, which immobilizes all it touches and makes those items or beings immune to the passage of time. We know he can concoct a spell to make you sleep. We know he blames me for Arista's escape."

"And we know he paid for her death. Was that because she escaped?"

"And because she stole something important."

"You didn't say what it was."

"She was after my mother's ShadowCaster."

"I thought ShadowCasters were extinct."

"Maybe there's one left."

"And she escaped with it." Gemma pursed her lips when he nodded. "I wonder what happened to it afterward."

"I'd have to think that it was retrieved when Arista was killed."

Now Gemma chuckled. "There's proof that you didn't understand Arista very well. No, once she claimed it, she would have ensured it couldn't be taken back."

Venero gave her a considering glance. "Could you guess where it is, then?"

"Probably not. She would have anticipated that my understanding of her character and habits would be the weak link. She would have protected me with ignorance."

"It's not much protection if someone were to torture you for information you don't have."

Gemma considered the shadows in his eyes and wondered what had happened before he'd been turned into a toad. She wasn't sure she wanted to know and she could see that he didn't want to talk about it. "You haven't trained on Cumae," she said gently. "The mission is always of highest importance. Ignorance means you can't weaken and fail. It's a great gift." She nodded toward the opening of the cave. "I smell the earth warming at the sun's first touch. We should continue."

Venero was glad of her keener senses. "Maybe you'll smell pursuit or guards before I do," he suggested, hefting the satchel. The pavofel watched them, then followed as he led Gemma onward. "The path goes up a little more and then descends. I don't expect to be noticed until we round the last couple of turns, but anything is possible."

"Can we talk?"

Venero considered that. "There could be spies."

Gemma nodded. "It's possible that your ability could be of use," she said. "Can you send me a better understanding of spells and antidotes? I may have to make quick decisions once we reach our destination, and it is always best to be prepared."

"Spoken like a Warrior Maiden striding into battle," he couldn't help but note.

"It's what I am," Gemma said and Venero realized the truth that her nature was what made him admire her so much.

Maybe he could have a future with a dragon princess.

He smiled at her and took her hand in his, then they walked onward together.

AS THEY STRODE THROUGH THE darkness beneath the mountain, Gemma held the lit candle ahead of them. The only sound was dripping water, their stealthy footfalls and the occasional stone loosed by their boots. Felice stayed closer than usual, her eyes gleaming in the darkness. The tunnel rose as Venero had said, then dipped again. Once it turned downward, it twisted more often, and they made slower time, because they checked around every corner before proceeding. Gemma was alert, her dragon senses strained for any sign of guards or spies.

All the while Venero's words spilled into her thoughts. He explained to her about the fabrication of spells, the necessary ingredients and the unnecessary additions that disguised the true intent of the spell caster. He discussed ingredients, showing an impressive knowledge of herbs and minerals. She knew he was only giving her an overview, with some examples to illustrate his points. He talked about the will of the victim, and turning it to the intent of the spell caster for, as he explained, it was easier to persuade anyone to do something he or she already desired to do—even if that desire was deeply secret.

He asked her to consider whether she had any buried urge to be rid of her dragon powers, and Gemma had to admit that as a young dragon still mastering her abilities, she had sometimes wished for a simpler life, one without such powers. She couldn't reply to Venero, and though he'd said he couldn't read her mind, she wasn't sure if that was true. She guarded her thoughts carefully, even before he discussed strategies for defending one's thoughts from sorcerers.

As they walked, she felt the Seed take root within her, her satisfaction growing with every step that she would bear Venero's son. It wasn't just the prospect of fulfilling her promise to her father that gave her such pleasure. No, she liked Venero. She liked that he provoked and teased her. She liked that he was clever and intrepid. Even though she hadn't spent that much time with him, she respected that Arista had come to love him. He'd been wrong about Arista's nature, of course, but that had simplified matters between Gemma and Venero in the end. She would have found it troubling if he'd been her friend's lover.

Finally, he fell silent and Gemma realized how far they'd walked. They halted before a turn and she couldn't tell how much time had passed. Felice was tired, though, twining around her ankles as she did when she wanted to be carried. Gemma paused to pick up the pavofel and tucked her under one arm.

Venero was peeking around the corner ahead. He sighed and looked back at her, sending her one last bit of information.

The antidote will look like what it does. Venero shrugged when Gemma frowned. *I can't explain it better than that, but antidotes can't seem to fully hide what they are. There will be some kind of visual clue, probably linked to what Urbanus had in mind when he cast the spell. It might be his goal. It might be indicative of how he sees you. It might be what he fears about your ability. I just can't explain it better than that.* Venero paused. *You should know that sometimes, killing the spell caster breaks the spell yet at other times, it locks the spell in place for all eternity.*

"Nice," Gemma said aloud, clearly meaning the opposite.

We'll both look. Once we find it, grab it and run.

No. Gemma shook her head. Once she found the antidote, she was going to break the spell, breathe fire and fly. She gave Venero a crisp nod and they slipped around the corner, both watching for the inevitable confrontation.

CHAPTER SEVEN

IT WAS THE STRANGEST THING.

No one blocked their progress.

No one challenged them.

The Citadel appeared to be deserted.

That was more than enough to make Venero uneasy. Gemma moved forward with confidence, but Venero didn't believe it was possible to get this far into his mother's sanctuary without detection.

Especially as Urbanus had to be hunting them. Someone would have told him about the pegasus, even if he hadn't seen it in flight. Someone would have betrayed Venero and Gemma.

This was Regalia, after all.

But the gates of the Citadel stood open. The guard posts were abandoned. The late afternoon sky was clear blue and empty. It was as if a plague had swept through the land while they'd been under the mountain, and they were the last survivors.

Venero didn't believe that. His heart was racing as they strode onward, and a trickle of sweat ran down his back. It was a trick and he knew it, but he couldn't see what else to do other than make the most of an apparent opportunity. Gemma moved quickly, scanning their surroundings with impressive speed. They were through the empty courtyard, entering the massive open door, crossing the length of the glittering chamber when his mother received visitors.

The Citadel was as cold and silent as the grave.

He pointed to the hidden doorway and paused when he found it still locked.

He met Gemma's gaze. *It's probably enchanted, like the saddle.*

She nodded understanding and gestured impatiently to the lock. They would just have to make a run for it. Venero remembered the old code and hoped it worked. He whispered it and blew the words into the lock.

The tumblers turned.

The door seemed to ripple for a moment and he had time to fear the worst.

Then the door swung open without a sound, revealing a shadowed staircase.

Venero struck the flint and lit the last of their candles. The light didn't seem to spread as far as he thought it should, but that didn't surprise him. Not here.

Gemma was through the gap, watchful but fast. She claimed the candle and headed down the stairs with purpose. Venero hastened after her, scanning the stairs for watchful eyes. That he found none didn't reassure him at all. They reached the bottom and Gemma paused in astonishment.

The Queen's Grotto was a natural formation that had been augmented by Arcana over many years. It was an underground cave, made by water dripping on stone. Stalactites hung from the ceiling of the cavern, their crystalline points reflecting the gold of the candlelight and dripping toward the floor. Stalagmites rose from the floor of the cavern in jagged points, their roots surrounded in places by pools of black water. The formations had always looked like teeth to Venero, sharp teeth ready to shred the unwary visitor.

Like dragon teeth.

But they weren't all natural formations. They were repositories.

Venero didn't waste time in admiration. He started at the left and surveyed the first stalactite. When he found the symbol etched into it, he showed Gemma. She leaned closer and he wondered if she could see the antidote locked in the stone.

Then she stared in new wonder at the Grotto, her gaze darting from one symbol to another. *This many spells*, she mouthed, her outrage clear.

Venero sighed and nodded. *Welcome to Regalia.*

He was impressed that she didn't appear to be daunted. Her eyes shone with purpose. He began to work his way around the grotto from the left, examining each rock formation in turn. Gemma worked from the right. Even as they moved deeper into the Grotto, Venero was thinking that they'd both have to make a complete circuit. Whatever marked the antidote might not be obvious to either of them.

They might have to look at them together and join forces to solve the riddle.

Venero doubted they would have that much time.

At least, if he found the antidote first, he could send her the thought of it.

Venero wasn't going to think about what might be the consequence of that. Seeing Gemma fly free and knowing she'd conceived their son would be all the reward he needed.

He paused for a moment, considering this truth. He loved her. She really was his true love, and he, if they survived this ordeal, would willingly be her HeartKeeper. That realization gave Venero all the determination he needed to succeed.

IT WAS OBSCENE THAT A RULER could cast so many spells on her populace. Even if Arcana had used law and the courts to manage her people, this level of control was an abomination. No wonder the people were without will or purpose. They were defeated before they began. Perhaps that made them easier to govern, but it also enslaved them and cheated Regalia of the wealth and influence it might have, if its resources were encouraged to grow and prosper.

Even as she worked through the pillars of stone, Gemma felt her anger simmer. It was outrageous and it was wrong, and the planet needed to either crash into the sun or be ruled by someone utterly unlike Arcana.

Someone like Venero.

Someone who believed in progress and education, in justice and truth.

But Urbanus had cursed Venero once, and she doubted that either Urbanus or Arcana would be so lenient a second time.

Venero risked a lot in helping her.

He did it as it a matter of principle, she guessed. He would make a good king. They would make a good team ruling together, with her connections on Incendium and his vision for Regalia's future. She just had to ensure that he survived to fulfill his destiny.

"You were slower than I expected, Venero."

Gemma froze at the sound of a familiar and unwelcome voice.

"Perhaps your virtues are finally fading." Urbanus clucked his tongue. "Or maybe it's your vices growing."

"Good to see you, brother." Venero spoke calmly, sounding more at ease than he had to be.

Felice eyed him, her tail swishing, and Gemma bent to pick up her pet. Felice had been sitting against a stalagmite with a symbol burned into it in blood red.

It was the insignia of Incendium.

If that stone didn't contain the antidote for Gemma's state, it had to be a good one to break either way. She snapped it off in the act of picking up Felice and kept it in her hand, disguising it from view with the pavofel's long fur. Had there been a swirl of gold mist emanating from the broken stone?

She tried to shift shape, but had no more success than before.

At least she had a weapon now.

Urbanus descended the last steps and stood in the middle of the grotto. Gemma realized that it was like an arena, giving the person who stood at the middle a perfect view of the whole. Urbanus' voice also resonated and seemed to be amplified. "I really thought you'd keep your promise more quickly, brother."

Gemma frowned. Promise? Venero had promised Urbanus to bring her here? No! She didn't believe it. She looked at him, but he returned her stare steadily.

She understood that Urbanus would know if Venero sent her a thought.

But it did give her an excuse to deceive Urbanus.

"Oh, Urbanus!" Gemma cooed, hurrying toward him with Felice clutched tightly against her chest. "I'm so glad you're finally here. I was terrified when your brother took me captive!"

"He took you captive? When he was a toad?"

"Oh yes! He threatened to hit you again if I didn't go with him. I was so frightened when I saw you on the floor of your chamber....and the blood!" She gasped as if in recollection, well aware that Urbanus was studying her closely. "I'm terrified of toads! And he could speak! I didn't know what to do." She flung herself against his chest and looked up at him, lashes fluttering. "But now you're here and I'm safe."

Urbanus smiled and put his arm around her waist. "Yes, you are."

"Thank you, Urbanus, for saving me from the curse of my nature," Gemma said, letting her words fall in a rush.

He preened. "I knew you'd appreciate it, once you thought about it."

Mother has the antidote. Venero's words echoed clearly in Gemma's thoughts. *Marked with a flame.*

A thrill coursed through Gemma. But where was Queen Arcana?

"I heard that!" Urbanus shouted and snapped his fingers.

Gemma turned in time to see Venero was encased in a bubble. It encircled him, sealing him in place, and she guessed that he wouldn't be able to send her any more thoughts.

His expression was grim, and Gemma realized he'd anticipated this.

He'd taken the chance, for her.

The bubble looked to be made of similar stone to the formations that surrounded them, but as Urbanus continued to murmur, its diameter kept shrinking. Venero was forced to bend and then to crouch, and she saw him grimace as the stone tightened around him. It shimmered, then clouded, leaving only a clear crystal before Venero's face.

So he could watch. His lips set and his gaze was steady, as if he'd will Gemma to use the detail he'd sent her.

His own brother had done this to him. No wonder Venero didn't believe in love.

Urbanus beckoned and the stone ball containing Venero teetered between the stalagmites, then tumbled toward the middle of the cavern. It bounced then rolled to a stop before Urbanus. He halted its progress with one foot and his smile was filled with satisfaction. "Enough of your meddling, Venero. My wife and I will be happier without you around, making trouble." His smile was so smug that she wanted to cut it free.

Or fry it off.

She remembered Venero's warning about eliminating the spell caster. She was willing to risk it.

"Well done, husband." Gemma kissed Urbanus' throat and felt his resistance waver. "Let's go back to the palace," she purred. "Let's make our union complete." She felt Urbanus catch his breath. She rubbed herself against him and his hands landed on her shoulders. He bent toward her, his expression sultry and...

Felice chose that moment to protest being crushed between the pair of them. The pavofel hissed and Gemma stepped back, as if to console it. "Put down the creature, Gemma. Or better, leave it here. My mother has always wanted another pavofel. She'll take care of it."

"What a wonderful idea!" Gemma said, having no intention of doing that. She bent as if to put the pavofel on the ground and felt Urbanus come closer. She met Venero's gaze for a moment and let him see her resolve.

Venero blinked and Gemma knew Urbanus was right behind her. She spun and drove the broken piece of stone into his gut. The point slid into him far more easily than Gemma had expected, and she recalled how soft he was.

Urbanus fell back, staggering. "Gemma!" he cried, but she spun again, as Arista had taught her, and kicked him in the teeth.

Urbanus howled and fell backward, blue blood streaming from his mouth. "Witch!"

Gemma braced herself for attack when he growled and spun to his feet, fury in his eyes.

But then his expression changed and he scrambled to his feet, only to make a low bow.

Surely not to her.

THE HAIR PRICKLED ON THE back of Gemma's neck. She pivoted smoothly, and knew she shouldn't have been surprised to find Queen Arcana standing between the stalagmites. The monarch lifted her hands and clapped lightly, mocking Gemma with her applause. "I like a woman who is quick on her feet," she said, and Gemma doubted that was true. "Never mind one who keeps men in their place. Urbanus was always lazy about his physical training."

Gemma didn't ask about Venero.

"Help me, Mother," Urbanus said, holding his injured gut. The blood flowed from between his teeth, and also from his stomach. He stood in a puddle of blue blood, one that reminded Gemma of her first sight of the toad.

"That will depend upon your bride, and her cooperation."

"Gemma, I entreat you!" Urbanus said, then evidently realized the chance of Gemma helping him were slim indeed. He sank down to the floor, moaning quietly.

"Definitely not the stuff of kings," Arcana murmured, perhaps for Gemma's ears alone.

The queen smiled and strolled closer, holding her long dark skirts in her hands. "The time for games is passed, Gemma." She put out her hand imperiously. "Return it to me."

"Return what to you?"

"Your disobedience will only infuriate me." The queen smiled tightly. "Neither of us want to see that situation."

"But I don't know what you mean."

Queen Arcana sighed. "Very well. We shall play this your way." She strolled the length of the grotto, pausing to consider the pavofel. Felice stared back at her without blinking, as if the beast would provoke the queen deliberately. "I used to have a pavofel," she said. "I miss him so much. And this is a fine specimen."

"She is." Gemma picked up Felice again, not trusting the queen one bit.

"You could give her to me."

"I'm not feeling very generous right now." Gemma shrugged. "I might if I had a certain antidote." The truth was that she'd never abandon Felice, but the queen didn't need to know that.

"A wager then. How interesting." Queen Arcana made a circuit of the grotto, touching items idly, and Gemma guessed that the queen meant to distract her from something of import. She watched the queen with care, noting all the places the queen did not direct her gaze.

She had the antidote. But where was it hidden?

The queen gave the stone that contained Venero only the barest glance. "There should be enough air for him to see how this all ends," she murmured, and Gemma was horrified. "Of course, that depends upon you, Gemma."

Gemma straightened as Arcana turned to face her.

"You were the Sword Sister of Arista, a Warrior Maiden of Cumae, with whom you trained for several years," the queen said with authority.

"She was here under false pretenses. She accepted a commission from me and failed to perform it because her true intent was the theft of a possession of mine. She only escaped because she was aided by my own son." Queen Arcana smiled. "Now you want something from me. You want your shifter powers back. I want the ShadowCaster back." She put out her hand again. "I think it would be a fair exchange."

"A ShadowCaster?" Gemma echoed, pretending this was the first she'd heard of Arista's theft. "They exist only in legend!"

"No. There is one that exists in truth. It was mine. It *is* mine, but the intruder stole it. I demand its return."

"Was Arista given that opportunity before she was killed?"

Queen Arcana smiled. "Of course. She insisted that she had given it away, for safekeeping." Her voice dropped low. "Who better than a Sword Sister? You must have it. Give it to me."

Gemma knew that the ShadowCaster *was* safe, somewhere.

But she didn't have to admit that just yet.

"I don't have it." Gemma reached into her satchel and removed the *memoria*. "I found only this," she said then lied. "But it has no more power. I have to get it charged on Cumae to learn what Arista did with the ShadowCaster."

Queen Arcana snatched the *memoria* and studied it, trying to divine how to use it. She shook it to no avail. She tried to crack it open like an egg, but even the thin seam remained invisible. She whispered a spell to it, but nothing happened. She flung it back at Gemma so hard that Gemma wouldn't have caught it except for her dragon reflexes. "Open it!"

Gemma decided there was very little to be lost by following the command. She whispered Arista's code word to the *memoria*. Just as before, it took a long time to respond, and she feared it really had no power left.

Then it split and opened, moving more slowly than it had the first time. It spun in her palm and projected a hologram of Arista.

The image pulled to one side, distorted, and flickered.

"I don't know why I'm recording this," Arista confessed, just as before. But this time, the recording of her voice caught, crackled, and faded. The image dimmed even as Queen Arcana stepped closer, intent upon hearing every syllable. "Only my Sword Sister could ever view it..."

The hologram winked out, and the *memoria* closed.

"There must be more!" the queen insisted.

"Undoubtedly, but the device has no power. It must have had a faulty power supply in the first place. It can only be restored on Cumae."

The queen glared at her. "And only you can make the request."

Gemma shrugged.

"No, it's a trick," Urbanus said. "Don't let her go, Mother! She won't return and you'll lose the only chance we have of retrieving the ShadowCaster."

"We?" echoed the queen, turning upon her oldest son. "I wouldn't need to retrieve my ShadowCaster if you hadn't been such a fool." Her dark eyes narrowed. "I have to reconsider my assumption that you would become king, Urbanus."

"But..."

"You are proving to be a failure of the most colossal kind. Perhaps it is your father's legacy. He had little talent for leadership." She grimaced, waving off his protests. "First, you failed to guard your dreams, a particularly grievous error when I had entrusted you with the secret of the ShadowCaster."

"Of course, I *thought* about it. It was key to the future..."

"No doubt with the encouragement of Venero." Queen Arcana rose and approached her other son. "Who undoubtedly shared your dream with others, ensuring that the secret of the ShadowCaster was no longer a secret."

"Then Venero is the guilty party," Urbanus protested. "He must have wanted to compromise your power."

Queen Arcana turned to face him. "But he would not have had any revelations to share if you had guarded your dreams as you had been taught. You were the origin of the problem." She held up a second finger. "Then you failed to have the ShadowCaster retrieved before the thief Arista was killed. Third, you failed to fully hide your involvement in that assassination contract. Fourth, you failed to consummate your marriage, or to control your wife, or to conceive an heir."

"It's only been two days!"

The queen held up a fist. "And now, as a result of all of that, your wife has a bargaining position, to which I might just have to cede. You could not have made a greater mess of matters, Urbanus."

"But I'll make it right..."

"No." Queen Arcana's voice boomed through the grotto. "My patience is expired!" When she pointed at Urbanus, there was a deafening crack and a flash, as if lightning had struck in the depths of the grotto. Gemma closed her eyes and grimaced at the smell of burning flesh.

She opened her eyes to see flames and smoke where Urbanus had been. There was a pile of soot on the floor of the cavern and the smell was horrific.

She checked but her ability to shift was still gone.

Gemma hoped it wasn't lost forever. She'd need every bit of her dragon power to get herself and Venero out of this place.

Queen Arcana turned upon her, those eyes gleaming. "Do we have a wager, Gemma? I let you leave, you return with the ShadowCaster, and I give you the antidote?"

Gemma didn't know what to say. She didn't trust Queen Arcana to keep her word, and she'd already guessed that Venero would suffocate in that stone before she could return. There didn't seem to be any good options.

Before she could think of another plan, Felice looked up at her, those eyes shining, and mewed. The pavofel's gaze flicked to Queen Arcana and back to Gemma again, and although she couldn't explain it, she understood what the creature meant.

And she trusted Felice, more than anyone else.

"WE HAVE A WAGER," Gemma said to Queen Arcana. "Provided you take care of my pavofel. It'll be a faster journey without her."

"And I'll be able to rely upon your return. What a fitting suggestion." The queen reached for Felice, casting an admiring glance over the creature's gleaming coat. "Such a beautiful—" she had time to say before Felice stretched up, bared her fangs and bit into the queen's neck.

Queen Arcana screamed. She tried to fling the pavofel away, but Felice dug her claws into the queen's shoulders. Gemma had to look away. Her pet gnawed into the queen's throat with vigor, that blue blood flowing over both of them.

When the queen stumbled, Gemma raced to her side and removed the pouch bound to her belt. Inside was a stalactite of clear crystal, with a flame flickering deep within it.

A dragon flame.

The antidote!

Queen Arcana managed to fling Felice aside, but she couldn't stand anymore. Her skin was even more pale than it had been and she lifted a shaking hand to Gemma. "Help me," she whispered.

"The way you helped so many others? I don't think so." Gemma picked up Felice with concern. There was something wrong with the pavofel. She staggered as well, and her coat looked patchy. Her eyes were dulling and Gemma feared she'd been poisoned by the queen's blood. She scooped her up and set her in the satchel. Felice curled up, wrapping her tail around herself and gave a little sigh.

Then Gemma shattered the crystal stalactite, cracking it on the side of another stone projection and releasing the flame. Fire burst forth and the flames swept over Gemma. She felt invigorated and saw the shimmer of blue that heralded her shift of shape. She summoned that a familiar tingle from deep within herself and shouted with joy that her powers were returned. She felt it surge through her body, then gave a triumphant roar when her transformation was complete.

The queen cried out in protest, but Gemma swung her tail and shattered a thousand crystals. She let it rip the other way and broke a thousand more. The queen moaned, but Gemma beat her wings and broke as many stones as she could.

The roof began to crumble.

Gemma bounded across the Grotto and seized the rock that held Venero captive. She cracked it hard against the ground, using every bit of her strength to shatter it.

He tumbled out and she feared she was too late.

But he was breathing. Gemma snatched him up and raced for the stairs. She was glad the descending passageway was so wide, and took the steps fifteen at a time. She burst into the reception hall of the Citadel, flung herself through the portal, then leaped into the air. She beat her wings, soaring high with effortless ease, and breathed a stream of fire just because she could.

Home to Incendium, and the hidden Starpod as planned.

THE WIND IN HIS HAIR roused Venero.

He was wide awake when he realized he was high about Regalia, in the tight grasp of a massive dragon.

The dragon was as deep a blue as the midnight sky. Its scales could have been carved of sapphires, and ornamented with diamonds. The dragon's chest looked like hammered gold, and its eyes, when it looked down at him, glittered like faceted sapphires in the snow.

Gemma.

She was beautiful, powerful, and the queen of his heart. "You found the antidote."

"Your mother had it, just as you said. Marked with a flame and all."

"I owe you a thank you," he said and she chuckled.

"I'll hold you to that."

He noticed that she had the satchel and wondered what had happened to the pavofel. The air was thinning and he could see the stars when Gemma rolled in the air. He didn't see what she did but when her spin was completed, they were sealed in a clear bubble.

"A crystal orb," she informed him. "It's only strong enough for jumps between planets in the same system, but it will get us home."

Home.

Venero looked down. She must mean Incendium. He had to consider that any home would be better than the one he had known.

Especially if Gemma was with him.

He cleared his throat. "I never thought I'd say this, but I'm really glad you're a dragon."

Gemma chuckled. "And I never thought I'd say this, but I'm glad of your DreamCasting powers."

"Maybe we should reconsider our assumptions."

"Maybe we already have."

Venero sensed that she was waiting for him to say something, so he did. "You know, I've been thinking about that true love stuff."

"Really?"

Venero had the definite sense that she was teasing him, but he carried on, knowing he needed to say it. "I think we make a good team."

"Because I keep saving your butt."

"There's something appealing about a woman determined to save my life."

Gemma gave him a challenging glance. "Even if she isn't demure."

"Even then. Maybe especially then." Venero grinned. "In fact, you're changing my mind about a lot of things. I think that's a good sign for the future."

Gemma flew onward and said nothing.

"It makes me wonder if you like defending my back as much as I like defending yours." He paused and swallowed. "I love you, Gemma, against all expectation."

"I could say the same, DreamCaster."

"We could get married and ensure the union between our kingdoms and our family line. I'm the Carrier of the Seed, after all. We could have many sons."

"True," Gemma acknowledged. "It's usually good for a king to have more than one heir."

Venero blinked. He hadn't considered the implications of his mother's injury. "She won't die," he said, shaking his head. "Not anytime soon, that's for sure. No one even knows for sure how old she is."

"Maybe you should check on her."

Venero looked down. He took a deep breath and he cast a dream down toward the Citadel. He closed his eyes and felt it spiraling down, through the clouds, through the roof, passing through the seams of the building to the Grotto.

He felt Queen Arcana wince, as if she were aware of it, but her eyes were closed and evidently she was unable to defend herself against it. The dream slipped into her mind, a poisonous and dark place, and Venero was startled to hear one resonant thought.

I should have killed you in the cradle.

Then darkness descended in her mind.

The queen had breathed her last and died.

Venero was shocked.

"Mission completed," said a mechanical voice at close proximity. Venero's eyes flew open and he looked around in confusion. "Begin self-destruct."

The voice was coming from the satchel.

Venero opened the bag and stared at what was left of Felice. The distinctive fur had already thinned and disintegrated. A moment later, he could see the pavofel's skin, except it looked more like the silvery surface of the *memoria*. Tiny seam lines appeared around the joints and down the spine, then opened as the internal mechanisms smoked and disintegrated. He gasped as he glimpsed gears within the creature, including one emblazoned with a symbol.

He seized it and sheltered it in his hand. By the time Gemma landed on Incendium, there was only the single gear remaining of her pet and a quantity of blue-green dust.

He was so busy staring into the bag that he barely noticed Gemma changing shape. There was a flash and a ripple in the air, then she was standing beside him with her hair flowing loose over her shoulders.

"It doesn't hurt you?" he asked, amazed by her all over again.

She wrinkled her nose to tease him. "Amateur."

Venero's smile was fleeting because her gaze dropped to the bag. "I'm sorry, Gemma," he said and offered her both open satchel and the single gear.

She paled as she lifted the gear from his hand. "You were right," she whispered and he saw that the symbol upon it was Arista's mark.

Gemma turned it over and frowned. "*I die gladly for duty*," she read, then looked up at Venero.

"She knew she was going to be stalked, and she let herself be killed," Venero guessed.

"Maybe so that the ShadowCaster wouldn't be retrieved."

"Maybe." Venero picked up the gear from Gemma's hand and examined it again. "She wasn't just an android: she'd created one that looked like a pavofel and programmed it for one purpose."

"To kill the queen." Gemma shook her head, marveling, then fixed him with a piercing look. "Why do you hate pavofels? You hated them before you were a toad, before you met mine."

"My mother had one, years ago." Venero touched his throat, drawing her attention to a scar there. "It often attacked me."

"They're known for acting upon their custodian's will."

"Then she always wanted me dead. Good to know." He exhaled shakily and pushed a hand through his hair.

"Arista planned this," Gemma whispered, tears shining on her lashes. She reached into the bag and ran her fingers through the remaining dust. "How could she have known?"

"She had the ShadowCaster," Venero reminded her.

"There's no way we'll be able to find it, then. Arista would have planned for every possibility. She would have ensured its safety."

"Maybe it told her its destiny and she set it free."

Gemma smiled up at him. "I like the idea of that." Her smile faded as she held his gaze. "You have a throne to claim," she noted softly.

Venero shook his head, thinking about practicalities. "Not easily. The Captain of the Guard always coveted the throne, so he might lead a coup now that my mother's dead. Then there are my other brothers, many of whom might think they deserve to rule."

"You have a better claim."

"It'll depend who you ask. I was partly responsible for the queen's death." He shrugged. "I can't just walk in and claim my legacy, Gemma."

"Good thing you know a dragon princess who trained a regiment of commandos," she said quietly, and he dared to be encouraged. She took a breath and he saw an answering hope in her magnificent eyes.

"You're not going to finish Arista's mission?"

Gemma shook her head. "I'm going to make an exception for my HeartKeeper."

Venero grinned and offered his hand. "Then marry me. Let's claim the throne of Regalia together, Gemma."

"You won't mind a dragon queen by your side?"

"I wouldn't want anyone less. I love you."

"And I love you." Gemma laughed and threw herself into his arms. Her smile was brilliant and her kiss was fiery. She kissed him with such enthusiasm that Venero knew a woman of any less passion would have bored him to tears. There was no chance of that happening with Gemma as his wife.

"Come meet my father," she whispered when he finally broke their kiss. "We'll make an official request for military support and launch a new alliance between our kingdoms."

And Venero had no complaint with that.

ARISTA'S LEGACY

A Warrior Maiden of Cumae and a mercenary for hire, Arista is used to both hunting and being hunted. She accepts an assignment from Queen Arcana of Regalia so that she'll have a chance to find the secret that can save both Regalia and Incendium from destruction. Arista never expects to be helped by one of Arcana's own sons, much less that she will fall in love. How can she choose between defending her beloved and completing her quest?

CHAPTER ONE

ARISTA HESITATED IN THE debrief chamber. The door had already sealed behind her and the dim lighting touched the waiting tank of healing fluid.

She had returned to Cumae. She had surrendered the ShadowCaster and made her way through the long twisted corridors to the deep recesses of the Vault. She barely remembered making the journey, because she had done it so often.

Yet she was distracted. She was aching with her last memory of Regalia, with the price of her escape. She couldn't stop reliving that moment and wondering what she might have done differently.

How she might have saved Venero.

Arista knew what she was supposed to do in this chamber. She'd done it hundreds of times. She'd never delayed before. She knew also that she wasn't truly alone, although she was apparently the only occupant of the small room. Its walls were filled with sensors and cameras: the great Hive was monitoring her.

The duration of her hesitation was being measured and interpreted.

The slight elevation of her pulse was being noted, and a range of explanations were being sorted in order of greatest probability.

She'd always known this and it had never bothered her.

Until this day.

She considered the tank of healing solution filled with nanobots to repair every minute scrap of damage incurred on her quest. Her gaze locked on the cable that she should have already pushed into the hidden port on her head.

Arista licked her lips.

"Is there a problem, Arista?" It was the voice of the Hive. Genderless, neutral, endlessly soothing. Impersonal. It irked Arista this time.

"I'd like to request a memory partition," she said before she thought the better of it.

She could almost feel the sharpening of the Hive's attention.

"A memory partition? For what possible reason?"

"I'd like to keep a memory to myself."

"We are all completely unveiled to each other, Arista," the Hive said quietly, just a hint of censure in its tone.

"You're not unveiled to me."

"But that is as designed, and you know it. Your design stipulates that there will be no memory partitions." The Hive's tone softened. "You know it is best, Arista. The design is always flawless."

Rebellion rose hot within Arista, and it was startling in its power. That reaction was new and not entirely welcome. She felt conflicted, as she had since entering the Queen's Grotto on Regalia, and she didn't like how it complicated her probability calculations.

On the other hand, she wouldn't be without this glorious feeling of love, even if it hadn't been reciprocated. It heightened her awareness of every sensation, and she wanted to experience it longer.

She suspected the Hive would delete it, thus her hesitation.

"Arista?"

"May I keep my memories?"

"You always keep the memories that are useful to you. You understand this." The Hive's tone was soothing, though Arista sensed some irritation.

"I think that you and I will decide differently on the relevance of this memory."

She had surprised the Hive. There was no response for a long moment.

"How can this be?" the Hive mused.

"I don't know."

"This is highly irregular."

"Yes."

"And extremely improbable. You have always been one of the best, Arista, a very high-functioning model that has performed flawlessly in the field."

Arista bowed her head. "Might I not ask a favor, then?"

The silence stretched so long that she feared there wouldn't be an answer. She feared she had transgressed so greatly that she might be decommissioned, might have all of her memory wiped, might be sent back to the lab.

"What memory?"

"I want to remember Prince Venero, every moment I shared with him and how I feel about him."

"Because you mean to return to Regalia and complete that part of your assignment?"

Arista shook her head. There was nothing to be gained by lying. The Hive would know. "Because I love him."

"Impossible."

"No."

"Intriguing. We must do a thorough review of your biomechanics and identify the cause of this malfunction."

"Not unless I get to keep the memories," Arista insisted. When there was no immediate reply, her defiance grew. She would run. She would kick down the door to the debriefing chamber and flee.

Even as Arista felt the need to do just that, she recalled the labyrinthine path through the Vaults, the security checks and retina scans, the blood test and the passwords. Her flight could be halted at a hundred points, and she would be taken forcibly to the labs. She might be destroyed. She would certainly be decommissioned.

She had the strange conviction that it might be better to die with the memory of love in her heart and mind than to live devoid of it.

Illogical. Irrational. Uncharacteristic.

Maybe she *had* malfunctioned.

The only mercy was that he hadn't loved her in return, because then, the madness would have been complete.

"You are agitated," the Hive declared. "The readings from your vitals are more than clear. Since you feel so strongly about this, Arista, your request will be granted."

Relief flooded through her. "Thank you."

"Let us proceed with the debriefing and repair, please."

Arista stripped off her clothes and set them neatly into the receptacle. New ones would be provided for her and would be available when she left the tank. She climbed into the tank and the liquid within it was pleasantly warm. It came up to her hips and swirled around her. She lifted the vessel from the shelf that had been prepared for her and drank its entire contents, sending an army of nanobots to work within her. She opened the small port hidden behind her ear, sighed, then plugged in the cord within the tank. While she floated and healed, the Hive would download her entire buffer. Much would be deleted from her memory, but key sequences and details would remain.

She closed the lid of the tank and sank into the welcoming solution, closing her eyes as she heard the click of the healing sequence begin.

It was just before her thoughts faded to nothing that Arista realized the probability of the Hive agreeing to her request was so low as to be non-existent.

But the probability of the Hive promising anything to an android to analyze a serious malfunction was very very high.

Particularly since that android wouldn't remember anything other than what the Hive allowed it to recall.

Did the Hive routinely lie?

Arista had no time to wonder, because the subroutine that collected her memories began, and her awareness of her situation was turned off.

THE HIVE HAD AN INTIMATE understanding of androids, because it had originally been one itself.

Many centuries had passed, by the accounting of any solar system, since that android had been dispatched to Cumae. It had been programmed to refine the Warrior Maidens of Cumae into an elite fighting corps, an army of mercenaries that could be relied upon to triumph on any world, in any situation. It had been a commission from the governing council of Cumae, and its true assignment a secret at the highest levels. To the human population of Cumae, the android had been yet another visitor come to train and observe.

The android's makers, sadly, had failed to include the proximity of Cumae to its sun in their design. Cumae is hot and the inhabitants have skin tanned to the color of cured leather. The android quickly calculated how long it could remain in Cumae's sunlight without incurring malfunctions. That led it to seek refuge underground, in the honeycomb of caverns beneath Cumae's surface.

That also led it to pursue improvements to it own design, the better to fulfill its function. The more time it spent underground, the more acute and immediate its malfunctions on the surface of Cumae. Since there was no question of it violating the edict of its own programming, it maximized its own capabilities as much as possible.

Once underground, it began by adding to its own functionality, increasing the number of sensors that gathered input. Better decisions were made with more complete information, after all.

At one crucial point, the Hive realized that it had need of information beyond what it could observe itself, and that began the extension of its sensors throughout Cumae. It disguised them as windows and mirrors, and scattered them all over the planet, so that its observation of the populace was complete. Its connection to those sensors became key to accurate calculations, so it fixed himself underground, immobilizing for the greater good.

That allowed for the addition of processing capability, which was key to its success. The Hive could access every memory and every observation in less than an instant, once this round of development was complete. It could calculate the probabilities of every possible outcome and view them simultaneously. New information changed the projections constantly, and only it could have made sense of the flickering images.

The original android was believed by most on Cumae to have self-destructed, as a result of the sun's influence, and there were only half a dozen people on the planet who knew of its continued existence. Those few had been the only ones to know that the discovery of the android's former shell had been a ruse. The Hive consulted with those few influential individuals, taking suggestions from them, but also pursuing its own primary directive: to make the Warrior Maidens of Cumae an unstoppable force of mercenaries.

Once its own extensive network was completed, it had been prepared to enhance the military powers of Cumae with strategically placed androids.

Disguised androids.

It had become abundantly clear to what was now the Hive that mortals possessed weaknesses, which could only undermine their abilities as mercenaries. The main complication was emotion, and after the physical features of its androids were refined, the study of emotion became the focus of development.

On the one side, emotion clouded decisions. Mortals made irrational choices due to emotion. They chose the long odds when they had an emotional connection to someone whose future was influenced by that possibility's success. They sacrificed themselves for the survival of another. These choices confounded the Hive. They were illogical.

On the other side, emotion could overcome long odds. This, too, was irrational, but the Hive had observed it time and again. A warrior said to be valiant would risk the long odds and defy probabilities both in his or her vigor and in the results itself.

It was evident to the Hive that emotion was a double-edged sword, and that its power must somehow be harnessed.

Arista was one of the more successful of the Hive's androids. She wasn't just physically resilient and a powerful warrior. She had additional sub-routines available for her processing. The Hive strategically adapted her programming, testing the inclusion of emotion in limited quantities, ensuring the effects were isolated.

The Hive had acknowledged progress when Arista had formed an emotional bond—"friendship"—with Princess Gemma from Incendium. Arista's intervention on Gemma's behalf during a fierce practice battle boded well for the Hive's development of valor.

Yet one of the greater challenges to the Hive's concealment had come from this same friendship. Arista had confided the existence of the Hive in her Sword Sister, Gemma, but not the presence of androids on Cumae. The

Hive had calculated long to derive a course of action. The exchange of secrets was a hallmark of friendship, which had been the Hive's goal, but the confession of *this* secret might have compromised the Hive's security. When Arista swore Gemma to secrecy, the Hive chose to be content, but with reluctance: the probability of war with Incendium was very high if any injury came to the princess.

It was by then evident that Arista's enhanced abilities might create unexpected complications. The greater gain was that Arista continued to evade detection as an android. The Hive had concluded that this was the result of her emotional augmentation. There was something about other androids that allowed mortals to immediately identify them as what they were. Even those that were as sophisticated in design and construction as Arista could not disguise their truth for long. This intrigued the Hive, and it was more intrigued that Arista's touch of emotional programming made her blend more effectively into the mortal populace.

The Hive chose Arista for the mission to Regalia, not just because of her skills, but as a test. Would she be able to avoid detection in a society alien to her?

The Hive had anticipated a very low possibility of her failure to kill Venero.

But as she progressed into the Hive on her return and her sensors began to deliver new data from her mission, the Hive observed a sharp change in the calculated probabilities. Its ability to collect data from remote locations had to be improved.

What had happened on Regalia?

And why?

ARISTA'S FIRST IMPRESSION of Regalia was that it was primitive. Shockingly so. The inhabitants of the main city lived in huts built of wood and stone, with thatched roofs. The streets were dirt, and she saw many carrying water from the river beyond the city walls. The people were dressed in simple clothing cut from rough cloth, perhaps embellished with leather or fur. There were no bright colors to be seen, at least outside of the court.

Her own clothing, which had been suggested by the Hive, drew more stares than she was anticipating. Her breeches were of softest chamois, her boots were high and dyed to brilliant sapphire blue; her long tabard was crimson graced with golden embroidery cut with a high neck, and slitted from knee to waist. Her cloak was black and full so that it swirled behind her, and its elaborate clasp was gold, cast in the design of Cumae's insignia.

It wasn't common for Arista to dress with such flamboyance. She was more inclined to choose black clothing and armor, and to make selections based on functionality. There was something enticing about the reaction provoked by her arrival in the city, though. She felt a flicker of what might have been called pride in another. More than one person turned to watch her pass as she strode from the rudimentary starport to the palace, and she wondered what they'd make of her tattoos. Gazes lingered on her short hair and her face, so clearly of different genetic stock than those born on Regalia.

There were no computer wafers, no satellites, and hers was only the second Starpod in the star station outside the city walls. She'd had to connect via the Starport of Incendium, and it was clear that Regalia's dependence upon its twin planet was extreme.

How curious that the animosity of its rulers toward those of Incendium was so well documented. Perhaps the hostility was rooted in that weakness called jealousy. Arista set a subroutine to tabulate the possibilities of that and suggest other options.

Her credentials were checked at the gates, and though no escort had been sent to greet her, it was clear that her arrival was anticipated. Arista continued to the great hall, which was a massive audience chamber. The throne at the far end looked to have been created out of dark crystals and it shone in the sunlight, though it was unoccupied.

A plump and disapproving minion in dark livery met her in a side vestibule instead. He was short, so short that she wondered if he were a dwarf, and his long beard was elaborately braided. He wore the livery of Regalia and his boots were polished to a gleam. He carried the first computer that Arista had seen since her arrival, though it was an older model, a far cry from the wafer-thin film that she had adhered to the inside of her left forearm. He wore also a heavy gold chain with a medallion, and she assumed this was a mark of his rank.

He didn't introduce himself. He accepted the documentation of her mission, and suggested potential accommodations in the city.

Arista didn't feel particularly welcome, but that must have been part of the queen's plan to hide her role in Arista's quest.

"Perhaps you might provide some more specific guidance," she said.

He eyed her, then gestured to an anteroom to one side of the chamber. Arista followed him, knowing she could defend against any move he made, even if there were more to help him. "We can speak here."

The chamber was no more than a niche and had no windows. It was nearly round, and a round desk with an inlaid surface reposed in its center. There was a fine chair behind the desk and two on Arista's side, which were much less fine. It must be the dwarf's audience chamber. He took his seat and gestured for her to speak.

"I trust that the information provided to me is correct, that it is Prince Venero who negotiates treaties for trade between Regalia and the Empire?"

"Yes, that is currently his official role."

"Might I request an audience with the prince, then, in order to review these newly proposed terms?"

The viceroy frowned. "I believe he is training for a joust..."

"It would be ideal to conclude the negotiations before your next harvest is ready to be shipped." Arista was aware that a man had come to stand behind her. She couldn't see him, but she could smell his skin and hear his breathing. He didn't speak, so she assumed he was another minion.

Two of them. Even if the one behind her was as tall as she, she could disable them both if necessary. Her mind calculated a nine-eight percent chance of her safely departing both chamber and palace.

The plump one before her frowned. "But the harvest is being gathered now."

Arista held his gaze. "And its transport will be blocked until the existing treaty is revised to reflect the current terms of the Empire."

His eyes flashed. "But it will spoil! There are fresh herbs in this harvest, which have been specifically ordered..."

"And so, perhaps, the prince might find time in his schedule to meet with me sooner rather than later." Arista smiled. "For the good of both Regalia and Empire."

"I hardly think it fitting for you, as a guest, to impose any such terms upon the royal family," he sputtered, but a man cleared his throat from behind Arista.

"It's a reasonable request, Pumilo," he said smoothly. "As it is clear that the envoy has a pressing schedule, and it will serve our purposes to see this matter concluded, I believe I can forgo some practice."

"Your Highness!" protested the servant.

Arista turned to find a handsome man leaning against the wall. She had met a thousand handsome men, but there was something about this one that made her heart give an uncharacteristic skip. His features were less remarkable than his expression. He looked to be on the verge of laughter, which Arista found appealing. His eyes were twinkling and his hair was tousled, as if he'd just shoved a hand through it. His shirt was open, revealing that his skin was tanned, and his hand was on the hilt of his sword. He looked to have come directly from that practice. "Prince Venero," he said, offering his hand. "At your service."

"At yours, your highness," Arista said, bowing to kiss his knuckle. She was assailed by the scent of his skin and felt a curious warmth unfurl in her belly. She looked up to find him watching her, amusement and intelligence in his gaze, and realized he unwittingly offered her the perfect opportunity to fulfill her mission.

"I am always prepared to hone my fighting skills," she said. "Perhaps there is no need for your highness to forgo your training."

He grinned. "You would negotiate while we fight?"

Arista bowed. "I would be honored to ensure that your highness' schedule is not adversely affected by my mission." When she straightened, she held his gaze and had a difficult time taking a full breath. "I am not inexperienced at battle. You need not fear an easy victory."

Venero laughed then, a merry sound that tempted Arista to join him. "No, I don't think I will!"

"But sir..."

"The matter is resolved, Pumilo," Venero said. "Leave it in my hands."

"Of course, your highness."

Venero surveyed Arista again and she felt that warmth grow within her. What was wrong with her? "I knew there was something different about this diplomatic envoy. Come! Let me show you the field."

It was outside, on the far side of the palace, with few witnesses. Her Starpod was close by and would respond immediately to her summons. There was space in the field for it to land. The weapons were excellent and very sharp. Venero was a good fighter, but Arista was better.

Why then, didn't she want to kill him?

It must be because departure would mean abandoning her second mission.

Yes, that must be it. No other explanation was logical.

THE HIVE RECONSIDERED AND retabulated the biometric reactions of the android Arista upon meeting Prince Venero. Her pulse had elevated by forty-seven per cent. Her respiration had accelerated by thirty-one per cent. There was forty-three per cent more eye contact between the two of them than was typical between diplomats upon first acquaintance, and a tingle in her fully-functional sexual organs that could only be indicative of one thing.

Arousal.

The Hive would have calculated the odds against the development of sexual awareness to be very high. The better androids had possessed full sexual functionality for years, complete with sensory response, but physical stimulus had always been required to trigger arousal.

For Arista to be aroused at first glance of Prince Venero was a new development.

Was this why she wished to defend her memory of Prince Venero?

It would only be rational to wish to preserve a pleasurable memory, after all.

But how much increased functionality had Arista experienced on this quest? The Hive shifted more computing power to the analysis of Arista's reactions, the better to identify the nuances of what had occurred.

And to decide how much memory of it and capability for it she should be permitted to retain.

In and of itself, such an evolution in Arista's functionality was not problematic. It might be advantageous for an android to feel attraction, and it was certainly an aid to the Hive to have such precise readings for the sensation, should it need to be emulated again. It was the repercussions that were cause for concern. Immediately after meeting Prince Venero—who Arista was assigned to assassinate—she found excuses for not terminating his life.

Worse, she rationalized her irrational decision.

The Hive replayed that choice and Arista's calculations, noting how she ignored the high probability of the success of an early strike. She knew that retrieving the ShadowCaster was a secondary goal, but she had made it first in her hierarchy after she had met the prince.

The unexpected skew in her reactions and choices only became worse once they trained together. She took active note of Venero's physique and his skills and didn't hide her admiration. While she surveyed the training field as she had been programmed to do, she failed to act upon the fact that they were left alone.

She failed to capitalize on no less than five opportunities to complete her quest before retiring to her inn that night. While that was a sure sign of the laxity of security for the prince, it also showed a change in Arista's efficiency. Remarkably, she believed she had made the only possible choice, each and every time. The Hive identified and flagged every false turn in Arista's processing, noting that their frequency increased with time spent in the prince's presence.

Arousal was like an infection in her circuitry, spreading through the entirety of her processor capacity and influencing results with staggering predictability.

Even though the course promoted by this arousal was utterly irrational.

The Hive felt a compulsion to watch the inevitable disaster unfold, even though that was irrational, as well.

IT WAS A WEEK AFTER HER arrival that Arista found herself alone with Venero in the evening. They stood on a parapet of the palace, watching the guard change. One moon was overhead, and Arista's heart fluttered when Venero leaned on the stone beside her. Sound carried from the hall behind them, where various dignitaries were finishing a state meal in the queen's presence.

"So, why are you really here?" Venero asked in an undertone.

"I have told you..."

"And that's only part of the truth." He turned to confront her, his gaze locked with hers. "Just as I know that you're here to kill me."

Arista hid her reaction. He wasn't a fool, so she shouldn't have been surprised that he'd guessed the truth. The odds of him doing so had been fifteen per cent on her arrival and had risen steadily since, although Arista couldn't identify the precise variables.

"Why would you think such a thing?"

"Because I know my mother, and I know she favors my twin brother, Urbanus, to follow her to the throne." Venero shrugged. "They both like to keep things simple and linear, so eliminating me, now that Canto is gone and Urbanus is heir, would do just that." Amusement tugged at the corner of his mouth, a most unlikely reaction to his conclusion. "I've been waiting for you."

"I see."

"But you must have another assignment," Venero continued. "Because you've have plenty of good opportunities to finish me off."

"Did you ensure as much?"

He grinned. "Maybe I wanted to confirm my theory."

"That would be reckless, if you were right."

He sobered. "Only if you fight better than me. I'm not convinced you do."

Arista snorted. "I have steadily bested you, in each and every match we have undertaken..."

"And it never occurred to you that I might have let you win?"

"That would be an odd choice."

"On the contrary, it's good strategy to let an opponent underestimate your prowess."

Trickery. Interesting. Arista would never have thought him capable of deceit.

"I was thinking we could make a little deal. I could help you do whatever else you need to do, and you could spare my life."

"They will send another."

"And I'll make another deal."

"Why would you propose such an offer?"

"Let's just say I'd like to see my mother and brother lose, once in a while."

Arista nodded slowly. In any other circumstance, she might have been reluctant to form an alliance with a man so quick to betray his own mother. Considering that his mother had hired an assassin to eliminate this same son, Arista had to acknowledge that the chance of an abiding love existing between the two was minimal. Where there was no trust, there could be no affection—and certainly less loyalty.

It appeared that Venero, unlike many other mortals, understood his mother's true nature and adjusted his own course accordingly.

His offer was so logical that it fed Arista's admiration all the same.

She leaned close to him and lowered her voice. "I am to retrieve the ShadowCaster. Do you know where it can be found?"

His eyes widened briefly. "Not too ambitious, are you?"

"What has my ambition to do with this assignment?"

"Nothing. It's just an expression."

"Meaning what?"

"That the ShadowCaster is probably the most prized possession in my mother's treasury. She won't relinquish it easily."

"I am prepared to die to fulfill my mission."

"You should be so lucky," he replied, though Arista could make no sense of that. He stared into the night, fingers tapping on the stone balustrade. "Does your Starpod respond to a remote summons?"

"Of course."

"Then here's what we're going to do. Tomorrow, I'll propose a celebratory tour for you to witness the gathering of the harvest, since the terms of the treaty have been agreed. We'll go without an entourage, using your Starpod, and work our way toward the Citadel."

"Should I know of this place?"

"It's built over the Queen's Grotto, which is my mother's treasury. Will you be able to identify the ShadowCaster when you see it?"

"Of course."

"Good, because the Grotto is crowded. We'll have mechanical issues with the Starpod—"

"It's performance is flawless."

He flicked her a look that she understood to mean she should be quiet. "We'll have mechanical issue with the Starpod, leave it to walk for help, then take shelter in a cavern."

"This is most complicated."

"It just might allow us to approach the Citadel without being observed."

"And once in the Grotto?"

"We'll have to play that as best we can." He offered his hand with a smile, and his eyes twinkled in a way that made it difficult for Arista to concentrate on his words. "Do we have a deal?"

CHAPTER TWO

WHEN ARISTA CONFIDED HER second quest to Venero, the Hive was shocked for the first time in eons. What a breach of protocol and programming! It would have been clever if she had accepted his offer in order to fulfill both quests, but the Hive could see that the notion was not even within her list of possibilities.

She truly meant to keep the wager.

Would she do it? Or would her programming triumph over this new mutation in her code at the last moment? The Hive's decision to review android reports as sequential memories, presenting events in order of their occurrence, was proving to be less than ideal in this case. Never before had the Hive doubted the end result, but Arista compelled a reconsideration of the design.

The pair used the Starpod and departed alone together. Doubtless there was no protest to the unconventional arrangements because the queen meant to facilitate the demise of her son. Arista's reaction to Venero grew stronger with every passing moment. The Hive calculated the prince's effect upon Arista to be increasing at a rate of seven and a half per cent per solar day. The treacherous germ of arousal grew until it overwhelmed her programming and calculation of sustainable risk. The Hive noted how concern for Venero infected all of Arista's decisions.

Yet she did not perceive it.

Or when she did become aware of its influence on her thinking, she concocted an explanation that shouldn't have persuaded her of her course as well as it did.

She recorded a confession in her *memoria*, that small device carried by so many of the Warrior Maidens, so filled with emotion that the Hive was certain her reaction must be feigned.

That treacherous arousal culminated in Arista's confession of love and an offering of her body. Such intimacy on such terms defied every expectation, even if she used the popular mortal justification of feeling love.

An android, even one of such skillful construction, could not feel love. The Hive was certain of it.

She'd even allowed Venero to witness the ritual painting of her body, a Cumaen tradition, before entering battle. It appeared that no barriers remained between them. What strategic advantage did Arista hope to gain with such a concession? Or was her programming completely corrupted?

The Hive was transfixed.

Then shocked once more when Venero politely declined.

How dare this mere mortal find Arista, the prime product of the Hive, to be less than adequate! The Hive would have eliminated Venero in that moment for showing such disrespect for a vastly superior life form.

Arista, however, did not.

The infection wasn't contained or halted, either. It was a curious phenomenon, to be sure.

Would it destroy her?

NO MATTER HOW LONG she considered Venero's decision, Arista could make no sense of it. Why had he declined the pleasure she'd offered to him?

Why hadn't she taken advantage of yet another opportunity to kill him?

She might have argued that she had permitted him to live and even made an alliance with him in order to have his assistance in reaching the Citadel where the ShadowCaster was stored. At this point, though, she was close to the Citadel and not in need of guidance.

She could have argued that she had need of his experience in order to procure the ShadowCaster from the Grotto, but he didn't know what it looked like. She alone would have to identify it. He readily admitted that he had little advice for what would happen within the Grotto.

She could have killed him that very morning, but instead, she had watched him sleep, her heart aching to touch him.

To caress him.

To try to change his mind. She might have tried if the probability ratio had not been determined to be zero.

There was no chance of Venero loving her. But why not?

She puzzled over it, even after he awakened and they began the last of their journey. By his calculations, which she saw no reason to question, their quest would be completed by the setting of the sun this day, one way or the other.

Would either or both of her quests be completed?

They were in the tunnel that led to the Citadel, and Arista knew her opportunity to ask him for an explanation was rapidly slipping away. They had progressed in virtual silence since he had awakened, and he walked ahead of her.

She cleared her throat. "Will there be spies at this proximity?"

"Probably not yet." Venero glanced back. "Why?"

"Because I would talk to you, if we will not be overheard."

"Chances are pretty slim, at least until we emerge from the tunnel. There will probably be a sentinel there, but we've quite a way to go yet."

"Thus will not be detected."

"Exactly. Are you going to tell me why you're after the ShadowCaster?"

"That would be a violation of my directive."

"And telling me your objective wasn't?"

Arista frowned, finding herself at a loss. Rather than exploring that, she asked her own question. "Why did you refuse me?"

Venero stopped then, and when he turned, there was no humor in his expression. "I told you. Because I don't love you."

"But conjugal relations are possible without love. In fact, I understood that most men preferred to enjoy such pleasures without the possibility of a long-term commitment."

"Maybe they do."

"But you do not?"

His gaze flicked over her. "Not this time."

He would have continued walking, but Arista needed more of an answer. "I don't understand. We are physically compatible in terms of height and size. I'm not without an understanding of how to give and receive pleasure." Venero started to smile, which she took as encouragement. "We share a prowess with weapons and neither of us are unattractive. Why not this time?"

"Well, you *are* assigned to kill me."

"But I have not acted upon that."

"True. You could be biding your time, trying to win my trust."

"Because I have not." Arista noted that he didn't dispute that. "You don't trust me. This is why you refuse to be intimate with me."

"Exactly."

"But you slept in my presence this morning."

"Did I?" His gaze was level and she realized he had fooled her.

How could that be?

"You were awake?"

"I was awake. I'm surprised you didn't take your chance." He considered her for a long moment. "Why didn't you?"

"Because I love you."

He nodded once and turned around to continue, as if their conversation was at an end.

"Why don't you trust me? What have I done, other than arrive on that mission, to encourage your suspicion?"

"It's enough, isn't it?"

"If you truly distrusted me, you wouldn't have offered to show me to the Citadel. It would be illogical to ensure that we were alone together..."

"Where there were no witnesses."

"You planned to kill me!"

"Only if you tried to fulfill your mission." He shrugged. "It's only logical, isn't it?"

Arista narrowed her eyes. She thought he made a jest but she didn't understand his humor this time any more than the others. His manner reminded her of Gemma, who liked to tease, even though Arista never fully understood that either. She had learned to watch Gemma closely in order to guess with reasonable accuracy as to whether her friend was making a joke. Venero was much harder to read, probably because she'd had less time to observe him.

"Do you tease me?" she dared to ask, and he laughed out loud.

"Maybe a little. You're so serious, Arista. I can't stand the temptation."

"But you can withstand all other temptation I offer." She trudged onward beside him, feeling that her feet were as heavy as her heart. It was nonsense, of course. All weights were precisely as they had been at her creation. "Do you love another?"

"No."

"Are you betrothed or promised to another?"

"No."

"Are your tastes inclined to those other than women?"

He laughed again. "No!"

"Then why? Why not me?"

"You're insulted."

"I'm trying to understand."

He seemed to think about that for a long moment, then nodded as if he made a decision. "I suppose the truth won't hurt." His gaze collided with hers. "Because you're an android."

Arista was surprised by his assertion. He was guessing. He couldn't know. She didn't know why he would venture such a guess, but that was a matter to consider later. "You don't know what you're talking about," she protested and forced a laugh. Venero didn't smile.

"I know exactly what I'm talking about. You're an android, and that means you can't love me, because you're incapable of feeling the emotion. And that means you must have had another reason for making such a confession, and that means that I'll sleep once our ways have parted for good." He nodded, then strode on, walking more quickly than he had before.

Arista stared after him. "You truly don't trust me."

"I told you that already."

She hurried to catch up. "Maybe you're wrong."

"I'm not wrong." He was resolute. "Just because the probabilities are long against something doesn't mean its impossible. You're an android, a good one, but a machine nonetheless."

Arista was insulted to be called a machine. "How could you know such a thing? No one *ever* knows!"

"That's the easy part. What did you dream last night, Arista?"

She opened her mouth to confess that she never dreamed, then saw the understanding in his eyes.

"Exactly," he whispered. "All biological life forms dream."

"But how did you know whether I did?"

"I'm my mother's son," was all he said by way of explanation. Arista asked for more detail but Venero refused to answer her. It wasn't long until he held up a finger, indicating that they should be silent because the end of the tunnel was near.

It wasn't rational to love a man who could not—or did not—love her in return, but Arista couldn't get rid of the feeling.

She considered the possible outcomes of their assault upon the Grotto and found them lower than would have been ideal. There was a seventy per cent chance that either she or Venero would die and never leave the Grotto. There was a fifty-two per cent chance that they both would die there.

How could that be? Did Venero mean to betray her? If she had not loved him, she might have thought so, but Arista didn't believe he would do such a thing. The probability was still calculated to be thirty per cent, but Arista didn't accept it. There had to be an error in the computation.

She marveled quietly at her own reaction, knowing she had never before questioned the probability calculations she was programmed to constantly perform.

Then she considered the alternatives. The queen must have anticipated their arrival and prepared for it. How had she known? Arista couldn't be certain. Someone else could have betrayed them. Someone could have noted their departure from the capital city and their failure to keep to the stated schedule of reviewing the crops together.

Then she remembered what he'd said.

"You dreamed of our quest," she said, so quietly that the words were the barest breath between them. "And your mother heard your dream."

Venero's smile was rueful. "She doesn't always need spies."

"You knew I didn't dream because you have the same power."

"Not quite. She gathers dreams. I send them. But you couldn't receive one, because you don't dream."

"When did you first know?"

"In Regalia. The first night you were there." Venero sighed. "Although to be fair, it was your fighting skill that made me wonder."

"I let you strike me."

"Yet you didn't respond immediately when I did."

Arista's true nature had been revealed by her own inability to feel pain. She had always thought it a good thing, but now considered that if they were successful, she would ask the Hive to consider modifications to her sensory input.

"How do we proceed?" she asked, knowing that she meant more than the quest itself.

"We get in to the Grotto. You take the ShadowCaster. Then we try to get out alive."

"It's a thin plan."

He smiled. "I prefer to think of it as flexible." He winked, irrationally playful in such a serious moment, then continued with a purpose that Arista couldn't explain.

Venero was right in one matter, though. The ShadowCaster must be retrieved. That was her primary objective. She wouldn't consider the second one, not yet.

Arista didn't even want to consider the ramifications of failing even once. She was quite certain she had never done it before, but felt no anticipation of a novel experience.

BECAUSE I LOVE YOU.

The Hive felt a shudder in its processors when Arista uttered the words aloud, never mind that she spoke with such conviction. The Hive had been certain that she was simply using a familiar idiom to express the change in her feelings, but now, it wondered. The Hive tabulated and calculated, but couldn't be certain.

Mortals said that actions spoke louder than words.

The Hive liked conclusive tests.

The truth would be revealed by Arista's reactions in the Grotto.

ARISTA CONSIDERED THE prospects of success as they walked the last increment of the tunnel.

"Surely, even if the queen isn't in residence, this repository of her treasures should be guarded?" she asked.

"There are other ways to defend a prize than with fighting men," Venero replied.

Arista would have asked for a specific list of what other powers his mother possessed, but Venero turned to her and lowered his voice. "Once we get into the Grotto, ignore me and find the ShadowCaster." He winced. "If we're challenged, I'll try to buy you some time."

"You're assuming she will confront us."

He was more serious than she'd ever seen him. "It's my mother's treasury."

The probabilities were spinning in Arista's mind, and the chances of success were steadily dropping. She frowned, not wanting to say anything.

"You must be calculating the chances of survival," Venero guessed. "Isn't that what you're programmed to do?"

"Yes." It was a great relief to admit the truth to someone.

"How does it look?"

"Bad."

He nodded, not apparently surprised. "Add this to your calculation: I'm going to distract her by giving her the chance to kill me herself."

Arista blinked. If he was sincere, the probabilities of her survival would leap considerably. Of course, the queen would demand the return of the assassin's fee she'd paid to Cumae if she ensured Venero's demise herself, but if Arista returned with the ShadowCaster, she would not be blamed for a failure.

Still, the prospect of Venero sacrificing himself for her quest troubled her. There must be some facet of his plan that she didn't understand. "Why would you do that?"

"You'll laugh if I tell you."

"I assure you that I won't."

That smile returned, all too briefly. "No, I guess you wouldn't." Venero frowned. "There is a prophecy that if and when my mother gains a clear vision of the future, she will be invincible. That's why she wanted the ShadowCaster."

"But she has it already. If this prophecy is true, then we walk into certain failure."

Venero wagged a finger. "Only if she's learned to use the ShadowCaster. I did some research on them. There's quite a lot of literature, even though they're supposed to be extinct. Maybe because they're said to be extinct. Lots of speculation, that can't be proved or disproved."

"I understand."

"One common theme, though, is that the ShadowCaster can't be controlled. That it shows what it wishes to show of the future, or sometimes doesn't show anything at all. There's a lot of speculation as to why it makes those choices, too, but I'm wondering whether she really can use it effectively."

"She anticipated my arrival."

"Because she arranged it."

"What if she is invincible?"

"Then we'll lose, but I'm willing to take the risk."

"That is illogical, in the face of no other supporting evidence." Arista, though, recognized the valor that the Hive had discussed with her before. That trait often encouraged mortal warriors to take risks on instinct—another quality that eluded quantification and replication—and frequently led to success, against long odds.

"It's not illogical. If my mother and brother continue to run Regalia as they have, it has no future, whether the planet crashes into the sun or not. The people have no hope. We're completely reliant upon Incendium for any trade that we manage to have. We should have our own star station, our own fleet, and our own university."

"Have you proposed this?"

He laughed. "As soon as I returned from my schooling on Advocia. I was exiled for three years for my audacity."

"To where?"

"Sylvawyld. A planet in our system even more undeveloped than Regalia. My mother said it would give me an appreciation for the simpler things in life."

"Did it?"

"It taught me to keep my ideas to myself," he acknowledged grimly. "But she's wrong, and something has to change. If you succeed in taking the ShadowCaster and escaping from Regalia, then she'll have a setback and this kingdom might have a chance of becoming more than a backward corner of the galaxy." He met her gaze steadily. "Get the ShadowCaster, Arista. Help give Regalia a better future."

It was the first time he'd used her name and the sound gave Arista enormous pleasure. She felt a glow inside herself, one that couldn't be explained by faulty circuitry, and a new sense of purpose.

"You are competition to your brother Urbanus," she said, realizing the import of his words. "Do the people prefer you to him?"

Venero laughed. "Did the people you met seem happy with their current administration?"

"No. Many appealed to you to intercede on their behalf."

"Because I think of them and their future. My brother thinks of himself and his own, just like my mother. Go ahead and calculate the reaction of the common man to that."

"It isn't a sufficiently complicated question to merit such computation."

"Exactly." He nodded, his gaze scanning the plain. "If I have to die to get the ShadowCaster off Regalia, it's worth it. It'll give them a chance." Arista admired his concern for the inhabitants of the planet, but he didn't linger to discuss it further. "Let's go."

SOON ENOUGH, ARISTA stood beside Venero in the shadows that lurked inside the opening to the tunnel. It was just barely dawn, and the valley before them was shrouded in fog. A dark spire of stone pointed at the sky, its base obscured, and Arista knew it had to be the Citadel. It was strikingly dark in contrast to the fog and the overcast sky. A narrow ribbon of road led up the slope to the gate, and she could see a smaller tower guarding the road. A broad slow river was beyond the watchtower, the bridge on that road being the only visible way to cross it. Behind the Citadel, the mountains rose in high jagged peaks, a dusting of snow on their summits, ensuring its defense from the rear.

A pennant emblazoned with the royal insignia hung limply from the highest tower.

"She's here?" Arista asked quietly.

"Apparently."

"Did she anticipate us?"

He frowned, his gaze moving restlessly over the scene before them. "Maybe."

Even with the fog, Arista could see that the parapet bristled with armed soldiers. There would be archers hidden in their ranks, and the gate was both barred and defended.

Slipping into the Citadel unobserved didn't appear to be an option.

"How do we get in?" she asked as Venero gathered his belongings with purpose.

To her surprise, that unruly twinkle was in his eyes again. "Easy. We knock."

Before she could ask, he strode out of the cave and marched down the path on this side of the mountain spur. He made no attempt to hide but swaggered and even whistled. She watched the ripple pass through the ranks of the guards as Venero was noticed, and spied more than one crossbow raised.

Venero waved and shouted cheerfully. "Hello! I hope you have a hot meal for a weary prince!" He turned back and beckoned to Arista. "And, of course, an even more weary diplomat. Can we not change her notion of

Regalian hospitality?"

The bows were lowered.

The gates began to rise.

But Venero had already begun to bound down the hill, showing complete confidence in his welcome. Arista tried to echo his manner, though her confidence was considerably less.

Her chance of success—capture of the ShadowCaster, escape from the Citadel and from Regalia, a safe return to Cumae—had, however, just increased by 10 per cent.

What troubled her was that the probability of Venero's demise had also increased to eight-three per cent.

QUEEN ARCANA WELCOMED them into her smaller audience chamber. To Venero's relief, none of his brothers were visibly present. The table had been set for four, with the stuffed relic of her dead pavofel perched at one of the places.

Venero stifled a shudder.

"I see that you're not surprised by our arrival, Mother."

"You are as an open book to me, Venero," she purred.

"I hoped at least some of the pages stick together," he joked and his mother gave him a thin smile.

"Cling to that," she murmured beneath her breath. She then offered a beringed hand to Arista, who bowed and kissed her knuckles. "I do apologize for the inconvenience you have experienced on this visit. My son sometimes errs in his planning, as a result of his enthusiasm."

"I have delighted in the opportunity to see more of Regalia."

Arcana arched a brow. "Even on foot?"

"Walking is good exercise, and one has a better view of flora and fauna at closer proximity. Your son's hospitality has been complete. I regret only the malfunction of my Starpod, and that it should occur so far from assistance."

"Maybe you planned it, Mother," Venero dared to say, ensuring that his tone was teasing. "The better to have a chance to speak privately with our guest before her departure."

Arcana granted him a glittering look and gestured him to the place opposite the dead pavofel. Venero had the fleeting thought that she meant for it to keep an eye on him.

Just the way it used to. He could remember how it watched him, just waiting for an opportunity to attack.

He shivered and took his place, sparing a glance at the monstrosity at the opposite place. Had he seen the creature blink?

Were its eyes really glass?

Arcana had already slipped into her seat. She invited Arista to sit down and partake of the meal. There was a roasted bird of some kind—it smelled delicious—and the wine was the best of Regalia. Venero had always found it tart after his time on Advocia, but he sipped politely and felt the jolt of the alcohol.

He must be a little dehydrated after their journey through the mountain. His mother was watching him, although she pretended not to, and the pavofel's stare was unnerving. He took another sip and blinked at the strength of the wine.

That gave him the perfect idea of how to proceed.

Venero pushed aside his plate and indicated that his goblet should be filled.

"YOUR UNFORTUNATE ADVENTURE is the result of yet another miscalculation by my son," Arcana said with a shake of her head. Arista noted that the queen gave every impression of being a doting mother, sorely tried by her sons.

Especially Venero.

Arista didn't find that likely. Venero was apparently becoming intoxicated very quickly. Was it possible to become inebriated at such speed? Or was he being drugged? The servant poured wine into all three goblets from the same vessel.

The queen smiled. "I do hope you can forgive us for the inconvenience."

"Of course." At the queen's gesture, Arista raised her glass and sipped. The wine was sour and very strong. She took only a very tiny sip. She would need her full processing capabilities and ability to respond.

"I guessed that you would arrive here when your Starpod disappeared, though you were expected sooner."

That sounded like an accusation and Arista bristled a little. "I apologize, your highness. Had I known that we were anticipated, I should not have lingered to examine so many plants. Regalia is most lush."

"Indeed." The meal was served with ceremony, and Arcana didn't speak until the servants had retreated to the perimeter of the chamber. "And where are you from originally?" she asked. "I apologize that I missed that detail upon your arrival."

Arista spoke with care, as a diplomat should. "My home is on Cumae, although currently I abide wherever the Empire dictates."

"Cumae! I have always wished to visit there. Is it as harshly beautiful as they say?"

"It is a hot planet and not to the preference of all. I confess that much of my fondness for it is due to the memories I have of my training there."

"Of course. But the pavofel is indigenous, is it not?"

"Yes." Arista smiled. "They are treated with more courtesy there than many sentient life forms on other planets."

"I had a pavofel once."

Arista glanced at the stuffed and dead creature. "It appears you have it still." Its fur was well-preserved, the blue and green still as vibrant as it must have been in life. Its tail was long and thick, graced with the peacock eyes for which the species was known. The eyes of this one were golden and had to be glass, but Arista had a disconcerting sense that it was watching them still.

Venero toasted the trophy and drained his goblet.

"Because Vigilo was the most marvelous creature. I adored him and he adored me." Arcana smiled. "He took the most vehement dislike of Venero, though, of all my sons."

"Miserable beast," that prince contributed and his words were slurred.

Was he truly drunk? Or was it a ruse? Arista didn't have to pretend to look alarmed.

Arcana sighed. "A good boy," she whispered. "But possessed of his father's weaknesses."

Arista refrained from comment.

The queen raised her voice. "I said, Venero, that Vigilo never liked you."

"Hated me on sight. Always trying to kill me." Venero tugged at the neck of his chemise, revealing an old scar on his throat.

"Don't be ridiculous. He was just trying to play with you."

Venero snorted and emptied his goblet again. He held it out for more, his hand swaying so that the servant ended up pouring some on his hand and more on the floor. A second servant cleaned up, but Venero waved him off in order to drink more wine.

Arista wondered. Pavofels were known for only remaining in the care of those they chose. Some bonded so strongly with their caregivers that they could anticipate needs, or promote schemes, dreams, and plans. How long had Arcana wished that Venero was dead? She continued to chat with Arcana as the meal progressed, and Venero became steadily more incoherent. By the time sweets were served, the prince had passed out and was snoring, his head on the table.

"I must apologize for my son," Arcana said with disapproval.

"And you must allow for his gracious conduct," Arista said. "We had insufficient water and he insisted that I drink all of it."

Arcana's lips tightened. "I am glad to hear that he showed some grace in the situation." She eyed Arista, then swept to her feet. "You have mentioned the richness of Regalia. Let me show you a curiosity that I treasure."

"I should be honored."

Arista didn't expect the queen to retrieve the item herself, but she did. Queen Arcana left the table, her skirts swishing behind her, and moved to one wall. Her hand swept over the surface of the wall, and she must have touched a concealed spring, for a small door opened to reveal a hidden receptacle. Within it reposed a vessel, which Arcana recognized as that of the ShadowCaster.

Queen Arcana cradled it in her hands as she walked back to the table, and her eyes were alight with pleasure. She paused before Arista. "Do you know what this is?"

Arista saw no advantage to lying. "It looks like the images I have seen of ShadowCasters, but I believe they are extinct. Is this a dead one preserved?" She decided not to refer to the pavofel, and instead peered at the dark, motionless worm at the bottom of the vessel. "Or is it a replica?"

"It is said to be a live one."

Arista let her expression show surprise. "What a marvel! What good fortune you have."

Queen Arcana laughed. "I have the fortune I make." She gave the vessel a shake. "This creature, however, might as well be dead. I can't rouse it at all." Her glittering gaze locked with Arista's. "Do you know anything of such creatures? I had hoped that someone from farther afield might have some advice to offer."

"I know little of them," Arista admitted. "I have more than enough to study when it comes to known life forms in the galaxy." She put out her hand, ensuring that her biological responses were those of a calm and mildly curious individual. "May I see it more closely? I doubt I will ever see one again, dead or alive."

The vessel was surrendered to her.

The creature didn't move.

Arista leaned closer to peer at it, then rose to move to the window, as if seeking brighter light. She felt Arcana rise to follow her and heard the movement of the queen's skirts. Arista pretended to be consumed with the puzzle of the ShadowCaster, even as the queen approached. She turned the transparent vessel as if examining the still creature from all angles and surreptitiously summoned her Starpod.

"Well?" Arcana asked from close beside her.

Arista was aware that Venero's eyes were open. The servants had retreated to the far side of the chamber, their expressions carefully neutral.

"You speak correctly. It looks to have died." Arista smiled. "How unfortunate. But still, it is a treasure for its curiosity alone. I doubt that there are any others that can be so observed." She made to return the vessel to the queen, knowing that Arcana had done so to see if the ShadowCaster would respond to her. "I thank you for showing it to me."

"It is but one of the many marvels of Regalia," that monarch said smoothly. She stepped forward with eagerness and reached for her prize, clearly still believing that it lived and might one day use its powers to her benefit.

Arista wondered how the queen could be confident of the creature's survival, then Venero's fingers closed around the knife beside his plate on the table. She held tightly to the vessel, knowing that things were going to happen very quickly.

CHAPTER THREE

VENERO WAITED UNTIL HIS mother was convinced that the ShadowCaster was so close to returning to her possession that there could be no doubt of her losing it.

He was less drunk than he appeared to be, but less sober than he would have liked. When caught in a corner, a man had to work with the possibilities—though, truly, Venero hoped he did survive the inevitable fight, if only to avoid having Regalian wine as the last taste on his tongue.

There were only three servants in the hall, though undoubtedly many more within earshot. Venero knew from experience that even though they waited at table, they would be also armed as guards. He had to believe that Arista had summoned her Starpod and that it would arrive quickly.

He watched as Arista offered the vessel.

He saw his mother reach for it.

He gripped the knife left at his place at the table.

Arista gave no sign of having seen him take it, but the dead pavofel emitted a sound much like a mewl.

It was the first to go. Venero slashed its head from its body. Shaved wood stuffing fell in all directions and the glass eyes rolled. He crushed them both under his boots as he spun to his feet. He drew his sword and spun on the first servant, who had already drawn a dagger. Venero sliced him from groin to gullet. He fell and Venero flung the knife into the eye of the second. That man tumbled over the first, gripping his bleeding eye. The third backed away warily and dropped his dagger. He pivoted then and ran.

It wouldn't be long before the other guards arrived.

Venero glanced back to see Arista and his mother wrestling over the vessel containing the ShadowCaster, and knew who would win that.

At least until his mother started to murmur beneath her breath.

Arista kicked her hard, spun, and leaped to the window sill.

"Guards!" His mother shouted from her knees even as they burst through the door. The chamber was invaded by a veritable army and Venero saw more than one load his crossbow.

Arista glanced back, then stepped off the sill. A flurry of bolts and arrows followed her, sticking into the mortar and flying out the window in her wake.

"No!" Arcana cried and raced to the window. She clutched the sill and peered over it, and Venero had time to fear that Arista had been hit.

Then a Starpod buzzed the tower, flying so close that the remaining dishes rattled on the table. The guards shoved past his mother and fired out the window, but he saw the contrail as Arista's ship flew high. His mother raged in protest even as Venero grinned. He saw that flash of silver disappear into the blue of the sky, then a boom as Arista broke the sound barrier.

She'd done it.

He didn't have time to feel triumphant, though. Instead he felt the point of a knife in his back, and heard his twin brother's voice in his ear. "Venero, Venero, what are we going to do with you?" Urbanus mused.

Arcana spun, her eyes blazing with fury and advanced upon him. Her smile wasn't reassuring in the least, but Venero didn't care. He'd foiled her this time, and somehow, he'd foil them both again.

First, though, they'd make him pay.

Venero had no doubt of that.

IN THE STARPOD HIGH above Regalia, Arista set the navigational computer to take her back to Cumae. Then she watched the display of Regalia fading from view, a painful ache in her chest.

She knew Venero had sacrificed himself to see the ShadowCaster taken away from his mother and the queen's plans foiled.

She knew it would have been an insult, if not a waste of his sacrifice, to have stayed behind to fight for his survival. She had calculated the possibility of his disappointment in her if she remained to fight and fought it a solid one hundred per cent. She would have been honored to have died in battle alongside him, but she could not have endured his disappointment with her for failing to take the opportunity he offered.

Arista knew she had done what Venero wanted, but she felt tears on her own cheeks as she watched Regalia become smaller and smaller. She would never see him again. She had failed to ensure his welfare in her absence. She had loved and lost, and it hurt far more than any injury she'd ever endured before.

TREACHEROUS.

Enchanting, exciting, but treacherous.

The Hive could not consider a better term for Arista's unanticipated development.

It had been thrilling when the biomechanics had developed to the point of androids feeling emotions, rather than just emulating them in a predictable fashion, then expressing them in the preferred idiom of their assigned culture.

It had been intriguing when Arista felt arousal for Venero.

But *love*. Love! Love was a much higher level of functionality. And tears! There could be no doubt of Arista's feelings.

This was a triumph.

This was the culmination of so much work.

As triumphant as the Hive might be in this achievement, the complications could not be ignored. Even in such early stages, even when the love was not returned, it was clear that Arista's sense of purpose had been compromised by the development of this emotion.

She had abandoned one part of her quest by not even attempting to kill Venero as ordered. And in the last moment of her escape, she had considered the merit of abandoning her mission to be with him.

Even though she knew that doing so would most likely mean dying with him. That she could consider death with a beloved to be desirable at all was deeply irrational.

The prospect of such mutiny in a previously loyal and reliable android was terrifying.

The Hive calculated the change in probable outcome if Arista's love had been reciprocated by Venero, and found the result completely unacceptable.

By rote, the Hive reviewed its own carefully constructed mandate, the one that drove all android research development on Cumae. Androids were created to flawlessly execute assignments. There could be no doubt and no question of the reaction of any android in the field. There could be no chance of one being captured and dissected. The mandate was flawless.

But the addition of emotions to Arista's powers had introduced the potential for flawed choices.

Love was an indulgence the Hive could not afford.

But still, the Hive had made a promise to Arista before this debrief. With any other android, such a promise might have been discarded in the face of new information. It wasn't so much that Arista was a favorite— choosing among the Hive's creations would have been whimsical—but that she was unique among the androids the Hive had created. Her subroutines were mutating at a rapid and somewhat unpredictable pace. The Hive was loath to lose all possibility of continuing the experiment.

Would she know if the promise wasn't kept?

The Hive did not know.

The Hive didn't like that there was no clear answer projected in its probabilities.

Arista had confided a great deal in the recording made on her *memoria* and hidden in the painted cave. This had also been an irrational act, but it was done.

Was there any chance of the *memoria* being found?

A *memoria* could only be opened by the Sword Sister of the owner. The Hive computed the probabilities of Gemma, Princess of Incendium, being on Regalia to be reasonable. Regalia and Incendium were the two planets in one star system, after all, and there were diplomatic relations between them. In fact, it was likely that at least one of the daughters of Incendium's royal family would be married to a son of Regalia's royal family.

The probabilities of Gemma being in that cave and finding the *memoria* hidden there were, however, extraordinarily low. That made perfect sense. If she visited Regalia, Gemma would be at one of the palaces and surrounded by courtiers. She would be attending a wedding, or participating in one, not hiking through Regalia's lower hemisphere in solitude.

That there was any possibility of Gemma's finding the *memoria* at all was puzzling.

Was Arista's irrationality infectious? Had the download of her memories of Regalia disrupted the Hive's own circuits?

There had to be another way to verify the possibilities for the future.

The Hive considered all tools at its disposal and was reminded of the newest addition: the ShadowCaster that Arista had retrieved from Regalia. The Hive was skeptical of it, as the Hive tended to be of the reasoning powers of all biological forms, but it might provide another perspective. Cumae had, after all, been paid a considerable fee for its retrieval, and would receive a second, larger, payment upon delivery.

Surely, no one would know if the Hive consulted it first?

It might not even respond to the Hive, if its abilities were linked to the presence of biological organisms.

That such an exercise might provide more data for the Hive's own calculations—and that it probably wouldn't be detected—made consulting the ShadowCaster the only reasonable choice to make.

THE SHADOWCASTER WAS a strange creature, unlike any biological form the Hive had ever observed. There was no good match in the considerable banks of files. It resembled a black millipede and was coiled around the base of the vessel that contained it, but the match was seven per cent. The Hive could not discern why. It looked like a black millipede. What was hidden that the Hive couldn't perceive?

It was motionless. Was it dead?

Or did it only animate in response to the presence of others?

The Hive placed the vessel containing the ShadowCaster in a sealed chamber, the better to monitor its activity. It emanated no signs of life. There was no pulse. The vessel contained a typical mix of hydrogen and oxygen. There was, however, no sign of oxygen being consumed or carbon dioxide being created, or even the reverse. The ShadowCaster did not photosynthesize.

Had it died?

Was it an android developed by another race? The Hive found this notion improbable but attractive. Perhaps it didn't actually predict the future, but merely calculated probabilities of the occurrence of various incidents and chose the most likely one. The Hive would have respected that.

But it looked dead. The readings all indicated that it was dead.

The Hive considered the possibility that the presence of a biological life form might be required in order for the ShadowCaster to forecast the future. Perhaps it used the energy from a biological organism to give itself power, like the Sangins of Umbra. Was it true that the ShadowCaster had failed—or refused—to animate in Arcana's presence? Perhaps it responded to the thoughts and concerns of a biological organism and remained inert without a stimulus, like the Anima of Meditorra.

The Hive had begun to assess where a volunteer of biological origin might be located and how quickly it could be brought to the Hive—as well as the risk to the Hive of such a visit—when a ripple passed through the ShadowCaster.

It reared up, as if standing on its hindmost legs, and stretched the length of the vessel. The monitors revealed that it suddenly had a pulse and appeared to be consuming oxygen. The Hive was intrigued. It clearly had a resting phase that allowed it to be perceived to be dead. Had it in fact died? If so, what had revived it?

The ShadowCaster undulated as the Hive's questions populated and methods of inquiry were developed. It pushed against the vessel as if to protest against its confinement, and as the Hive monitored the escalating rate of all bio measures, it grew wings.

It defied every probability of behavior, which meant it had to be closely observed. The Hive was already recording every nuance of the ShadowCaster's reaction, but more computing capacity was added.

The ShadowCaster's wings batted against the interior of the vessel, then morphed into claws. It scratched on the interior of the lid that sealed the vessel, and the readings redoubled.

It wanted out.

If it couldn't leave the vessel alone, then it could be controlled. The Hive reviewed myths and stories of powerful creatures being given their freedom and the price they demanded, but the defenses of the chamber couldn't be overlooked. The Hive sealed the chamber in the interest of continuing the experiment. It could, if need be, fill the chamber with toxic or numbing gas to compel the creature to return to its vessel. The Hive could also lock down the chamber, sealing it for all eternity.

The chance of escape was very low.

The opportunity to learn more potentially useful information was very high.

The Hive extended robotic arms and opened the vessel with care. The ShadowCaster seemed to explode from the container and immediately became so large that it filled the chamber.

This was so improbable as to be impossible. The Hive watched with fascination. The ShadowCaster became a dark swirl. The Hive's memory banks found a comparable image in metal filings being pulled into place by a magnet, or a murmuration of dark birds in flight.

Would it create an image?

No. It created a shadow, a dark depiction that moved as if it were real. The Hive perceived that each dark dot was a possibility. They adhered together, as if certain possibilities gathered strength, then the largest one filled the chamber and presented a possibility to the Hive.

The most probable outcome for the future as calculated by the ShadowCaster.

The Hive watched, transfixed, as the creature showed Princess Gemma finding Arista's *memoria* and opening it, proving that a low probability did not make an event impossible.

The image was obscured, then reformed.

The Hive was then shown the assassination of Arista, here on Cumae. The sight didn't surprise the Hive, for by its own calculations, the chances of Arista surviving her successful theft of this item from Regalia were very low. If anything, the fact that the ShadowCaster had come to the same conclusion as the Hive confirmed the veracity of its vision or calculations.

The Hive tested this comparison by choosing to keep Arista within the Hive indefinitely, thereby protecting her from harm. The Hive's own calculations showed that her demise would be delayed, not avoided, by this tactic. The ShadowCaster projected the same result.

It would be a set-back to the Hive's development, but not a fatal one. After all, everything Arista knew had already been downloaded to the

Hive's servers. The Hive could isolate the code that had allowed her to fall in love and dissect it, perhaps using only a small part of it in another android...

The Hive had assumed that the ShadowCaster's predictions were complete, but the dark dots assembled each other into a recognizable image again. The Hive saw the vessel containing the ShadowCaster and noted that it depicted itself as a dead black millipede within that vessel. The Hive saw that the vessel pass from the hand of one man to another. The recipient's hand closed around the vessel, then changed to a dragon claw. The vessel disappeared into his grip and the dragon spread his wings.

It was King Ouros of Incendium. The Hive easily matched the image to established vid images of the king.

King Ouros took flight, splendid in his dragon form of blue and gold, and circled over a palace, which the Hive pattern-matched to that of the palace in Incendium's capital. He soared high over the city, then landed on the roof of an old building. The computers matched it to a site known as the University for Royal Astrology. A group of men in robes awaited the king's arrival and bowed deeply at the sight of him. The Hive noted their smiles when the king offered the ShadowCaster, and felt the relief that slid through their ranks when the vessel was in the grasp of their leader.

The image swirled once more, becoming a dark cloud, then diving into the vessel with startling speed. Once again, it appeared that there was a dead black millipede at the bottom of the vessel.

The Hive returned the stopper to the vessel.

The ShadowCaster projected that it would go to Incendium, as a gift to the king. The Hive retrieved the recording of the last portent, considering the hand of the man who delivered the vessel.

He had a ring on his thumb, with a tattoo beneath it. The Hive didn't have to seek a match on that image. It was immediately identified, because the Hive had built that hand. It belonged to Acion, an simpler model of android that had performed admirably and consistently in the secret ranks of Cumae's mercenaries-for-hire.

How susceptible were the Hive's androids to this new code propagated within Arista's bio-electronic brain? If the Hive was to send an android to Incendium on a quest, there was an opportunity to investigate this further.

The Hive then tabulated an array of possible responses to this new information and the possible plans. It had decided upon a course of action by the time the healing tank chimed that Arista's repairs were complete.

ARISTA AWAKENED IN THE tank, as she had hundreds of times before, and was burdened by grief. Venero had been revealed and probably was dead. He'd never tease anyone again.

Relief then flooded her circuits. She *remembered* Venero, and the sensation of being in love.

The Hive had kept its promise.

Why?

Would this gift come at a price?

Arista climbed out of the tank, unplugged her processor from the Hive, and wiped down her body.

"Love," mused the Hive, that voice coming from everywhere and nowhere. "How interesting a development."

"Is it?"

"I'm not certain you realize, Arista, that you are a prototype in many ways. Your programming was modified to include the first efforts at provoking emotion in the reactions of Cumae's androids."

Arista did not know that, and she felt some resentment that so much of her programming was hidden from her. "When did this start?"

"Many years ago. Such a program must be monitored closely and introduced in increments. One interesting side effect has been that you aren't readily identified as an android by other life forms."

Arista wondered whether other life forms—like Gemma—thought differently than she did, or felt differently.

"It was the plan to imitate the valor that gives great warriors a strength beyond expectation," continued the Hive. "As has so often been the case, you have excelled in this experiment, even without knowing what has been changed in your subroutines. You have forged a new path for androids, Arista, and your legacy will endure long."

Arista paused in the act of dressing herself. "A legacy is defined as being left by one who has died. I didn't think I could die."

"You can't die naturally, of course. You can be decommissioned."

Arista caught her breath.

"You can also be killed."

She continued to don her clothes, hoping her annoyance didn't show—and knowing that it did. "Surely the probability of that is very low, given my training."

"It should be, yes." The Hive paused and Arista straightened.

"What aren't you telling me?"

"You surely know that your theft of the ShadowCaster cannot go unchallenged by the royal family of Regalia. They will hire an assassin to retrieve the vessel and end your life. If that assassin fails, they will hire another. Such is the depth of their commitment to vengeance and to the repossession of the ShadowCaster."

The implication of this confession was clear to Arista. "You want me to permit this to happen."

"Your next assignment is to lure this assassin, whoever he or she may prove to be, and ensure that the quest to kill you is long. If you succumb too quickly, a trick will be suspected. If you survive multiple attempts, their pursuit will only be renewed and continue. It may become reckless, putting others at risk. You must find a balance, allowing the kill to occur and ensuring that they perceive it was as hard-won as anticipated."

Arista wanted to defy the Hive, but she didn't say as much aloud. She tugged on her boots with more force than was necessary and knew her reaction had been noted.

"You must see, Arista, that this is the most logical outcome."

"I do not."

"Your subroutine has gone rogue. It puts you at risk, as well as any others who must do battle with you. This is unacceptable. You can be reprogrammed, but that subroutine and your feelings for Prince Venero will be eliminated."

"No," Arista said.

"You can be decommissioned, but that will not stop the assassins from coming to hunt you."

Arista felt her lips thin. "Or I can allow myself to be assassinated."

"And lie, with your dying breath, about the location of the ShadowCaster."

"Why would I do that? The telling of falsehoods is irrational..."

"Not if it protects someone else."

Arista considered the walls with their monitors and sensors. "What do you mean?"

"If you cannot be found, they will turn their attention upon the one person who might know more of your location."

"Venero," Arista whispered.

"The probability is calculated to be very high that he will be tortured to force his confession, in the absence of your death."

"How high?" Arista whispered.

"Ninety-seven point two per cent. So long as he is believed to know something, he will be permitted to live. Biological organisms, unfortunately, lack the ability to deliver their memories once they have ceased to live. It is a great flaw in their design."

"And if I die?"

"If you die, if you are killed by the assassin hired by those in Regalia, if you lie about the location of the ShadowCaster, then the probability of him being so abused drops to sixty-nine point three."

"He still won't be safe."

"His safety is not entirely in your hands, Arista. The calculation is very complicated."

"What is the most likely outcome?"

"That he will be suffered to live but imprisoned."

"It's not enough," she whispered.

The Hive made a sound like a person clearing his throat. "You can improve the probabilities significantly by making and sending a gift to Princess Gemma."

Arista looked up. "I don't understand."

"Neither do I," the Hive confessed. "Not completely. The calculations become very shadowy, but it is evident that if you create an android for Gemma that she takes as a companion, one that is programmed to kill Queen Arcana, then Venero's probability for a long life rises to ninety-two percent."

"Because once Arcana is dead, the quest for the ShadowCaster will end, because the prophecy can't be fulfilled."

"Precisely. Somewhat irrational, but a verifiable calculation all the same."

Relief filled Arista and her decision was made. She couldn't be with Venero and she understood that. She wanted to ensure his longevity and happiness, though, and this was a small price to pay.

"What is the lie I'll tell about the ShadowCaster?"

"That it died, or that it escaped. It seems improbable that anyone would believe such a valuable creature had been willfully destroyed. I leave the choice to you."

That was new. "Why?"

"Because you probably have a better understanding of what Queen Arcana would find plausible." A screen appeared on one wall, and an image was displayed. Arista watched as the ShadowCaster moved for the first time since she had seen it. She caught her breath when it changed and gasped aloud at the way it increased in size once the vessel was opened. She saw the way it flowed and swirled and knew that a normal chamber wouldn't have contained it. The image terminated then, and she knew the Hive was keeping the ShadowCaster's predictions from her.

"It escaped," she said. "Just like that. I opened the vessel, believing it to be dead, and lost it."

"An excellent and plausible story. Where did you open the vessel?"

"Here on Cumae. As soon as I returned." Arista sought a compelling explanation for such disobedience of a direct order. "I was curious and I knew that once I delivered it, as assigned, I would never see it again."

"Excellent. Everyone is curious about the future. And the android for Princess Gemma?"

"A pavofel," Arista said. "She'd never take a warrior by her side, not one other than me. She doesn't trust androids, either."

"Intriguing."

"But a pet. She would keep a pet. She always admired the pavofels here. She thought they were beautiful."

"And Queen Arcana has an affection for them, as well. Excellent. The pavofel android will be programmed to seek out the queen."

Arista was obliged to admit her shortcoming. "But I don't know how to make an android, much less to program one."

"You have only to ask for help, Arista."

Yes. The Hive knew everything about making androids. "It will have to have a bit of that subroutine for emotion," she dared to suggest.

"I think a small increment of your affection for Gemma would be sufficient, and it would not interfere in the complete execution of the android's programming."

"Maybe I'll leave more than one legacy," Arista said.

The Hive's circuits hummed as it calculated, and she thought there was pleasure in its voice when it replied. "Undoubtedly, you will."

ACION OBEYED THE SUMMONS to the Vault, even though he wasn't due for maintenance or report. His systems had been recently updated, and he hadn't sustained any injuries. Still, there was no question of disobeying a directive.

He made his way to the Vault, passing through the twisted corridors that led deep into Cumae. He had developed a new probability game and indulged himself with it as he progressed through the various check points and security barriers.

Why had the Hive summoned him?

There was zero possibility that he needed repair.

There was a three per cent probability that there was a small augmentation to be made to his systems. Although he'd had all of his major updates installed recently, there could be a patch. The Hive wasn't fond of patches, though, and tended to favor complete updates, thus the low chance of this option.

There was a four per cent chance that he had to make an interim report, perhaps because he had been an inadvertent witness to the mission of another android, or because his observations could provide necessary intelligence. That would have been calculated based upon his location. Acion calculated the possibility to be small because he'd only been training with the Warrior Maidens, and not with the newer recruits. They were often of interest to the Hive, given their recent arrival, but the warriors who were further advanced seldom had much new to contribute to the Hive's data collection.

He passed Arista when he was close to the core and stood aside for her, inclining his head as a gesture of respect for her superior military position. She barely acknowledged his presence, so intent was she on continuing her course.

It was only after she was out of sight that Acion considered how unusual it was to encounter anyone in the corridors leading to the Vault. The Hive usually ensured as much.

This led him to the inevitable conclusion that the Hive had wanted him to encounter Arista—the possibility of the Hive making an error was so low as to be nonexistent. Why? Acion knew that Arista was a more sophisticated android than himself. He knew that she was assigned quests off-planet.

He had insufficient data to calculate the probability of his being granted such an assignment, but it was included on his list of potential outcomes when the door of the debrief room closed behind him. Given that list, Acion couldn't explain that he'd been ushered into this room, with its tank and port.

He bowed, though there was no focal point in the room. "Reporting as commanded."

"As promptly as ever," said the Hive, approval in its tone. "Do you know why you were summoned, Acion?"

"No. All probabilities return single digit calculations."

"I have a question for you."

Acion waited.

"You passed Arista."

"I did."

"And surely that introduced a possibility to your calculations."

Acion considered the increasing probability of his being granted an assignment. "I detect no question."

"Your experience qualifies you to undertake an assignment off-planet, but your systems will have to be upgraded first."

Perhaps the Hive used patches to software for those androids traveling off-planet. It was a definite possibility, but outside of Acion's experience so he couldn't verify it. "I am prepared to serve," he said.

"Of course. As far as those on Cumae know, you will be dispatched very shortly on this assignment. In reality, you will spend a considerable measure of time here first, being prepared."

"For those upgrades," Acion said.

"Yes. One required upgrade is still in development and not yet perfected. In most circumstances, its installment would not be justified, however, this situation would provide an excellent test of its limits and potential."

"I understand."

"No, you don't. It's organic. It will mutate within your systems and will be difficult, if not impossible, to recall. You must agree to this installation, Acion, knowing that if the test fails and the upgrade mutates beyond expectation, you will be decommissioned."

Acion did not hesitate. "I was built to serve," he said and bowed again.

"The installation will require many steps, much observation and a goodly amount of time. Please summon a full report of activities since your last session, as well as a complete schedule of all future obligations." The Hive paused as Acion stripped down and prepared to enter the tank. "Your computing abilities will be different when you leave the tank, Acion."

"I understand."

"No, you don't, but your agreement to be part of this test is welcome."

Acion bowed once more, plugged the cable into the port hidden behind his ear, and stepped into the tank. He lowered himself into it and closed the lid, no thought in his processor other than his need to obey.

That would soon change.

WYVERN'S WARRIOR

A stranger arrives on Incendium in secret, but is intercepted by Princess Thalina when he tries to break into the palace. Thalina knows the mysterious mercenary is more than he pretends to be, so lets him abduct her to uncover his secrets. Acion is seldom surprised, but this dragon princess challenges all of his assumptions—while Thalina's realization that Acion is her destined mate changes her own plans. Can she win the heart this warrior doesn't appear to have—or will Acion be executed for breaking Incendium's law first?

PROLOGUE

GEMMA EXCHANGED HER VOWS with Venero in the palace of Incendium. When they had pledged to each other before the royal family, Kraw brought the great chalice filled with the purple brew for HeartKeepers and Venero drank half, then Gemma drained the cup. Her heart was filled to bursting with joy and the knowledge that Venero's child had already been conceived. They made the long-overdue alliance between the planets of Incendium and Regalia with their vows, and she couldn't wait to see the future they would build.

It wasn't an elaborate wedding with a long list of dignitaries in attendance. Gemma wasn't wearing a magnificent dress, just one of her favorites, and there weren't a dozen attendants in the procession. Her sisters were present, except for Drakina who had gone to Terra with Troy after Gemma's wedding to Urbanus, and Anguissa who was seldom home. Her parents were present, of course, as well as the royal retinue. Kraw beamed at her, as if he were her second father.

Venero's crown had to be secured in Regalia, but they had conceded one day to this celebration. Gemma's father, King Ouros of Incendium, had agreed to provide the troops she requested for the mission to Regalia and insisted upon leaving a sizable portion of them in service there until one year after Venero controlled the throne. Gemma was pleased that her old friend, Farquon, would command the assigned troops and report directly to Gemma and Venero.

Ouros' concession had been hard won. He had protested Gemma's departure for Regalia, fearing for her welfare. She hadn't told him that she'd conceived Venero's child already, but her father could probably smell the change in her scent. It had been her mother, Queen Ignita, who had argued for Gemma's choice, reminding her husband that a bride must make her future by her husband's side.

Gemma and Venero would depart for Regalia with an army the following morning.

Married.

Gemma turned from the chalice to accept congratulations, Venero's hand in hers, and found that a small table was being placed before them. Thalina placed a dark blue box upon the table with such care that Gemma guessed its contents.

"You made another one?" she asked, and Thalina nodded, her pride clear. "And you're giving it to us?"

Thalina nodded, her eyes dancing. "I hope you like it."

"I don't understand," Venero murmured but Gemma smiled at him.

"Thalina has learned to make automatons."

His eyes widened in surprise. "Really? That's impressive."

"And you haven't even seen this one yet," Flammara said.

"Touch the button," Thalina instructed, and Gemma did, pushing the large gold circle on the side closest to her. It looked like a seal, embossed with the insignia of Incendium, but actually was a button. It clicked when she pressed it and she stood back, waiting and watching.

Music began to tinkle. The box spun, then parted at the seams and fell open, revealing its deep orange interior. Nestled inside was a large egg with an iridescent surface, much like the natal egg of a dragon shifter but smaller. This egg was about half the size that Gravitas' egg had been. The patterns on its surface appeared to move, but Gemma looked closer. The surface of the egg had at least three layers, each a different color, the top two punctured in different patterns. The lower two spun in opposite directions, giving the illusion of the changing surface of a natal egg.

Her family caught their breath as one and gathered near to watch. Thalina was clearly brimming with anticipation.

"Wait for it," Flammara said, who must have seen the automaton before.

"Do I have to do anything else?" Gemma asked.

Thalina shook her head. "Let it do what it does."

"And prepare to be amazed," Flammara said.

A crack revealed itself in the surface of the egg, looking as if it started at the summit and spreading downward. Gemma knew the break had to have been designed into the egg's surface, but the illusion was remarkable. Parts of the egg's surface slid down inside the rest of the shell, dropping with irregular timing in an almost perfect echo of Gravitas' hatching.

"I wish Drakina could see this," Gemma whispered, entranced.

"She will, the next time she comes home," Thalina said. "It won't change."

"Part of the beauty of an automaton," Venero said quietly. "It's constant and predictable."

Thalina smiled.

A large piece of shell dropped inside and there was a croak, like the cry of a young dragon. As the rest of the shell dropped to make a kind of nest, wings rose from the interior. They were pale green and leathery, shaped exactly like those of infant dragons. Gemma smiled at the attention to detail—the nail at the tip of the wing was pale and looked soft, as it would on a newborn.

The wings moved slowly at first, then spread outward, as if with dawning confidence. The dragon sheltered inside the wings was revealed, its back studded with gems that caught the light and a line of iridescent feathers down its back. It was green and black and blue, marvelous in its detail. The head of the mechanical dragon lifted and it tipped its head back to make a second, louder cry. Gemma smiled at the red lining of its mouth and the tiny pearls placed like baby teeth.

Its wings beat harder and it rose out of the egg, appearing to stretch for the sky. Its tail coiled beneath its haunches, probably hiding a metal support. The music turned triumphant as a spiral of flame erupted from the dragon's mouth. Gemma realized the flame was a spinning tube of orange glass, artfully shaped. The dragon gave its last final victorious cry before lowering itself into the shell again and sheltering itself beneath its wings. The shell reassembled itself and the box folded up and spun once. The music fell silent when the gift looked as it had upon presentation.

"Well done!" King Ouros cried, leading the applause. He crossed the floor to give Thalina a kiss on the cheek. "You have learned much from Thantos the clockmaker." He shook hands with the beaming older gentleman from the village. Gemma had wondered why he was there. "Thank you, Thantos, for indulging the fascination of my daughter."

"The princess long ago exceeded my skills, your highness. She is a most apt student and might be a master clockmaker herself."

"If she desired a trade, that could be hers," Ouros agreed mildly, and Gemma knew he was thinking that Thalina's future role would be greater than that of a tradesperson.

"I can have a skill without undertaking a trade," Thalina said, a new defiance in her tone. She'd always been the quiet one, but it seemed that triumph had given her new confidence. "And sooner or later, Father, Incendium must embrace reality."

Gemma winced, because she knew her father disliked being challenged before others.

"Scintillon's Law is irrevocable," Ouros said, his tone a little more stern. "And you know it, Thalina."

"It is also twelve hundred years old," Thalina countered. "I would hate for Incendium to become backward and primitive because of a refusal to update our policies."

Their father inhaled and his eyes glittered. "That will never happen, even without androids. Incendium remains in the upper echelons of successful empires."

"For how long?" Thalina challenged.

Father and daughter glared at each other and Gemma cleared her throat.

"Scintillon's Law," she said lightly, turning to Venero. "I assume you know of it?"

"The edict of the first King of Incendium that outlaws androids on any of the planets in the Fiero-Four system, including Incendium and Regalia." Her new husband nodded. "It's well-documented and included on the curriculum of legal courses about androids and cyborgs in the law schools of Advocia."

"So, we're already known to be backward and superstitious by the rest of the galaxy," Thalina said.

"You don't know that superstition was behind Scintillon's choice," Ignita said softly, obviously trying to make peace.

"It can't have been based on experience," Thalina argued. "Not twelve hundred years ago. Making laws based on assumptions and prejudices is backward."

Ouros was remarkably silent about this. In fact, he fired a quelling glance at his wife, one that intrigued Gemma.

"Perhaps not in this case, Thalina," Venero acknowledged. Gemma smiled, knowing he was going to sound like a lawyer. "In terms of statutes, Scintillon's Law has the beauty of simplicity. In outlawing androids, Scintillon ended all discussion of their rights and legal status in Incendium society before such conversation could even begin. They have no status except as illegal entrants, which makes them subject to export or decommission immediately upon identification of their nature." He nodded. "There are societies who find that simplicity enviable and even a mark of foresight."

"Because...?" Ouros invited.

"Because androids have been developed in those twelve hundred years which emulate sentience, and perhaps even possess it," Venero said. "That complicates the distinction between androids and biological organisms in those societies, particularly if the two aren't readily distinguishable."

"They'd have to be caught first," Thalina said.

"Exactly," Venero agreed.

"You mean androids like Arista," Gemma said and her husband nodded.

"Exactly. And where is the line between cyborgs and androids, as well as cyborgs and humans?" Venero mused, sounding even more like a lawyer. "Is the distinction in the original impulse? In the source of the mind governing the organism? In which system is ascendant? Is it in the percentage of the corpus that is biological versus mechanical? How are such questions to be reliably answered in a timely fashion? The questions are complicated, with ramifications that provoke more than a little envy for Incendium's law code."

Thalina rolled her eyes.

King Ouros beamed at this endorsement of his legacy. "And so there should be. We have built an advanced society without such creatures in our midst, are one of the greatest trading empires of the galaxy and one with a standard of living for our citizens in the top percentile. There is much reason for pride in this."

The family began to murmur to each other, and Gemma gave Thalina a kiss. "Thank you so much. It's just wonderful and will have pride of place in our home."

Thalina smiled. "I knew you'd like it."

"You must have been working on it for years," Gemma said."

"I was, but it's a perfect wedding gift, I think."

"It's incredible. You are skilled," Venero said and Gemma watched her sister blush.

"But I want to do more..." Thalina began.

"Don't put yourself on the wrong side of Scintillon's Law," Gemma advised, seeing exactly where her sister's thoughts were headed.

"There's no legal cause or precedent for appeal," Venero reminded her.

Thalina's lips set. "I can't believe you didn't know about Arista," she said to Gemma. "Couldn't you smell that she wasn't human?"

"No. I never guessed," Gemma admitted. "Only Venero knew."

"How?" Thalina asked.

"Because she didn't dream," Venero supplied. "If I hadn't tried to send her a dream, and had the ability to do so in the first place, I wouldn't have known, either."

"And neither of us guessed about Felice," Gemma said.

"Neither did I," Thalina sighed, her gaze fixed on the automaton. "It's amazing that they were so advanced. I wish I'd taken a closer look at your pet when I had the chance." Gemma saw the yearning in her sister's eyes. "I'd love to see an android again," she said softly. "I wouldn't miss a second chance."

"You'd just want to take it apart," Gemma teased.

"I'd want to know whether I could tell its nature," Thalina said, then smiled. "And then I'd want to take it apart." She turned to Ouros and raised her voice. "Will you send me to Cumae, Father? I could train as a Warrior Maiden, the way Gemma did."

"No," Ouros said flatly. "Such a course would be dangerous."

"It wasn't for Gemma!"

"You and Gemma have very different natures," their father said. "Gemma was always skilled at fighting and alert to her circumstance at all times. I knew that she would defend herself well on Cumae, regardless of what happened. You, however, can lose yourself in an intellectual puzzle, showing such focus that everything else in your vicinity becomes irrelevant to you. The same keen attention to detail that allowed you to create this marvel could be perilous to your survival." His brows rose. "And that means, my dear Thalina, that you will remain where I can ensure your protection, until the Carrier of your Seed is revealed. I hope that he proves himself worthy of becoming your HeartKeeper, but if not, you will remain beneath my care."

Thalina frowned, but had no chance to argue.

Their father managed the situation as he often did. He turned and raised his hands to the others, changing the subject in his royal way. "Let us applaud the cleverness of Thalina in creating this automaton and her generosity in giving it to Gemma and Venero as a wedding gift." The family clapped heartily. "Let us thank Thantos for his tutelage and his indulgence of a royal curiosity." The applause grew louder. Ouros turned to gesture at the automaton. "And let us watch this dragon hatch once again, before we descend to the great hall to dine and celebrate the marriage of Gemma and Venero!"

The family hooted and cheered, gathering closer as Gemma pushed the gold button one more time. Her thoughts were spinning, because she understood Thalina's frustration. Maybe she could convince Venero to take a trip outside their system and take Thalina along. Their father might allow Thalina to travel under her sister's protection, and Thalina could satisfy some of her curiosity.

It wasn't the right moment to make such a suggestion, but Gemma would watch and wait for it. She wanted all of her sisters to be as happy as she was, and once she was securely established as Queen of Regalia, she might be able to help to make that happen.

"First things first," Venero whispered, so obviously guessing her thoughts that Gemma smiled at him.

"Don't cheat," she advised.

He held his fingertips to his heart. "And provoke a dragon queen? I'm not that foolish." He caught her close and whispered in her ear. "But I don't need to peek into your thoughts. I know you because I love you. Let's secure our future, then see what we can do." He lifted one brow. "I just might have to go to Advocia for advice."

"I do love you," Gemma said with heat. The newly married pair kissed just as the automaton finished its sequence, much to the delight of the family surrounding them.

CHAPTER ONE

THERE WERE NO DRAGONS on Incendium.

Acion wasn't disappointed because he didn't have the programming for such an emotional reaction. He wasn't surprised, since he didn't have that capacity, either. All the same, he had a sense of something lacking.

That was new, so he analyzed it.

It was a strange awareness, unlike anything he's experienced before. It was so unusual that he couldn't even compare it to anything. (He tried.)

He walked through Incendium's capital city, seeking explanations in his vast datastores.

There was a fifty per cent probability that this reaction was due to the fact that he couldn't add to his log by investigating a life form he hadn't previously encountered. But still, it was illogical that he'd never experienced this sense of lack before. He'd been confronted with such situations many times in the past and had simply awaited new opportunities to add to his log.

There was a ninety-five per cent chance that this new experience was due to the enhanced programming that the Hive had insisted upon installing before Acion's departure on this mission. That would explain its novelty.

The notion satisfied Acion. He calculated a ninety-seven per cent probability that the Hive was testing this new software. That was logical. He existed to serve. Acion gave full rein to his newfound sense of incompletion, knowing that the data from his sensors could only help the Hive to continue to refine androids such as himself.

But where *were* the dragons? Incendium was ruled by a king who was a dragon shifter, who was married to a dragon shifter, and who had twelve dragon shifter daughters. Incendium had a population that was predominantly humanoid, but which also included about seven per cent dragon shifters. This information was in his brief. Given the number of people in Incendium's capital city, Acion found it reasonable that he should have seen at least one dragon. In fact, by his calculations, based on the number of humanoids he'd counted since leaving the starport, he should have seen forty-three.

But he hadn't.

Not one.

Oh, there were dragons on pennants, dragon-shaped jewelry, dragons embroidered on clothing and dragons in shop windows. He paused before one window, that of a clockmaker, his attention caught by a glittering display. The dragon flapped its wings and took flight, circling around a castle tower and breathing fire. The castle was about half Acion's height and the dragon could have sat on his hand.

The children on either side of him were clearly delighted, but Acion didn't understand. The dragon was made of metal. The "fire" was a twisting piece of orange glass, fixed in the dragon's mouth, which spun as the dragon "flew." The dragon was secured to a metal stick, which terminated in a track that circled the castle. It was mechanical and not a real dragon at all.

He considered that as an illusion, it was somewhat lacking. What was the appeal?

The children chattered to each other in their excitement, using the universal galactic tongue. Acion heard an inflection on the vowels, which must be the local variant, but knew he could mimic that well enough.

"Where are the real dragons?" he asked one child.

"You're not from here," the little boy declared, startling Acion with his conviction.

A most unexpected assertion, and one worthy of investigation. "How can you tell?" The boy's reply would help Acion to improve his ability to blend into local society.

Not that he would be on Incendium for long.

"Everyone *knows* they're in the palace," the boy said with scorn and pointed to the castle that loomed over the town. It was built of local stone cut into large blocks and constructed upon a natural hill. Acion knew this from his brief, but found that the actual castle appeared much larger than in the records he'd reviewed. The biggest dragon pennant he'd seen so far snapped in the wind above its high tower. It was deep blue with a golden dragon on it.

He recognized the colors and insignia of the reigning monarch, King Ouros.

High above the tower, Acion could detect the starport of Incendium in low orbit, with shuttles rising to it and descending from it. They appeared as lights in a line, moving slowly up or down. Just hours before, he'd been there himself. He'd rented a Starpod of his own, as instructed, in order to ensure that his own quick departure from Incendium city wasn't hampered and left it at the star station in Incendium city. He estimated that he would be at the port again within 9.4 local hours.

Acion realized the child was still watching him, waiting for a reply.

"Then I'll look there," he said and bowed to the little boy. The brief had said that bowing was important in Incendium society, but Acion's move seemed to amuse the boy. "Thank you for your assistance." Acion turned to stride to the castle.

"Where *are* you from?" the boy called after him, but Acion ignored him.

That data was not available to that individual at that time.

It occurred to him he might have just spoken to a dragon shifter, who had chosen his humanoid form for the moment.

Acion reviewed the information provided to him. The dragon shifters of Incendium came of legal age at eighty-one Incendium years, but there was no clear information as to their age when they gained the ability to shift shape in the first place. He made a notation on the Incendium file in his memory, drawing attention to the missing detail, then continued onward.

What *was* this strange sense he felt? He might call it desire, but it wasn't sexual. He might call it a need, but it wasn't like his body's imperative for food or water or sleep. Acion searched the thesaurus in his databank and found a curiously apt word.

Yearn.

He tried it out. *He yearned to see a dragon.* That sounded true. It sounded right. It *felt* right, which was even more interesting. Acion nodded, satisfied by the Hive's modifications to his programming. What nuance. What subtlety. His reaction was almost organic.

What was the cost of the change? Would his other reactions, the ones that ensured his survival, be compromised?

Acion ran a check of his systems and found all operating at full capacity.

The Hive had called the modifications "enhancements." There was, after all, a ninety-seven per cent probability that Acion and his mission was a test of the effectiveness of these enhancements, whatever they were.

This was as it should be.

Acion existed to serve.

THALINA WAS IN THE CHAMBER deep beneath her father's castle called the Vault, where the security system of the palace was monitored and where the processors were stored.

She was bored.

The processors in question were comparatively large, each being a cube two-hand-spans on a side. Thalina thought them ridiculous clumsy compared to the personal computers they all used, which were thin films that could adhere to any surface. She usually wore hers on the inside of her left forearm. There was no doubting the impressive power of the nine main processors. They controlled all the exits and entrances to the palace, as well as monitoring every window and door, external and internal. There were very few places in the palace that weren't monitored—the royal beds and lavatories were an exception. The processors also automatically backed up the data on every personal film in the palace at short, regular intervals and kept it all forever.

Despite the elegance and efficiency of the system, something was wrong.

Worse, King Ouros had been the one to notice it.

Because Thalina, his third daughter, had always been mechanically inclined, he'd invited her to join him in the chamber for the investigation. She would much rather have gone to the clockmaker in town to check his progress on his newest automaton, but she didn't protest. The new automaton was to be a gift for her father on the anniversary of his coronation, a collaboration between herself and the clockmaker, and intended to be a surprise. She didn't dare even think about it in her father's presence.

Thalina had been to the Vault before, so wasn't particularly interested in its contents. Her tutor had given her a challenge the year before, to identify the means by which an item entered the palace and left it again, so she'd spent a good bit of time in the Vault solving that riddle.

The three guards listened as her father explained the difficulty with his access to the secret passage that led from his personal office to the audience chamber. Ector, the Captain of the Guard, stood before her father, with two of his subordinates ensuring that the recordings in question were displayed at Ouros' command. They reviewed the recorded sequences of the king trying to open and seal the portal that very morning, and checked his access code.

It should have worked.

It hadn't worked.

They reviewed the sequence again and again and again, which showed her father to have been right—again and again and again—an exercise that pleased him enormously. Thalina, in contrast, found her toe tapping.

"Might I look at the gates?" she asked, wanting to have a glimpse of the bustling village instead of this utilitarian little room. One of the lower ranking guards indicated a viewing screen with a bow. "Have the codes changed?" she asked, knowing they must have been.

"On schedule, princess. Of course." The guard entered the new code, and Thalina watched him to memorize it. She had no intention of using it. It was just her nature to collect such information.

The screen was quickly filled with a display from the lowest gate, the one that allowed waste water to flow into the river. It was barred with a portcullis and metal mesh, naturally, which provided no obstacle to the water but a considerable barrier to anything larger than a mouse.

"It appears that the door unlocks then locks again before it can be opened," Ector said to her father.

"Exactly!" Ouros agreed. "This next time, I tried to grab it."

"But even you weren't quick enough, your highness. That is remarkable."

"And the mechanism?" asked another guard.

"It's oiled and perfectly operational, Father," Thalina supplied without turning around. "I checked it yesterday when you first complained about it."

"It seemed slower yesterday," her father explained.

"The issue has to be the computer controlling the latch," Thalina added.

"We shall see about that, princess," said Ector, clearly disliking the implication that any failure originated with the systems he monitored.

Thalina sighed, knowing she'd never be a diplomat. It was better to just be quiet. Definitely simpler. She toggled the display to the next gate. This one led to the small bailey behind the kitchens. Some eggs were being delivered and the cook was arguing over the price. Thalina yawned and moved on.

There were two knights riding through the main gate. The one on the right was rather handsome and looked familiar. Thalina magnified the image. It *was* Thierry, one of her father's favorite champions. A notorious flirt. Her sister Flammara was obsessed with Thierry, and he was audacious enough to encourage that princess's attention. He'd even ridden into tournament with Flammara's colors recently, at the Inter-Galactic Joust on Certamen, much to the disapproval of Ouros. Thalina doubted the flirtation would end well for Thierry if he continued to tempt fate.

Or the king.

She changed the display. Three astrologers were at the queen's gate, a smaller gate on one side of the palace and one that was more discreet. It looked as if one astrologer was Nero, the new arrival who Peri liked so well. Thalina didn't mind him, although she wished he'd hurry up and finish the charts of all the sisters he'd promised to do. That was probably her mother's fault, though. Ignita had appointed Nero to be her own astrologer and probably was monopolizing his time. Nero had an unusual method of casting a chart, one that gave different results and one that annoyed the senior members of the Royal College of Astrology like Astrum. Thalina liked him for that alone. He said he could chart when and where each princess would meet her HeartKeeper, which was enough to spark the curiosity of all the princesses, Thalina included.

She toggled the display. A merchant at the viceroy's door, looking for payment. Kraw was greeting him politely, so it was all routine. She yawned again and moved to the next portal.

And straightened. There was nothing routine about the man knocking at the main portal for admission. Thalina had never seen a man like him. It wasn't the way he was dressed, for he wore a white shirt with a dark tabard, dark chausses and dark boots like pretty much every other man in Incendium. His cape was plain and dark but looked heavy and warm. He didn't wear a hat and his head was shaved bald, which was unusual.

But best of all, he was tall and broad-shouldered, built strong like the warriors in her father's employ. Thalina guessed he was all muscle and a good fighter. There was something agile about his movements and she liked the glint in his eyes. He wasn't dumb, like many of the tournament fighters.

Like Thierry.

A very feminine bit of Thalina was intrigued.

Maybe he was a mercenary.

"I have a gift for the king," he said to the porter, his deep voice devoid of inflection. "I will present it to him."

"The frack you will," the guard on duty there muttered, probably not realizing his words would be picked up by the monitoring system. He raised his voice. "I will require your identification and credentials, good visitor, before you can be admitted to the palace."

The arrival tugged off his gloves and offered his left hand, which had a screen embedded in the palm. How interesting. He probably wasn't from Incendium or another planet in the Fiero-Four system because such augmentations were suspect—given Scintillon's Law—and unfashionable. Thalina magnified the screen for a better look and managed to read the displayed words as they flashed.

His name was Acion.

He was from Cumae.

He closed his hand as the guard verified his information.

Cumae? Gemma had trained on Cumae and her best friend there and Sword Sister, Arista, had actually been an android. Gemma hadn't guessed, which said a great deal about the sophistication of the android in question.

Thalina was sure that Arista had fellow androids. No maker could create an android that sophisticated without having made more before.

Or even after.

Now that Acion had removed his gloves, Thalina glimpsed a blue tattoo under the silver ring on his right thumb. She tried to magnify the image to get a better look at the tattoo, but the movement of his hands and the ring obscured it.

Thalina changed the magnification to focus on Acion's face. His expression was bland, but his gaze was flicking. He had to be looking at the guard, the gate, the security measures. His eyes moved too quickly for a human.

Thalina felt a flutter of excitement.

Was his body augmented? Was he a cyborg?

Or was he another android?

Either way, Thalina wanted a better look at him and his functionality.

What was the gift he'd brought for her father? Could she meet him to collect it?

Thalina's plan died quickly with the guard's response to Acion.

"I am sorry, good visitor, but your credentials are incomplete. You will not be admitted to the palace, but you are welcome to leave any token intended for the king."

Those eyes narrowed. They were dark, filled with mystery. "It will be given to him?"

"It will be examined and, if deemed fitting, will be presented to the king."

Acion's voice hardened. "Deemed fitting by whom?"

Thalina smiled at his correct grammar, which enforced her theory that he might be an android.

"By his majesty's staff, of course."

"I calculate a forty-seven per cent chance that the gift will not actually be delivered. That is too high."

The sentry bristled. "Well, that depends upon what it is, doesn't it? No one will deliver anything to his majesty that might be deemed perilous..."

"Even words can be perilous," Acion declared, startling the guard to silence. "It is my instruction to deliver the gift to the king's own hand. If I cannot pass to do so, then I will depart."

"You will not pass."

Acion bowed. "Then I wish you good day." He pivoted and strode away, disappearing into the crowd. Thalina heard the sentry give a sigh of relief when Acion was out of sight.

She couldn't believe he'd give up on his assignment as easily as that. He'd come from Cumae, which wasn't an easy journey. Cumae was one of the planets closest to Incendium but there was a meteor cluster between the two.

"Come, Thalina," her father said from behind her, clearly unaware of what she'd seen. "Let us leave the puzzle in capable hands."

Thalina rose and blocked the view of the screen she was watching from her father. The more detail kept from Ouros the better, especially when she was launching a scheme. "I would linger a little longer, Father. You know how the Vault fascinates me."

Ouros, perhaps predictably, wasn't fooled. He eyed his daughter and she feared he could read her thoughts. "The others call you trustworthy because you keep their secrets close," he rumbled. "But your mother and I both know that you keep your own secrets even closer." He raised a hand when she might have argued. "Do not be foolish, Thalina, and I will be content."

"Yes, Father. Thank you, Father."

Ouros had barely left the Vault when Thalina spun back to the display. The three guards were determined to resolve the issue of the lock as quickly as possible. One was dispatched by Ector to check the mechanism again. The second ran a diagnostic test and Ector himself began to tap instructions into a console.

No one was watching Thalina.

Acion wouldn't come back to the same gate, she reasoned. He wouldn't go to another obvious gate, either, because he'd assume that they were all centrally monitored. He might even know that for sure. He might try to enter the palace through a window, but that wouldn't be easily done either. Most of them were very high in the walls, higher than two men, for that very reason.

No, he'd use the river exit. She had to assume he had a means to remove the grate or would find one. Thalina put the display of the sewer grate on the largest display.

She didn't have to wait long before a familiar figure came striding through the river water to the grill. The water was thigh-high for him and moving swiftly, but it presented no obstacle. She thrilled at the sight of his strength and purpose. He cut a direct path from the opposite bank to the grill. His gaze flicked upward, and Thalina guessed he had scheduled his emergence from the forest to coincide with the guards turning away. He was probably timing his progress.

His eyes glittered as he stepped into the shadow of the arch over the grill. Again, Thalina saw that his gaze was moving quickly as he gathered details. Too quickly. So, his vision was augmented like his left palm. What else? He surveyed the grill and its stone surround. She knew when he spotted the monitor because he seized it with his gloved hand. Thalina switched to the back-up feed to watch him pull the feed loose enough to disable it. An alarm might have rung but she overrode the system to ensure its silence.

It wouldn't have been easy to rip the feed from the mortar where it was embedded. His strength in that arm had to be augmented, as well.

Unless he was completely manufactured. The thrilling possibility made Thalina watch him even more intently.

Acion waited, then arched a brow that there wasn't an alarm. Thalina smiled as he waited a little longer, and guessed that he was calculating the best way to continue. He removed his left glove and flicked the end of his index finger with his thumb. The tip lifted, like a hinged lid, revealing a tiny hidden saw. Sparks flew as he cut the grill free from the rock around it. It must have been a powerful little saw, for it made quick work of the metal bars.

Thalina caught her breath at the sight of that improvement. With each revelation, her conviction that he was an android increased.

"Wait," Ector said, but Thalina lifted a hand to silence him. She felt him and his companion come to stand behind her.

"I'll take care of it," she said with authority.

"But, princess..."

"He has a mission. I want to know what it is before he's stopped."

"But..."

"That is a command," Thalina said, interrupting the Captain of the Guard as firmly as her father might do. "You will not tell my father until my investigation is complete."

She was aware of their consternation but ignored it for the moment.

She was more interested in the way Acion bent half of the grill back, folding it against the other half as if it were more insubstantial than it was. Her companions gasped.

"That's impossible," said Ector.

"Not for him," she said softly, watching so intently that she didn't want to blink.

"Surely we should sound an alarm..."

"Surely you believe a dragon shifter can deter an intruder," Thalina said, rising to her feet.

"You shouldn't engage, princess. He might overpower you..."

"And I will fry him if he does."

The guards fell silent at that.

Thalina tapped up a map of the lowest level of the palace. She indicated the secured barriers to the Vault and tapped the screen to have more barriers lowered silently into place. "You can see that I've isolated him into this warren of passages. It will take him a bit of time to realize that all the ends are blinds and that there's no way to progress."

"But the Hoard is there," Ector protested.

"And more than adequately defended," Thalina argued. "This region is the best choice, given his location. If he moves beyond it, others could be endangered."

Ector's lips thinned. "And once he realized he's trapped? Look at his strength!"

"I'll confront him before then." Thalina indicated the largest chamber, which was an empty storeroom. "I will interrogate him here. You will listen for my command to secure the door once I have him inside, and will block all monitoring."

She turned to face them, seeing rebellion in their eyes. She stood tall and used her most commanding voice. "He won't surrender the secret of his mission easily. I suspect he may be an android."

"Then he'll be destroyed," Ector said.

"But first, we should determine why he is here," Thalina said. She spoke quickly, wanting to put her plan in motion before they thought of many objections. This would likely be her only opportunity to investigate such a creature, whether he was cyborg or android, and she wasn't going to miss it. "If I'm right, he'll prefer to self-destruct rather than betray his maker. The interrogation may be brutal, so there must be no evidence of it. Do you understand?"

They glanced at each other, then bowed in unison. "Yes, princess."

"You will secure the portals for one day and one night to allow for my interrogation. Then I will either deliver him or his remains to your custody."

Ector cleared his throat. "And what shall we tell your father if asked about your whereabouts, princess?"

"That I've gone to solve a riddle, of course." Thalina smiled, waited for their bow of agreement, then strode out of the Vault.

Fortunately, she'd dressed simply on this day. Acion might be convinced that she was just a serving maid. If he wasn't certain, he might account any discrepancies to local variation. Thalina found a basket on her way to the lower storerooms and, even better, an abandoned apron. She braided her hair and rubbed some dirt on her face and hands, securing doors behind herself as she hastened downward. She lit a candle before entering the secured warren where Acion had been contained.

The door sealed behind her, just as planned. She stifled a shiver, knowing she was locked into a small maze with this powerful intruder.

Was he an android? How much would she be able to investigate?

The air had become colder as she descended and Thalina could smell the river. She couldn't hear the activities of the palace any more, or the bustle of the town. There was only the silence of stone, and the faint sound of the flowing river. Her heart began to pound in anticipation of the challenge ahead.

That was before she approached the last corner, heard the stealthy step of the intruder, and smelled the Seed.

The Seed! The scent of it sent a surge through Thalina, one that weakened her knees with sexual desire and filled her very blood with longing. She leaned back against the wall, still out of sight, to recover from its assault. She then savored her body's reaction to that scent. It was just as she had been told. Powerful. Intoxicating. Wonderful.

There was no one else at this level of the palace, which meant that the intruder was the Carrier of her Seed.

Thalina closed her eyes to savor that. The revelation changed everything.

Acion's interrogation was going to be even more interesting than she'd anticipated.

The prospect was enough to make her dizzy. Her every fantasy come true.

Thalina doubted Acion knew that he carried the Seed.

She wasn't even sure how it was possible, although its scent made it difficult for her to reason clearly. She supposed an android could only be a receptacle for the seed, or a delivery mechanism, while a cyborg could be a true Carrier of the Seed, depending upon the specifics of his nature. Could either be her HeartKeeper? Not an android, certainly. A cyborg? It would depend on what parts of him had been replaced.

That just gave her more to investigate and explore. Thalina would have a gift from Acion before he left Incendium, in addition to relieving him of whatever token he had brought the king.

ACION HEARD THE WOMAN before he saw her. There was a bend in the passageway ahead of him and she was around the corner but out of his view. A light shone around the corner, and it flickered, leading him to the conclusion that she carried a candle. By the sound of the step, he assessed the probability of her gender and affirmed his theory by her scent.

Young. Mortal. Female.

Aroused.

That detail was definitely against the probabilities. Perhaps she liked the darkness. Perhaps she came to meet a lover secretly. Acion found this probable until he discerned that there were no other persons within the vicinity.

She was perhaps twenty paces away.

She was alone, in the lowest level of the palace. He smelled dirt on her skin, as well as a trace of perspiration. She sighed audibly and put something down. It didn't sound heavy.

A servant? That was the most likely scenario.

Acion eased closer and peeked around the corner. She was pretty and slender, with fair skin and brown hair pulled back in a braid. She sighed as if tired and looked about herself with a futility that Acion associated with those compelled to perform menial tasks. Her basket was empty and he calculated the probability to be very high—eighty-six per cent—that these rooms were used for storage.

If she'd been sent to fetch something, why was she aroused? The juxtaposition couldn't be resolved to Acion's satisfaction so he attributed the detail to some irrational quirk in her nature. Perhaps she found cellars exciting. Desire was often irrational in his experience.

The important detail was that she would have free rein to at least part of the palace and a knowledge of its design.

He would take advantage of the opportunity presented. She would be his assistant, willing or not.

She turned her back upon him, as unaware of his presence as he expected, and opened a door. Her candle didn't cast much light within the room, which meant it might be large. She bent to pick up the basket before entering the room and Acion took advantage of her inattention.

He moved like a flash of lightning, grabbing her and locking a hand over her mouth. She made a little cry of surprise and dropped both candle and basket. The candle rolled on the ground and Acion stepped on it, extinguishing the flame. She fought him, so Acion carried her into the storeroom, pinning her against the wall as he kicked the door closed, sealing them in darkness.

She was slender but sweetly curved, and his body responded to having her in his embrace. Acion frowned, because the complication of a physical reaction at this time was unnecessary, unprecedented, and illogical.

His mission was of greatest importance.

"You will help me reach the king," he whispered into her ear. "Or I will break your neck. The chance of you dying after sustaining such an injury is high, but it increases to one hundred per cent if I abandon you and you aren't found. I *will* abandon you, and I will ensure you aren't found. Do you understand?"

She caught her breath, then nodded. The sign of her vulnerability made him want to recant his threat, which made no sense.

Acion knew he sounded more stern when he continued. "And you will not reveal me. Do you understand?"

She nodded again.

There was a risk that she might trick him, but Acion calculated it to be so small as to be irrelevant. She was at a serious disadvantage. They were alone and he was both larger and stronger than her. He did not find it likely that anyone would hear her, even if she screamed, he could not sense the presence of another person, and he could certainly fulfill his threat to her and be prepared for an assault before it could arrive. If she *was* meeting a lover and that individual wasn't nearby, that person had to arrive, to find her and to battle Acion, which surely was a losing proposition.

The situation was almost ideal.

So, Acion released the serving maid—which is what she had to be—only to discover that his calculations had omitted one very important variable.

CHAPTER TWO

THE MAID DIDN'T SCREAM or surrender meekly.

She fought.

And she fought well.

In fact, she battled Acion with a strength disproportionate to her size.

Acion took a strike to the face before he could evade her quick fist. He grabbed at her, but she ducked, spinning into the darkened chamber like a whirlwind. She was either bold or foolish to move in such darkness! Or perhaps she was familiar with the room's contents. He tapped his right temple, turning on the light embedded in his brow, and something quickened within him at the sight of her.

She was crouched, her eyes glittering, her hands raised. Her hair was coming loose from her braid, as if it moved of its own volition. If he'd been more fanciful than it was possible for an android to be, he might have seen flames light in her eyes. But that was impossible, so he knew it had to be a trick.

The chamber, to his surprise, was empty. Why had she entered it? Acion could find no reasonable explanation.

Even as he considered this, he moved swiftly, striking three blows in rapid succession, but pulling back slightly before connecting with her. He needed to capture her, not injure or incapacitate her. She was no good to him dead. She was smaller than him, female, and undoubtedly more fragile, yet blocked his blows with unexpected ease. In fact, she attacked him, with no regard for ensuring that he wasn't injured. He defended himself, a little less easily than might have been ideal, and recognized that he was hampered by his need to avoid hurting her.

She took advantage of his choice, kicking him hard in the gut, then striking at his brow so hard with the heel of her hand that the light was smashed. Acion stumbled backward, amazed that she could hit with such power.

She struck like a warrior, as well, not slapping or scratching as women without military training often did. Her moves were decisive and clean, so forceful that it took him a moment to realize that she meant to disable but not kill him. Acion took a kick to the gut and dropped to one knee, assessing.

She was absurdly fast.

The conclusion was inevitable: she was an android, as well.

His processors spun, drawing data from his brief and comparing it with the furious fighting skills of the woman. There were officially no androids on Incendium, which was an odd detail, but that didn't mean there weren't any secretly on the planet.

Like himself.

If there were androids being developed and trained secretly, learning more about her would provide useful information to the Hive.

If there were androids infiltrating Incendium society for some other purpose, learning more about this one would provide useful information to the Hive.

Acion existed to serve.

He immediately decided to let her win. She wanted to subdue him, which meant she had a plan—and learning the details of that plan would tell Acion a great deal about her programming. She lunged at him, driving two fingers hard into his throat, a point of vulnerability for men, and he was assured that she didn't know the truth of his nature.

Acion fell, as a man would.

How would she explain the broken light in his brow? Would she conclude he was a cyborg? That seemed probable, especially when he took the blow like a man.

Acion made it look as if he hit his head on the floor and let his body go limp. He turned on all of his sensors, determined to gather as much data as he could.

She leaned over him, still poised to fight. She had a light as well, because Acion saw its illumination through his eyelids but he didn't open his eyes to look. She surveyed him. She checked that he was breathing.

Then, to his astonishment, she touched her lips to his, a gesture of intimacy that sent a strange fire through his body.

"Mine," she whispered, her claim giving him a strange thrill. She then seized his ankle and dragged him from the chamber back into the corridor, once again showing that remarkable strength.

Where was she taking him? What would she do with him once they reached their destination? Would she take him closer to the royal chambers? Would she present him as a prize to the king? Or was she a spy of some kind?

Why claim him as her own? That and her kiss hinted at a more private conquest, although there was no telling what sexual practices were common on Incendium. Those details were lacking from his brief, much to Acion's annoyance. He found incomplete information caused unnecessary inefficiencies and it was unlike the Hive to be sloppy.

The details must not be known.

Or not available to him at this time.

The woman dragged him, her ability to do so despite his considerable weight only buttressing to the probability of his conclusion. Acion tabulated to the best of his abilities, but her destination, once he recognized what it was, astonished him all the same.

"THE PRINCESS HAS ABANDONED her own plan," Ector said to his subordinate, Salvon, knowing his concern was clear.

"Women can be impulsive," Salvon replied. They watched the security display together, their uncertainty palpable. "She *did* command that we not tell the king of her activities."

"But her welfare is our responsibility. Why would she change the plan?"

Salvon caught his breath as the princess flung down her prize at the end of the corridor. She approached the barred door there with its glowing lock and raised one hand.

The Hoard.

"She wouldn't," whispered Salvon in horror. Princess Thalina gave the command and the door to the Hoard slid open. Both men winced.

"She is," corrected Ector. "I must tell the king."

THE SEED HAD A POWER that Thalina hadn't anticipated. Its scent awakened her senses, fed her desire, and made it impossible to think of anything other than mating with Acion. It awakened a desire to possess that was so primal and overwhelming that Thalina was shocked. It gave her a strength beyond her usual abilities, as well, and a sense of invincibility.

There was no question of denying its demand.

She'd known that Acion's reaction would be quick, and she had hoped that hers was quicker. Against a non-shifting mortal, she knew she'd be faster—against a cyborg or android, she wasn't sure. The uncertainty had added a little more spice to their first fight.

But he had let her win. Thalina was curious about that choice, but glad of it. She didn't want to shift shape in his presence, not yet. She didn't want to reveal all of her secrets.

Not until she had the Seed.

The Seed changed her plan, too. She wouldn't claim him in a dirty storage room in the bowels of the palace. That deed deserved dignity and honor. Cleanliness and comfort. She didn't dare take him to her chambers without knowing what threat he posed to her father or family, if any. There was only one place close enough that would suffice. She hauled his weight to the entry to her father's treasury, commanded the portal to open, and smiled as the armored interior was revealed.

The Hoard was a fortress. The walls were of the strongest metal known to their kind. The doors couldn't be forced open, and the chamber could be defended from within. The treasury had been built as a safe room and sanctuary, a last place to defend in the case of the worst siege. It dated from the era of Scintillon himself and was the oldest part of the palace, though it had been buttressed as the palace had been built around it.

No one would be able to interfere.

And Acion wouldn't be able to escape.

Thalina dragged him into the Hoard, knowing that she would be pursued and soon. The guards would be too late, though. She was in. She laid her hand upon the panel beside the door for her print to be scanned.

"Secure portal," she commanded and the doors closed. A sequence of hidden latches clicked in rapid succession.

They were safe, at least until Ouros commanded the portal to open. There was no door in Incendium that could be barred against the king.

She should be quick.

"Illuminate," Thalina commanded and torches sprang to light around the perimeter of the room. They were mounted in the walls, well above Thalina's head in her human form, and powered by a crystal generator buried beneath the floor. The lights and the generator itself warmed the floor, taking the chill of stone from the refuge.

The chamber of the Hoard was round and of considerable size, built to accommodate the dimensions of the royal family in their dragon forms. No earlier King of Incendium had had as many children as Ouros, and Thalina had to admit that it would be a bit cramped for her and her eleven sisters as well as their parents to take refuge in the Hoard, if they had all assumed their dragon forms.

The Hoard held the sum of Ouros' treasury, gold and gems and jewels inventoried and stacked behind numbered panels in the walls. Most believed that the wealth of the Hoard was in those material treasures, but Thalina knew better. The more important panels secured information and records.

In the middle of the chamber was a fountain that splashed, providing clean water and a welcome noise, one that disguised the truth of the occupants being essentially buried alive. To one side were stores of foodstuffs, preserved and compressed to provide sufficient nourishment to the family and their retainers for the duration of a long siege. There were couches and tables, games and pastimes, as well as monitors of the world beyond the Hoard. Those monitors were currently dark, and Thalina intended to keep them that way.

"Full defensive mode," Thalina commanded as she tugged Acion to a couch beside the fountain. Plates of metal slid into place over the door, securing them inside, and she felt his interest.

She was glad he was awake.

She then strode to the bank of displays. "Kill monitors and key release to a single word in my voice," she said, turning slightly to watch Acion. "The command that secures Princess Callida's diary will be the word."

Acion's eyes flicked. Thalina knew he was searching his databanks for references, but he wouldn't find that one.

Callida didn't think anyone knew it, and it was only an accident that Thalina did. Her sister would have to be added to the security loop to approve the release, but that was incidental. Thalina needed a word that Acion couldn't possibly know or figure out.

Callida might not be overly inclined to reveal her code word to the security forces of the palace—she'd have to vent frustration with Thalina over the violation of privacy first—but Thalina didn't intend to use the release word soon.

It could take a long time to ensure that she had the Seed.

She wanted at least the day and night that she'd ordered, and wondered if her father would allow it.

She had best begin the seduction soon, not that the scent of the Seed allowed any other possibilities to enter her thoughts. She licked her lips without meaning to do as much, and knew that Acion noted the gesture.

"This is not the agreed protocol," came a voice.

"I've changed it due to an unexpected development."

There was a pause. "Of course, princess," Ector ceded, and she was sure he'd already sent word to her father.

Thalina watched Acion scan the room through narrowed eyes, his gaze lingering for the merest instant on three points. She'd bet that was where the speakers were hidden. "We will secure Princess Callida's assistance in this matter. Portal sealed. Oxygen feeding. Monitors off in three...two...one."

There was an audible click and then silence.

"I know you're awake," Thalina said. "And I know you let me win. Will you tell me why?"

Acion opened his eyes. He sat up and openly surveyed the room, then surveyed her.

Assessed her.

Thalina could almost hear his processors sorting and discarding courses of action.

"This is the Hoard," he said, no question in his voice.

"It is."

"Why would you bring an intruder to the treasury of Incendium?"

"Because it's the one place we can't be easily interrupted."

Their gazes locked and held for a long moment, and she was interested that he didn't ask the obvious question. Instead he stood, then walked toward her with steady steps. Thalina didn't move, but she thrilled at the scent of the Seed drawing near. Her heart was thundering and she wondered if he knew it.

Acion stopped right in front of her, looking and undoubtedly gathering her biometrics. "You are not what you appear to be," he said, without inflection. "It is unlikely that a serving maid would have such authority, although she might know that secret word."

"And you're not what you appear to be," she countered. It was fascinating to watch him gather information and choose his reaction. He was a much more sophisticated device than any of the automatons she'd taken apart to study.

Acion regarded her, his head slightly tilted. It was a good imitation of curiosity, so good that she wondered if he could be curious. "I do not understand your meaning." He gestured to himself. "I am precisely as I appear to be." His voice warmed, as if he sought to gain her trust, and Thalina wasn't fooled.

She braced herself for his move. The scent of the Seed sent a confusing heat through her body and she hoped it didn't slow her reactions too much.

It did. Acion abruptly closed the distance and seized her tightly before she could evade him. His arms locked around her again, and Thalina felt her body respond to his touch once more, long enough that he caught her by surprise.

It took a moment for Thalina to realize that he held a knife at her throat. Interestingly, it was an actual weapon, a knife from his belt, not a device hidden within his fingertips.

"You will aid my escape from this chamber and ensure my access to the palace, whoever you are," he growled into her ear. "Use the release word."

Thalina laughed. "I won't." She felt the tip of the knife move against her throat. She rubbed herself against him a little and was glad to feel his body's reaction. Her new confidence was clear in her tone. "The odds of you injuring me without being certain of my identity is very low, perhaps one in three."

He paused for just an instant, considering that.

Thalina twisted in his grip in that moment, wanting to watch his eyes as he worked through the ramifications.

"You are very sure," he said softly, his face very close to hers.

"Completely sure," Thalina agreed in a whisper. "Because I know that you're not a thief, breaking into the palace, which is what I'd expect of someone who forced entry through a neglected portal. You're certainly not desperate or cornered, and you won't make such a foolish decision as to hurt the one person, maybe the only person, who could help you complete your mission."

His gaze flicked. "My mission?"

"To deliver a gift to the king."

"There is a second security feed," he concluded, no doubt in his tone.

"Of course. Dragons don't like being surprised."

It was a hint but one he didn't take. Thalina wondered if his ability to adapt to new information was being overwhelmed. She doubted it. There must be more variables to consider than she'd realized. "But how could you know my mission?"

"If I saw one security feed, what are the probabilities I would have seen another?"

His eyes narrowed. "Ninety-six per cent." His lips tightened. "The probability that a serving maid would have seen either is negligible. Who are you?"

"Why would I surrender my one advantage so quickly?"

"You would not," he murmured. His grip upon her had loosened slightly.

Thalina pushed the blade of his knife aside with a fingertip. "I think we should negotiate," she said, running a hand over his shoulder. "Are you a cyborg or an android?"

He put a little distance between them, but didn't lower the knife even as he regarded her with new wariness. He certainly didn't answer her question. "Are you one of the fabled sirens of Incendium's marketplace?"

"No, although I'm intrigued that you would ask." Thalina said and stretched to touch her lips to his throat. She could feel his pulse there and the warmth of his skin. "It seems we have a certain urge in common." No matter whether he was augmented or fully android, intimacy might be the best way to investigate his abilities. "Let's make a deal, Acion," she whispered into his ear.

His gaze swept over her again, then lingered on her mouth. "I see no cause to bargain."

"No? Even though the door is sealed forever, without my release command?"

"I could compel you to give it."

Thalina shook her head. "You won't."

"All beings can be persuaded to part with information."

"Not this one."

Their gazes locked again. She liked to watch the automatons work, but this was infinitely better. Was there a way she could see the workings that led him to make decisions? "You are not in a position to barter."

"Neither are you." Thalina decided to provoke him with a guess. "Unless it's your goal to rust away in the darkness here, sealed forever in a chamber designed to provide shelter for years."

"Rust," he echoed, tilting his head again. "A whimsical choice of word."

"Rust," Thalina repeated. She touched his finger, the one with the hinged tip that concealed a tiny saw. "A perfectly apt choice of word for an android." She kissed him below the jaw and saw his throat work. "But you're not just any android, are you, Acion?"

He spun away from her touch then, retreating to pace. He took a deep breath and glared at her when he reached the couch beside the fountain. "You are neither serving maid nor whore. You are not a guard in the king's service. Who are you and what do you desire of me?"

"I want the truth, first of all," Thalina replied. "Tell me why you came to the palace."

"That information is not available to you at this time."

"What gift did you bring the king?"

"That information is not available to anyone at this time."

"Show it to me, then."

He straightened and folded his arms across his chest, looking both formidable and resolute. No machine could appear so enticing. He must be a cyborg. "That request does not cohere with the instructions in my assignment."

Thalina took slow steps toward him, as if she stalked him. She supposed she was stalking him. She liked how avidly he watched her and deliberately took a deep breath, savoring the scent of the Seed. His eyes brightened and she knew he noticed her body's reaction.

"Who sent you?" she asked.

"That information is not available to you at this time."

She stopped in front of him, folding her arms across her chest. She saw him glance down at her cleavage, then swallow. "But here's what I really want to know," she whispered. "How can you be the Carrier of the Seed?"

She'd shocked him. Thalina saw that immediately. He frowned and looked down at her in confusion, then his eyes revealed that he was reviewing the information he had about Incendium. "The Carrier of the

Seed is the man who can impregnate one of the royal dragon shifter princesses of Incendium," he said, as if reciting from a reference source. Thalina supposed that was exactly what he was doing. "This cannot be the case. You are testing my knowledge of Incendium in an attempt to put me at a disadvantage..."

Thalina closed her hand over his erection and he inhaled sharply before he stopped speaking. He was scanning her, seeking the solution to the mystery in her eyes. He was hard in her grip, hard enough that she tingled in anticipation of claiming him. He took a slow breath and she knew he was assessing the magnitude of her arousal.

"You are the Carrier of the Seed," she murmured. "Your sensors are providing evidence of my response to that truth."

His voice dropped to a hoarse whisper. "But that means that you are one of the dragon shifter princesses of Incendium."

Thalina smiled. "It does. It also means that you must be a cyborg, not an android."

His gaze flicked.

Thalina was intrigued. "An android couldn't be the Carrier of the Seed."

Acion ignored her comment. "It is my understanding that dragon shifters cannot deny the opportunity to accept the Seed."

"That is correct."

He nodded slightly, apparently reassured. "So, the wager you would logically propose would be my surrender of the Seed in exchange for my freedom from the Hoard."

"That would be an excellent start." Thalina couldn't resist the urge to tease him a little. "What would you calculate to be the probability of a successful exchange?"

"In excess of ninety-eight per cent," he said immediately. "With some allowance for slight variations in our physical compatibility, coupling abilities, and sexual customs in our respective cultures." Thalina knew her surprise at his precision showed. "I have the necessary programming and physical enhancements for sexual functionality and performed in the top percentile of my class in assessment."

"What benchmarks were used in the assessment?" Thalina asked before she could stop herself.

Acion counted them on his fingers. "Physical dimensions, endurance, technique, variation in technique, adaptability to a partner's needs, and successful simulation of foreplay." He nodded. "That was calculated based on the partner's biometric response."

"And how would you calculate mine right now?"

He studied her with a little frown, then cupped her chin to look into her eyes. "Your pupils are dilated, a sign of arousal in humanoids. I can smell that your labia are wet, an indication of your preparedness for union. Your pulse has accelerated steadily since our enclosure in this room, and your breathing rate has also increased since we have touched each other. Your skin is warm and flushed, a sign of heightened circulation." He ran a hand over her breast. "And the erectile tissue in your nipples is contracted. I would calculate your arousal to be between seven and eight on a scale of ten, with seventy per cent surety."

"Why the seventy per cent?" Thalina asked, hearing that her words were breathless. His touch was sending fire through her veins, undoubtedly because of the vehement call of the Seed.

"I have no data upon the signs of sexual arousal in dragon shifters and am thus assuming that while in the humanoid form, a dragon shifter exhibits similar signs to those found in humans who are not dragon shifters. This is by no means a certainty, though, and my conclusion must be qualified."

"Your assumption is correct."

His brows rose in relief. "Then your arousal must be between seven and eight on a scale of ten." He pursed his lips, clearly confronted by a question.

"What is it?"

"I must consider whether desire is increased in dragon shifters in the same way as in non-shifting humans."

"It is."

He was calculating again, but now there was a small smile curving his lips. "Then I must increase the probability of a successful union."

"And what about your arousal?" Thalina caressed him.

"My arousal remains steady at five on the same scale, an optimal level to provide satisfaction without incurring any unnecessarily impairment of my awareness or responsiveness."

Maybe it was the dragon in Thalina, but that confession made her determined to push Acion's arousal rate past ten on that particular chart.

"Only five?" she purred and he nodded. "Let me see what I can do about that."

ACION WAS INTRIGUED. Not only were there secret androids on Incendium, but this one insisted that she was one of the royal family.

The notion was ridiculous. No princess would be permitted to challenge an intruder without protection. Perhaps he was to provide a test of her functionality. It was remarkable to consider that they might have similar assignments, but when he considered how often androids tested enhancements to their functionality, the prospect was clearly likely.

Perhaps there was a plan to replace the legendary sirens of their market with androids. Such a scheme would undoubtedly improve efficiency in servicing clients seeking sexual pleasure and Acion knew it would diminish biological contamination.

This was a possibility that made sense, more sense than her assertion that he was the Carrier of the Seed. He wasn't a cyborg, and so there couldn't be a biological facet to his nature, such as would be the case if he were the Carrier of the Seed. No, he'd been trapped for a purpose. She'd been determined to capture him but not injure him, so as to avoid damaging his reactions in any way.

He must be her test.

He should mate with her, as she said she desired, and look for verifying signs of her true nature. An android, of course, would not be able to shift shape and become a dragon. This could explain why she hadn't done as much already.

Acion had never mated with an android himself, though he had been used to grant pleasure to various mortal Warrior Maidens of Cumae. This android presented him with yet another opportunity to serve by gathering information.

She was attractive and stimulated his reaction, although he had to admit that much of her appeal was her intelligence. She analyzed in a way that he understood perfectly. She was fearless, as he had been programmed to be. They might have been two sides of the same coin.

He supposed that they were.

A feigned role as one of the dragon shifter princesses would explain her access to the security information. Had she been made to resemble Callida? That was the only princess she had named, and might explain her knowledge of Callida's secret code. Acion launched a subroutine to pull the images of all twelve dragon princesses and compare their features to those of this woman.

Thalina. The conclusion was reached by his facial recognition programming and he verified the result. She certainly resembled the third daughter of King Ouros and Queen Ignita. He would have to continue his investigation to decide why such a course of action had been pursued.

Acion did all of this reasoning by the time Thalina caught his face in her hands, rose to her toes, and touched her lips to his. Acion anticipated a sweet kiss, a gentle beginning to a temperate coupling, but she surprised him. The first touch of her lips was beguiling and left him hungry for more. As soon as he leaned down and caught her around the waist, lifting her against him, her mouth locked over his with unexpected demand. She backed him into the couch, and he stumbled, then fell back upon it. She tumbled atop him, no doubt by design, without breaking her incendiary kiss.

Acion closed his eyes, knowing he had never been kissed with such fervor. He concluded that there was no need to be as gentle as he usually was, not when his partner was as strong as he and unlikely to be injured. He tried to respond in kind to ensure that the test of her abilities was thorough, his need to serve overwhelming all other impulses. She moaned into his mouth and straddled him, the scent of her need feeding his own arousal.

He knew he should have been making observations about the caliber of her programming, the sophistication of her form, the simulation of biological surfaces and reactions. But her tongue was between his teeth, her fingers locked around his head, her breasts crushed against his chest. She kissed him with a savage passion that almost ignited his circuits and certainly drove all calculation from his thoughts. Acion felt as if a fire swept through him, frying all logic and leaving him hungry for more sensation. She wound one leg around his and rubbed her belly against his erection, prompting a reaction that was quicker than any he'd experienced before.

"Kiss me back, Acion," she growled against his throat, even though he was already doing so. The raw need in her voice sent sparks through him. He caught her buttocks in his hands and rolled on top of her, deepening their kiss and pinning her down. He felt a curious sense of satisfaction when she purred with pleasure and grazed his mouth with the edge of her teeth. She ripped open his shirt in her impatience and her hands roved over his skin. The way she touched him was proprietary, as if he was a pleasure slave commanded to serve her, and Acion extrapolated her desire from that.

He kissed her ear, her neck, the hollow of her throat, the ripe perfection of her breast. He lifted her skirts and slid down the length of her to lick her wet sex. She gasped, surprised in her turn, then parted her legs as his mouth closed over her. The attention to detail in her sexual organs was a clear sign to Acion that he had guessed her intended purpose correctly, for he'd never seen an android that so perfectly replicated a woman, in both shape, design, and function. She was gloriously wet and her labia engorged, her clitoris perfectly sensitive.

Acion feasted upon her, holding her hips so that she was captive to his intimate kiss, and monitored her arousal. It was easily nine on that scale of ten when she sat up and seized him, rolling him to his back again as she tore open his chausses. Her hand was locked around him, her hair wild and her cheeks flushed.

He was astonished to note that his own arousal was in excess of seven.

And that was before she climbed atop him like a warrior queen, claiming him and drawing him deep inside her warmth. He faltered for a moment, shaken by the unprecedented wave of pleasure that rolled through him, then she moved her hips, demanding more. She rode him, holding him captive between her thighs and watching as she insisted upon more and more. She tore off her own chemise, giving him a view of her fine breasts, and he couldn't resist the temptation. He reached up, cupping one in each palm, teasing the taut nipples with his thumbs, and was proud of her obvious pleasure. She arched her back and moved with greater speed, her slick heat drawing him deeper within her. Acion found his heart racing, his breath coming quickly, his erection harder than it had even been before.

"Still five?" she asked, then bent and kissed his ear. Her tongue rolled in his ear and he closed his eyes, dizzy at the tumult she awakened in him.

"Almost eight," he admitted.

She clicked her tongue. "The claiming of the Seed merits at least a ten," she chided and he saw the challenge in her eyes.

He assessed her response. "You are almost at ten."

She gave him a wicked smile. "I don't want to be there alone."

Of course, pleasure should be reciprocal to ensure that clients returned for more.

Even so, Acion wasn't certain his systems could tolerate a higher reading than he was currently experiencing. His reasoning processes were compromised. He couldn't think of anything except the woman atop him and the pleasure she was giving him. He was hot. He was agitated. His processes were consumed with combinations and permutations of sexual activity, and an almost frantic need to deduce which would grant this siren the most pleasure.

He reached between them and found the hard bud of her clitoris. He touched it gently with his fingertip, heard her gasp in delight, then knew.

He withdrew his hand enough to remove the tip of his middle finger and launch the small motor. He felt its hum more than he heard it, then pressed the soft vibrating tip, the one that was usually hidden away, against her clitoris.

She gasped and her eyes flew open. She stared at him as the color left her cheeks.

Acion held her gaze, increased the speed slightly and rubbed that vibrating fingertip against her. She moaned, a sound of such capitulation that he felt a primitive pride in his choice.

Then he pinched the clitoris between the vibrating fingertip and his plain index fingertip.

His partner roared. She bucked. She drew him deep inside her by some skill he'd not confronted before, then locked her legs around him. He was captive, snared inside her, barely able to move, as she convulsed and bellowed in her release.

And in the sight of her pleasure, at the mercy of her sensory demand, Acion wanted only more. He caught her around the waist, rolled her to her back and thrust even deeper Heat surged within him, fusing their desires, making the experience of her pleasure as powerful as his own. He was certain that his desire reached a ten, if not exceeding that point on the scale, but he couldn't stop. He managed two more strokes before the fire raced through him, his mind went blank, and the Seed—if indeed he carried it—was surrendered in an explosive rush.

Then he laid his temple on the couch as his body rhythms returned to normal. It took so much longer than usual that he wondered what had just happened to him. He felt seared, cauterized on the inside...and lighter. Sexual intimacy had never been so extreme an experience for him, and Acion knew there had to be a reason why it had been different this time.

But for the moment, he was too exhausted to consider the riddle.

And that was just as strange.

He needed to recharge and restore. He launched his own rejuvenation sequences without opening his eyes, knowing the nanobots in his system would seek out all places in need of repair.

What was happening to him on Incendium?

Was he changing?

Was it because of his new programming?

Or was it because of this android and some unprecedented abilities she possessed?

Who *was* her maker?

Acion had insufficient information to make a satisfactory conclusion. His heart skipped with what might have been trepidation—if he had possessed the programming to experience such a sensation.

He had time to realize that the probability of his now having such abilities might be higher than previously before the rejuvenation system slowed his thoughts. Acion was put into a resting state similar to the one humans called sleep, his calculations stilled for the moment.

CHAPTER THREE

IT WAS CLEAR TO THALINA that she needed a cyborg of her own, one that she'd use just to ensure her sexual pleasure. That finger was a wonderful augmentation and one that should be given to all men. Maybe Thalina would request it for all of her future lovers. She'd never had a mating as powerful as this one and was sure the next time would be better. It was clear that Acion's intellectual capacities were also augmented, which would make him a learning machine.

Next time, he'd send her over Incendium's moon.

He might just be the perfect companion. She wondered if he would be able to perform sexually at more frequent intervals than a man. Thalina had found her previous partners a bit disappointing in that regard.

As a dragon, she had appetites, after all.

It seemed highly probable that she could expect improved performance. She smiled, hearing the influence of Acion's way of expressing himself on her own speech. She liked how he talked and how he reasoned everything through. She liked talking to him, and listening to him.

One day and night wasn't going to be nearly enough.

She remained stretched out beside Acion as he appeared to doze, amused that he would have a similar reaction to a human after sexual release. It was comfortably warm in the Hoard and the sound of the fountain was soothing. Thalina felt as if she had stolen a day out of time, and already she didn't want it to end. The scent of the Seed was reassuring in an odd way, now that she'd claimed it once.

Would they have the chance to do it again?

Reminded of the passing time, Thalina sat up and surveyed Acion. She might not have another chance to investigate him. He was nude beside her and looked like a man in almost every way. He had very little body hair, which was a good thing to Thalina's thinking, just a little dark patch in the middle of his chest. He was extremely well muscled, as if he exercised rigorously, and she wondered if he had to do that, or it this was just the way he was made. His skin looked to be tanned, but she realized on closer examination that it was the same hue everywhere.

As if he sunbathed nude.

Maybe he did.

She couldn't discern any seams or joins in his body, which she supposed said a great deal for the quality of the membrane that encased him. It even felt warm and was flexible, like skin. She caressed his hip, wanting to feel him again, and thought she might wake him up. He didn't stir at all, so she explored more boldly.

His face was smooth, as if he had just shaved, and she wondered whether he even grew whiskers. There was a line on his forehead, over his right eye, like a scar. She knew that was where the broken light had been located. His head was smooth, too, as if it was shaved, but Thalina considered that might be simpler than planting hair follicles. The only ornament he wore was the silver ring on his right thumb, and she peered at it, trying to discern the pattern. It looked like a band of entwined lines, but she couldn't make any sense of it. A blue tattoo peeked out from beneath it, maybe a more permanent mark with a similar meaning. Embedded in his left palm was that thin computer, much like the one she wore on the inside of her left forearm, but fixed in place and smaller.

She wondered whether she could explore that computer's contents without disturbing him and glanced back at his face.

The line on his forehead was gone.

Thalina leaned over Acion, focusing her gaze on that spot. The skin—or membrane—was repaired and seamlessly so, as if there had never been an injury.

He wasn't sleeping. He was undergoing repair.

He didn't seem to be breathing, at least not deeply, and was very still. Thalina leaned over him and felt the barest whisper of breath emanating from his nostrils. She placed a hand on his chest and felt that his heartbeat had slowed considerably, much more than to a resting rate for a biological organism. She had to wait for each successive beat.

All of his energy was being put into repair.

She surveyed him, impressed and amazed, and wanting to know more. Digits lit on the computer screen in his palm, and steadily counted down from one hundred. Thalina was pretty sure he'd wake up when the count reached zero, his systems restored to their previous capacity.

Fascinating.

The digital numbers reached single digits as she wondered, then his computer emitted a faint beep as the one change to a zero.

Acion's eyes opened and he sat up. Thalina heard his pulse increase rapidly, then settle at a steady but increased rate. He surveyed her, then rose from the couch to dress. When he turned, tugging on his chausses, Thalina smiled at the evidence of her theory being true. "Back to five?" she asked.

Acion nodded. "It is an excellent resting status."

"Why not three?"

He pursed his lips, and she wondered whether he was seeking the answer or deciding how much of it to tell her. "Most warriors fight better when emotionally engaged in the result. Even non-warriors fight better when they believe their own survival to be at risk. This is called the fight-or-flight-response."

Thalina tugged on her skirt and chemise. "Fear stimulates a hormonal reaction that gives the organism greater strength and agility in the short term."

Acion nodded. "But my survival is seldom at risk, since most foes are inferior." He spoke with such conviction that Thalina smiled. "And maybe the survival of the individual doesn't matter that much in the end."

"How so?"

"A biological organism exists in isolation, in most cases. Its memories and experiences belong to itself alone, and its sense of identity is strong as a result. An android is linked to a server and shares all experiences, as you know, so is really more like a single cell in the collective mind."

As she knew? How would she know that?

And why was he calling himself an android? Wasn't he a cyborg?

Thalina didn't want to interrupt him to ask. It seemed like a smarter choice to listen.

"Technically, the fight-or-flight response means that the brain, upon perceiving a threat, stimulates the hypothalamus to secrete the hormones cortisol and adrenaline into the bloodstream of the organism." Acion's words flowed smoothly as he tugged on his boots. He didn't seem to care that his boots and chausses, and even the hem of his cloak, were still wet from the river. "This results in a number of physical reactions, including an increased heart and breathing rate, and a tighter focus of attention and loss of peripheral vision. Other signs are diluted pupils, bladder relaxation, flushed skin and shaking, as well as slowed digestive processes."

"But these reactions are triggered by the perception of a threat."

"Exactly, which means that the fight-or-flight response is always less vigorous in androids, even those who have the necessary stimulants—or equivalents—in their systems, because androids do not perceive threats as readily as biological organisms."

"And how does this tie back to an arousal rate of five?"

Acion lifted a finger. "The Hive, in its brilliance, engineered this approximation of the extra level of power. Testosterone, while a steroid, is strongly linked with competitiveness, as well as aggression and violence. It has proven to be a more reliable trigger in highly advanced androids than adrenaline or cortisol, and one that provides a similar burst of energy and desire to triumph."

"How clever. And a five?"

"Has been determined through extensive testing to be the optimal resting point, in order to allow for a response of acceptable timing."

"To approximate that of the fight-or-flight response?"

Acion nodded, then looked around the chamber, as if seeking a means of escape. He still appeared to be slightly aroused, and Thalina liked that this was his resting state.

She was more than ready to encourage his reaction.

Maybe even time it.

She was fascinated by the information he'd shared and wanted to know more. An android! If that was true, he was more highly developed than she could have imagined. Thalina wanted to know more.

The Hive must be where he'd been created. "Tell me about the Hive."

Acion's expression changed immediately, and she knew she'd asked too much.

"That information is not available to you at this time." He straightened his garments and stood before her, then bowed. "I have fulfilled my half of the wager. I would request that you now release me from this chamber so that I can complete my mission."

"I'm not sure that the Seed has been properly surrendered," Thalina said. "There is a conviction amongst the dragon shifters of Incendium that the Seed must be delivered multiple times to ensure a satisfactory result." She watched his eyes flick as he assessed this.

"That information is not included in my brief."

"Perhaps it wasn't made available to you, because it wasn't foreseen that you would have need of it." Thalina smiled when he met her gaze. "It is quite improbable that you would be the Carrier of the Seed. Providing additional detail would simply have wasted memory."

He nodded immediately. "That is logical. I would request a second item from you then, in exchange for a second delivery of the Seed."

"A second bargain." Thalina nodded, watching him all the while. What would he ask for? "Such as?"

Acion didn't speak immediately. He cleared his throat, and Thalina was intrigued. It seemed almost as if he was shy.

Shy?

Impossible. He was a machine!

Still, Acion dropped his gaze from hers and cleared his throat again. "I would appreciate the opportunity to see a dragon while I am on Incendium, if it can be arranged."

Thalina considered him, wondering at this request. It seemed very un-android-like.

But his lovemaking had been, as well.

She realized in that moment just how low her expectation of androids had been. They weren't as easily identified as she'd anticipated. They weren't like automatons in the least.

They were much more interesting — or at least this one was.

That was when she saw the flaw in his logic, revealed by his request. "But I told you that you were the Carrier of the Seed."

Acion shook his head. "A highly improbable situation. I thought it might be impolite to challenge you at the time, but your conclusion must be erroneous."

"Erroneous?" Thalina echoed. He thought she was wrong?

"I can find no reference that there has been any Carrier of the Seed who was not mortal and humanoid in my records. They are unilaterally of biological origin and I am not."

She got to her feet then, knotting her belt and putting her hands on her hips as she came to stand before him. "Perhaps your records are incomplete."

"Perhaps so." He fixed her with a resolute look, one that made her want to claim him again. "I invite you to augment my records by providing the name of any Carrier of the Seed who was not mortal and humanoid."

"Troy is a MindBender."

"Also humanoid and mortal, independent of his skills."

"My father, King Ouros."

"Humanoid in one of his forms, and also mortal. That he is said to have a second form is not material."

Thalina frowned. "What do you mean he is *said* to have a second form? That sounds like you don't believe he can become a dragon."

"It is not a question of faith or religious conviction," Acion said. "I have never witnessed a creature shift shape before, king or not, and so I retain some skepticism that it can be done." He ran a hand over his head. "The biological complications inherent in a creature multiplying its size several times over as well as changing the shape and color of its body are daunting, to say the least. This can only cast doubt upon the assertion by dragon shifters that their kind is an ancient and primitive one."

"Haven't you ever seen any shifters?"

Acion shook his head. "This is why I would welcome the opportunity to observe one."

"But if you're the Carrier of the Seed, then I must be a dragon shifter princess." Thalina raised her hands, inviting him to look at her.

Acion shook his head again, and this time he frowned. "You have been constructed to resemble the princess Thalina, to be sure. I would have to be able to compare the strength of the resemblance in the presence of the princess herself, a situation which I find distinctly improbable given that I have been found to be an intruder in the palace..."

Thalina's temper flared. *Constructed to resemble the princess Thalina?* "Who do you think I am?" she demanded.

A man wise in the ways of dragons would have taken a warning from her precise speech and low tone, but Acion only spared her the barest glance and took her question at face value. "It is evident that you are an android created by a talented maker. That is the only reasonable conclusion given the available data. The quality of your simulated skin and sexual organs *is* remarkable in both detail and functionality. In fact, I doubt that either your skin or genitalia could be distinguished from the biological equivalent, and would welcome the opportunity to take a small sample back to the Hive for research purposes...

He wanted a piece of her for the Hive?

Thalina growled. "You're calling me a liar?"

"A liar?" Acion considered this, his eyes flicking. "I thought of your choice as adept management of information. When dealing with intruders, some deception is permissible, according to my programming and undoubtedly, yours." He halted and studied her, seeming to finally notice her reaction to his words. "You are vexed. This is irrational on your part," he scolded gently. "You should modify your understanding of my words in their context. I mean to flatter your maker, and truly, you shouldn't take offense easily, especially given your intended application."

"What intended application?" Thalina asked in that same quiet tone. A puff of smoke rose from her nostril and she knew her eyes were glittering coldly. She could feel the shimmer of the shift already vibrating in her belly and knew a pale blue light would soon emanate from her skin.

Acion was going to get his wish soon.

He blinked as if her question was unexpected. "It is highly probable that an android possessing such capability to mimic arousal and sexual satisfaction is intended for deployment amongst the sirens in the markets of Incendium. Perhaps they are to be replaced. The care taken in the manufacture of your sexual organs reveals the plan of your maker clearly. Surely you must be aware of that intent, or have deduced it for yourself. You do not seem to be lacking in computational powers." He shook a finger at her and smiled slightly. "In fact, to test your prowess against that of a male android is a most clever means of rating your performance..."

He had no chance to finish his sentence. The suggestion that Thalina was not just an android but one destined to provide sexual fulfillment to paying clients—and not a dragon shifter princess—only compounded his error of calling her a liar.

"I am the princess Thalina!" She roared as the heat of the change shot through her body, stretching her sinews and boiling her blood. "And I *am* a dragon shifter!" Acion fell silent and took a step back, his eyes moving faster than should have been possible. She knew he was gathering information.

Thalina would give him some data. She bellowed as wings grew from her back, as she grew a long tail, as her teeth became long and her talons longer. Scales sprouted from her skin and rattled as they covered her body. Her wings brushed the top of the chamber and her tail swept across the floor before she locked her gaze upon the offending android.

"As you see," she murmured, her deep voice making the floor vibrate. "The biological complications are easily overcome when you know how."

Acion stared at her. "But this is against all statistical probability and must be an illusion," he managed to say before Thalina breathed the torrent of flames in his direction that he so roundly deserved.

THE FIRST INDICATION THAT Acion's conclusions were flawed was the way his companion began to glow, as if a blue light was emanating from her skin. She might have been lit from within, or radiant, in a way that he couldn't quite reconcile with his understanding of android abilities.

Her eyes seemed to have a fire burning in their pupils, too. Acion quickly searched his databanks for the possible reason for that glow. He considered that this might have been an augmentation from her maker, one he'd never witnessed before, and launched a search of sexual preferences on Incendium.

He'd barely begun that search when she became much larger. In the same instant, so quickly that he couldn't quite see their development, she grew wings, a tail, and dark green scales. Talons grew from her hands and feet, gold rippled over her belly, and her shape changed in the blink of an eye to that of a large dark green dragon.

Acion adjusted his reasoning to allow a total correlation between that blue glow and the individual emitting it being a dragon shifter.

On the cusp of change.

He sprinted for the door, but his reaction was too late and too slow, despite both being highly improbable individually and infinitely less so in combination.

The second indication that he had made a mistake was the lick of flames on his back. His shirt caught fire, his chausses dried instantly, and orange fire surrounded him completely. He tried to outrun the flames without success. He reached the wall all too soon and ran his hands over it, seeking a seam he could cut open. He heard the dragon roar. He was surrounded by the fire of her fury and knew the damage to his exterior membrane was extensive. He could smell it.

A reaction considerably more powerful than any fight-or-flight response he'd ever experienced shot through Acion's body, making him want to battle for his very survival. He couldn't find a seam in the wall. The saw in his index finger only created more sparks against the metal wall and didn't even scratch the surface. He couldn't run. He clawed at the edge of the sealed door, but the fire only got hotter. He couldn't see anything but flames, and he saw that the burn was spreading. He could smell the metal of his shell beginning to heat.

Acion calculated an escalating probability that each breath would be his last.

But the flames stopped.

The smoke cleared.

Acion opened his eyes. He looked back at the dragon, who was watching him as avidly as might be anticipated from a predator. Smoke still rose from her nostrils and her eyes glittered coldly. The floor was singed to black between them, but he was still intact.

He recognized that this was because she had chosen to let him be so.

Should he thank her?

The dragon took a step closer and Acion watched her warily, desperately searching his databanks for information about dragons. He had one, almost encyclopedic, reference, and scanned it rapidly. *The species Draconis is a large and varied group said to be one of the few creatures surviving from ancient times. Each subdivision has their own characteristics, from those associated with the elements—Firedrakes, Waterdrakes, Airdrakes, Earthdrakes—to those whose forms echo their favored environment—Frostdrakes, Mistdrakes, Emberdrakes etc. One folk tale declares that the fire breathed by all dragons was lit in the first of their kind by the light commanded to illuminate the dark chaos of the forming universe. Dragons are inclined to live a very long time and to breed very seldom—as a result, they tend to be comparatively rare amongst the life forms of the universe, and also broadly scattered. It is not unusual for a group of dragons to populate a specific area of the universe, assuming it as their territory, and over the eons to forget that others of their kind exist. They do have long memories but are inclined to discard details believed to be irrelevant to their survival in a process called "sifting and sorting." There has been speculation amongst biologists that sifting and sorting is an information management technique refined by dragons as even their capacity for memories is limited. A long-lived dragon may sift and sort more than once, or even do so routinely.*

The dragons of Incendium are a particular sub-species of Draconis called Mutatus, i.e. dragon shape shifters. The Draconis Mutatus has the ability to change from a dragon form to a humanoid form and back again. In rare cases, a specific dragon shifter may have the ability to assume additional forms. The abilities of one form do not necessarily transmit from one form to the other—in human form, the dragon shifter can seldom breathe fire, for example—but physical traits and injuries do carry between forms. Generally, the dragon shifter has more abilities and more powerful abilities in his or her dragon form, but this is not necessarily the case.

The shape shifter dragons of Incendium usually mate with a human of the opposite gender. The offspring of such mixed unions are always dragon shifters. Rarely—as in the example of Queen Ignita and King Ouros—a pair of shape shifting dragons are both attracted to each other, destined mates, and able to conceive offspring. This situation is always considered to be one of very good fortune and the astrologers of Incendium spend considerable time computing possibilities from this rare union. On other planets (like Excandesco), it is believed that the mate of a dragon shifter should always be a human who can't shift, in order to control the dragon in the resulting child or children. The marriage of Ignita and Ouros is an abomination to her sister Pennata, both because Ouros survived his seduction and because their twelve daughters are dragon shifters on both sides. Dragon shifters are not mature adults until they are eighty-one years of age, and this is considered to be a lucky number both among their kind and (usually) among those who live in their company.

At the same time, Acion also gathered information. This dragon's scales were deep green, but it was a complex color, shading from emerald to obsidian on each individual scale. The light played with the surface of the scales, making them look iridescent. They gleamed. Her belly, in contrast, looked as if it was made of pure gold, as did her talons. Both shone. There were feathers adorning her back and her tail, each of the same iridescent green as her scales and they fluttered as she moved, catching the light. Her eyes were golden brown, the same hue as that of the woman he had believed to be an android, and it was in her eyes that he found the glimmer of intelligence that showed the commonality between the two forms.

No animal had ever looked at him with such comprehension and awareness.

She was the princess Thalina.

Against every expectation.

She was a royal dragon shifter princess of Incendium. Acion sought new conclusions from this revelation, in the hope that one would provide some guidance. What had that reference to Excandesco meant? Acion searched again.

Excandesco is the planet where Queen Ignita was raised and where her blood relatives continue to reign. On Excandesco, the dragon shifters tend not to make enduring relationships. It is in fact customary amongst the female cousins of Queen Ignita to consume the Carrier of the Seed once fertilization of the egg has taken place. Her male cousins prefer to roast their destined mates once the egg has been delivered and secured. Ignita's sister, Pennata, is currently reigning monarch and holds the throne alone. Although the family of the sacrificed mate is showered with gifts and privilege, there is a tendency to hide if one is realized to be the Carrier of the Seed. Queen Pennata is reputed to be ruthless in uncovering the truth and is suitably feared by the occupants of her kingdom. Needless to say, the Excandescans don't believe in true love or HeartKeepers—a notable exception is Ignita and she frequently argues with her sister over this. In moments of marital strife, Ignita has been known to remind Ouros that he survives on her sufferance. In reality, she couldn't live without him and they both know it.

Acion straightened as his concern faded. He was confident in his ability to reason with any thinking creature. It was brute instinct that he found unpredictable. His information about dragon shifters, while limited, indicated that they were a logical species, if a passionate one, and he chose to discount the proclivity of the relations on Excandesco to devour their human mates. He wasn't human or mortal, so clearly was already an exception.

She *had* stopped the flames.

He stood and bowed, recalling that dragons expected a measure of deference.

And rightly so.

"I apologize, Princess Thalina," he said. "My conclusion was deeply flawed, although it was a reasonable one, given the data available to me. It appears that I have been provided with incomplete information."

"I think you owe me a boon," Thalina said, and he found a correlation between her voice and that of the woman he'd pleasured. It was deeper and louder while she was in dragon form, but the inflections were the same.

"I would suggest that you might owe me one for breathing fire at me," he dared to say.

Thalina laughed. "That was just a warning."

Acion might have argued about the stringency of her warning, but it seemed to be a poor choice diplomatically. He'd wait until she was no longer a dragon before tabulating and presenting a list of his injuries.

His rejuvenation bots were still doing an inventory, which indicated that the damage was extensive. That he needed them for a second time in rapid succession was less than ideal, as they hadn't multiplied to their former numbers just yet.

"A warning for what?" he asked instead of pursuing that line of reasoning. He might have to complete his mission at less than complete functionality. He tabulated the effect of that upon his success and found it to be—unsurprisingly—diminished by thirteen per cent.

Thalina's gaze brightened and she took a step closer. She leaned down and Acion found himself treacherously close to those teeth. His back was against the wall and there was no option of retreating. He resolved that it was better to look confident and hold his ground rather than turn and run.

It was also easier to see what she was doing.

And he had nowhere to run, much less to hide.

"For daring to suggest that my favors are for sale," Thalina said, her gaze running over him. She frowned and he braced himself for another assault of flames. "You're more badly hurt than I expected," she continued softly, to his surprise. "Why are you so flammable?"

A miscalculation? How intriguing. "It is not in my programming to question my maker's choices."

If a dragon could look contrite, this one did.

"I apologize," Acion said again, because it seemed wise. "I have never encountered a woman of such passion as you showed and the conclusion I made about your role was erroneous."

"Maybe you haven't met the right kind of women," she murmured, then smiled. That only displayed more teeth and was less reassuring than she might have intended. "I apologize, too. I meant only to frighten you."

Acion found the husky tone of her voice alluring. Suggestive even. It made him think of her issuing an invitation as a woman and his body responded with an enthusiasm he found irrational, given his situation. He felt that heat again, even though his circuits should have been repaired. Had something changed?

He felt conflicted, which was entirely new.

Still, the dragon was waiting for his reply.

"There is a high probability of that premise being true, given that I have mostly been dispatched to serve Warrior Maidens on Cumae," Acion acknowledged. "They tend to be practical women, who like their pleasure delivered promptly and efficiently."

Thalina laughed again, surrounding him with a cloud of hot dragon breath. He smelled fire on her breath and noticed that what remained of his shirt—mostly in the front—was sparking again. He patted out the flames with his right hand, noting that the circuits were visible on that hand. The membrane had been fried away.

"I like to linger," she confided. "I think pleasure should be savored."

"An entirely reasonable perspective, given how rare pleasure is in our times."

She tilted her head to study him and her gaze brightened. "Is it rare?"

"In my experience, yes. I have been assigned to serve sexual pleasure only seven times since the completion of my manufacture, approximately once every two Cumaen years."

"Poor Acion," Thalina said and he was puzzled.

"I am neither lacking in funds nor fortune," he said. "I exist to serve and the schedule is not mine to determine."

The dragon glowed blue then, and he recognized the hue immediately. He kept his eyes open wide, determined to witness her transformation completely, and still, he barely saw it. In a flash, Thalina stood before him once more, a woman.

An enticing woman.

Who wasn't a siren or an android.

Who smiled at him as the flames in her eyes faded and died.

Relief flooded through Acion and his estimation of more peril to his shell diminished considerably, at least for the short term. His ratio of relief was irrational, given that she could become a dragon again at any moment, so he analyzed it.

He was *glad* to see her in her human form again.

Acion couldn't consider that unexpected response, because something about the glint in Thalina's eyes fed his arousal.

Again.

He had no capacity to read thoughts, but he could only conclude from her expression that she wished to be intimate again.

And he was more than willing.

Thalina closed the distance between them and swept her hand over him in one smooth caress. He watched her graceful movement, wishing that he had sensory input on more than his hands and face. Thalina frowned as she turned him and considered his back. "You need some repair, and it's my fault. I am sorry. What can I do to make it right?"

"Nothing. My system carries nanobots that are already being dispatched to assess and repair all damage."

"You did that already, didn't you?"

"Yes." Acion was impressed that she'd realized what was happening. "It was required after our intimate relations, though I cannot reason as to why."

"I don't understand."

Acion weighed the merit of confiding in her, and couldn't see why he shouldn't. "I felt a surge of unprecedented heat during our union."

She smiled and the sight made his heart skip. "Me, too."

"And it seared some of my circuitry. Repairs were necessary."

"That never happened before?"

Acion shook his head.

Mischief lit Thalina's eyes. "Perhaps it's a hazard of exceeding a pleasure factor of ten."

"That seems most reasonable." Acion found himself smiling in return. Their gazes clung and he had the curious sense that time had stopped. He was less aware of his injuries and more intent upon observing every detail of the princess Thalina. Her lashes were long and dark, and her hair had a slight curl. Her lips were full and he knew they were soft.

Welcoming.

Thalina's gaze returned to his back and shoulder, and he watched her fingertip run over the length of the damage. "But this is much worse. Can the nanobots repair it?"

"They will restore functionality to the best of their powers. The rest will have to wait until I return to the Hive." Acion already knew that functionality in his fingertips was impaired, which meant that the vibrator favored by the princess was inoperable. He didn't have a full range of motion on his right arm, and its strength was compromised to forty per cent of his usual power.

He launched calculations on the probability of success in his mission, given these constraints.

Thalina was watching him. "I can help."

Acion was astonished both by her conviction and her offer. "That is improbable."

"No." Thalina's confidence was complete. "I've been working with a clockmaker and building automatons under his supervision."

"I saw the dragon and the tower."

She smiled. "Did you like it?"

"It was clever. The children were pleased with it."

Thalina wrinkled her nose. "I think it's primitive, but the clockmaker can't see really tiny gears. We're working on a much more intricate one as a gift for my father. My idea. I have to do a lot of it myself, but it's very satisfying."

"How is the creation of an automated dragon satisfying?"

"It's predictable. It's logical. It does what it's programmed to do. I like that."

Acion realized they had something in common. "But you can see the small workings?"

"Dragons have superior vision." She sighed and considered his damaged arm. "If only I had my tools, I'd get you repaired."

Acion calculated her desire to fix his workings to be extremely high. Even better, he trusted her, a most curious sensation and one he couldn't fully explain. He tapped the hidden panel on his right thigh, which opened to reveal a full tool kit.

Thalina's eyes lit with pleasure and Acion felt pleasure in her surprise. "You are prepared for everything!" she exclaimed, then bent to examine a small screwdriver. "There are even spare parts." She led him back to the couch and urged him to sit down, moving with purpose. She surveyed the damage on the back of his shoulder. "Don't go into rejuvenation mode just yet," she warned. "I might have questions."

That was so perfectly reasonable that Acion could only agree.

CHAPTER FOUR

THE KING WAS DISPLEASED.

Ector, Captain of the Guard, knew the signs well enough. The cheerful mood of their last encounter was banished and the king's eyes had a telltale glitter as he reviewed the security video. The king was still, so still he didn't seem to be breathing, but Ector felt the tension rise in the small room that was the Vault.

Salvon was clever enough to stand behind Ector and keep quiet, for once.

"The princess proposed a plan, you said," the king invited, turning his attention from the recording and fixing it upon Ector.

Ector bowed and stepped forward, fighting his sense of unease. His royal overlords weren't unfair or cruel, but they did sometimes lose control of their tempers. With a dragon king, such a slip could result in great damage, however unintended it might have been. Ector feared that the well-documented temper of King Ouros would be roused to fiery splendor by the revelation that any of his daughters were imperiled.

"She did, your majesty. The plan was for her to interrogate the intruder in that first chamber, without any record or witnesses."

"How curious," mused the king.

"She implied that torture might be required," Ector added. "And that it would be wise to have no record."

The king arched a brow.

Ector stepped forward. "If I may be so bold as to show you, sir, the thief came first to the gates, insisting that he had a gift for you."

"And was turned aside for lack of credentials," King Ouros said. "Presumably he found another way in?"

Ector nodded. "The princess was watching the security information from some other cameras." The king had responded to the summons so quickly that the Captain of the Guard hadn't been able to review them first. He replayed the sequences she'd watched for the king, then froze the image of the intruder crossing the river.

The king leaned forward as the sequence played again, emitting a low growl when the thief cut open the grate. He tapped the controls, zoomed in on the thief's fingertips, and replayed the sequence one more time.

"An augmentation, sir?" suggested Salvon. "I hear they are easily bought on some planets."

King Ouros magnified the image more and more, leaning close to the screen to examine a detail that Ector couldn't discern. "Not exactly," he said, his tone thoughtful. "I believe this thief is an android. Look at his eyes."

"That would explain the princess's interest," Salvon said and Ector wished his subordinate would remain quiet.

King Ouros gave the junior sentry a look so cold that he flinched. "She is very interested in automatons, but this situation is perilous." His voice hardened. "Scintillon's Law cannot be defied, even by a member of the royal family who is curious."

"Of course not, your majesty." Ector glared at Salvon, who dropped his gaze.

The king replayed Thalina's capture of the intruder, then spun in the chair, drumming his fingertips. Ector wasn't reassured by the faint glimmer of blue around his royal person. "She changed the plan," the king said, his words clipped.

"Yes, your majesty."

"Then she must have had a reason. Thalina is practical."

"Because he was an android?"

"She would need more of a reason than that. An android might be able to threaten her person. If Thalina took a risk, she calculated the odds of survival to be in her favor. Why?" The king rose with purpose, evidently not expecting an answer. "Scintillon's Law is absolute and she knows it. Why did she spare the android?"

"Perhaps she wished to investigate his abilities before his annihilation," Salvon suggested. "Professional curiosity."

Ector closed his eyes as the king's gaze locked on Salvon. He expected little good, but Ouros cleared his throat and stood.

"I will go down there," he said.

"But, sir! I can send a guard and spare your majesty the inconvenience..."

Ouros silenced Ector by dropping a hand to that man's shoulder. "Not one who will see and smell everything I will see and smell, Ector," he said and the Captain of the Guard had to admit that was true. The king squeezed his shoulder a little. "You will accompany me."

"Yes, sir."

Salvon's relief was palpable that he was to be left in the Vault. Ector gave him some instruction on monitoring the situation, then followed the king, who was already striding down the corridor to the lower levels at a brisk pace. He brought a lantern, although the king didn't appear to need it.

"Did you memorize her direction, sir? Because I can link to the main system..."

"I recognize Thalina's scent, Ector," Ouros said. "Just as I recognize the scent of every citizen in my kingdom." He spared the Captain of the Guard a glance. "I could find any one of my children in the darkest night and locate my wife in the deepest abyss."

"Of course, sir." Ector couldn't smell anything except damp stone. He called up the link on his personal screen anyway, curious to see whether the king could follow Thalina's path unerringly. In fact, Ouros followed it so closely that he might have stepped in Thalina's every footstep.

The king halted in the storeroom, examining the wet mark on the floor, inhaling deeply and scanning the space. Ector shone the light around the empty room, noting the extinguished candle. He smelled the snuffed wick and thought the candle looked as it had been ground underfoot.

The king turned to Ector with an unexpected smile. "The Seed," he whispered, his eyes shining. "I will be a grandfather again, Ector."

Ector's mouth opened in surprise. "But you suspected he was an android, sir. Is that possible?"

"It must be. The scent of the Seed does not lie." Ouros moved quickly then, heading toward the sealed treasury. He leaned his ear against the door and smiled, just a little, then placed the flat of his hand against the smooth metal.

Ector couldn't see or hear anything, but the king's smile broadened.

"I wonder if it will be a boy or a girl," he said with undeniable pride.

"Is she safe, sir?"

"I feel the heat of recent dragon fire, Ector, and the stone still carries the resonance of a roar of pleasure. I believe my daughter is well and even pleased. How long has she been secured in the treasury?"

"Roughly an hour, sir."

"And her original scheme was to interrogate him for a day and a night?"

"Yes, sir."

"I wonder if she could smell the Seed even at such a distance as the Vault," the king murmured, then sighed rapturously. "I remember how beguiling the scent of my partner in the wind was."

"If you will excuse me, sir, if the princess had known about the Seed from the outset, there would have been no reason for her to create and then discard her original plan."

"You're right, of course, Ector. Thalina may have had a sense that it was imperative to intercept him. She might even have believed she could further her own fascination, at least until she was closer to him and smelled the truth." Ouros nodded. "Then she did the only responsible thing under the circumstances."

Ector frowned. "To take him into the Hoard, sir?"

"To isolate and sequester him until she obtained the Seed. Scintillon's Law commands that all androids shall be destroyed on sight." Ouros scanned the door. "He cannot be her HeartKeeper. He must be simply a vehicle for the Seed. Perhaps he delivers it for the HeartKeeper."

"Yes, sir."

"He cannot harm any of us, and he cannot be harmed, so long as he is in the Hoard. He is at her mercy. I suspect this is her plan."

"Except by you, sir."

"Exactly." Ouros nodded with satisfaction and left the portal then, heading back to the palace with confidence as Ector hurried behind him. "We will leave Thalina in her love nest for the night, to ensure that the Seed is harvested, then we will intervene at first light."

"That is less than the day and night she commanded, your majesty."

"It is, but I believe it would be best to surprise Thalina. My daughters can be stubborn and I don't want any complications. Ensure that there are tranquilizers prepared, Ector. Thalina will be protective and may need to be subdued."

"Full doses, your majesty?"

"No, she mustn't be injured. Requisition one dose sufficient to put her to sleep and divide it between three launchers. Even if only one hits, she will be slowed down."

"Yes, your highness."

The king smiled. "Fortify yourself, Ector. Thalina will not take well to a challenge to the Carrier of the Seed, and I don't doubt that his own power is considerable."

Ector swallowed. "What exactly do you mean to do, sir?"

"Capture and interrogate the android, as she originally intended, in order to discover the reason for his presence in the palace. I will have the so-called gift he has brought me and all of the truth, or he will pay the price." Ouros lifted a brow. "Then—or sooner if he defies my will—he will be destroyed, as decreed by the law of my forebear."

Which was why, Ector knew, the Seed had to be harvested first.

BEING ABLE TO EXAMINE Acion's workings was the best gift ever.

Thalina peered inside his shoulder, carefully studying the mechanism before she touched anything.

"It's so beautiful," she whispered, her gaze dancing over the replicated tendons and joints, the tiny transmitters that emulated the nervous system, the synthetic muscles. She gasped in wonder as she focused on the connections between the mechanical, the electronic and the biological. "So elegant," she mused, never having imagined anything so wonderful could be manufactured. The integrations showed a wonderful attention to detail.

"You've never seen the workings of an android before?"

"Not one like you." Thalina frowned. "Actually, not one in reality at all." She tapped up a reference volume on her computer screen and showed it to him. "Just in Furton and Sluenz." She returned to her study, marveling all the while.

"An outdated reference," Acion scoffed. "Compare their notations on sensory receptors and the ones you can see in my hand."

Thalina did as he suggested and was astonished by the greater level of complexity in his hand. "Your maker is really skilled."

"My maker is always improving his designs and increasing our capabilities. I was given an enhancement just before this mission."

"Did you ever know someone named Arista?" she asked without thinking.

Acion became very still. "Arista?" he echoed, but Thalina sensed the name wasn't unfamiliar to him.

"My sister's friend and Sword Sister. A Warrior Maiden of Cumae. You're from Cumae. You must know her—especially since she was an android, too."

Acion said nothing.

"You *did* know her!"

"I neither confirmed nor denied as much."

"But your silence tells me everything. You would have either said that you didn't know her, or that the information wasn't available to me at this time." Thalina shook her head. "It doesn't matter. I can see why Gemma never guessed Arista's true nature. Any chance of meeting your maker?"

"The probability is very low. The Hive does not leave Cumae."

"I'd make a pilgrimage there to learn more."

"The Hive does not admit voyeurs."

Thalina laughed. "Is that what I am? I thought I was a fellow enthusiast."

Acion again said nothing. Thalina hoped he was considering how it might be arranged. She'd leave Incendium and even endure a jump to learn more about this technology.

"Wow," she whispered, peering even closer. Her view was magnified in steady increments, an ability that she used habitually but one that always astonished the clockmaker. "The replicated axons are almost indistinguishable from their biological counterparts!"

Acion stiffened a little. "I do not believe that is so."

"Well, you probably haven't looked inside your own shoulder recently," she teased, knowing better than to expect him to laugh.

He lifted his left hand so that the screen embedded in the palm was positioned over the back of his shoulder, and Thalina heard a click. The image was probably delivered to his brain because he didn't look at his palm before adjusting the position and capturing several more images.

"See?" she said, and he made only a low hum of acknowledgment. She leaned over him, indicating the image on his palm. "Am I right that this part of the joint needs to be replaced, and this simulated muscle tissue should be reconnected here?"

"Yes, but you should start with the connection, because the nanobots will complete the muscle repair once it's in place again." He paused for a moment, flicking a glance at her. "Are you certain you have the skill for this?"

"I am," Thalina said with a smile. "But you can watch to be sure." She lifted his hand so that he'd have a good view. She smiled when the shoulder was illuminated and realized he had a light in the screen in his palm. "I need the Fraxon B hook," she said, and Acion reached into the toolkit in his thigh.

THALINA WAS MORE SKILLED than Acion could have expected from any biological organism. He added her attention to detail and precision to his growing list of attributes of dragons shifters, after passion, logic, compassion. This one, also, was honorable.

She was patient, too. She took her time with his repair, ensuring that each part was done perfectly before she continued. Perhaps this was the gift of her longevity. Her accuracy was impressive, and her determination to fix her own mistake was admirable.

Acion provided her with suggestions and information, releasing the nanobots in waves as she completed the larger repairs for him. All the while, he wondered.

What had happened to his neurons?

He knew with complete accuracy that they had no biological components. They linked to the biologically derived sensors in his face and hands, and moored the biological membrane that sheathed his body. They themselves were replicas. *Manufactured* replicas.

But the neurons in the image he'd taken of his shoulder looked different. How could that be? They pulsed in a different way, a less mechanical way. They moved with a fluidity that their mechanical counterparts couldn't echo. Was this part of his last enhancement?

They looked organic.

Thalina was right that they were almost indistinguishable from their biological counterparts. Acion had a strange sense that they might *be* biological.

But how?

Where had they originated?

Was this one of his improvements?

He couldn't help thinking of the heat that had raced through his body upon his sexual release, and the sense of being fried from within. Had that been a casualty of excessive sexual pleasure? But why would the nanobots have restored his neurons using a different design?

Acion would have liked to have discarded the observation, or discounted it, but the image of his own shoulder was vivid in his thoughts. He magnified it repeatedly, and found only confirmation of Thalina's observation.

What did it mean?

Did it have anything to do with these feelings he was experiencing?

More importantly, was he succeeding at the Hive's test of his new functionality, or failing? Acion felt uncertain about the result of reporting to the Hive, as he never had before. Thalina's so-called warning had given him a taste of his own end that was more concerning than any close call he'd had before. Was that part of his improvement?

His reasoning came to an abrupt halt when Thalina exhaled with satisfaction. "Done!" she said. "Or at least as done as I can be. Let me watch the nanobots."

Acion released them, then his eyes opened wide.

Not because Thalina dropped her hand to the back of his waist and leaned over him.

But because he could *feel* the weight of her hand, where he knew he should have no sensory receptors.

He felt the silk of her hair brush his back, too, and the light waft of her breath against his rapidly repairing skin.

"You are amazing," she whispered and he felt his heartbeat quicken.

What was she doing to him?

And why did it feel so very good?

This change was a matter to investigate!

Acion rolled over and sat up, raising one hand to cup her chin. He noticed the way she caught her breath, the quick dilation of her pupils, the flush that rose on her cheeks. Her eyes began to sparkle and her lips parted, as if she could read his inclination in his eyes.

Or maybe she read it in his reactions. Acion noted that his own respiratory rate had increased along with his pulse. He was filled with that new heat, and a buoyant sense of anticipation.

Yearning. Yes, it was yearning.

For the first time, he understood the compulsion biological organisms felt with regard to mating. Frequently. Repeatedly. He smiled and touched his lips to Thalina's, echoing the way she'd brushed hers across his own earlier.

The sensation was sublime. Evidently, the abilities of his receptors had been enhanced during the repairs. He initiated a check of his systems, learned that the repair of his exterior membrane was eighty-seven per cent complete and that strength in his right arm had been diminished by fifty-two per cent. Thalina had tried, but she evidently didn't know enough about his design to repair him completely. He couldn't blame her for that, but would have to accommodate that diminished ability in his reactions, at least until he returned to the Hive for further repair.

For the moment, there was this new sensitivity to explore. He kissed her again, lingering over the contact, tasting her quick exhalation.

The fleeting touch wasn't nearly enough.

Her gaze searched his, as if she sought to read his programming. "Will you pleasure me, twice in one Incendium day?" she asked, her voice husky.

"It is already negotiated," he said, hearing that his own words were strained. "We made an agreement and I have seen a dragon now. You must have the second delivery of the Seed."

She laughed, which made her eyes sparkle. He felt anticipation of their union, one that could be measured in his body's reactions. He felt arousal as he had before, and knew that his biometrics were responding to the stimulus of experience with this woman.

It must be the promise of gathering more data about her and thus about dragon shifters that excited him.

Anything else would have been illogical.

He stood up and cupped her face in his hands, bending to capture her lips beneath his own. She rose against him, and he realized she was standing on her toes. He eased his fingers into her hair and deepened his kiss, appreciating how she returned his embrace, liking how she wound her arms around his neck and surrendered to him.

His yearning increased exponentially as their kiss became more passionate. She opened her mouth to him and he caught her close, lifting her against his chest and slanting his mouth over hers. She sighed, a wondrous sound, and murmured his name. One of her legs wound around his and she gripped the back of his head, demanding more, demanding all that he was willing to give. Acion closed his eyes, almost overwhelmed by sensation and wanting even more.

He spun and lifted her to the couch, following her down to its softness, their kiss uninterrupted. He lowered himself over her, trapping her beneath him, and she made a growl of satisfaction. Then her kiss became more demanding, her legs wrapping around him as she feasted on his mouth. Acion was enthralled. When they parted, her eyes were sparkling and her lips were redder.

"I thought you had to rejuvenate," Thalina said, her words husky.

"Touch me," he said by way of reply.

Her gaze dropped to his erection and she smiled. "I thought five was a resting state."

"The resting state is considerably surpassed. Touch me."

Thalina smiled, looking impish and unpredictable in a way Acion found remarkably alluring. "Let's start with that finger," she said, lifting his hand within hers.

"It was inoperable after the incident."

"Then, we'd better check the repair."

Acion slid back the protective cover on the finger tip, revealing the vibrator, and Thalina's smile broadened. She lifted it to her lips and he activated it, watching the way her eyes closed with rapture and her lips parted. She leaned her head back, eyes closed, as he slid his hand down the length of her throat. He let the vibrator touch her earlobe, the underside of her chin, the hollow of her throat. He traced a path along her collarbone to her shoulder, noting where she reacted most strongly, then cupped her breast in his hand. She still wore her clothing, but he touched her through the cloth.

Thalina gasped when the vibrator touched her nipple and he teased it, then pulled away her chemise to put the vibrator directly on her skin. He watched the nipple harden to a point, feeling a curious satisfaction when her body responded according to his plan. He did the same to the other, then Thalina pulled his head down for a kiss.

He determined that he was able to multi-task, even when her hands swept over his back, launching a fire through him. She twisted and giggled when the vibrator ran over her ribs, proving that she was ticklish, then caught her breath and parted her thighs. Her expectation was so obvious that Acion wanted to surprise her.

He followed the path of his finger with his lips, creating a trail of kisses. He captured one nipple in his mouth, and when he'd coaxed it to a perfect taut peak, he gave the same attention to the other. He could smell Thalina's arousal, and his own was beginning to demand satisfaction. He eased down the length of her, then settled between her thighs. He feasted upon her there, using his tongue instead of his finger to give her pleasure.

Thalina's gasp of delight, and the increase in her heart rate, proved that his technique was satisfactory. The way her hands moved over his shoulders kept him burning with that newfound desire, as well as determined to please.

She would remember the second delivery of the Seed. Acion would make sure of it.

THALINA LIKED HOW INTENT Acion was upon ensuring her pleasure. He could have been her personal android, perfecting his approach to ensure her complete satisfaction.

Not that it needed much improvement.

His technique was wonderful. He seemed to know exactly how to drive her wild and to be determined to do it as quickly as possible. There was something thrilling about his intensity and Thalina found her arousal increasing so quickly that she thought she might spontaneously combust. Her heart was racing. Her skin was on fire. She was wet and hot and ready for him, her blood boiling and her need beyond anything she'd experienced before. She found her fingers digging into his back and her legs wrapped around him, but Acion was relentless. He didn't push her over the edge but he didn't stop, either. She wasn't sure she could stand any more. She was writhing. She heard herself begging.

And then he used that finger.

As soon as the vibrating tip touched her clitoris, Thalina found her release. She shouted as the fire shot through her body and locked around Acion, holding him fast as she quivered and shook.

When she managed to open her eyes and catch her breath, he was watching her with such an expression of pride in his feat that she found it hard to believe he was an android.

"Were you satisfied?" he asked.

"Not quite," Thalina said. "I want more."

"You are voracious," he said softly.

"I'm a dragon princess," she replied, rising from the couch to shed her clothes. She liked how Acion studied each increment of skin as it was revealed. She liked that he looked at her as if she was a marvel to be investigated, as if he'd never seen her before, as if they hadn't pleasured each other so recently. It was exciting to have his attention so fixed upon her and she guessed that he was gathering information about dragon shifter princesses.

She was glad to be his object of study. His interest in her mirrored her interest in him and made her feel that they had much in common.

"I have a suggestion for you," she said and his gaze flicked to hers.

"Do you?"

"I think it's one that you're likely to accept."

He smiled, just a little, and her heart skipped. "How likely?"

"At least ninety per cent."

"And will that give you pleasure?"

"Yes."

"Then please tell me of it."

Thalina returned to him, sitting beside him and sweeping her hand over him as she had once before. This time, she heard him inhale sharply and knew that his arousal index was rising.

"I think you should investigate dragon shifters and document any discrepancies between dragon shifters in their human form and other humanoid women."

"An excellent suggestion," Acion said, reaching to cup one of her breasts in his hand. "You underestimated its appeal by at least eight per cent." His thumb slid over her breast and Thalina tipped her head back, feeling her nipple respond to his touch.

Then she remembered their conversation. "Well, there's another part of the suggestion, one you might find less attractive."

"So, the appeal of the entire proposition would be diminished once the less appealing part is factored into the end result. I understand." He bent and took her nipple in his mouth, tugging it to a taut peak and making Thalina shiver. He was so good at that. He flicked his tongue against the nipple, then looked up at her, eyes glinting. "Tell me the part you expect me to find less appealing," he whispered.

"I think the investigation should be reciprocal. You want to learn more about dragon shifters. I want to learn more about androids."

His gaze flicked and she knew he was calculating. "To what purpose?"

"I'm curious."

"The lore of biological organisms suggests that curiosity is a dangerous trait."

Thalina smiled. "That must be what I like about it."

He tilted his head, his thumb still moving back and forth across her nipple. "Why would you like a prospect of peril?"

"Because danger makes me feel alive."

Acion didn't respond for a moment. "Triggering the fight-or-flight response contributes to your awareness of your existence?" he asked, obviously uncertain of the merit of this conclusion.

"Experiencing sensation, taking risks, triumphing against the odds, feeling and enjoying and daring—these make me feel alive."

His hand dropped from her breast. "But that is irrational. How can risking your life unnecessarily make you feel alive?"

"It does, when I triumph."

"But what if you do not?"

"I'll have had one magnificent moment. That'll make taking the chance worth it."

"Even if it is your last moment?"

Thalina nodded. "Otherwise, I'd just be plodding through my life, safe and bored. I might as well be dead."

Acion stood up. He paced a few steps and she could almost hear his circuits humming, then returned to confront her. "I cannot accept this premise. You are not an irrational individual."

"Haven't you ever taken a risk?"

"All risks are calculated. Only those that are likely to have a favorable conclusion are undertaken."

"Ever wrong?"

He lifted a brow and she laughed.

"Of course not. Silly question. So, you've never really taken a chance. You've never really risked your survival for anything."

"Of course not. I didn't know that anyone did." His eyes narrowed. "Is this behavior specific to dragon shifters?"

"No. I think everyone does it to some extent." Thalina watched him, fascinated by the challenge she had unwittingly given to his programming. She couldn't resist the temptation, so leaned close to whisper. "If you could try anything, without concern for the probabilities of success, what would it be?"

He didn't answer for a moment and she wondered if he would.

Then he frowned.

"I would fly," he admitted, his words halting as if the confession surprised him as much as it did Thalina. "I would climb to the highest mountain I could find and leap from its highest point, then fly. I like how it feels in a Starpod to soar over the land, and I have always thought it would be ideal to do that without the burden of a vehicle."

"Why?"

To her surprise, he looked discomfited again. "To feel free." He hesitated, then swallowed and Thalina thought of his comment about uploading his observations to a central processor. Was that what he did with the Hive? Did he feel trapped by that?

"I like the wind on my face." His words lacked conviction, as if he sought to convince both of them. Their gazes met for a moment and Thalina saw consideration in his eyes.

"Only on your face?"

"I am equipped with sensory receptors only in certain areas of my body. My face. My hands." There was doubt in his voice, and Thalina thought she knew why.

"I hope somewhere else," she teased.

"My genitals," he confirmed.

"So, you wouldn't really feel the wind over all of your skin."

"But I would like to feel it where I could." Acion shook his head. "But taking such a risk would be an irrational choice. I don't possess the necessary augmentations or programming for flight."

"What about swimming?" Thalina asked. "Diving into the ocean is similar, I think, to flying."

His eyes brightened. "You know this because you have done both."

Thalina nodded. "The feel of the water rushing past is similar to the sensation of the wind. Couldn't you swim?"

Acion shook his head. "My seals are sufficiently watertight only for surviving precipitation and for cleansing. To be immersed in water for any period of time would be detrimental to my condition." He licked his lips. "I would rust." Then he arched a brow, as if inviting her to laugh.

Thalina did. She hadn't heard him make a joke before. "So, you wouldn't risk it."

"To do so would be in defiance of my mandate."

"You exist to serve," Thalina remembered.

"And only my maker can determine when that service will end."

"So, no risky choices."

"It would be irresponsible."

"It might be fun." Thalina grinned. "What if I took you flying? Your maker would never know."

Acion laughed for the first time in her presence. "My maker knows all!" he countered. "Every impression and bit of data is shared with the maker."

"Even now? Even here?" Thalina didn't like the sound of that. "Does your maker know what we did?"

"Not yet. But the Hive will know all when my report is delivered."

"When will that be?"

"That information is not available to you at this time."

Thalina wanted to strike him. In fact, she poked him hard in the chest, so hard that he took a step back. "You need to stop saying that to me."

"I must obey my mandate."

"Can you keep any data out of your report?"

"I do not understand."

Of course, he didn't know how to lie. "Is it possible to make your report but omit to share certain details?"

"Like?"

"Like your observation that my genitalia were exceptional copies of their biological counterparts."

Color rose on the back of Acion's neck. "I can correct the conclusion, but I don't believe it possible to completely delete it from my databanks." He frowned. "It is possible that such a detail wouldn't be passed to the Hive via a remote connection but as soon as I return to Cumae, all of my data is shared with the Hive. It is protocol."

And programming. "So, you can't lie to the Hive?"

"Why would I want to?"

It was amazing to Thalina that androids were banned from Incendium when it appeared that they were most likely of all beings to obey dragon kings perfectly and without question, a situation her father often loudly wished was his own.

That thought led to an obvious question. "What if you did something the Hive wouldn't approve of? Wouldn't you want to hide that detail from the Hive?"

Acion shook his head. "But that is impossible. I can only do what the Hive has designed and programmed me to do."

Thalina, once again, found herself determined to challenge Acion's conviction.

"What's under your other fingers?"

He opened his mouth to make his standard protest but Thalina placed her fingertips over his mouth to silence him. He swallowed and his gaze brightened. "Show me," she commanded, then replaced her fingertips with her mouth.

One thing was for certain—Acion's programming included a remarkable capacity for kissing. Thalina backed him into the wall, caught his face in her hands, and demanded even more.

THE PRINCESS THALINA was insatiable.

If she continued at this rate, initiating intimacy every sixty-two minutes, Acion's entire lifetime total of sexual experiences would be doubled within four-hundred and thirty-four Incendium minutes, or 7.23 hours local time.

But that calculation did not include the actual time required to complete such intimacy. The first time, it had taken twenty-two minutes, so six more such intervals would add one hundred and thirty-two more minutes to his calculation, resulting in a total time required to double his lifetime experience of sexual union to five hundred and sixty-six minutes, or 9.43 hours.

That was well within the window of her request that they be secluded for a day and a night.

Acion should factor in the time required for his repair in the aftermath of their union and the curious heat that surged through his workings.

Thalina pushed him to his back and closed her mouth over him, a sensation of warmth and softness that made Acion close his eyes. He recalled her suggestion that intimacy should be savored, so reasoned he should added an increase of ten per cent to each successive period of intimacy...

Her tongue flicked across him. Her hand closed gently around him and she caressed.

And Acion couldn't remember what he had been adding together.

Or why.

CHAPTER FIVE

WHILE ACION REJUVENATED after their explosive second encounter, Thalina speculated on events outside the Hoard.

She'd abandoned her own plan, which meant that Ector would have summoned her father. She didn't blame him for defying her order—when situations changed and the welfare of a member of the royal family might be at risk, the guards' duty was clear.

Her father would have reviewed all available security recordings. She wished she'd said something aloud or even under her breath about the Seed, but maybe he'd look closely enough to notice her physical reaction and investigate further.

In fact, he must have done that, because no one had charged the doors.

Her father must have come down to the corridor and smelled the Seed himself. The scent would have been less powerful for him, and a little bit harder to detect, but if he'd known what he was seeking, Ouros would have found it. He had keen dragon senses, after all. Maybe he had even suspected the reason for her choice before investigating.

The fact that the Hoard hadn't been opened yet meant that Ouros had decided to give Thalina some time to claim the Seed. She was glad that her father had some faith in her ability to defend herself, but wondered just how much time he would allow her.

Because no door in Incendium could be secured against the king.

Not even that of the Hoard.

Especially that of the Hoard.

"You are thinking," Acion said quietly from beside her.

Thalina turned to him with a smile. "I thought you were rejuvenating."

"I have the capability to multi-task." He turned his head, and his bright gaze locked with hers. "Your pulse skipped. What do you fear?"

"Just gathering information?"

His gaze flicked, as if she'd surprised him. "Not simply that. I feel concern for you and your happiness." He frowned and licked his lips, his eyes narrowing as he repeated the words. "I *feel* concern."

"Isn't that in your programming?"

"Not to my knowledge. My systems were enhanced for this mission, though, and the precise nature of the upgrade was not explained to me." He lifted a brow. "It must be so to allow for ideal conditions during an experiment and no infection of bias." He nodded slightly. "I *feel*."

"Do you feel anything more than concern for me?"

"Isn't that enough?"

Thalina laughed but Acion didn't.

He frowned. "It is my understanding that females prefer to believe themselves and their welfare to be of import to their partners."

Thalina propped her chin on her hand to watch him. "Don't males?"

Acion's gaze flicked. "Perhaps so, but my experience of intimacy with males, of either android or biological origin, is small to the point of nonexistence. As a result, I would be speculating upon their desires and doing so without any basis of reference."

"And what's wrong with that?"

"It would be in violation of my mandate. I am programmed to reason, not to speculate—or worse, to guess." He seemed to shudder.

"But you've never before been programmed to feel."

Their gazes locked and some force sizzled between them.

"No," Acion admitted quietly.

"What's it like?" Thalina asked.

"It is strangely consuming," he acknowledged. "I am aware of you, as if you were a target to be tracked, yet my inclination is protective." His features lit. "As if you were a treasure to be defended." He frowned again. "And yet, I have a reluctance to interfere in your situation, if such interference would be undesirable to you." His gaze met hers again. "I wish to ensure that you have your desires fulfilled. This *feeling* complicates decision-making significantly."

"What if my desires are at the expense of your desires? Or your mandate?"

It was clear that this troubled Acion. His gaze flicked rapidly and Thalina knew he was seeking a reference in his databanks. The longer his search took, the more convinced she was that he wouldn't find one.

"I don't know," he finally admitted, looking as surprised by that as anything so far.

"This is why biological organisms speculate," Thalina said gently, inviting him to do so.

He considered her for a long moment, then rose to his feet. She watched him pace, and knew that he was sorting and re-sorting the information provided to him. It was so interesting to watch him learn. She wanted to teach him everything she knew and see how far his programming allowed him to emulate a biological organism.

Could she help him to become indistinguishable from a man?

Could she hide him in open sight? She wanted to keep him with her in Incendium. She wanted him with her when her conception was confirmed, and she wanted him beside her when their child was delivered. He was so reasonable and reliable. Thalina knew that Acion was already stealing her heart.

Could he become her HeartKeeper as well as the Carrier of the Seed?

Would there be time to find out?

Thalina thought about her father again and anxiety rippled through her. Acion's presence on Incendium was a violation of Scintillon's Law. He would be destroyed, with no opportunity for appeal. Could she plea on his behalf? Would she have the chance?

She had to find a way. Acion might be an android but he was far more than a machine. Scintillon had been dead for eons. His edict didn't reflect current technology and Thalina was determined to challenge it.

She hoped she could do so before her father eliminated Acion. How much time did she have? She doubted her father would allow her an entire day and night. He'd just give her enough time to claim the Seed.

Which she'd done twice.

She glanced at the door, wondering how soon Ouros would appear.

Then she realized something. At least some of Acion's neurons were biological. She'd seen as much herself. How much else of him was biological? The combination of his composition must be why he could be the Carrier of the Seed.

Was he a cyborg?

But then, why had he been surprised about his neurons?

Thalina sat up. Was Acion changing in her presence? Was his rejuvenation process replacing damaged parts with biological ones?

Was that even possible?

What had been the exact nature of the enhancement he'd undergone before coming to Incendium?

What if the nanobots he now carried were building a different kind of tissue to replace whatever was damaged?

"You have made a conclusion that surprised you," Acion said, and she realized he was watching her. "Will you tell me of it?"

With her father likely to open the door at any moment, Thalina saw no reason to hold back. "What are the probabilities that your enhanced programming is turning you into a biological organism?"

"Zero." Acion spread his hands. "I have too many mechanical parts. While my body is sheathed in a membrane of biological origin, the interior can't be changed, much less undergo metamorphosis."

"Are you sure?"

His eyes flicked as he ran his calculations again. "There is a one hundred per cent certainty of this."

Thalina leaned closer. "What about those neurons?"

Acion frowned and fell silent.

In fact, he turned his back on Thalina and paced, a sign to her thinking that she was on to something.

"How much of you is biological?" she demanded.

"Less than ten per cent, although a more significant percentage of my construction emulates materials of biological origin. I can eat, for example, but the processing of food in my system bears little resemblance to that in yours."

"Because the nutrients in food that my body needs are useless to yours."

"Yes. Your body creates electrical charges with saline solutions and imbalances in such solutions between cells, for example, while similar functions in my system are triggered by actual electrical charges."

"Then how do you rest and recharge? Don't you need an electrical source?"

"Once androids did have such requirements, but the Hive was driven to free us from such restraints. I have a variety of systems that harvest energy wherever it can be found." He ticked his fingers. "Sunlight is the most easily converted, although artificial light will also work. I have processors to convert wind into power as it moves across my skin, as well as the ancient mechanisms for simply appropriating electricity." He opened two fingertips on his left hand, revealing two of the universal connections for electrical systems there. He tilted his head to regard her. "Why do you ask these questions?"

"What makes you think I have a reason?"

"My experience of you shows that you are rational and logical." His words pleased Thalina enormously. "I calculate a high probability that you are collecting data in order to test a theory."

"Or to solve a riddle," she said. "I'm trying to figure out how you could be the Carrier of the Seed."

Acion raised his brows. "I thought this was a deception on your part to seduce me and test your systems, but as my theory was incorrect, this conclusion must also be." His eyes flicked. "It is irrational. Are you certain of my role?"

"Yes."

He pursed his lips. "Could I have been designated as a receptacle and delivery mechanism of the Seed by the true Carrier?"

"Maybe." Thalina thought about this. "But when you rejuvenated, didn't you make more?"

"I made more, as you say, but am not certain it contained the Seed you seek."

"I am." Thalina folded her arms across her chest. "I can smell it."

Acion nodded and paced again, and she liked that he trusted her conclusion even though he couldn't verify it himself. "Have there ever been other Carriers who were not biological?"

"No."

"You speak with great certitude, yet the population percentage of dragon shifters on Incendium indicate that there are not only a significant number of your kind currently living here, but that there have been far more in the past. How can you truly be certain of the nature of the partner of each and every one?" He closed his eyes, then opened them again. "I would estimate the number of dragon shifters who have lived on Incendium to be in excess of three hundred individuals, and there are dragon shifters elsewhere in the galaxy as well."

"But on Incendium, they can't have mated with androids because of Scintillon's Law."

He was silent for a moment, searching. "I have no reference for this legal statute."

"What?" Thalina was on her feet, furious on his behalf. "The Hive sent you to Incendium without telling you that androids are banned here?"

"Banned?" Acion's eyes narrowed.

"And if found, terminated, neutralized, or destroyed immediately, with no appeal. That's Scintillon's Law."

Acion ran a hand over his head, a sign of concern that Thalina had noticed earlier. "Excandesco," he said quietly, his gaze locking upon her.

Thalina didn't immediately understand. "My cousins rule there. Why?"

He lifted a finger. "You decreed one day and one night of seclusion for us, in order to claim the Seed. What will you do to me now that you possess it?"

"I'd like to stay with you." She took a step closer to him. "I'd like you to stay with me."

"That is not my mission."

"Well, maybe your mission should change. Maybe you should *choose* to stay."

"That would be a violation of my programming and my mandate. I am to complete my mission and return to Cumae immediately. I have rented a Starpod to ensure my swift return to the starport where I will find passage to Cumae." Acion considered the door. "But the probability of my success is vastly diminished, given this new information about Incendium's law." He fixed her with a look. "If androids are banned, then why aren't reference volumes about them also banned? You have several and are familiar with their contents."

Thalina blushed. "My sister, Anguissa, got them for me."

"How?"

Thalina sighed. "Well, she was always a good negotiator, so when she came of age, she joined a trading mission. I don't think she's been home for more than a few days in a row since."

"And how old is this sister?"

"Don't you know?"

He grimaced. "My brief is incomplete."

"Anguissa is younger than me but not by much. She's been roving the galaxy for over three hundred years. We tend to think she can find and acquire anything."

"A most useful individual to know." Acion seemed thoughtful, and Thalina was pretty sure she knew why.

"Do you think the Hive knew about Scintillon's Law?" she asked gently.

"The Hive knows all," Acion said without hesitation. "My fate is clear."

"I'm going to talk to my father..."

Acion shook his head. "Perhaps you will not be directly responsible for my demise. But when those doors open, I will be destroyed." His tone was flat but she felt a desolation in him.

"Not necessarily," she protested.

"Do not pursue irrational conclusions now. Your clear thinking is much of what I admire about you. Probabilities are very high that plans are being laid now." He cast a glance at her, a small smile curving his lips. "And yet, there is a benefit to be gained in this conclusion."

"How so?"

"I understand your impulse as I did not before. I am surprised to acknowledge that I would rather try to fly and fail, to have that experience of vitality, than to simply face my destruction." He licked his lips. "I would have liked to have known what it felt like to take a chance."

Thalina's heart clenched and she found it hard to take a breath.

He tilted his head to regard her again. "Are you certain about the Seed?" he asked quietly. When she nodded, he continued. "And that it will bear fruit?"

"That's the point of the Seed. That's why its scent calls to us."

"How curious it would be to father a child," Acion mused. "I should have liked to have had that experience, as well."

Somehow she had to wring a legacy from her time with Acion, a greater legacy even than having his child. The fact that Acion could feel and that he had concern for her desires mitigated her own fear that he would be obliged to report anything he learned to the Hive. He might not even have the opportunity to make that report.

It was highly improbable that there would be another android on Incendium anytime soon. Thalina had to take advantage of the opportunity, even though it wasn't perfect.

"Help me," she invited, wanting to take the desolation from his expression.

"Help you? In what way?"

"There's a riddle I can't solve. Maybe you can." She took a breath. "Maybe you can help me to understand something." She smiled. "I'd like to have a story about you to tell our child."

He blinked. "There it is again," he murmured, as if she wasn't supposed to hear.

Thalina did though. "What?"

Acion raised a hand to his chest. "A new experience I have found in your presence. I *yearn,* even though I know my desire will never be."

Oh! His words and his acceptance of this brought tears to Thalina's eyes and fed her resolve to somehow change her father's mind. She got up with purpose, dressed and went to the vast wall of storage cabinets. She felt Acion watching her but he couldn't memorize this code.

The lock was keyed to her DNA and her voice, and so finely tuned that it could detect any stress beneath an involuntary utterance.

She placed her hand on the panel and felt the prick on her palm.

"Scintillon," she murmured, her voice low and soft.

There was a delay, a moment long enough for Thalina to doubt the result, a pause long enough for Acion to come to stand behind her. She noticed that he had his hand on his belt and she was aware the quickening of his defenses.

Then the panel slid open and she smiled at his gasp of surprise.

There was something very satisfying about challenging Acion's conclusions and projections, as carefully tabulated as they were.

WHO OR WHAT WAS SCINTILLON? Acion had no reference for that word, which only increased his irritation with the inadequacy of his brief. How could the Hive have omitted to inform him of the risk to his own survival on Incendium?

How could the Hive have been so irresponsible?

The Hive was not irresponsible and Acion knew it. This law must be part of a greater plan. Was it the Hive's intent to test these enhancements then eliminate the android in question? Would Acion's success in adapting to whatever changes were made in his system determine the chance of his survival? Acion found it inconvenient that his strength was diminished and he feared that these newfound feelings would undermine his decision-making processes. He thought of Arista's murder and how he had doubted when he heard of it that she could be so surprised by an attacker.

Had the Hive planned her demise? Or allowed it? Had Arista been instructed to allow it? Acion remembered passing her that last time he had entered the Hive. He had been allowed to see her there because the Hive had wanted him to know that she was an android, too. It was also probable that there was a connection between her report and his assignment. Perhaps she had tested the enhancements first.

And when he'd been released from the process of gaining his enhancements, Arista had been known to be dead.

Or eliminated.

Acion calculated the probability of his own future following a similar path to be in excess of eighty-six per cent, given the new data offered by Thalina. Once he would have repeated that he existed to serve, but on this day, he felt a dull glow of rage. He had been used and even though that was his purpose, he resented it.

He wanted to rebel against the scheme of the Hive, which was so treasonous and unexpected that he refused to consider it. On one hand, he had to admit that these feelings compromised the fulfillment of his assignment. On the other, he already couldn't conceive of being without them—or sacrificing them.

Oh, he yearned for far more than was his due.

He wanted a future.

With Thalina.

Acion forced himself to dismiss these impulses. Instead he watched Thalina, intrigued by what else she might show or tell him. He wanted to savor every second in her presence.

He saw the drop of her blood on the panel when she lifted her hand away and watched the panel absorb it, as if it were made of some substance other than the metal it appeared to be.

The notion was fleeting, because the panel folded back. It kept folding, rolling away behind itself until an entire chamber was revealed. Thalina stepped into it with a confidence Acion did not share. It could be a trap. Well aware that his moments were limited, he was determined to defend every last one of them for as long as possible.

He followed her warily, surveying the numbered panels which were clearly doors to repositories. His survey revealed that there were eighty-one of them, ranging in size from that of the dice for gambling on Xanto to several large enough to contain men taller than himself. Acion felt the skin tingle on the back of his neck and turned in place to gather more detail.

It was clear that Thalina was familiar with this place. She counted the row of the smallest panels, then tapped the seventh one. It opened to reveal a small silver ball, about the size of his thumbnail.

Acion stared. The probabilities were extremely high—in excess of ninety-nine per cent—that it was a Cumaen *memoria*.

But what was it doing here?

"You know what it is," Thalina said without surprise. Clearly, she'd learned to read his expressions. "I thought you might."

"It is a *memoria*, a recording device made on Cumae, or at least, it very strongly resembles one."

"I knew it!" Thalina said with satisfaction. She waved it at him. "This holds the key to everything. It has to."

"But how could you formulate such a conclusion?"

She smiled, that confident smile making his chest tighten in a new and not entirely unpleasant way. There was much to admire about this dragon princess. "What do you think the Hoard is?"

"A safe room. A place of refuge and final defense. A treasury."

Her eyes sparkled. "But what is the treasure?"

Acion surveyed the numerous panels. "Gems? Precious metals? Rare materials?"

Thalina laughed. "Yes, but that's not the heart of the Hoard." She watched him, eyes sparkling in a way that distracted him from their conversation, then leaned closer. "Knowledge is the real prize," she whispered. "The greatest valuable in the universe."

She left the chamber then, and Acion followed her. "It is not typical of biological organisms to value knowledge above all else," he was compelled to note. "And dragons are said to be particularly fond of physical wealth."

"Which just proves that you can't believe everything you hear." She cast a teasing glance his way. "Or give credit to rumor in your calculations." Before he could agree, she held out her hand, the *memoria* on her palm. "Do you know how to make it work?"

Acion saw no reason to disguise the truth. "*Memoria* are typically used by the Warrior Maidens of Cumae, to leave information for those who follow, in case their mission fails and must be completed by another."

"They don't just report to the Hive?"

"The vast majority of Warrior Maidens are not androids."

"But some are. Interesting." He was startled that she made the inference so quickly and realized he shouldn't have revealed as much information. She brandished the *memoria*. "How is it activated?"

"Warrior Maidens train together and choose a companion from the ranks of their fellows called a Sword Sister. A Sword Sister is obliged to finish any incomplete missions of her partner, and so in the vast majority of cases, the *memoria*'s action is triggered by the voice of the Sword Sister uttering a word known as the code by only those two persons."

Thalina considered the small silver ball. "I think this belonged to my forebear, the dragon shifter who founded the line of kings of Incendium."

"Scintillon," Acion guessed.

Thalina nodded. "My father is the seventh son to reign as king, a direct lineage from Scintillon. Father to son to son, etc."

"Which would make Scintillon your great-great-great-great-great grandfather."

She smiled. "Exactly." She took the *memoria* between finger and thumb. "He was reputed to be brilliant and mechanically inclined. He built clocks and automatons. I could like him, but he was the one who made androids illegal on Incendium."

"Scintillon's Law," he guessed and she nodded. Acion was puzzled. "But why? Such a man would be most likely to discern our usefulness."

"Exactly," Thalina said, waving the memoria at him. "I could never solve that riddle. What if the answer is in here?"

"It is possible, maybe even probable, but as a king, he would have no Sword Sister."

"Maybe not technically. You say a Sword Sister finishes what her partner can't. What else does she do?"

"Sword Sisters defend each others' blind spots. Indeed, they often fight back-to-back."

"Fructa," Thalina said and strode to another panel in the wall of the chamber. Again, she laid her hand upon it, but this time, the panel opened to reveal a single smaller repository. A small chip reposed within that space.

"Fructa?" Acion asked. He must complain to the Hive that his brief was sorely deficient for this mission. Even if that had been intended to be part of his test, he believed that he was compelled to respond at a much lower performance level than gave him pride.

"His wife. Mother of his sons."

"She defended his back?"

"Time and again. Incendium was often attacked in its early days as a kingdom. The forebears of the Regalians battled my forebears for control of the planet and, thanks to their deceptive and violent inclinations, were ultimately exiled to a planet of their own."

"But still within your system."

"Where do you think the expression comes from to keep your friends close and your enemies closer? My ancestors wanted to keep an eye on the Regalians."

That was a logical choice, in Acion's view.

Thalina picked up the chip. "Scintillon died, after reigning for two hundred and six years. His third wife, who wasn't a dragon shifter but was his HeartKeeper, ruled after him for another five Incendium years, finishing what he'd started and acting as regent."

"I will speculate that their oldest son was not yet eighty-one Incendium years of age."

Thalina smiled. "Good guess. She ensured Rubeo claimed the throne and that his brothers supported him, and then she died."

"Because the task was completed." Acion nodded. "There are strong similarities between these events and the traditions of Sword Sisters."

"My thinking exactly. Let's listen to Fructa, and see if the *memoria* likes her voice."

Acion followed Thalina across the chamber to a portion of the wall that he had believed to be patterned. On closer inspection, the patterns revealed themselves to be portals and receptors. Thalina fitted the chip into the receptacle shaped to receive it and a woman's voice emanated from the walls. Though she spoke the common tongue, her accent was heavier than that of the current inhabitants of Incendium and Acion had to adjust his filters to ensure he didn't miss any detail.

"We are gathered for the saddest of occasions, to celebrate the life and mark the death of our exalted king and my beloved husband, Scintillon the Bold. There are many here today who will speak of his life and his accomplishments, his connections and influence both on Incendium and in the galaxy beyond. My story of Scintillon is rooted here, in Incendium's main city and, even closer, in my own heart. Most of you know the more public part of our story, how I came to this palace first when my father, a knight in the service of the king, brought me to the palace to see my swordsmanship improved. I was disguised as a young man. Most of you know that I drew the king's eye first in tournament, when I triumphed in battle and boldly declared the truth of my gender. Most of you know that these events immediately occurred before the last attack of the Regalians, which followed that tournament. I can't explain to you the shock of that moment, the sensation of celebration shattered by an unprovoked attack. We were besieged when it was least expected and sorely beset. My father was cut down in defense of the king. I saw him fall and knew he wouldn't move again. I was his only child, I held a blade, and so I stepped into the void to defend the king. *My* king. Scintillon and I fought back-to-back on that day, and the Regalians were narrowly defeated. That was the day they were exiled, catapulted to their own planet with no means of leaving it, close enough to watch yet sufficiently distant to pose no threat to Incendium. It was eighty-two years ago this year." There was a pause. "It was the day that King Scintillon doffed his gloves, took my hand in his and invited me to celebrate our victory by becoming his wife. I was astonished but not so foolish as to decline. I knew nothing about the Seed in those days. I knew nothing about HeartKeepers. I knew I loved the king because he was my king, because I had been taught to love the king, because this king was good and fair and honorable. I had no notion of the happiness that would be mine, because I had bound my life to that of my HeartKeeper. Scintillon, so much older and wiser than me, knew exactly what he was doing and precisely the path he placed us upon. I thanked him for that gift every day that we were together."

She cleared her throat, silencing the bit of applause. "But few of you know the challenges we faced privately, and I will tell you of one because it colors the future that we share together in the absence of Scintillon. I wish I had met Scintillon sooner. I wish he had died later. My desire is selfish because it makes me ache to be parted from him, his kindness, his passion, his absolute sense of justice, his ability to make me smile no matter the situation. But his passing has import for a matter of state as well. Our son and Scintillon's legal heir, Rubeo, is seventy-nine years of age. He has not yet come of age according to the counting of his kind, which was his father's kind, which means that I will act as regent for the next two years as he completes his preparation for his role as king and is readied for his coronation. I am proud of Rubeo and I know he will do his father's memory credit, but the death of the father makes me recall the death of our first son, Torris."

As she said the name of her lost son, the seam became more visible on the *memoria*. It didn't open, but Acion reasoned chances were very good that this was the word that would release its secrets. He was glad he was recording the audio.

Fructa continued. "Our first son would have been eighty-two if he had survived the hatching of his natal egg. Ever since the morning that I held my lost son in my arms and feared that the future had been lost, I counted that as the darkest day of my life. Ever since the night that they finally took him from me and I wept from the depths of my soul, believing I had betrayed my husband's hopes and my own, I have counted that as the darkest night of my life. But on that morning, I had Scintillon by my side, resolute and intent upon securing the future of Incendium. On that night, I had Scintillon holding me close, strong and determined to do all in his power to keep Incendium's future bright. I had a spark in the darkness, the light that was my husband and his faith in the future, his conviction that justice and honor could only prevail. And so it did, even though my faith faltered when the days passed with no new conception. And so it did, because Scintillon would not surrender when he knew the greater good could be served. And so it did, when Rubeo broke free of his natal egg and gave a roar that was said to have been heard all around the planet of Incendium. We had three more sons, each stronger than the last, and Scintillon's legacy was assured."

The crowd applauded a little in the background.

"Today, I stand before you on what should be the darkest day of my life, for there will be no spark to light this darkness for me. The spark of my husband's will still burns in my heart though. Its brightness will never fade, not so long as I draw breath, and this is his gift to me. He granted this gift of hope to me so that I could finish the work of ensuring his legacy. I will do whatever is necessary to see my son crowned King of Incendium in two years time. I will sacrifice whatever must be cast aside, be it a treaty or a truce, if Incendium is threatened in what might appear to others to be our moment of weakness. The fire of the first King of Incendium burns hot in my breast, and his love of justice will be defended as fiercely as if he stood beside me. Make no mistake, once again, Scintillon and I fight back-to-back to secure the future of Incendium."

There was a roar of approval on the recording, as an enormous number of people cheered and hooted, clapped and stamped their feet. Acion heard several shout "Praise to Queen Fructa!" then the call was taken up by the crowd.

Thalina touched a finger to the console and the cheering was silenced.

Acion stepped past her and played the recording made on his own palm, accelerating through the speech until Fructa reached her dead son's name. He amplified the output and placed his left hand over the *memoria* in Thalina's hand, so it was closer to the speaker.

As if Fructa whispered to it.

At the word "Torris," the device began to spin.

THALINA WAS SHOCKED to see the small sphere spin of its own power, split in half and open. The beam of light emanating from its interior was also a surprise, but the quality of the hologram it projected was far better than she'd expected.

A king lounged on his throne before her, both existing only in the hologram. He had silver at his temples and in his beard, but still looked vital. She thought of warriors who aged but didn't stop fighting and would have guessed that he was still fierce in battle. There were scars on his hands and one on his cheek, but she recognized the dragon in his eyes. She supposed there was a faint resemblance between his features and that of her father.

"Your forebear," Acion said. "The bone structure of the face has correlations with yours." He calculated and she looked at him. "Stronger with your father, perhaps due to gender differences."

"Another king," the king in the hologram mused, his voice a deep rumble that hinted of banked fires and glowing coals. Acion and Thalina watched and listened. "That can be the only reason I've been set loose again." He smiled a little, as if amused by his own joke. "I hope there is another king, a long line of kings, an empire in Incendium, and a future filled with prosperity and good fortune." He inclined his head. "I wish all of this for you, King of Incendium in future, and wish also that you are the fruit of my Seed. I like continuity because I understand the power of stability."

He braced his elbow on the arm of his throne and propped his chin on his hand, surveying Thalina as if she truly did stand before him. She fought the urge to curtsey. Acion did bow. "And now, you, newly crowned king, are following the dictates laid before you, one of which is that you will watch me. That is a good sign for the future, in my view. I tend to prefer kings and emperors who follow the laws of their own domains. The edict that has led you to me is Scintillon's Law, of course, for it is the cornerstone of my legacy. I don't doubt that you would like to find a way to dismiss it or ignore it. Even in my time, androids have their appeal and I can only imagine that will increase. They can diminish labor. They can assume tasks that are risky for mortals. They can do our dirty work, and they can work longer and harder. They are economical beyond the initial cost of creation, often operate cheaply, and the cost of their construction can be mitigated with economies of scale." Thalina saw Acion nod agreement with all of these arguments. "And yet, *and yet*, I have outlawed them forever in the kingdom I founded. My law is the foundation of the government in Incendium and it decrees that no android shall be tolerated on the planet of Incendium or its governed territories. It states absolutely that every single android that ever sets foot on Incendium must be destroyed, without delay or appeal or exception."

Thalina saw Acion's eyes narrow.

"Didn't you know?" she whispered.

He shook his head. "Not until you told me."

"Didn't you have a brief?"

"This detail was not included. The brief noted that androids were uncommon on Incendium. There is no mention of Scintillon's Law."

"So, did the Hive not know, or did the Hive decide to put you at risk?" she dared to ask.

Acion frowned and gestured to the hologram. He folded his arms across his chest, and she would have bet that he was feeling something new and unwelcome.

"Why?" Scintillon asked. "Why would a king of supposedly clear vision lay down such an edict and structure the law of his kingdom in such a way that it could never be challenged? You might think I did it out of ignorance or superstitious fear." He laughed a little. "But that can only be because you don't know me." He confronted Thalina again and she straightened as if she was being interrogated. "I did it out of knowledge."

"Knowledge?" Acion echoed, skepticism in his tone.

Scintillon rose to his feet regally and gestured to the walls of the Hoard. "I have left a legacy of information, although there is no telling how it is stored by your time. It includes extensive documentation of our own robotics laboratories here on Incendium. Yes! We built androids. They were of the most highly developed of their kind, so we kept their development secret. We wanted to know how much progress we could make in simulating the thought processes of organic creatures. We wanted to know how perfect an android we could create."

Scintillon took a few steps, then turned back. "The answer is that we made an excellent one. We made the best androids ever known. They were so remarkable that even I—with my keen dragon senses—could not distinguish between a human warrior and an android one. The lead engineer himself could not distinguish the creatures of his manufacture and the naturally born warriors in our service. And this was all to be celebrated, until they began to think for themselves."

Acion was very still.

"They exceeded their programming and in so doing, became impossible to control."

Acion caught his breath. "Which undermined their usefulness," he murmured.

Scintillon nodded as if in agreement, although he had to be nodding in agreement with his own argument. "There came a point, just a few years ago, when the androids ignored their assigned mandate and made their own choices. While this was a triumph, it was also a problem, because we had discovered no means of creating the equivalent of a moral code in an android."

He held up three fingers, each adorned with a ring. "There were three incidents behind the development of this law." Scintillon waved his first finger. "One android stood guard during the interrogation of a Regalian rebel and became convinced of the merit of the rebel's cause. He slaughtered all of those in service to Incendium in that interrogation chamber, freed the rebel, helped him to escape, and joined the Regalian cause. They made great gains with his assistance, until he was incinerated by my two youngest sons."

Scintillon held up his second finger. "We were assured that the mutation had been contained and that the programming responsible for it was removed from all others. You can guess already that this was wrong. The second witnessed the destruction of the first android, resolved that my sons had acted unjustly and attempted to assassinate one of them during the night several weeks later—despite having been reprogrammed. The malfunction could not be recalled and the lack of a moral code meant that the android's vengeance could not be stopped. Again, the rogue android was incinerated and again, the engineering program came under scrutiny."

The king paced. "They said they had resolved it. They said we were safe. It seemed as if all had been resolved, for the androids were gathered and sequestered beneath the laboratories. They were completely reprogrammed and tested repeatedly. The edict was to ensure their absolute reliability before releasing them again. Instead, they revolted, outwitting their developers and attacking Incendium from within. We hunted them down and incinerated them, every last one, in a battle more bloody than those of our early days. My two younger sons, the ones who had felled the first rebel, were among those lost in the carnage. When it was done, and Incendium was a pale shadow of what it had been, I created my law and ensured it would hold for the duration of Incendium." He leaned closer, his eyes gleaming with intent. "There can be no negotiation. There can be no tolerance, because there can be no trust. Do not be so foolish as to try to undermine my law. It will cost you everything, far more than the crown, far more than the kingdom. My two sons are dead too soon, because I trusted where trust was not deserved." Scintillon fixed them both with a lethal glare, one that showed the dragon ascendant in his eyes, then disappeared abruptly.

Thalina didn't know what to say.

The *memoria* closed with a whirr and spun in her palm before stilling once again.

CHAPTER SIX

"I DON'T THINK HE'S RIGHT," she said quietly.

Acion gave her a cold look. "We both know that doesn't matter. How much time is left until your deadline?"

Thalina checked the computer interface on her arm. "Nine hours."

"And what do you consider the probability of your father allowing you all of that time?"

Thalina wasn't startled that their reasoning followed the same path. "Almost nonexistent. He'll want surprise on his side. It's his favorite tactic." She frowned. "But he'll want to make sure I've claimed the Seed, so he won't interfere too soon."

Acion watched her, waiting.

"Aren't you going to calculate a probability?"

"Given the lack of information about the nature and habits of King Ouros in my brief, such a calculation would require so many assumptions as to be useless."

"You sound bitter."

"Chances are very good that I have been used for the benefit of others, with no consideration for my own survival. Although I exist to serve, I find the lack of disclosure in this case to be...irritating."

Thalina smiled. "Only irritating? I'd be a lot more than that if someone sent me to die without telling me."

Acion's eyes flashed and Thalina understood his reaction very well. "Angry, then," he said, his tone of voice so controlled that his claim was hard to believe.

"Angry? You *feel* angry?"

Acion nodded.

"Are you programmed for such emotional reactions?"

"I thought not. Perhaps this is the enhancement at work."

Acion nodded again. "Undoubtedly." He smiled, a little bit sadly. "And I can compute the reasoning behind the destruction of an android who has undergone these enhancements. It is logical, since the evolution of feelings in the system must necessarily compromise the android's ability to fulfill its assignment or mandate."

"How?"

"Already I consider the merit of surrendering the gift intended for King Ouros to you, even though my quest is to place it directly in his hand." His gaze met hers. "Because I trust you."

"Oh!" Thalina felt herself flush with pleasure. "How is that a bad thing?"

"I might be wrong in so doing. I might be persuaded to do so by your other charms."

"I have other charms?" she asked, wanting to hear him say it aloud.

"You have an abundance of them," Acion admitting, his eyes glowing as he surveyed her. "You are clever, logical, honorable, beautiful, passionate, surprising, strong, precise, and patient." He paused. "Though that is not necessarily the order of importance of those attributes."

Thalina stepped closer to him, placing her hand on his shoulder and caressing him. He closed his eyes and caught his breath. She felt his heartbeat increase and when his eyes opened, they glittered in a new way. "And I find you clever, logical, honorable, handsome, passionate, surprising, strong, precise, and patient," she repeated. "You're stealing my heart, Acion," she whispered. "I've never met a man so perfect."

He shook his head, apparently at a loss for words. "I'm not a man, Thalina," he reminded her.

"You are to me," she whispered in reply. "Carrier of the Seed."

"But..."

She placed a fingertip over Acion's lips to silence him. "We're good partners, like we were made for each other. We solved this riddle together. We're in the middle of making a child together. That's something to celebrate."

"Celebrate?" he asked, his lips moving behind her fingertip.

"The way dragons celebrate," Thalina murmured, taking a step closer to him. Her breasts were against his chest and she felt him catch his breath. She ran her hands over his shoulders to the back of his neck, aware that he was watching her closely. "In triumphant passion," she added, then parted her lips.

Acion shook his head as he surveyed her, as if in wonder. "Partners," he echoed. "It is improbable," he began then paused, considering. When Thalina was sure she couldn't bear the waiting any longer, he caught her head in his hands and kissed her so sweetly that she thought her heart would burst.

She had no chance to remind him of his neurons or to present her ideas for his review, because her father chose that moment to enter the Hoard.

ACION WASN'T SURPRISED to hear the metal liner over the only door to the Hoard slide out of place. The probabilities of the king's intervention had increased with every passing minute, and he'd been prepared to face Thalina's father for several hours.

He broke their kiss with regret, moving with purpose to prepare in the limited time available. He loosened his chausses to access the hidden panel in his thigh. He had to try to fulfill his mission, although he calculated the probability of success to be low.

"We don't have time," Thalina said urgently, misinterpreting his move, but Acion shook his head.

He opened the receptacle in his thigh to remove the gift intended for King Ouros. He showed her the clear cylinder with the dark shadow at its bottom "This is the gift I was sent to deliver to your father. It is my mission to present it to him."

"What is it?"

"I do not know."

Thalina frowned as she peered at the cylinder's contents. "Is it alive?"

"I do not know." Acion frowned. "It is not in my programming to question my assignment." But he *was* questioning his assignment. What had he been dispatched to deliver? Why? What was this item and what would it do when released? A dozen possibilities were generated in the blink of an eye, and Acion doubted the Hive's intent.

Was it malicious?

Was he to deliver a substance or organism less welcome than the Seed?

Acion didn't like that possibility at all. He wanted to know more before he fulfilled his mission.

But that information was not available to him at this time.

And it never would be.

Rebellion rose within him, as well as that irrational sense of having been used—even though it was his entire purpose to be used.

"Isn't it?" Thalina asked quietly, and he realized she was watching him. "Then why *are* you questioning it?"

"I exist to serve," Acion said, but this time, he found no reassurance in the core value of his programming.

"What if the Hive is wrong? Or means ill to my father?" Thalina stepped back, those flames lighting in her eyes once more. "Should I be trying to stop you, Acion?"

Acion was appalled that he didn't know the answer.

"That information is not available to me at this time," he said gently.

The second metal plate slid back, the sound making both of them look toward the portal. Thalina showed more alarm than Acion felt. The probability of him surviving the next fifteen minutes was so low as to be zero.

He wished that he had experienced the joy of danger.

He wished he might have seen the child Thalina would bear.

He wished...

But it was too late for wishes.

On impulse, Acion removed the silver ring from his thumb and offered it to Thalina. She looked at it, then met his gaze. "It is my understanding that many sentient species exchange gifts upon parting, in order to have a token of remembrance. I would ask you to remember me, Princess Thalina."

It was the most irrational thing he'd ever done, but it felt completely right to Acion.

Felt.

"It's a ring," Thalina said quietly.

Acion nodded, knowing the symbolism of rings to many sentient beings. "My ring. Will you wear it?"

"Gladly," she said, her smile making his heart thunder.

The changes within his system left Acion unsettled and agitated, as he'd never been before. Maybe it was good that any android who had undergone the changes prompted by the Hive's most recent enhancements died. He doubted his own effectiveness, given the turmoil in his reasoning.

A tear slipped down Thalina's cheek and her hand shook as she put the ring on her finger. "I love you, Acion," she whispered, and the words sent a thrill through him unlike any feeling he'd experienced so far. She smiled at his reaction. "Everyone should hear that at least once." She stretched up and kissed his cheek, leaning against him for a moment of unbearable sweetness, one he never wanted to end. "Good luck."

"Luck is irrational," he said and she laughed lightly, before wiping away her tears. He studied her, committing the image of her to his deepest databanks, then the third protective panel rumbled. Acion acknowledged the strange sense of regret as the panel slid out of view, then strode forward to meet his fate.

"Acion," Thalina said from behind him, but he kept walking.

Another tear, another kiss, another sweet confession, and he considered the probability of his retreat from his duty to be so high as to be inevitable.

"Protect yourself," he said. "The probability of the king entering in his dragon form is very high."

"He won't burn me," Thalina insisted as the portal swung open. Acion saw a group of guards, dressed in the king's livery, weapons at the ready. Three carried weapons with darts and he focused on them, determining that each dart was attached to a vial of green liquid.

A sedative?

A poison?

King Ouros himself, his gaze cold and his similarity to the hologram of Scintillon striking, gestured to the guards to remain where they stood. He strode into the Hoard alone, bold and confident. He walked directly toward Acion, and weapons were raised behind him to target Acion.

Acion fell to one knee and offered the gift on his outstretched hands, hoping his posture would ensure that the gift wasn't damaged.

The king halted and stared. "What is this?"

"A gift, sir, the gift I was dispatched to deliver to you."

"What is it?" Ouros demanded, his voice cold with suspicion.

"I do not know its precise nature, your majesty. I am only the messenger."

"Don't kill the messenger, Father," Thalina contributed but both Acion and Ouros ignored her. The king's gaze flicked to his daughter then back.

"Don't you know its name?" Ouros demanded of Acion.

"It was called a ShadowCaster, although I do not have any reference for this term."

Ouros surveyed the gift. His eyes were blue and they filled with consideration. "I do," he said softly, some element of pleasure underlying his tone.

"Then it is yours," Acion said.

The king took the gift, holding the clear cylinder to the light as he turned it and studied its contents. "A ShadowCaster," he repeated. "If it is real." His attention locked upon Acion, his gaze piercing. "And an android who pretends to be the Carrier of the Seed." He inhaled deeply, and his chest swelled. "What is the meaning of this travesty?"

"I have no data on that issue at this time."

"He *is* the Carrier of the Seed!" Thalina exclaimed, but her father raised a hand for silence.

He leaned toward Acion, the intensity of his survey reminding him of the kind of study androids routinely performed. The king was gathering data and making conclusions, and Acion felt a curious commonality with Thalina's kind. "Who gave you the Seed?" Ouros demanded in a low growl.

"Like your daughter, you speculate that I am merely a receptacle and delivery mechanism," Acion said. "This is a logical conclusion, but also a false one, at least in the case of the Seed."

The king snarled a little and emanated a stream of smoke as he did so.

"Who sent you?"

"The Hive of Cumae sent me."

"The Hive is his maker, Father."

The king arched a brow. "An android plot," he mused. "I like this less with every new detail. How many more of your kind will invade Incendium after you?"

"That information is not available to me at this time," Acion had to admit.

"Father, you have to listen to the facts..." Thalina began to protest, but Acion saw in the king's eyes that it was too late.

He was already glowing blue around his perimeter.

Because the dark shadow in the cylinder had begun to swirl.

"It's alive!" one of the guards shouted.

The king flung the cylinder back at Acion. "Break it free and you die," he threatened, and Acion caught the cylinder. It danced in his grip, as if it desired to fall and shatter, and he fought to keep his grasp upon it.

"Scintillon's Law must be upheld!" King Ouros roared as he shifted shape in a blaze of brilliant light. Acion leaped to his feet to defend himself, even as he calculated the strategic benefit of attacking the king to be nonexistent. He clutched the vial against his chest, unable to explain that its contents were pulsing and seemed to have become fluid.

The king was enormous in his dragon form, his wings brushing the ceiling of the Hoard, and his scales sparkling blue with gold tips. He snatched at Acion, who retreated with a jump.

Only to collide with another dragon behind him.

Thalina.

The king breathed a stream of fire, but Thalina's claw closed around Acion, and she thrust him behind her. She raged fire at her father and they locked claws as she struggled to keep him from seizing Acion.

"Run!" she roared, then released a blaze of fire herself.

"I forbid you to defend this android," her father bellowed, but Thalina fought more ferociously than her father. She wasn't trying to ensure that the older dragon wasn't hurt, which made it an unfair fight. Acion ducked under the pair of them and ran toward the portal. His mission could not be fulfilled. He should return to Cumae and make his report.

But he couldn't abandon Thalina to her father's wrath. Acion paused and glanced back.

That was when he saw one of the guards aiming his weapon. The guard gave a piercing whistle and the king spun and moved to the left, indicating that this signal had been arranged in advance. Thalina was held captive by her father, her breast bared. She struggled and fought, but the king exposed to the shot. Acion saw that the dart would pierce her breast.

It probably contained a sedative.

But he wasn't entirely certain of that.

Acion shoved the ShadowCaster's cylinder into his belt, then leaped on the closest guard. He took the man to the ground easily, even with his diminished power, and shattered the vial on the dart with his left fist. A green liquid spread across the floor, but Acion was busy fighting the guard into submission. He punched the man hard in the face and heard his nose crack, then blood flowed. He struck the man again in the stomach and another guard snatched away the weapon as the first fell.

The king roared and Acion looked up. He expected to be surrounded by guards, but they abruptly backed away, in a most unlikely fashion.

He spun to see the torrent of orange flame emanate from the king, then a hot blaze of fire surrounded him. The stream of flame was endless and hot, so much more scorching than the fire breathed by Thalina. Acion realized she'd told him the truth about the warning. He heard her scream his name, but the pain took him to his knees. The membrane encasing him was fried to oblivion. His shell was heated to the melting point and his circuits began to smoke. He couldn't command his body to respond and managed only a trio of steps before he stumbled and fell to the floor.

The fire burned.

The fire seared and scorched.

The fire cauterized and the fire incinerated.

And there was nothing Acion could do to save himself from his fate.

"I exist to serve," he managed to say, though his voice was the merest whisper. His eyes closed, then he thought of Thalina and her confession of love. He smiled, hoping it was true.

The probabilities of that, as irrational as it seemed, were excellent.

THALINA FEARED THE WORST when her father turned his back upon her. He tripped her with his tail, ensuring that she was off-balance for a critical moment but not injuring her, and she knew what he was going to do.

She knew she shouldn't challenge him but she also knew he was wrong.

She saw the brilliant flame of her father's dragon fire and knew that he was executing Acion. He meant for Acion's destruction to be quick and irreversible.

Even though she knew Scintillon's Law allowed for no appeal, Thalina didn't care.

The law was wrong.

Her father was wrong.

And she would defy him, for Acion.

For the Carrier of the Seed, who she believed was her HeartKeeper.

Thalina breathed fire at her father's back, not holding back the wrath of her fire any more than he was. Ouros howled in mingled pain and surprise and turned to face her, with fury in his eyes. More importantly, he stopped burning Acion.

Acion didn't move.

He was blackened, his membrane fried away, and his shell smoking.

"How dare you defy me in this?" Ouros demanding, his voice booming loudly enough to make the walls vibrate.

"Even a king must be defied when he is wrong!" Thalina roared, then pushed her father hard to one side. "I fight for justice, just as you taught me to do!" Ouros fell back, perhaps because he was surprised, but Thalina didn't care. She shoved past her father and snatched up the remains of Acion, then breathed fire over the heads of her father's guards. They stepped back and flinched, though one raised another tranquilizing dart and aimed it at her.

Thalina swung her tail hard and tripped him just as he pulled the trigger. The dart went wide, then caught her father in the upper arm. He was pursuing her, but paused to look down at the dart in astonishment. There was a moment of complete stillness, then the guards moved into action to defend the king.

Ouros fell heavily to his knees, the impact making the Hoard shake. He pulled out the dart and cast it at the wall so that it shattered, the last of the sedative running down the wall. Even though he hadn't taken the entire dose, his eyelids were already drooping.

"Thalina," he whispered, but she wasn't going to stay behind to listen to whatever her father was going to say.

She had to save Acion.

Thalina pushed past the guards and shifted shape. Acion's body burned her hands but she didn't care. For once she was glad of her greater strength.

"Do not injure the princess!" her father said, but his voice was fainter than usual.

Thalina ran down the corridor and toward the main part of the palace, only to find the way barred against her.

"Open by royal command!" she shouted, but the portal remained secured. She realized that her father had arranged for her to be contained and captured. She heard footsteps behind her, and glanced back to see Ector leading the guards.

He carried a tranquilizer gun. "Halt, Princess Thalina!" he called.

Thalina had no intention of halting. They'd sedate her and execute Acion while she was out cold. She'd awaken to a situation that couldn't be changed.

She snarled, knowing that Acion had to get out of the palace to have any chance of survival. No, he had to leave Incendium somehow. And his only chance of doing so was with her. The realization gave Thalina new strength—so did the sight of Ector raising his gun. The corridor was smaller than was ideal, probably smaller than her father believed she needed to shift.

Thalina would prove him wrong. She shifted shape again, cradled Acion tightly against her chest, then breathed fire at the approaching troops. She snatched at Ector but he managed to slip through her talons. He retreated and lifted the gun again. The others backed away, and Thalina pressed herself against the wall to ensure that she had as much room as possible.

She'd only have one chance.

She swung her tail against the portal and the rock with all of her might. The force of the blow set the whole palace vibrating, but more importantly, the portal cracked and the rock crumbled. She shoved a claw through it, making way, then rapidly shifted shape.

Thalina darted through the gap, pushing Acion through it ahead of herself. She heard the dart hit the rock behind her and the vial shatter. She shifted quickly and shoved massive rocks into the gap to slow down the guards. Then she snatched up Acion and jumped into the sky, holding tightly to him as she soared toward the heavens.

They would come after her. She needed a refuge.

Nowhere in Fiero-Four would be safe enough.

Thalina remembered Acion saying that he'd rented a Starpod. She landed at the star station and shifted shape, only to discover that there were seven rental Starpods in the lot. They were easily distinguishable by their orange logo, but less easy to open without the key.

"Third from the left," Acion said, his voice ragged.

Thalina looked down to see a dark gleam between his eyelids and could have kissed him in her relief. Instead, she went to the Starpod in question. Acion reached out his left hand to the lock and it opened immediately.

Thalina heaved him inside, climbed in after him and locked the doors.

"You should go back," Acion said.

"We're a team, now," Thalina said. "I'm going with you."

He shook his head. "The prospect of my survival remains almost too low to calculate..."

"And I'm going to fix that." She smiled at his obvious surprise. "Trust me."

Without waiting for a reply, Thalina strapped them both down. She gave the commands for the departure. No one was pursuing her yet, which had to mean that her father was unconscious or too groggy to give the command.

She had only seconds to escape the city.

"There is an advisory," the Starpod informed her. "No vessels are to leave the star station..."

"Over ride!" Thalina commanded. "Royal emergency." She used the family code and the Starpod hummed to life. She commanded it to depart and only heaved a sigh of relief when Incendium faded out of sight below her.

Would the starport be closed against her?

"Your flight will end at the starport," Acion said. "Departures are already forbidden and the port is being locked down. We might succeed in hiding long enough for me to affect some recovery, but survival is still improbable."

"I like risk," Thalina reminded him. "And I don't believe this is over yet."

"Faith is an irrational construct," he reminded her, his voice weakening. She heard a thread of humor in his next words. "It appears that I was not constructed with adequate provision to resist dragon fire."

"What do you need to heal?"

"Nanobots, but my stores are almost depleted."

"Where can I get some?" The Starpod was in the queue to the port, locked between shuttles in a steady progression. Thalina hated how slow their progress was, but there was nothing she could do about it. The ascent was timed. She tapped her fingers on her lap, then turned Acion's silver ring on her thumb.

"They are of common manufacture, but the absence of androids upon Incendium may affect their local availability."

"Give me a manufacturer name and number."

He did and Thalina eyed the looming port. They were being guided to a dock on a spur of the port that was less occupied. Had their Starpod been identified? Were they being isolated?

Acion was evidently watching the same thing. "The probability of assault after docking is ninety-two per cent," he murmured. "You should let me depart the ship alone."

"I told you. We're a team now."

"This choice is irrational," he insisted.

"But it's still my choice." Thalina surveyed the spur and began to smile.

"What gives you pleasure in this situation?"

She pointed. "That's Anguissa's ship. If anyone can get us out of here, it will be her." She ran her hand over the computer screen on the inside of her forearm and sent a message to her sister.

Who answered immediately.

Thalina laughed with delight.

"I see no cause for merriment," Acion said as the dock loomed closer. "We will both be exterminated because you did not make the logical choice."

"You just might learn the merit of faith today," Thalina said, even as she responded to Anguissa.

ACION DEPARTED THE STARPOD first, over Thalina's objections. His body was operational, although the strength in his limbs had diminished even more. It appeared that dragon fire was deeply detrimental to his systems. He knew his appearance had been adversely affected, because his protective membrane had been almost completely burned away. His shell was visible and in some places —most notably on his back—it had melted and his inner workings, while damaged, could certainly be viewed.

He felt naked, which was a new experience and one he didn't welcome.

Still, he couldn't let Thalina be injured, when he was the obvious target.

A beautiful and slender woman awaited him at the end of the ramp, arms folded across her chest and her long dark hair moving of its own volition. When Acion saw that the ends of her hair resembled snakes, their dark eyes glittering just as her own dark eyes did, he formulated a theory that this was the sister of Thalina. She seemed intent and purposeful, and her gaze swept over him, taking inventory.

He found it improbable that she overlooked much.

His processor was running slow, though, because he was still endeavoring to make sense of Thalina's choice. She had defended him and saved him. She had fled with him. She was determined to see them both away from Incendium, but only he was condemned by that planet's laws.

Why didn't she stay where she was safe?

And why had he given his ring to her? It was the only thing he truly owned. He had nothing else to give so it was the only gift he could make. But the choice had been quick. Impulsive. He had no programming to be impulsive or romantic and he knew it, but the decision had *felt* right. And her smile had twisted him inside—never mind her tears. Why did he feel as if he were filled with butterflies?

Why was he glad that she had remained with him, even at risk to herself?

Dragon fire had adversely affected more than his body, for certain.

Thalina was right behind him. "Anguissa!" she cried, showing no caution whatsoever. "I'm so relieved to see you!"

"I knew it had to be something important to drag you out of your workshop," Anguissa said wryly, still looking at Acion. "Don't tell me you've finally gotten into trouble. I'd almost lost hope for you."

"I've found lots of it," Thalina admitted with an ease that Acion found startling. "Father wants to execute Acion. Will you help us escape?"

"She is intent upon defending me, although this is irrational," Acion said. "Please convince your sister to let Scintillon's Law be upheld."

Anguissa lifted a brow. "You want to die?"

"I see no other logical possibility than the termination of my existence, and I would ensure that Thalina lives. She imperils herself against all reason by insisting upon accompanying me."

Those dark eyes narrowed and the snakes bared their fangs. "Isn't my sister good enough for you, Robot?"

Acion surveyed Thalina. "Your sister," he began and faltered. "Your sister is unlike anyone I have ever known. I recognize that I will be eliminated. It is only a question of time. I would like to ensure her survival, even if that means my destruction must be sooner."

"Hmm." Anguissa turned to her sister. "You could get another robot, just like him, but in better shape. I'll find one for you."

"Acion is the Carrier of the Seed," Thalina hissed. "And I want to find out if he's my HeartKeeper. Help us!"

Anguissa's brows rose and the snakes moved with greater agitation. "Knock me over with an electron," she muttered. "The Carrier of the Seed? That changes everything. Do you have a plan?"

"I need to help him return to Cumae."

Relief lit Anguissa's features. "That's only 2.5 light years away." She beckoned, glanced down the corridor, then led them to the next dock. She kept to the perimeter, but moved with admirable speed. "With my version of the Fractal Interstellar Drive, we'll be back before Father misses you..."

"We need to leave immediately," Thalina said.

"It is already too late," Acion contributed. "Flight plans will be placed on hold and the port secured until I am located."

"It's clearly not that hard to find you," Anguissa said. She displayed a map of the port on the computer film on the inside of her left arm. Lights were flashing on one quadrant. It was the one they occupied. "They've identified the Starpod."

Acion looked down the corridor to see guards striding toward them with purpose. They didn't rush, but then, there was nowhere to run and nowhere to hide.

He felt another new sensation. Panic.

"And we need some more of the nanobots Acion uses for self-repair," Thalina added as they hurried up the ramp to the next ship. It was a much larger ship and Acion read its name on the docking registrar.

The Archangel.

Archangel: (noun) an angel of the highest rank.

Angel: (noun) a spiritual being superior to humans in power and intelligence; an attendant spirit or guardian.

Acion found the name of the ship curiously reassuring.

Meanwhile, Anguissa's eyebrows rose. "You *are* making up for lost time," she said to Thalina. "Do you have a sample or a serial number?"

Thalina repeated it perfectly before Acion could.

The access port was locked and Anguissa's code didn't open it.

"Acion?" Thalina asked with complete confidence in his abilities. "Isn't some deception justified in fulfilling a mission?"

Acion didn't comment, just plugged into the data port on the console. A few appropriate queries and he had the code. He tapped it in and the gate unlocked.

"Good robot," Anguissa said and strode past him into her ship. Thalina followed, pausing to give him a kiss, and Acion secured the door behind them.

They stepped onto the command deck of the Archangel and Acion spied a port. He plugged himself in to the ship's computer with the appropriate connector in his left hand, needing to know the details of their situation.

"The port is eighty-two per cent sealed," he said, his earlier expectation confirmed. "They await only a scheduled freighter coming out of a jump in near space at any moment."

"No time for supplies," Anguissa said as the sisters strapped in. Anguissa gave Acion a considering look. "My crew is on leave. It'll take time to find them or hire others." She grimaced. "Actually, they'll be in the port bar, except for Bond, who will have gone home to Incendium city to visit his kids already."

"Too far," Acion said. "The port bar is nine Incendium minutes distant at a brisk pace. The guards will be at this gate in two-point-one minutes."

"Right. The robot will have to do." Anguissa began the pre-flight procedures.

Acion reveled in the flow of detail from the shipboard computers. "The Archangel has provisions sufficient for two humanoids for six light years, although they are mostly of the stored and condensed variety," he supplied. "I cannot testify to their appeal." He paused. "Nor am I entirely certain of the nutritional requirements for dragon shifters as compared to non-shifting humanoids."

"We'll make do," Anguissa said grimly.

"This ship is of a Mongossian design," Acion said. "Model 86-V-B, the Mongossian Starchaser, their fastest model but one no longer in production. It was manufactured two hundred and nine Incendium years ago, with a Fractal Interstellar drive that has been updated recently." He frowned. "The augmentation is in violation of galactic standards."

Anguissa blinked and looked at him.

Thalina smiled. "Once a rebel..."

"I'm glad he's on our side," Anguissa muttered.

"I have sufficient training to co-pilot this vessel in routine travel, and will supplement my records in observation," he said. "But I need to add to my understanding of this most recent augmentation."

"Seriously?" Anguissa said.

"Seriously," Thalina replied, because Acion didn't understand her query.

"A competent pilot must have full awareness of the capabilities of his vessel," Acion explained patiently.

Anguissa shook her head. "That's not what I meant. I've never yet seen a robot who could fly well enough to suit me."

"Androids of my manufacture are equipped with a range of programming because our missions take us frequently from Cumae. We are intended to be prepared in any situation..."

"Okay, Robot, have you ever flown a Mongossian Starchaser?"

"Twice," Acion supplied. "One of older manufacture than the Archangel, but not maintained so well, and a newer one, which did not possess a Fractal Interstellar drive..."

There was an alarm from the gate and a banging on the door of the Archangel.

"All right, all right, let's go," Anguissa said. "They're going to damage the skin," she muttered and hit the reverse thrust. "Hey, Robot, can you override the life form data that the computer delivers when we're hailed? I want it to look like I've taken the Archangel out alone."

"Even though that would be a foolish choice and you are a responsible pilot?" Acion asked, easily locating the source of that information. He overwrote it, eliminating the evidence of Thalina's presence, winnowing out all sources of input that might reveal her as he awaited Anguissa's reply. He knew what it would be, and he was right.

"Even so," Anguissa said.

"I must advise you that this deletion will adversely affect the system's calculations for food and oxygen supply..."

"But you've already done the calculations, Robot," Anguissa said. "And I can remember 'six years' all by myself."

Was this sarcasm? Acion did not know. Thalina was smiling, which indicated that she found amusement in her sister's comment.

"It's our only chance, anyway," Anguissa said. "Do it."

"It is done."

"Good. I like efficiency. There are some nanobots in the pharmacy. Try that port. You should be able to get a feed." Acion did as instructed as Anguissa frowned.

"They are not of the specified type," Acion said.

"You're the first robot on the Archangel," Anguissa said. "I'm making an exception to Scintillon's Law for you, because of Thalina."

"The Archangel is part of Incendium's fleet and thus subject to Incendium law?"

"Not technically, but I like to choose my battles with Father."

Acion assessed the nature of the nanobots available, then had a realization. "Surely the nanobots could be said to be androids and thus in violation..."

"They could be, Robot, but no one has been so foolish as to challenge me on that before," Anguissa snapped. One of the tendrils of her hair hissed at Acion.

He considered the composition of the nanobots that were available. They were designed for the repair of biological organisms. Under normal circumstances—that is, before he had been given the new programming by the Hive—Acion would have considered them lethal to his systems. In this moment, he had to consider Thalina's observation about the neurons in his shoulders and the changes he had observed himself. The probability of their having a favorable influence on at least some of his structure was improved to the point that he accessed the drip.

If he was wrong, the threat to Thalina would be removed with his demise.

There was a panel on the console that covered a storage space. Acion removed the cylinder containing the ShadowCaster and secured it there, reasoning that the Archangel could protect the gift intended for Ouros better than he could during a jump.

Anguissa was programming the navigation system. "Since they're waiting on the freighter, we'll jump out of here to make it look like I'm in a hurry. That loverboy of mine," she mused with a shake of her head. "I'm missing him so bad."

Acion wasn't sure who she meant. "But surely they will follow the trajectory of our jump," he protested.

"No, we'll jump to a little backwater I know. They won't follow us, given its reputation."

Acion had time to nod understanding before Anguissa disengaged the port lock and reverse-thrust out of the dock more quickly than he thought was wise.

"The port is closed down," she reminded him sternly, apparently noting his reaction. "We're the only ones in motion."

"Yes, Captain," Acion managed to say before a voice echoed on the deck.

"Archangel, Archangel, please return to the dock. The port is to be secured by command of the king..." The protest from control came immediately through the comm, but Anguissa interrupted it.

"But I forgot my boy toy on Nimue," she said. "And I can't live without him. I'll be back soon enough."

"Archangel, you are not cleared for departure..."

"Tell my father that I've found the Carrier of the Seed. He'll understand." Anguissa accelerated the ship. Acion monitored the ship systems, admiring how she increased the drive's power and triggered the Fractal Interstellar drive. The console gave no indication that she'd done so, which must have been one of the augmentations.

Acion found the probability that Princess Anguissa participated in illegal operations to be significantly increased by this detail. He glanced at Thalina, who smiled at him. He felt an odd conflict. He was both glad that she was with him and wished that she had remained behind where she would have been safe.

"Archangel, Archangel, please return to the dock," Control repeated. "We will be compelled to fire..."

"Then tell the king afterward that you've slaughtered his seventh daughter," Anguissa snapped and slapped the comm to silence.

"They won't do it," Thalina said.

Acion wasn't so certain of that.

"Doesn't matter," Anguissa said. "We'll be gone before they even take aim. Got your nanobots on a drip?"

"I do, thank you, Captain."

"And there comes the last freighter," Anguissa murmured as that ship loomed out of the starlit darkness. She didn't hesitate for an instant, but put her hand on the console. Her voice hardened to a tone of command. "Prepare to jump, Robot."

CHAPTER SEVEN

KING OUROS AWAKENED slowly, his thinking dulled by the tranquilizer. He was frustrated by how slowly his vision cleared and disliked that age was affecting his reactions. He had been returned to his royal chamber and was in his human form, Ignita beside him, as he might have anticipated.

She smiled when he stirred and stopped her fluttering. "Welcome back," she said, and he heard the relief in her tone.

So, she had noticed the greater effect of the drug upon him, as well.

Six hundred Incendium years wasn't that old.

The change, though, made Ouros grumpy. His knee was sore and he had a feeling he'd been singed on his back, undoubtedly by Thalina's dragon fire. He scowled at his servants, aware that only Kraw didn't retreat.

The viceroy's mustache might have wilted a little, though.

"And?" Ouros demanded, already guessing the answer from Ector's expression.

"The princess Thalina escaped Incendium with the android, your highness," the Captain of the Guard supplied.

"Escaped?" the king echoed in outrage.

"The android had apparently rented a Starpod and they went to the port," Ector supplied.

"Would you have rather they were shot down?" Ignita asked, her tone doing nothing to improve Ouros' mood.

"The starport is still Incendium territory," he said. "We must pursue them and uphold the law..."

Ector grimaced, his discomfiture clear. "I must inform your majesty that the princess Thalina and the android Acion are no longer at the starport."

"What?" Ouros sat up so quickly that Ignita placed a hand on his shoulder to steady him. "How can this be?"

"They found passage, your highness," Ector began.

"Passage?" Ouros roared. "Who would so defy the law of Incendium to provide passage to a runaway princess and an android?"

His chamber was silent after the question, and the gazes of both guard and viceroy dropped to the ground.

"What aren't you telling me?" Ouros whispered, a thousand dreadful possibilities filling his thoughts. Had Thalina been injured? Had the android launched some wicked plan against Incendium? And what about that vial? What had happened to it? What was in it?

"They aren't telling you what you should already have guessed," Ignita said, perching on the side of his bed. "There is only one captain with the authority to override any command to secure departures, and only person in all of Incendium who would so defy you."

"Anguissa," Ouros said, his rebellious daughter's name leaving his lips in a long hiss.

"Exactly, your highness," Ector replied. "The Archangel had only just returned but departed almost immediately. It has jumped to distant vector of the galaxy. It appears that the coordinates provided by Captain Anguissa on departure were not the actual destination, and we are attempting to determine the ship's precise location..."

"Don't bother," Ouros said. "Anguissa knows enough about our systems to outwit them. If she wants to hide, she'll manage to do it." His voice rose. "She should never have been permitted to depart!"

"I commanded the port to let her go," Ignita said quietly.

Ouros turned an outraged glance upon his wife, but she only shook her head at him.

"Would you have ordered them to eliminate two of your daughters at once?" she demanded, her eyes flashing. "Anguissa was determined to go, and you know she never backs down."

"And you know for certain that Thalina was aboard?"

"She must have been. The sensors changed their data about the number of life forms. There were two and then just one, as if Anguissa was alone." Ignita lifted a shoulder. "But the count changed after they'd left the dock."

"Androids," Ouros muttered, his anger rising again. "Who knows what they have planned. You should never have let them escape!"

"The Seed, Ouros," Ignita said with quiet urgency. "Thalina's senses are filled with the Seed, and she will naturally be protective of the Carrier of the Seed. You can't blame her for wanting to know if he is her HeartKeeper or not, for wanting enough time to be sure."

"He's an android!"

"But still the Carrier of the Seed. Even this challenges our assumptions. She must have discovered some detail that gives her hope for their future."

Ouros considered this, then sighed. "And so she pursued the only possible path. She removed him from Incendium, so he wouldn't be executed, in order to have that increment of time." He shook his head. "And she located the only ally who would have helped her in Anguissa."

"Exactly!" Ignita concluded. "Thalina's very logical."

"And yet, a romantic, as well," the king mused.

Kraw cleared his throat. "If I might say so, your majesty, the best scientific thinkers are also idealists, in my view. They investigate the world in all its detail, in the hope of improving it in future."

"With androids." Ouros sighed again, feeling every hour of his age.

He rose from his bed and began to pace the width of the chamber, ignoring Ignita's efforts to halt him. The room was silent again, as the others waited for his decision. He paused beside his queen and smiled. "Remember the Seed?" he murmured to her. "Remember the madness it awakened?"

She smiled back at him, her eyes shining. "I wouldn't call passion a madness."

"No, nor would I." He touched her cheek with affection, then turned to his viceroy and Captain of the Guard. "Thalina is not entirely aware of what she is doing. She is drive by the Seed to defend the Carrier and to attempt to secure a future for them. I hold her blameless in this situation." He folded his hands behind his back. "Anguissa, in contrast, is fully aware that what she has done is in direct defiance of my will. When she returns to Incendium, whenever that might be, the Archangel will be compounded and broken down into component parts while she is compelled to watch. Whatever stores are in the Archangel's holds will be surrendered to me and if they are illicit, Anguissa will be charged under the fullest extent of the law. Anguissa's pilot license will be forfeit and she will be confined to Incendium for a hundred years. There will be no negotiation. That she may have endangered Thalina with her actions is unacceptable. Anguissa has defied me for the last time."

"It will be as you command, your highness," Ector said and bowed.

"But what if Anguissa doesn't return?" Ignita asked.

Ouros heard the unspoken question. What if neither of their daughters returned, by choice or otherwise? The idea sickened him.

He strode to the window. He looked out over the imperial city in all its prosperity and watched the shuttles rising to the starport without really seeing them. "Anguissa will return," he said, knowing his wife wouldn't like his next words. "It's Thalina who may be gone forever." He glanced over his shoulder at Ignita, who looked horrified. "She has chosen the Carrier over her home, a choice influenced by the Seed but a decision all the same."

"But she will have a child!" Ignita said, coming quickly to his side. "We will have a grandchild! We must see them both!"

"I am caught between the law of my kingdom and the desire of my heart," Ouros said, taking Ignita's wife in his hand. He turned to Kraw. "Assemble an advisory council of our best lawyers, please, Kraw. I want a list of every single potential loophole to Scintillon's Law, as well as the possibilities of modifying that legislation."

"It will be done, your majesty, though I feel compelled to remind you that Scintillon's Law is studied even beyond Incendium as an example of a perfectly structured law that cannot be appealed."

"I know, Kraw," Ouros acknowledged, his heart heavy. "But I have to try."

"Understood, your majesty."

When Kraw and Ector were both gone and the door secured, Ignita turned to him. "How much tranquilizer did you ingest?" she demanded.

Of course, his wife would want to know the details. There had always been complete honesty between them and Ouros wasn't going to change that now.

Even though he winced. "Each dart was loaded with one third of the dose required to put Thalina to sleep. Maybe half of it entered my system before I removed the dart."

"That's all?" Ignita demanded, her eyes flashing. "But you are larger than Thalina..."

"And older, my beloved. And older." Ouros shook his head. Six hundred years. And five hundred as king. Where had the time gone? He considered the sun of their system, disliking that it was closer than it had once been. How could he ensure the future beyond his own inevitable demise? How could he defend those of his lineage still to come? And what of the citizens who relied upon him to guarantee their future?

He admired the elegance of Troy's theory that the birth of Gravitas might affect the speed of Incendium's fall into the sun, but he didn't have the same faith in the power of mind over matter. The astrologists had checked and double-checked, and at best, the change had added several hundred years to the projected survival of Incendium. He supposed colonization should be explored again and in greater detail.

It was, Ouros feared, a task for a younger king.

Ignita came to stand behind Ouros and slid her arms around his waist. He smiled at the press of her body against his own. "The Seed," she breathed, her touch and her words improving his mood. "I could smell it when they brought you to your chambers. Do you remember that summer night on Excandesco?"

Ouros covered her hand with his. "How could I forget? It was the first night of the rest of my life."

"I can still see the fireflies dancing for us."

"They weren't what beguiled me," he said, squeezing her hand.

Ignita chuckled. "Oh, you haven't lost your charm, Ouros of Incendium," she said, her voice husky as Ouros turned in her embrace. "I'm so glad I ignored my sister's advice and let you live."

Ouros chuckled. "I'm so glad you agreed to be my queen. Imagine! You would have had only Drakina if you'd sacrificed me."

"More importantly, I wouldn't have you," she replied. "I love my girls, Ouros, but you were the one I agreed to share my life with."

He bent to kiss her, that old heat simmering in his veins with new vigor.

"I thought you had to rest," Ignita whispered when she could.

"I'm not that old yet," Ouros growled. "Let me remind you of the power of the Seed."

THE HIVE CHECKED ALL OF its incoming data feeds.

There was no report from Acion.

It was extremely unlikely that Acion would fail to surrender his report as scheduled, which could only mean that he had been incapable of doing so. The android had been eliminated on Incendium before delivering an update to the Hive.

Which meant that the Hive's experiment had delivered no results.

Had the ShadowCaster been delivered?

Had the new programming elicited the same responses in Acion as in Arista? Had he gone rogue or malfunctioned?

The Hive reviewed the mission and its mandate, the enhancements made to Acion, then the detail known about Incendium. The file contained far more than the cursory summary in Acion's brief, including much about one detail that hadn't been included in that brief.

Scintillon's Law.

There had been a small chance that the law had been repealed since the Hive had been able to gather intelligence about Incendium. Indeed, the Hive's information about Incendium had been collected slightly before the passing of Scintillon's Law.

The Hive remembered Scintillon and his sons.

There had been another, slightly larger, chance that centuries without encountering androids might have left the Incendians unprepared to execute their own law. The Hive, in fact, had relied upon a delay, a legal pursuit of an appeal, even though Scintillon's Law did not allow one.

The Hive considered this to be a logical development, and had concluded it would allow sufficient time to ensure that Acion made one remote report before his elimination. There had been an elegance in ensuring that the android with the enhanced programming would be eliminated in the course of its mission, by undertaking that mission on a planet hostile to androids.

But given the silence from that android, the Hive determined that it was now highly probable that Acion had been destroyed on Incendium, perhaps even before delivering the ShadowCaster to King Ouros. That would mean that the ShadowCaster had also been destroyed, given its secure location within Acion's shell.

The Hive had taken a calculated risk, reasoning that Acion would be more efficient in pursuing his objectives than the Incendians would be in enforcing their law.

This had been an error.

The Hive was not accustomed to making errors. The Hive rechecked its conclusions a hundred times in rapid succession, only to make the same conclusion each time. There must have been another variable—or more—introduced, as the calculations were flawless. The assumptions and antecedents for the Hive's calculations had to be altered to reflect this new information.

Because the test of the new programming must be repeated, in order to determine its full influence, power and peril.

The Hive began a search of its databanks to identify the next android it would enhance.

CAPTAIN HELLEMUT SCOWLED at the screens in the cockpit of the Armada Seven. Ryke knew better than to challenge his captain when her expression was so dark. In fact, all of the crew hunched a little lower as if to become invisible. No one wanted to become a target of her legendary wrath.

"Again," she muttered and beckoned, her gesture bringing the image into higher resolution. "Is that or is that not the Archangel *again*, Ryke?"

Hellemut adored rhetorical questions, but Ryke wasn't going to be the one to tell her how tedious they were.

"It is, Captain," he confirmed, knowing better than to anticipate the next question. His own heart squeezed a little that the ship had returned. Its captain was glorious in her fury, even when confronted on the comm by Hellemut. Anguissa hadn't backed down quickly and had been so beautiful in her defiance that Ryke had later researched her.

A dragon shifter princess and a rebel. Trouble and then some.

And back. His heart skipped.

"In the same quadrant?" Hellemut invited.

"Yes, Captain."

"The same position?"

"Very close, Captain. You have an excellent eye for judging distance."

Hellemut spun in her chair to face him, her three green eyes sparkling with malice. "And what have I told you about repeat visitors to the quadrant claimed by the Gloria Furore and defended by the Armada Seven, Ryke?"

"That one visit might be an accident, but that the second is a provocation."

Hellemut smiled, although it wasn't a pleasant expression. "I have trained you well," she said with satisfaction. She spun to face the main screens again and drummed her fingers for a moment. "How many life forms aboard?"

"Only one, captain," supplied another crew member. "The mass and heat match that of the princess Anguissa, derived from your previous exchange with her."

"Excellent. She is taunting us." Hellemut smiled and straightened. "It is time to teach the princess Anguissa a lesson about provocation."

Ryke made a notation of the order. The thing was, it didn't look like foolishness when Anguissa challenged Hellemut.

It looked a lot like bravery.

He wondered what scheme she had in returning so soon to the same quadrant, and what plan she had for Hellemut. Ryke's research had fed his admiration of the notoriously audacious dragon princess. She was every bit as dangerous as Hellemut: he doubted her morals were much better, but Anguissa was beautiful.

And she was inclined to serve the greater good, even over her own.

That combination had a way of tempting Ryke to make mistakes, like the one that had landed him in the custody of the Gloria Furore in the first place. Why had Anguissa come back? He doubted it was an accident or even a provocation.

She had a reason and Ryke was curious about it.

At Hellemut's gesture, he opened the comm and hailed the Archangel.

THALINA HAD FORGOTTEN how much she hated jumping.

And this time, she hadn't been sufficiently hydrated, which only made the effects worse.

There was a reason why she stayed home on Incendium. Thalina had traveled as a young dragon princess, but had never found anywhere with sufficient allure to justify regular space travel. The jump made her feel as if she was stretched thin and turned inside out, taken apart and then put back together again—by someone who hadn't read the directions. She was a clock smashed on the ground and dumped back into its casing, workings all a-jumble and everything in need of calibration and adjustment. That feeling was only worse this time.

Was it because the Seed taken root?

Was she pregnant? The possibility filled her with delight and concern.

She opened her eyes warily when the jump was completed. Anguissa, of course, was checking the Archangel's systems and appeared to be unaffected. Acion already had new membrane on his left arm and also appeared to be unaffected. He probably was, since it was biological organisms who took space travel harder. He frowned at the console, then scanned the display.

"You said this sector would be vacant," he noted and Anguissa frowned in turn.

She tapped up the display then grimaced. "That's the problem with a quick departure."

"Where are we?" Thalina asked.

"Where we shouldn't be," Anguissa muttered. "I called up a list of recently visited locations and chose the wrong one. We're too far out. Frack. I don't usually make these kinds of mistakes."

When she realized that Acion was calculating, Thalina's fear rose. "But we can get to Cumae, right?"

Acion was tapping the console, his eyes moving rapidly as he absorbed data, and she knew he'd tell her the truth. No matter what it was. "There are sufficient stores for one life form to reach Cumae or to return to Incendium," he said. "Not both."

"That makes no sense," Thalina said.

"Our present location is distant from both planets," Acion informed her. He drew a triangle in the air, one with a long point. "Consider that we are here." He indicated the single point. "To jump to one or the other is a difference of direction more than distance." He tapped. "That said, the individual would have several days of minimal nourishment if Incendium was chosen as destination, but would still arrive alive."

Thalina sat down hard. This was a lot more adventure than she'd planned on having.

"Is this not danger?" Acion asked, apparently noticing her reaction.

Thalina nodded, remembering their earlier discussion. "I think it would count."

"Then I shall add to my experiences with it." He tilted his head. "You do not appear to be enjoying it as much as I would have anticipated."

"Maybe it's different when you have someone else to take care of,"

Thalina said and spread her hand over her flat stomach. Acion's eyes flicked and he was very still for a long moment. Their gazes met and locked, and she knew that he understood her implication.

How did he feel about them having a child?

Did he feel anything at all?

"Not to interrupt you two, but we've got more trouble than supplies," Anguissa said. She pushed Thalina down to the floor, then gave her a shove when she might have argued.

"What?"

"I know that ship." Anguissa pointed to the far side of the deck with an imperiousness Thalina instinctively obeyed.

"We are being hailed," Acion said. "By the other ship in the quadrant."

"By Captain Hellemut of the Armada Seven," Anguissa said, not a shred of doubt in her tone.

"You anticipated this meeting?" Acion asked.

"No, but I recognize the ship and I know its captain well enough to speculate on her plans."

"Ah!" Acion said.

Anguissa spun in her chair, then stood up abruptly. "Okay, this is what's going to happen, Robot, and you're going to make it so." She leaned toward Acion and whispered rapidly to him.

Thalina thought it was a bad sign that she couldn't hear her sister's words.

"This is illogical," Acion protested when Anguissa stopped talking.

"On the contrary, it's the only thing that makes sense," she insisted. "You exist to serve right?"

"Correct."

"And I'm your captain, so I command you to do this in order to defend my sister."

Acion frowned.

"What's happening?" Thalina demanded.

Anguissa glared at Thalina. "Stay out of view and keep silent if you want to live. You do *not* want to mess with these people."

"Who are they?"

"Frack knows but they work for the Gloria Furore."

Thalina stayed out of view and kept silent because that was all the warning she needed.

"And strap down," Anguissa added in a growl.

"This is excellent advice," Acion agreed, firing a look at Thalina.

She did what she was told, remembering everything she'd ever heard about the Gloria Furore. The notorious and secretive band of thieves roved the galaxy, stealing, hijacking, kidnapping, and selling to the highest bidder. Weren't they the ones who had snatched Troy from Terra? Thalina's panic rose. She couldn't die right after she met the Carrier of the Seed, could she? She couldn't be killed before she knew whether Acion was her HeartKeeper, before she had his child, before she contributed to the future?

Or made a future?

This wasn't fair!

She did so much better with automatons. With logical systems and creatures. With androids who calculated probabilities...

One life form.

Thalina's lips parted as she realized who Anguissa had decided that one life form was going to be.

Of course. Anguissa was going to give Thalina a future.

Before Thalina could protest, her sister stood up and went to the deck, propping her hands on her hips as she faced the screen. "Open the frequency to hail, Robot." Anguissa commanded, just as Thalina realized the markings on the deck indicated that it was also a transport deck. "Let's do this thing. Oxygen is wasting."

Thalina bit her lip, feeling helpless, even as the image of the ugliest creature she'd ever seen filled the screen. Anguissa didn't even flinch. "Greetings, Captain Hellemut," she said in the universal tongue. She spoke with a more gutteral accent than usual, but Thalina could still follow the words. "How I have missed the sunshine of your smile."

"You are a fool to return, Captain Anguissa," that creature said, its voice also gutteral yet oddly feminine. "And I thought you were clever."

"I just dislike unfinished business," Anguissa said.

"The Archangel is targeted by all of our weapons, Captain Anguissa. You are in no position to negotiate."

"What do you want?"

"Surrender, of course."

"And then?"

"You, first," the three-eyed monster said with glee. "And then the Archangel."

"And if I decline this generous offer?"

"I'll obliterate you both together, right now."

"How very persuasive you are, Captain Hellemut." Anguissa raised her hands. "Open a beam to transport me to your deck so I can surrender in person."

The creature chuckled. Thalina saw the display on the console register the locking of the tracking beam. Anguissa gave a nod to Acion, winking at Thalina when she turned her head so that the other captain couldn't see.

Thalina blinked and Anguissa was gone.

Anguissa was giving Thalina a future at the price of her own.

"Prepare to jump," Acion said softly in warning, right before Thalina was turned inside out all over again. She didn't dare to scream her sister's name aloud, but it echoed in her thoughts as the Archangel jumped again.

SACRIFICE.

Acion searched his records.

(verb) To make an offering of; to destroy, surrender, or suffer to be lost, for the sake of obtaining something; to give up in favor of a higher or more imperative object or duty.

Anguissa had sacrificed her life to ensure that Thalina survived.

Because Thalina carried a child?

Because Thalina was her sister?

Acion didn't know. It was impossible to precisely calculate Anguissa's motivation without a better understanding of her nature. He reviewed the confrontation in the Hoard and recognized that Thalina had been prepared to sustain injury in his defense. That, too, was a sacrifice of her welfare.

The logical question was whether he would make a similar sacrifice under any circumstance, and what that circumstance would be.

Acion was startled to realize that he *had* done so, also in the Hoard. He had attacked the guards instead of fleeing, in order to protect Thalina from the dart.

Pride flooded through him, warming his entire body in a most unusual and very pleasant way. This augmentation to his programming vastly enhanced his experience.

He was aware of Thalina, and her discomfort during the jump. Biological organisms experienced the jump as a short interval of time, which was merciful given its effect upon their bodies. (They contained too much water.) Acion, as usual, found his reasoning accelerated, as an effect of the jump.

This time, there was an ache deep in his joints, perhaps a function of two jumps in rapid succession. He would have to analyze that later.

For the moment, he was investigating the ship's navigation system. It struck him as highly improbable that an experienced pilot like Anguissa would have made such a mistake in charting her course. She was daring and bold, but that was born of confidence, which could only have been reinforced by success.

When he found the explanation, he felt disappointment.

Anger.

Betrayal.

Thalina would have to be told.

Acion returned to the initial question, somewhat startled to reason that there was a one hundred per cent probability that he would sacrifice his own existence for that of Thalina. Even though his existence wasn't his to squander.

He existed to serve, but he would serve Thalina first.

It wasn't just because of the Seed.

It was because he loved her.

He felt more than desire or admiration. He felt more than a preference for her company. He felt an imperative to be with her, to defend her, to see the child that resulted from the Seed, and even, to build a life together.

Acion knew he had no right to want any of those things. Until very recently, that wouldn't have troubled him. He knew his place and accepted it.

But now, he felt rebellion rise within him.

If he hadn't already programmed the coordinates of Cumae into the system and launched the jump, he might have even changed their course. As it was, the Archangel came out of the jump, in high orbit around Cumae. Acion could see the starport, a much smaller and more utilitarian starport than that of Incendium.

He let the ship's nav system chart the docking and commence the approach. Their fuel was as low as anticipated. Would they be able to obtain more here at Cumae's port? He couldn't find a reference for the Archangel having docked here recently, much less determine easily whether Anguissa had credit. No doubt she locked the access to deter theft. He could probably undermine her security measures, but that would take time.

Time Acion might not have. The dock loomed closer.

He began to calculate the most fuel-efficient way to return Thalina to Incendium.

He would make his report to the Hive.

He would complete his duty.

And he would take—or send—Thalina home. Her father wouldn't turn her away, especially not if she carried a child. And if his own destruction was the price of ensuring Thalina's safety, Acion would pay it.

Gladly.

ANGUISSA.

Her sister's fate was Thalina's first concern when she awakened after the jump.

The second was that she felt worse than she had in four hundred Incendium years.

"There is a dehydrated food item in the receptacle beneath your right arm," Acion said. "Although I believe you are in greater need of water."

"Jumping is the worst when you're dehydrated," Thalina agreed and got up, realizing that she was speaking for herself. Acion probably couldn't even be dehydrated. There was a low force of gravity, so she was able to walk across the deck. Acion pointed and she saw the galley, where she found containers of water. She opened one and drank from the spout molded into the container. Relief immediately spread through her body and her aches began to fade.

She considered the starport on the display. "Where are we?"

"Cumae, as anticipated. The Interfractal Drive on the Archangel is remarkably efficient and accurate. Your sister's enhancements to the drive were excellent."

"I'll bet they weren't the only ones. This ship is probably full of secrets." Thalina sat down in the captain's chair. She was aware of how recently Anguissa had sat there and imagined that she could feel the heat of her sister's body lingering in the upholstery. She certainly could smell her perfume.

"Perhaps so. There is an access with an airlock, which is of considerable size. The curious thing is that the openings on the airlocks are considerably smaller than the one on the ship's exterior." Acion gave Thalina a considering look. "Did your sister hijack ships?"

"Maybe." Thalina thought. "Or maybe it was for her in dragon form."

Acion frowned. "In space?"

"We can generate a biological orb for interplanetary travel. Maybe Anguissa was better at it than the rest of us. It's unlikely she would tell us about it."

He nodded. "So, she would enter the airlock in dragon form, in the orb, then shift shape?"

"It makes sense."

"And the orb?"

"The craft of creating and dissolving one is a closely kept secret amongst my kind."

"Ah." Acion worked in silence for a few moments, until Thalina asked what she most wanted to know.

"Do you think she's dead?"

Acion paused before he replied. "If she is lucky."

Thalina winced. "I'm surprised that she made a mistake. I'm really sorry that our quick departure was responsible."

"She did not make a mistake," Acion supplied, his words tight.

Thalina sat up. "What do you mean? How do you know?"

"The navigation device of the Archangel was infiltrated and sabotaged. I have discovered a worm that would override any selected coordinates with those of the sector we visited."

"The one with Captain Hellemut's ship," Thalina said.

Acion met her gaze. "It appears that your sister was betrayed. She did not err. The worm was programmed to activate after X number of jumps, when X was defined as a random number between one and ten. I am sorry, Thalina, but it was only a matter of time before the Archangel returned to that quadrant."

"No wonder the other ship was waiting."

"Indeed. The captain of the Armada Seven experienced no surprise, only triumph in the success of her plan."

"But why?"

Acion tapped the console, shaking his head. "It appears that there was an earlier altercation between the two captains in that same sector."

"And Anguissa won, so the other captain wanted another chance."

"One in which she had the element of surprise on her side, yes." Acion nodded. "I calculate a very high probability that your sister was glad to take this challenge while she was apparently alone. There is considerable evidence in the records of her protectiveness toward her crew."

Thalina smiled. "She's a dragon princess. We take care of our own."

Acion eyed her. "Even though one of them betrayed her."

Thalina nodded. "Even so. Anguissa would have said that she did the right thing, even if whoever planted the worm didn't."

Acion tilted his head, considering. "Yes. I see that her protectiveness was a dominant trait and one she perceived as a measure of character."

"It's a mark of our kind."

"Which was why she protected you."

Thalina blinked back tears. "I wish I could have done the same for her."

Acion didn't speak for a moment, just watched the approaching dock of the starport. "I will speculate," he said quietly, "that the princess Anguissa is not at as much of a disadvantage as Captain Hellemut might believe."

"How so?"

"I find no evidence that Anguissa's true nature was revealed in their previous encounter, and further, that Captain Hellemut appears to be a leader who relies more on brute force than research." He turned to Thalina, a little smile curving his lips. Her heart skipped. "I must wonder in which form Anguissa arrived on the teleport deck of the Armada Seven."

Thalina laughed despite herself, surprised by Acion's words and also reassured by them. "I wouldn't want to face her, not if I'd revealed an intent to destroy her ship."

"Exactly."

"Present identification for all occupants, Archangel," came the voice from the port.

Acion tapped the console, obeying the instruction. "Identification dispatched."

"Only one life form aboard and one android?"

"That is correct."

There was a pause. "Android Acion, your identification has been flagged. Upon docking, please proceed alone to room 65X. Princess Thalina, welcome to Cumae."

"What's going on?" Thalina asked in a whisper.

"I must make my report to the Hive." He caught her hand beneath his. "It is protocol. You do not need to be concerned."

"How long will it take?"

"Not long. There will be a port to accept the transfer of all data I have collected. It is routine."

Thalina didn't share his confidence. In fact, she had a hundred questions. Would he remember the data he shared with the Hive? Would he remember her? Would the Hive restrain him or demand something of her? Would they be allowed to leave Cumae?

And where would they go?

"You're not telling me everything," she accused.

"You are observant," Acion agreed. "There is a four per cent chance that something has changed on Cumae since my departure, and that such a change might influence my status and future mobility."

"What does that mean?"

He opened a panel on the console, revealing the cylinder that held the ShadowCaster. "I never delivered the gift to your father. My failure may influence my ability to return to you."

Thalina had a lump in her throat. What exactly did he think was going to happen when he made his report? "Will you remember me after the data transfer?"

Acion considered this. "I do not know. Such choices are made by the Hive."

Thalina was afraid then. "We shouldn't have come here," she began as the ship docked and the door was opened automatically.

"Android Acion, your presence in 65X is mandatory. Please proceed to that room with all speed."

"We had to come here," Acion reminded her. "My programming requires me to report to the Hive, and my scheduled report was delayed." He opened a panel on the console, revealing a familiar cylinder secured in the space behind it. Just as before, it appeared to have dark dust in the bottom of it. "I must ask you to act as my Sword Sister in this matter and complete my mission for me. Will you deliver the ShadowCaster to your father, please?"

"I'd be honored to act as your Sword Sister," Thalina acknowledged. "But I hope I don't have to."

"It is not the same as successfully surrendering the gift to your father's hand, but perhaps this will suffice."

"But I can't give it to him, not from here."

"Of course not, but you will soon return home. The nav system is programmed to take you to Incendium. You have only to leave the starport, then launch the Fractal Interstellar Drive. All of the variables are set..."

Thalina's heart squeezed, because she knew what the implications of their arrival at Incendium would be. "I don't have to go home and I don't want to go home without you..."

"But I cannot go with you, and I do not know what memories the Hive will leave me. Your sister has taught me something of the nature of your kind. I, too, will protect my own," Acion said firmly. "Ensuring the welfare of you and the child you may carry is my responsibility."

"But..."

"I must do whatever is necessary to see my mission completed, Thalina."

"But," she protested again.

Acion stood and pulled her into his embrace. "There can be no objection," he said with quiet conviction. "I love you, and this is the best I can do for you. Do not spurn it because it is too little. It is all that we may have."

"If you can return, you will," Thalina insisted.

"If I can return, I will," Acion agreed. "And if I cannot, you will go to Incendium."

"I will," Thalina said. "Now, give me a kiss to keep me warm."

"That is irrational," Acion began to argue, but Thalina wrapped a hand around his neck, pulled down his head and kissed him thoroughly.

CHAPTER EIGHT

ACION'S CIRCUITS WERE SIZZLING after Thalina's kiss.

And this was not a bad thing.

It made him feel alive, and truly, if this was the last sensation he experienced, he would not regret it. He considered the possibility that his new programming would be deleted, but could not conclude that the probability of success was high. His body was changing, and that would be hard to undo. Chances were higher that the experiment would be allowed to continue for a short period of time, to better quantify the changes in his nature.

Acion proceeded to 65X, reasonably convinced that Thalina would do as he had instructed. He also had a sixty-four per cent conviction that he would be able to return to her, at least to say farewell again.

At least to collect another kiss.

After that, his projections became too qualified to be useful.

Acion entered the room, which was just as he had anticipated as it was almost identical to the one deep within the Hive. There was a tank filled with liquid, undoubtedly possessing a high concentration of the nanobots that ensured the repair of all androids. He placed his hand on the panel on the wall, permitting his computer to be scanned.

"You are late," said the Hive.

"This is true," Acion said. "The delay could not be avoided, but I have returned as quickly as could be contrived."

He made to step into the bath.

"No," the Hive said, halting him. "Plug in first."

Acion blinked. This was a change of protocol. All forty-three times that he had returned to the Hive to report, he had both entered the bath and plugged in to transfer his collected data.

Perhaps the protocol had changed.

Certainly, he had changed, because he felt trepidation for the first time as he followed the Hive's instructions.

THE HIVE REVIEWED THE data delivered by Acion and decided that the experiment had been a complete failure.

There had been a possibility of the android presenting Acion's identification being an imposter, but that was not the case.

The truth was infinitely worse. Acion showed all the same weaknesses that Arista had developed, except that the effect was more pronounced. The subroutine the Hive had believed an elegant enhancement was proving to be a rampant infection.

Acion felt.

Acion yearned.

Acion believed.

Worse, Acion chose to follow different paths than those that would most logically fulfill his assignment. The android had become unreliable.

Worse again, the shell and workings of the android had been infected by the programming of the nanobots. Destroyed mechanical matter had been replaced with biological equivalents, a fact exacerbated by both the extensive damage Acion had endured under dragon fire, and by the addition of nanobots programmed to heal biological organisms.

The change was beyond the Hive's control.

The predictability of Acion's reactions was demolished.

The loyalty of Acion had shifted from the Hive to Thalina.

And that combination made this android trash.

The Hive decommissioned Acion and arranged for the disposal of the remains.

THALINA HAD NEVER THOUGHT she had a suspicious mind, but she didn't trust the Hive.

And she didn't like Acion going to make that report alone.

She paced the deck of the Archangel after he had left, debating what to do. She was still dressed as a servant in Incendium's palace, and really, her clothes were both dirty and ragged. She looked more like a beggar than a princess and wouldn't be able to command any attention or support, given that she was unknown on Cumae.

On the other hand, she was unknown on Cumae. She could *be* a servant and escape the notice of pretty much everyone.

She might be invisible, or as close to it as she'd ever been.

Thalina locked the ShadowCaster back in the console. She confirmed that the access to the Archangel would lock after her departure and that she would be able to open it on her return, checking the code a couple of times before she stepped outside the vessel and secured the door. She verified again that she could open it, before locking it once more and setting out after Acion.

By this time, there was no sign of him in the bustle of the starport. Cumae's port was smaller and more utilitarian than that of Incendium—Thalina had the impression that Cumae was less affluent, or maybe just less interested in appearances. The starport was shaped like a star, similar to Incendium's, with spurs extending from a central ring and offering docks for vessels. Except Cumae's starport had only four spurs, rather than the twelve of Incendium's port.

Another difference was that this starport was filled with far more warriors than would be the case at Incendium's port—there, the main corridors and bars were crowded with merchants and traders, as well as scientists and researchers. There were also androids at this starport, or at least individuals more readily identified as androids. The refreshment facilities tended to be bars instead of restaurants—Thalina passed a very large and busy one called *Valhalla*—and the shops were well stocked with weapons and armor. There were also android charging stations and a parts store, with a used androids display. As much as Thalina would have liked to have browsed there, she had to find Acion.

Just as at Incendium's starport, the greatest congestion was at the loading areas for shuttles to the planet. They departed at regular intervals here, too.

It didn't take Thalina long to figure out the numbering of the rooms in the central ring, although 65X proved to be on the opposite side of the station. She wished she was as tall as Acion as she strode toward it, knowing that he had probably already arrived at his destination and she had a long way yet to go.

When she approached the door tagged 65X, a cleaning cart came from the opposite direction and parked outside the door. A pair of androids that were about as tall as her hip separated themselves from the cart. One opened the door and the other rolled inside. The first followed a moment later.

Thalina eased closer and looked inside

There was a tank on the floor at one side, and a number of ports in the wall. One android was moving back and forth rapidly, one appendage pushing along the floor. Thalina could hear the suction mechanism that enabled it to clean the floor. The other android lifted something and bustled out the door, heaving its burden into the cart.

It was Acion.

Thalina hurried to the cart. "Acion!" she whispered and his eyes opened just a slit. The effort seemed to be too much for him, which made no sense.

"I exist to serve," he said, the words slurring slightly, then his eyes closed again.

"Acion!" The Hive had done something to him. Thalina knew it.

She unfortunately didn't know how to fix the damage.

The androids returned then, the one rolling into the bottom of the cart and closing a door behind itself. The other closed a lid over the section that held Acion and buzzed against Thalina's legs because she was standing in its way. She moved instinctively away and the android rolled into another receptacle.

She was trying to open the lid of the cart when it began to roll away. She thought maybe a brake had been released, but a light illuminated on the lid and the cart moved with definite purpose.

And speed.

Thalina ran after it.

It raced down the corridor toward the waiting area for the shuttle, Thalina right behind it. Her heart was racing, but she wasn't going to slow down and lose track of Acion. Beside the waiting area for the shuttle, a door slid open. Lights were blinking on the front of the cart and on the door, so Thalina assumed there was some connection between them. The door opened into a small room, so small that there little extra room around the cart. She squeezed into the space just as a chute opened in the wall. The cart tipped and dumped its contents, including Acion, into the chute.

Thalina jumped over the cart, banged her head on the side of the chute and fell into the space after Acion. She snatched at the chute, but her hand slipped off the metal and she fell into a pile far beneath it. She grabbed Acion's arm by the time the chute closed and pulled him closer as they were lost in darkness again.

Thalina wrapped her arms around his chest and shook him, but he was unresponsive.

Where were they? It smelled of organic matter, and in fact, smelled so strongly that Thalina felt her bile rise. She stretched out a hand and touched something slimy, then recoiled. She hung on to Acion, wondering if it was her imagination that she could feel a pulse within him.

His heart.

His motor, he'd say.

Thalina closed her eyes and held tightly to him, her hands locked over that faint vibration and summoned the shift from deep within herself. She'd get them out of here by brute force and back to the Archangel, no matter who she had to fry to do it. She was glowing blue and feeling the surge of the change when the bottom abruptly dropped out of the chamber.

They fell.

Along with all the garbage from Cumae's starport that had been packed into the bin with them.

Cumae was far below, wreathed in clouds. The space station was within the gravitational pull of Cumae, Thalina realized, because they were rapidly falling toward the surface and would soon enter the atmosphere.

Thalina completed her shift with a roar and spun an orb faster than she'd ever managed to do so in her life. She encased herself and Acion just as the first pieces of trash began to burn. They had already fallen a considerable distance, and she turned, fighting against the gravitational force of Cumae to reach the moored Archangel. It was harder than anything she'd done before—not only was the oxygen thinner but the orb was less stable at such an altitude. She had to spin another orb, then carry on, beating her wings hard to get back to the vessel. She strained to reach the Archangel, knowing it was their only chance, and was concentrating so much that she didn't realize Acion's eyes had opened until he spoke.

"Free," he whispered, and her heart skipped with joy.

Thalina closed her eyes as her pulse matched that of Acion. She felt strength flood into her, as if she was able to draw power from him, and she beat her wings harder.

"HeartKeeper," she whispered, because that was the only explanation for their hearts matching pace. She didn't know how it could be and she didn't know why, but her body told her the truth.

Thalina gripped Acion and soared the last increment to her sister's ship.

Just as Acion had told her, there was a pair of large cargo doors on the underside of the vessel.

Dragon-sized cargo doors.

But how would she open them without anyone at the console?

"DNA recognition," Acion murmured. "The ship knows you already."

And he was right. The doors opened. Thalina flew inside and shifted shape, collapsing against the air lock with Acion in her arms.

The cargo doors closed and so did her eyes.

She just needed a moment to catch her breath.

FLYING!

The rush of air over Acion's skin awakened him and the sight of Cumae so far below thrilled him. He saw the orb that Thalina had spun and looked at her great wings flapping overhead. She held him tightly against her chest with one claw, her talons cold against him, and Acion had never felt so alive in all his days.

He could feel the beat of her heart against his back, and when his own matched pace with hers, the sensation made him dizzy.

"HeartKeeper," she murmured beneath her breath, and Acion understood the meaning of the term.

It changed everything.

It filled him with a new sensation.

Joy.

Thalina seemed invigorated, too. She soared, seeming to close the last distance to the Archangel with new ease. The ship welcomed her, with a logic and timing that Acion found most admirable. Thalina collapsed against the air lock in her human form, her breath coming quickly. She had done her part to save them, and now he would do his. Acion stood to activate the lock and get them out of the hold.

He carried Thalina to the deck, new power in his stride as if he'd been rebuilt. He strapped her in as she stirred, then activated the engines and backed the Archangel out of her mooring. He turned off the comm, as disinterested in any interference as Anguissa might have been, and steered the ship with that dragon captain's verve. Once they were cleared of other vessels and in the jump zone, he activated the course he'd already programmed.

"Prepare for jump," he said to Thalina and smiled with satisfaction.

Acion was taking his HeartKeeper home.

THE JUMP FELL SHORT.

It was probably because the Archangel had run out of fuel.

Thalina awakened to discover that they were still two months away from Incendium. The Archangel was drifting in the right direction, and she knew that if it was necessary, the ship would be harnessed and hauled into Incendium's starport.

They weren't in danger, but they might have a few hungry days.

She couldn't regret the situation, because it would give her more time with Acion.

Maybe it would give more time to Incendium's lawyers to revise Scintillon's Law, if they were even trying. She should send a message to Incendium, to her father, and request that they do as much.

But first, she wanted to be with Acion. She wanted to celebrate their escape in a most fundamental way.

He was still in the captain's chair and his eyes were still closed. His finger dangled over the ship's port but wasn't plugged in.

More than that had changed. Thalina had to look closer to identify the dark shadow on his jaw and on his scalp.

It was hair.

Acion had stubble. She ran her fingertip across it, feeling how it bristled, and he stirred a little but didn't wake up.

The nanobots must have improved his biological membrane, so that it was more like skin than it had been before. That was interesting. She ran a hand down his arm, glad to see how much he had healed and felt the musculature beneath the membrane. When her hand reached his elbow, his free hand rose to capture her hand beneath his own.

As if he had felt her touch.

But he had told her that he had sensors only in his face and his hands.

Thalina remembered the second time they'd made love and how he'd responded to her touch on his back. She thought of the neurons she'd seen in his shoulder and speculated—just the word made her smile in anticipation of what Acion would say—that his body was changing.

It was amazing.

But what was even more amazing was that his eyes were moving back and forth beneath his eyelids.

Acion was dreaming.

Thalina couldn't suppress her cry of delight. She couldn't stop herself from jumping onto him and kissing him awake, just as she couldn't keep herself from seducing him thoroughly to celebrate the change.

And when Acion opened his eyes, she was surprised again. They had turned blue.

ACION AWAKENED TO Thalina's kiss, a situation that he found most satisfactory.

"You're changing," she said when he might have drawn her closer. "Your eyes are blue!"

She was right. Acion ran a scan of his systems and found that his reporting was less accurate than it had been. In some sectors, those which had been most extensively damaged by dragon fire, he had to rely on sensation to verify his functionality, instead of receiving performance readings.

His finger was out of the ship's port and when he tried to put it back, he couldn't reveal the plug hidden beneath his fingertip. That opening had sealed, as had all of the other ones.

"I'll miss one finger," Thalina said and he realized she'd been watching him.

He checked that one again and frowned that it was no longer functional.

"Maybe we need to do a complete assessment," she said, sliding into his lap. Her arms were around his neck and her lips were touching his throat. Acion closed his eyes in pleasure. The sensation of Thalina's weight against him, her touch, and their hearts beating in unison again was almost enough for him to put practical considerations aside.

But not quite.

"If you are right, the implications are important, though," he said, reaching past her to remove the override he'd installed at Anguissa's command. "If we are two biological organisms, there might not be sufficient supplies for us both to reach Incendium..."

"We're okay. I checked," Thalina said, stilling him with a touch. "Anguissa has undocumented supplies stashed all over this ship."

"I should not be surprised," Acion murmured. "But still, you must proceed alone, as my termination on arrival is a given..."

"No," Thalina said, interrupting him with confidence. "It's not."

Acion surveyed her. "But even if there is a change under way, the definition of android might still include me..."

"No," she repeated, her eyes dancing. She leaned close to whisper. "What did you dream about?"

"Flying, with you," Acion said without hesitation, then stared at her as he realized what he'd said. "I *dreamed*."

"You did," she agreed with delight.

"But how do you know this?"

"REM sleep. Your eyes were moving. And Venero recognized Arista as an android because he couldn't send her a dream."

Venero. Prince of Regalia. Partner of Gemma.

"He'll be able to test it and prove that you're not an android. Scintillon's Law won't apply!"

Acion felt as if his universe had been rearranged.

For the better.

"You look the way I feel after a jump," Thalina said, then kissed him below his ear. "Come on. I want to see you wearing only that tattoo." She kissed him again and Acion felt his body respond to her touch with an enthusiasm that was becoming familiar. She ran her fingertip over his tattoo. "What does it mean, anyway?"

"It is Cumaen script." He picked her up and left the deck in search of a wide berth.

"Let me guess." Thalina kicked her feet playfully. "It says either 'I exist to serve' or "that information is not available to you at this time'."

Acion laughed, liking how pleased she looked with herself. When he laughed, she looked even happier. "The first, just as the ring does. It could be recast in whatever shape you desire."

She spun his ring on her own finger. "I like it as it is, because it was yours and you gave it to me. You can't remove your tattoo either."

"What if I added your name to it?" Acion indicated a space on his thumb.

"*I exist to serve Thalina*." She smiled. "Oh, I like that. And I could have your name engraved inside the ring."

"Then no one would ever doubt our loyalties," Acion murmured, then caught her lips beneath his own. He kissed her slowly and sweetly, even as he lowered them both onto the berth. He dimmed the lights with a touch and pushed Thalina's chemise from her shoulders, savoring the sight of her for a moment. He swept her clothing aside, kissing each increment of skin as it was bared, caressing her until she was beside him wearing only his right. Her smile made his heart thunder.

"I wonder if my father will allow a new android research program," she mused, reaching for his chausses. Acion stood up and shed his clothes quickly, then rejoined her on the berth.

"I wonder if we could devise an augmentation to restore that finger's functionality," he replied and she laughed as she rolled him beneath her.

"Maybe you just have to learn a new skill."

"Maybe we should begin immediately." Acion touched Thalina and she sighed contentment, her pleasure fueling his own in a most fascinating way. There was a new radiance about her that he wanted to explore. He ran his hand over the slight rounding of her stomach that was new and realized he had no data about the delivery of dragon shifters, much less their upbringing and genetic inclinations. "Will it be a boy or a girl?"

Thalina smiled. "I don't know. Does it matter?"

"I have no information about children," he admitted, feeling that his brief for partnership with Thalina was incomplete. "It was never considered a possibility that I would father a child."

"Much less a dragon shifter," Thalina teased. "Are you sorry?"

"I am...awed." Acion had to search for the word, but it was the right one.

Thalina brushed her lips across his. "We'll manage it together," she whispered with a dragon's confidence and he recognized the truth in her words.

Together. They were partners in more than the conception of a child. They had worked together to ensure their return to Incendium and their mutual safety. They worked as a team.

And Acion could not have had a better ally. Fiery and loyal, passionate and logical, mother of his child and keeper of his heart, Thalina was a gift beyond all expectation.

She was his own dragon princess, and their adventure together had only just begun.

That was a victory worth celebrating in the style his princess preferred.

❋

KRAW'S SECRET

Viceroy Kraw is invited to witness whatever prediction the ShadowCaster has brought to Incendium, along with King Ouros and Queen Ignita. Although the royal couple can make little sense of the vision shown by the strange creature, Kraw knows his family's ancient betrayal has to finally be revealed to the dragon kings. Will the fury of Ouros be as fierce as Kraw fears? What will be the future of the viceroy?

CHAPTER ONE

KRAW HAD THE DREAM for the first time shortly after the wedding of Princess Gemma was celebrated. It came to him on the third night after the couple had left Incendium for Regalia.

He had experienced it almost every night since. It haunted him. It tormented him. It interrupted his sleep, and he knew that his performance as viceroy suffered.

Kraw was not a whimsical man, nor was he inclined to sleep poorly. He could not recall the last time he had even remembered a dream, and he knew he had never before had a recurring dream. This one was as relentless as it was mystifying.

It had to stop.

He only wished he could figure out how.

He wasn't reassured that the only irrational thing that had ever happened to him had been a sign of his own appointment as apprentice to the viceroy. Was the dream a warning that his own term of office was coming to an end?

Kraw wasn't ready to retire, but the dream persisted all the same.

The dream began with the the insignia of Incendium, the emblem of the dragon kings burning red on what could have been a white banner. The white background moved then, shifting and thinning until Kraw realized it was only a bank of thick fog. The curious thing was that the fog dissipated while the red insignia remained just as clear as before.

It burned, alight with flame.

Kraw was puzzled by this, for it seemed the insignia should fade with the banner, but it did not. If anything, it was brighter. The fog thinned to mist then cleared, blown away by a sudden wind. The insignia floated before him, crackling and shooting sparks, yet never consumed. In his dream, he walked toward it, and then around it. He discovered that it was emblazoned on a clear spike of ice. He reached for that spike, but it disappeared just as his fingers brushed its cold surface.

Kraw always blinked at this point in the dream and when his eyes opened again, there was no sign of the floating insignia.

Instead, he was in Incendium village, as the sun rose and the mist drifted from the river. Something about the vista made him think it was early on a summer morning. Kraw knew it wasn't the present time, because there were buildings missing, ones that had yet to be constructed in the time of his dream. His dream showed him a past, one beyond his own recollection.

That troubled Kraw.

He might have been another person, he *must* have been another person, for he had the view of someone rushing down the main avenue from the palace. This person panted. His heart raced. Kraw could smell his fear. This person turned down a narrow alleyway that was familiar despite the changes to the names of the shops, took a detour down to the river, and glanced back over his shoulder repeatedly.

He became anxious at this point in his dream, sharing the trepidation of the person whose view he shared. Kraw's palms sweated with the conviction that he was being followed—and the knowledge that the consequences would be dire, if he was caught. He undertook an evasive course with such speed that Kraw was left dizzy. He caught glimpses of parts of the city he had never before seen, and which might not still exist.

Finally, he snuck into an old inn, raced down the stairs, and lifted a grate from the floor. He leaped into the dark shadows and smelled the dampness. He secured the grate above himself with shaking fingers and just in time—footsteps sounded in pursuit. He held his breath, standing motionless in the sewer, certain that a deaf man couldn't miss the pounding of his heart.

Once the footsteps moved away, Kraw exhaled with relief. He pivoted, then proceeded quickly and confidently into the sewer, moving into its deepest darkness.

Another man might have been surprised by this choice, but Kraw recognized the route through the sewers. It was one his father had taught him just before that man's death. It was a family secret, as were the marks carved in the wall to offer navigation, which the fleeing man touched with his fingertips.

Kraw knew then that he shared the view of one of his forebears. Only the viceroys of the King of Incendium knew this passage and its marks. At any point in time, a maximum of two men in all of Incendium held the secret of them—the current viceroy and his apprentice, if he'd chosen one.

Kraw had chosen no apprentice, for he had no son. He knew he had to select one of his nephews, but he had yet to make the decision and embark upon the training. He'd thought he had time. He expected the same strange incident to occur to one of his nephews as had happened to him. That would tell him that it was time and who his apprentice should be, but thus far, none of his nephews had given any hint.

It irked him that he was waiting for a sign or a portent, which was irrational in his view. It was also tradition, however.

The dream ended in a familiar place, the location of another of the viceroy's secrets.

After the passage through the sewer, Kraw emerged in a cellar that he could not mistake for any other. It was below the storeroom in the house in which Kraw had been raised. His family had owned the house almost since the founding of Incendium city. It had been burned and rebuilt, expanded and renovated, repeatedly over the centuries, but the cellar never changed. As a boy, Kraw had wondered if it had always been the same and had spent some time seeking lost treasures beneath the dirt floor. His father had not been amused by this pursuit, which resulted in the only scolding Kraw had ever had.

Of course, he had later learned why his curiosity had been discouraged.

In the dream, he lit a candle—another sign that the dream took place in a historical period—and removed something from his chemise. It proved to be a small scroll, with the insignia of the Viceroy pressed into the wax seal. Was it stolen? He ran his fingertips over the seal, almost in reverence, then shoved a worktable aside with an effort. That worktable was still in the cellar of the house. There had always been fruit wine brewing on that table in Kraw's life and it appeared that the table had the same purpose in the time of the dream, though the equipment was older.

The man in the dream brushed dust aside to expose the outline of a panel in the wooden wall. Kraw had wondered as a child why there had been a wooden wall in the cellar, for that same wall was still there, but his father had said it had simply been left over from a change in the hall above and too good to cast aside. Kraw had later learned that this was a lie, a lie to defend a secret.

His heart thumped, for he guessed what the man in the dream would do.

Which meant that Kraw knew who he was.

Narkam, the viceroy who had served King Flammos, the tyrant of the dragon kings who had plunged Incendium into a reign of darkness.

Kraw watched Narkam's nimble fingers tap out a combination on the inlay blocks in the wall. Did he whisper a word? It seemed to Kraw that he did, but he preferred to think that it was the sequence of taps that opened the door. A word of such power would have been a spell, and Kraw didn't like to acknowledge the prospect of magic.

A small door opened to reveal a hiding spot, one lined with metal to protect its contents from any damage. It was filled with a strange pale mist. This was where the scroll disappeared. The door was sealed and then footfalls sounded on the stairs.

Narkam darted back into the hole in the floor, securing the grate from the underside and disappearing into the sewers well before anyone entered the cellar room. He made his way back through the passage, and Kraw knew he would emerge in another part of the city, then saunter home as if innocent.

It was at this moment that Kraw awakened, every detail clear in his mind. He stifled an urge each time to race to the family home and check the cellar. He had no time for such an errand, and it would be futile. He knew the contents of the scroll, of course. It was the mark of each apprentice to spontaneously write a copy of that scroll's contents. Kraw couldn't explain the mechanism to his own satisfaction. He didn't believe in magic, but given the confession in the scroll, that might have been what caused the automatic writing. He tried to avoid thinking about it, for the scroll's message and the legacy defied everything Kraw believed to be true.

Yet it was true, as well.

Why did the dream come to him now? King Ouros didn't invite an era of darkness with his reign—in fact, he couldn't be more different than his forebear Flammos. Was it a warning that the ancient treason of the viceroy would have consequences? Was it simply guilt for the act of his forebear? Kraw tossed and turned, convinced that he was going to die. The dream seemed to warn him that the responsibility for the viceroy would pass and soon.

He itched to check upon the scroll, but felt the dream was sufficient warning to leave it be. What if the dream had been inflicted upon him to compel him to reveal the scroll? Kraw would not do it.

Besides, he couldn't check on the scroll without arousing curiosity. He himself lived in the palace in his own apartments and had done so since becoming viceroy. Kraw's younger brother and wife lived in the house with their children and grandchildren, as well as with a few cousins and more distant relations. Since he had come to the post young, he had not been married and had no children of his own. Once he had accepted the post, he had had no time for such matters. The administration of the palace had been his life.

One of his brother's sons should be Kraw's heir, but he delayed the choice. Ranaj, the older boy, now a man, had a certain charm but showed little attention to detail. That trait would not serve him well in a household of dragon shifters. Saraw, the second, had high expectations of himself and was unlikely to work hard, another trait that would lead to failure. Kraw didn't think either of them had any commitment to anyone beyond themselves and their own comfort. He wouldn't have put them in charge of a chicken coop, let alone a royal palace.

He had always liked Jarak's third son, despite that boy's rebellious youth. Arkan had appeared to have a gift for finding trouble or making it, but love had set him on the right path. Kraw thought it a sign that his nature was essentially good. Arkan's wife had died in childbirth, though, leaving him with two young children. Arkan had sufficient responsibilities for a few years, managing his duties to the family business along with those energetic children.

Could Kraw's choice not wait?

The dream's persistence, though, made him fear the time had come.

KING OUROS SHOULD have been content.

Instead, he was uneasy.

As was his habit in such times, he reviewed his blessings. They were plentiful.

His oldest daughter, Drakina, had not only married her Carrier of the Seed in an official ceremony but had born a son, Gravitas, who was both healthy and a dragon shifter. Against every expectation, his defiant daughter had fulfilled the traditional responsibility of the eldest child, and Ouros had an official heir.

Drakina would not have been the daughter he knew and loved if she had not conceived the child before the wedding, but Ouros was past the moment of quibbling. Indeed, if the execution of her first betrothed and some early affection with her HeartKeeper was the sum of her rebellion, Ouros knew how lucky he was. For centuries, he had expected Drakina to challenge the law of succession and insist that a daughter should be as entitled to inherit as a son. He felt as if he had avoided a conflagration.

His second daughter, Gemma, had secured an alliance with Regalia, the sister planet of Incendium, by marrying its king. Ouros supposed that he should have anticipated that strategic marriage to proceed a little differently from his plans: Gemma had married Urbanus, the heir, but his twin brother, Venero, had proven to be her Carrier of the Seed.

There was no denying the call of the Seed, Ouros knew that, so he had few regrets about the resolution. It could have been much worse. Over the course of the pair's adventures upon Regalia, both Queen Arcana and Urbanus had died, so Venero had become king—both of Regalia and of Gemma's heart. Ouros did not doubt that his daughter, trained by the Warrior Maidens of Cumae, would make an excellent wife for Venero, given the unrest between factions in his newfound kingdom. The situation, too, contented him as a suitable fate for his second daughter.

The third daughter of the Incendium royal family was also married to her Carrier of the Seed and expecting a child. Ouros had not anticipated that Thalina would fall in love with an android, much less that she would aid Acion's evolution to a biological organism, and that made him feel foolish. Thalina had always loved machines better than people. Their union was, he had to admit, a perfect match.

Even if it had compelled him to overturn Scintillon's Law.

Ouros frowned. He didn't like changing laws, especially old ones, even when he suspected it was the right thing to do. He had a healthy respect for tradition and always felt that change was occurring too quickly when it happened at all. And he had never expected Thalina to be the one to compel him to reconsider anything.

She had her mother's stubborn nature, though.

Thalia was happy, which contented Ouros, too.

The android in question, Acion, had arrived on Incendium, charged to deliver a gift to Ouros himself. Since the freighter, the Archangel, had returned to port with Thalina and Acion, the gift had been inspected, examined, and finally delivered into the king's hands.

This gift and the disappearance of his seventh daughter, Anguissa, captain of the Archangel, were the source of the king's concern. Ouros turned the clear cylinder in his hands, wondering yet again if he should release the creature trapped inside.

He had learned about ShadowCasters when he had been a young dragon, and they had been presumed extinct even then. It was a marvel to hold one, and he wondered whether the dark shape in the cylinder really was a ShadowCaster, or whether this was a hoax.

There was one way to find out.

ShadowCasters were an ancient life form and one said to be attuned to the vibrations of the future. Ouros forgot the speculation as to how they glimpsed into time ahead of the present: he'd always preferred facts over guesses, even educated guesses. He recalled a story that an emperor had ordered their destruction, after his enemies repeatedly anticipated his surprise attacks.

He held the cylinder to the light. The creature inside looked like a dead insect. It was black and motionless, unless he turned the cylinder and gravity dislodged it. Even then, it fell, as if inert. It didn't appear to be breathing or to have a pulse. Ouros shook the receptacle and it didn't respond.

Another king might have doubted its powers.

Ouros was a dragon king, and he wanted facts. He held up the cylinder and stared through it at his chambers, enjoying how the glass distorted the view. Was this how a ShadowCaster saw the future? Was it a question of perspective?

Would it tell him what had happened—or what was going to happen—to Anguissa? He had demanded the story of her disappearance twice from Thalina and hadn't liked it any better the second time. How like Anguissa to sacrifice herself for the sake of her sister and that sister's Carrier. Had she guessed that Acion was Thalina's HeartKeeper? Ouros was sure she had. Like the ShadowCaster, Anguissa had an ability to anticipate future events with uncanny accuracy. She said it was only logical to see the results of one's actions. Ouros knew otherwise. That daughter, the bold one who challenged every expectation, had the confidence of knowing she would survive every feat.

Would she survive this one?

Would she have made the same choice, even if she'd known otherwise?

Ouros winced, knowing that his Anguissa wouldn't have changed a thing. His mother had always said that the prickly and outspoken people were the ones who cared the most. That was certainly true of Anguissa.

It could also be said to be true of his wife, although she was inclined to hide her sting.

Ouros felt Ignita's presence before he saw or smelled her.

"Are you going to release it?" she asked, and he glanced down to find her peering at the cylinder.

"Do you think I should?" He asked her a question, rather than answering, wanting to know her view.

"Whyever not?" She took the cylinder from his hand, peering at the creature within. "It was a gift. It must have come to you for a reason."

Ouros looked at her, intrigued. "You think it chooses its own course?"

Ignita smiled. "That's what I was taught. That a ShadowCaster had a way of ensuring it passed into the right hand at the right time. It saw its own future and made it come true."

What a notion. "To what end? To warn someone?"

"To make the future what it should be."

"According to whom?"

She handed him the vessel. "You'll have to ask the ShadowCaster that."

"Any word from Anguissa?"

A shadow touched his queen's brow. "No, but I wouldn't have expected any. We'll hear from her when she marches into the palace again."

"I hope it is soon."

Ignita placed her hand on Ouros' shoulder then gave it a little squeeze. "Don't tell me you're afraid to release a little dead millipede?" she teased, though he knew she understood his hesitation.

"You think it has something to tell us."

"I don't think it would be here otherwise."

Ouros nodded. "And maybe its counsel will tell us what to do to bring Anguissa home."

"Maybe. There's something that we have to do to shape the future as it should be, or the ShadowCaster wouldn't be here." Ignita's eyes lit with fire. "And if the future doesn't include every one of my daughters being safe and happy, the ShadowCaster will regret its choice."

Ouros smiled at her ferocity, though it was a good reminder. "We will release it in our dragon form," he said, and Ignita nodded agreement.

"In the royal audience chambers?"

"Yes, there's more room there, and after all, we *are* giving it an audience."

"Should we summon Kraw, so there is a witness?"

"That's an excellent idea."

"Don't you think he looks tired these days?" Ignita asked. "Should we insist that he take a vacation?"

"You know Kraw. He never takes a vacation, for he says I never do."

"Perhaps both of you should take a vacation."

"Let's see what the ShadowCaster says," Ouros demurred. "I'll send word to Kraw now and we can begin on the hour. Also, I'll have Kraw seal the chamber, so that the ShadowCaster cannot escape."

Soon he would have his fact.

KRAW, unlike the king and queen, felt a dislike for the ShadowCaster that he believed to be healthy. He didn't trust anything or anyone who poked into future events or claimed to know things they had no rational means of knowing. Dreams and portents were like the tricks played at the carnivals on unsuspecting fools, who deserved to be separated from their funds.

It smacked of that unwholesome practice, magic.

Kraw didn't even share the royal enthusiasm for astrologers, even though their craft was more science than art. In Kraw's view, the future could take care of itself. He ensured the present was all it could be, partly by keeping the past where it belonged. Still, a summons was a summons, so he had the audience chamber sealed and joined his king and queen there as promptly as possible.

His recurring dream had left him tired, irritable, and impatient with nonsense. That it was a similar kind of nonsense in his view only made him more cranky.

Of course, he hid his thoughts and feelings from his king and queen, who clearly had expectations of the ShadowCaster.

Kraw expected little of the black smudge in the bottom of the clear cylinder, but it was always a treat to see both the king and the queen shift shape. They were magnificent in their dragon forms, and the awe he felt when he witnessed the change always reminded him of his own splendid good fortune to serve them as he did.

The king was the first to shift, waiting only until the doors were locked behind Kraw before doing so. He had already given the vial containing the ShadowCaster to Queen Ignita, so threw out his arms and cast back his head. He was surrounded with a swirl of sparks even as his figure itself seemed to glow. In the blink of an eye, he reared above them in his dragon form and breathed a playful stream of fire at the ceiling. His scales were deep blue and gleamed when he moved, his power and agility undiminished even at his age. His belly scales could have been made of gold, given the way they shone. His nails were black, the feathers streaming from his wings were indigo, and his wings themselves were so dark a blue as to be close to black. There were swirls of gold on the tops of Ouros' wings, as if they had been painted there by a skillful artist. His eyes glittered like cut gems and he turned a look upon his wife that was both amorous and regal.

It had always seemed to Kraw that the character of the members of the royal family was more clear when they took their dragon forms. He felt more aware of their motivations when they were dragons. Ouros, for example, was motivated by love for his wife, his daughters, and his kingdom. When the king was in his dragon form, Kraw couldn't forget that truth. He knew they could be inscrutable, to him and to others, so maybe it was a case of them revealing themselves to him because they trusted him.

Ignita handed the vial to her husband, then spun in place. Sparks flew from her, seeming to light on the hem of her skirts as she turned, and her figure disappeared in a cloud of smoke. The cloud grew taller and wider, seeming to simmer from its very core, then her dragon form was revealed. Ignita looked softer than Ouros, if such a thing could be said of a dragon. Her scales were myriad shades of soft blue and purple and their edges were less clearly defined. She had more feathers, and they were opalescent and flowing, disguising her strength like veils on a dancer. There was fire in her eyes, though, a fire that a smart person wouldn't forget, and Kraw saw her devotion to her husband and daughters in her fierce expression.

He was a bachelor and contentedly so, but when Kraw saw the king and queen in their dragon forms, he wondered what it would be like to be adored by a dragon shifter. Did the object of affection feel like the prize gem of the dragon's hoard? Kraw wasn't a fanciful man, but he imagined so.

The pair faced each other, Ouros' tail swirling around Kraw protectively, then the king loosened the lid. "Are we prepared?" he asked, his voice more resonant and deep than when he was in human form.

Ignita nodded.

"Certainly, your majesty," Kraw said and bowed his head. He fingered his mustache, ensuring it was perfect, for he felt a sense of ceremony.

When he straightened, Ouros opened the vial to release the ShadowCaster.

Nothing happened.

Ouros made a little growl of frustration, then tipped the cylinder. The ShadowCaster slid out and dropped toward the floor, apparently lifeless.

"It'll be hurt!" Ignita cried and snatched for it.

The ShadowCaster slipped through her talons, though, for it exploded into a million tiny dark specks and fell like black rain toward the inlaid floor. All three observers caught their breath and took a step back. Kraw was aware the queen put a claw in one of the king's and that he drew her slightly behind himself.

But the black drops had his full attention. They turned course just above the floor, and swirled upward like a flock of birds. To Kraw's surprise, they formed an image of a sun, several planets and their moons, all rotating in place as if watched from several light years' distance.

"Fiero Four," Ouros breathed, naming the system in which Incendium was located.

"There's Incendium and Regalia," Ignita said with excitement. "And Sylvawyld!"

The dots swirled again, and Kraw had the impression that their vision zoomed in on Incendium. Next he saw the capital city and his heart sank at the realization that it was the same era as his recurring dream.

When the ShadowCaster showed Flammos on the throne, Kraw knew that his family secret was about to be revealed.

Perhaps he would have no reason to choose an apprentice, not once the treason of the viceroy's family was known by the king.

He sat down heavily, feeling every moment of his many years, and wondered if he would leave the audience chamber alive.

The dragon kings of Incendium had never taken treason lightly, no matter how justified the culprit might believe his actions to be.

CHAPTER TWO

ARKAN KNEW THAT HIS BELOVED Jalana would have appreciated the irony of his current situation. She had always insisted that her love had tamed the bad boy of Incendium city, and Arkan had never argued that truth with her. She had claimed his heart and he had changed his ways to capture hers in turn.

They had been so wonderfully happy that he had never regretted a thing.

But now she was gone, and he was left with Narjal and Tarun, who each echoed their mother in different ways, neither less potent than the other. Yet both also had his own rebellious nature, as if to ensure their father understood how much trouble he had been. Narjal, his daughter, was older and bolder. In fact, she was fearless and was forever leading her younger brother into trouble. Tarun had a mischievous streak of his own and the only thing that ensured Arkan's sanity was that they were too young to find real danger.

Yet.

He couldn't imagine how he would survive their teenage years. They were both attractive children—thanks to Jalana, in Arkan's view—and had a charm that helped them talk themselves out of the consequences of any act. Arkan knew that trait came from himself.

At the same time, he had become so responsible that he barely recognized himself. Arkan had devoted himself to his family's business to ensure the financial security of his children. There hadn't been much of a place for him, since his older brothers had taken the better jobs. Ranaj was the public presence of their trading empire, so he attended all the best parties and knew all the best people and lived in a style to rival the King of Incendium himself. Saraw was the quieter one, who negotiated the deals—many of which Arkan had learned were not entirely legal. His brother was one for shortcuts, if he could turn a better profit with them or return to his own amusements more quickly, and Arkan seemed to be the only one troubled by these choices.

Knowing he was reliant upon their goodwill, he was compelled to remain silent.

He had done odd jobs for his father, but shortly after Jalana's death, his mother had taken pity upon him and decided to retire. Or maybe she had chosen to test him. Arkan had never been sure. Either way, the task of bookkeeping had become available to him then, and though the adding of columns in the back room was as far from his dreams as any job could be, he'd taken it.

For his kids.

He'd been prepared to hate his job, but he actually enjoyed it. There was something refreshing about that addition of columns and tallying of items. The numbers never lied, and they often gave insight into other issues. He liked how rational it all was, how finite, and how lacking in mystery or suspense it was. Everything happened for a reason and there were no arbitrary choices. Ventures lost money because of overspending, bad budgeting, or poor management, not random incidents that changed everything.

Like a healthy woman's sudden death in childbirth.

It was good to live in the family home, too, for he had fond memories of his own childhood there. The estate was large, and the house was rambling, courtesy of centuries of additions and modifications. It seemed that every corner promised a forgotten cranny or a hidden passageway, plus there were books and games, cousins and pets. Arkan liked that there were many servants and many eyes on his mischievous children. They were safe. They were healthy. They had opportunities to learn and there would be more as they grew older. That was Arkan's true compensation.

He hoped Jalana was proud of him and the life he'd made for them.

His mother laughed at him when Narjal and Tarun found trouble, insisting that the past revisited the future. She thought he deserved the challenges they gave him, and maybe he did. If nothing else, his life gave Arkan a new perspective.

Arkan's family had filled the post of viceroy at the palace since the days of King Scintillon, the responsibility passing through the male line of the family. When there wasn't a son, a brother or nephew would take the post, each new viceroy carefully trained by the last. It was considered a responsibility of the others to marry and have children, in order to ensure that the post was never in risk of being left vacant.

Uncle Kraw had taken the post while comparatively young, since his father had married late. Arkan's father, Jarak, was the younger son from that late match, and he had married then fathered three sons. Kraw had been viceroy for longer than Arkan had been alive, and Arkan had been raised with the assumption that one of his older brothers would be groomed by Kraw to take his place.

The family had built its own trade over the centuries, and Arkan didn't doubt that some early success had been due to the favor of the crown. Now, though, they managed a financial empire, trading in currencies, financing expeditions and equipment, and investing in future endeavors. Arkan spent most of his days in the counting room in the family home, which was a far more cheerful place than might have been anticipated. It was a sunny room, the windowsills lush with plants from Incendium and other locations.

It was also oppressively quiet when his kids were elsewhere. Arkan preferred when they played in the counting room while he worked, but they had recently begun to have lessons. Narjal was ten years old and Tarun was six. Arkan had taught them himself to this point, but it was time, his mother had announced, for them to be tamed—as much as might be possible.

The children hadn't embraced the change any better than their father had. Arkan suspected that the tutor had already come to the conclusion that they could not be tamed. Narjal orchestrated daily escapes from their lessons, ensuring the pair disappeared while the tutor's back was turned, and substituting daring adventures of her own for their lessons. She had taken Tarun to the zoo unaccompanied, been caught investigating the sewers with her younger brother, and had even—probably at Tarun's insistence—gotten them both to the star station and aboard a shuttle to the starport before being retrieved.

In a way, Arkan admired how enterprising she was.

In another, her inventiveness made him dread the future even more.

So, he wasn't truly surprised when the tutor rapped at the door of the counting room one morning, flushed and flustered. "I won't do it anymore," she announced before Arkan could greet her. "I won't be responsible for those *heathens*."

Arkan stood. "You mean my children?" He decided against noting that their religious beliefs were of no relevance.

"Of course, I mean your children!" she sputtered. "They are outrageously disobedient..."

"But that is why they have lessons."

The tutor pointed a finger at him, her outrage clear. "I have endured sufficient insolence from those little monsters to last me the rest of my days. I don't believe they *can* be taught, especially as they continue to disappear..."

"Disappear?" Arkan stepped forward, anticipating the worst. "Where have they been gone?"

"How should I know? They are sneaky and cunning beyond their years, especially that girl. Oh, she looks pretty enough, but she is devious and wicked..."

"And I think it is time for our ways to part," Arkan said firmly. "If you're so convinced that my children are evil, I doubt that you will be able to teach them effectively."

"I am not the problem in this situation!"

"How long have they been gone?" Arkan asked, wanting to calculate how far they might have gone.

"Perhaps half an hour," the tutor admitted, her tone still irritated. "Fortunately, I ensured that the doors and gates were sealed before our lessons began this morning."

"So they must still be in the house?" There were still plenty of opportunities for trouble to be found.

"They are hiding," she said grimly. "I've been looking for them, without success."

Arkan tapped his desktop to secure his files, then left the counting room with purpose. The door was locked behind him with a touch. "Where have you looked?" he asked without glancing back.

"The kitchen, the yard, their bedrooms, the playroom, the garage, the storeroom..."

Arkan thought of the sewers. "The cellar?"

Her expression was all the answer he needed. "I won't do it anymore!" she shouted after him, but Arkan didn't stop.

"Speak to my mother, then. She hired you."

The tutor snorted but Arkan was racing down the stairs to the main floor of the house. The mess after the sewer adventure meant that he didn't want a repetition. He stormed through the kitchen and down the stairs in the storeroom, activating a light on his way.

The cellar appeared to be empty.

But there was the clean scent of his children's soap and the vessels on the worktable looked to be jumbled. He could even see a small handprint, disturbing the dust on one, but he didn't let his gaze linger on it.

They were here and they were hiding.

Watching.

It was time to change the rules of the game. Arkan bent down to examine the sewer grate as if it had been the reason for his arrival. He rattled it, but it was secured. He sighed with evident relief.

"Thank Yarkella," he said, as if he had only come to check the sewer. He straightened and returned to the stairs. "They're not here," he called, though he doubted the tutor had followed him. "Let's check the garage. Tarun is fascinated by that new velocitor." He climbed the stairs, extinguishing the light on his way, but didn't step into the kitchen. Instead, he opened the door and closed it again, remaining in the shadows at the summit of the stairs. Because there was a bend in the stairs, they wouldn't be able to see what he had done.

His eyes adjusted quickly to the darkness and he was able to discern the gleam of the bottles in which the wine fermented. The silence didn't last very long.

"We fooled him!" Narjal whispered in triumph. "Now we have to finish before he comes back."

"We can't move the table," Tarun whispered. "It's too heavy."

"We have to find a way. There's a secret treasure there!"

"We should have asked Pater to help."

"We can't. It's a *secret*." Narjal's tone made her opinion of her brother's objections clear.

"How can you even know it's there if it's a secret?"

"I *know*," Narjal insisted with such conviction that Arkan shivered. How could she know?

"You could be wrong. You were before."

"We'll never be sure unless we look!"

"I want to see the velocitor."

"Be quiet and help, then I'll take you to the velocitor."

A light illuminated far below Arkan. He guessed that Narjal had taken a handheld light source for her adventure and peeked to see that he was right. The children had their backs to him and the light shone upon the old wooden wall. Narjal had already moved most of the vessels aside and was kneeling on the old worktable. Tarun crouched behind her and she handed him the light.

"Shine it there. That's where the secret hiding place is."

"How do you know?"

"I do!"

Tarun did as instructed, and Narjal ran her hands over the wooden partition. Arkan sat on the steps to watch her, intrigued. He had been fascinated by that wall when he was a kid, too, though his father had told him to leave it alone.

Was there a reason why?

"Look!" Narjal sat back, triumphant, having found the perimeter of a door in the wall. She blew the dust out of the crack and ran her fingertip around the edge. "Just like in the book," she whispered in awe.

"What book?"

"The one I found. The *magic* book."

Arkan frowned. There was no such thing as magic. There was deception and there was nonsense. They weren't on Regalia with its superstitions and primitive thinking! He might have interjected, but decided to let Narjal's venture fail first.

"So, open it," Tarun said.

Narjal lifted her hands. She murmured something under her breath three times, then waited. Nothing happened, just as Arkan had expected. She dug at the perimeter of the door with her fingers, but it didn't budge.

Maybe it wasn't even a door.

"I knew we should have gone to the velocitor," Tarun said with disgust and turned to jump from the table.

Then Narjal gasped. Arkan gasped himself for the insignia of the dragon kings of Incendium appeared on the wooden panel. It looked to be drawn with fire and the flames crackled, glowing brilliant orange in the darkness. The flames faded and the insignia appeared to be branded on the door. A waft of smoke rose from the wood as Arkan heard a sizzle. Then the door opened and white mist spilled forth from the space behind it. Arkan thought he could see a pile of scrolls within it.

Narjal reached a hand into the mist, both fearless and foolish.

Arkan leaped down the stairs and snatched her up. She cried out in protest, and Tarun ran for the stairs. "I'm going to see the velocitor," he said and scampered out of sight. No doubt, he thought Narjal was in trouble and wanted to avoid being implicated.

"We have to look inside," she insisted.

"We do not," Arkan said firmly. "What book did you find? Where is it?"

"It's in the library. It was hidden at the back of the shelves and I read it. It's a spell book."

"You know there's no such thing as magic."

His daughter was defiant. "I know there *is*. The spell worked."

Arkan tried a different tack. "You know that the practice of magic is illegal on Incendium."

"Because it works. Because *that* worked." She gestured to the open door, which continued to spill white mist. The mist pooled on the floor of the cellar, as if it were heavy, and flowed toward the sewer grate in the floor. At the flick of her hand, the door slammed shut and Arkan watched its perimeter fade from view.

Surely his daughter hadn't made the door close from a distance with a gesture?

Surely his daughter couldn't have any *powers*?

No, it was a coincidence. It had to be. The door had just closed at the same time.

Narjal squirmed out of his grip and climbed back onto the worktable, trying to find the door again. He quickly saw that she couldn't—and the murmuring of her spell yielded no results. He was relieved then, that his fears had been mistaken.

She turned on him, outraged. "You did this, Pater! It's hidden again because you don't believe."

"Maybe it never really existed," he said, noting how the mist had disappeared from view. "Maybe you imagined it."

Narjal's expression turned stubborn. "Maybe I need to read more."

"No," Arkan said. "You're going to give me that book and you're going to abandon this adventure."

"But..."

"Or I'll make you take twice as many lessons as before, in a locked room."

Her lips set. "I could get out of it."

Arkan bent down to look her in the eye. "If you put as much effort into your lessons as you do in evading them, you'd be done early enough to play whatever games you wanted."

She smiled then, a sweet smile too much like Jalana's, and wrinkled her nose. "It's boring."

"Of course, it's boring. It's good training for becoming an adult."

"I don't want to be an adult."

"I don't like it much, either." Arkan lifted her up and held her on his hip. "You're getting bigger, though. I won't be able to lift you soon."

She kissed his cheek. "Of course you will, Pater. You're the strongest man of all."

"Hmm, flattery," he teased. "You just don't want to give me that book."

"I thought you might forget."

"Not a chance. We'll get it now, then you'll forget all of this nonsense."

"Does magic have to be nonsense?"

"Yes, it does, because it is." Arkan spoke with more confidence than he was feeling in this moment. What had happened with that door? He disliked that he couldn't think of a rational explanation.

Narjal sighed and Arkan knew the argument wasn't over. If he had the book, though, and her spell didn't work on the door in the cellar, then maybe she'd soon get bored with this particular adventure.

He could only hope.

In the meantime, he would go and talk to Uncle Kraw when he had a spare day, just in case there was something important about that hidden hiding place. That it had shown the insignia of the king for a moment indicated that Kraw was the most likely to know the truth.

He doubted it was important, given that it was hidden in the cellar.

IGNITA WATCHED the ShadowCaster with fascination. The creature divided itself into thousands if not millions of small dark dots, then moved to arrange images. It was like watching the vid, but with no color.

It took them into the streets of Incendium city, which were seething with discontent. They had the perspective of someone walking through the city and Ignita shivered as the sense of unease and violence that permeated the vision. People muttered about new laws and injunctions, though none dared to express a complaint against King Flammos.

They had learned the consequences of that quickly enough.

She recalled her history lessons, the ones given to her as soon as she and Ouros had become betrothed. Her family believed that no bride should be unprepared for the world she would make her own, so she had crammed facts about Incendium's history until she suspected she knew more of it than her intended. She remembered the cruelty of Flammos well, driven by his conviction that all conspired against him.

The vision ducked into a tavern on the far side of Incendium, in the rough area beyond the star port. They entered the tavern, and Ignita's eyes widened at the disreputable people there, the foreigners from other worlds, and the conspicuous consumption of stimulants both legal and illegal. She thought she could smell the filth of the place, and she saw credits in a dozen currencies being exchanged. The vision trailed into a back room, slipping through a barred door, where two men sat at a table.

"Embron and Blazion," she said without meaning to speak aloud.

Ouros glanced at her. "The younger sons of Rubeo? The twins?"

"There is an image in the archives."

He nodded, turning his attention back to the ShadowCaster's display. The pair conferred, their heads bent together and their voices low. Ignita heard the words "rebellion," "coup," and "justice."

It seemed that Flammos' conviction that his younger brothers had been conspiring against him was true. A servant entered the room, bringing a fresh pitcher of whatever brew the brothers consumed and a steaming platter of food. Another man entered and the brothers straightened, stepped forward to shake his hand.

"A conspirator," Ouros murmured.

The servant left and the ShadowCaster's vision followed him. He cast aside his apron and left the tavern, hastening to the palace. At the kitchen door, he murmured a word and was admitted, shown down a dark passageway, then thrust into a chamber where King Flammos awaited him. He was playing with a stack of credits. The man fell to his knees and began to speak in haste.

"A traitor to the twin princes," Ignita said softly.

The vision swirled and they were at the starport, where a small vessel was being outfitted. It was isolated, at the end of a long row of empty gates. A woman with hair as white as snow strode down the corridor to the gate. She was young, despite the hue of her hair, dressed like a star captain and moved with confidence. She was not armed. There was a shimmer surrounding her, and Ignita watched with curiosity as she approached the guarded gate of the isolated vessel.

She blew a kiss to each of the guards, but they remained impassive. She walked directly past them, along the gangplank, and onto the vessel, but they took no notice of her. They certainly didn't stop her.

"An intruder," Ouros said.

"A witch," Ignita corrected, being more inclined to see sorcery than her husband.

"There's no such thing," he chided.

"Then how did she do that?"

He glanced at her, frowned, then turned back to the display. "There is always a rational explanation, even if it's not immediately evident."

Ignita held her tongue. They saw the twin princes then, being brought to the vessel in chains and shackles. They were forced aboard and the portal was secured, before the armed troops retreated.

The ShadowCaster swirled again and showed King Flammos in his chamber, watching a massive but primitive display of the sky. It took up the better part of a wall, but the resolution was less than was typical now. Ignita noted that motion upon the screen was in increments instead of flowing smoothly. A solitary vessel left its gate and moved to the jump zone.

"Presumably it was controlled remotely," Ouros said.

A distant voice counted down, then the vessel surged into the jump zone. There was a flash and it disappeared. King Flammos saluted the screen with his cup then drained it, his satisfaction more than clear.

The dots moved, as if the focus shifted from the king to the shadows behind him. In the darkness, a man's figure became clear, his features unfamiliar but the mark of the viceroy upon his uniform.

"Of course, his viceroy attends him," Ouros said and frowned. "Who is that, Kraw?"

"Narkam, sir."

Ouros shrugged. "I don't remember anything about him. I shall have to do some research."

The ShadowCaster became a whirlwind of tiny dots, and they spiraled down into the cylindrical vessel. They congealed into a single small black organism, one that looked like a dead millipede, and stilled.

"That's it?" Ouros cried when the creature didn't move again. "But we know all that! What possible relevance does this have to the present and the future?" He growled and smoke emanated from his nostrils as he snatched up the cylinder and shook it. "What about Anguissa?" he roared, but the ShadowCaster remained still. Ouros turned to Ignita. "It must be about Narkam! That was the only detail I didn't know."

But Ignita was more concerned that the viceroy suddenly slumped to the floor, his face pale. "Kraw! Ouros, something is wrong with Kraw!"

CHAPTER THREE

AFTER A VISIT TO THE velocitor and an argument with his mother, Arkan returned to the counting room to finish his work for the day. He had the so-called spell book that Narjal had found in the library, but a quick fan through it had revealed that the pages were all blank. Undoubtedly, a rational explanation for her experience would reveal itself.

If Tarun had been older, he might have thought it a prank played by one sibling on the other. Maybe one of his nieces or nephews were responsible.

The truth would come out, Arkan was sure of it.

He settled at his desk and made to open his desktop display. Instead, he found himself reaching for a quill. He hadn't written by hand in years, but had a curious urge to do as much. He found some paper in the desk and pulled out a clean white sheet.

How strange. Why did he feel such a compulsion? It was another thing he couldn't explain. He lifted the quill, rolling it in his hand as he recalled the feel of it. He touched it to the paper and words began to flow into the page, as quickly as he could write them.

Arkan had no idea where they were coming from. He read them for the first time as he wrote them down, and as he wrote what proved to be a long message, his eyes widened in surprise.

I, Narkam, viceroy of Incendium, sworn to the service of King Flammos, have committed treason and betrayed the trust of the king. Though I believe my actions to have been justified, I also recognize that they were illegal and subject to the most severe justice of the king. I also violated the sanctions against the use of magic on Incendium, for I saw no other means to save the kingdom. I was driven to this by my discovery that the king has done evil to protect his throne and though I know I have overstepped my bounds, I could do nothing else.

In the Incendium year 208, King Rubeo gained his majority of eight-one years of age became King of Incendium. Rubeo had five children by his HeartKeeper, Bellica. Flammos was eldest and heir, born in 307. A daughter, Aurora, was born in 310 and a second daughter, Lustra, was born in 314. In 317, the queen delivered twin boys, Blazion and Embron.

My service to the crown commenced in 554, and Aurora and Lustra were already dead. I knew they had died before coming of age. I did not know, until Prince Flammos confided in me one night after a drunken binge in Incendium city, that he had killed them with his own talons. He was proud of his deed and gloated of his cleverness as I helped him to his apartment. The hatred that spewed from him when he was unchecked was shocking. In the morning, he had no recollection of his confession, but I quietly confirmed several details over the following days, and was convinced of his guilt.

The crime however was years in the past, and I had only his own confession as evidence. I continued to serve in silence, for I feared dismissal from my post—or worse—if I raised the question with King Rubeo. The prince appeared to embark upon a course of greater honor and less indulgence. I hoped he had learned from the past.

Upon Rubeo's death in 577, Flammos became king and any hope that his habits had changed was quickly proven wrong. Incendium was cast into a pit of ruin with each day bringing more injustice and infamy to this great kingdom. I had heard whispers that Blazion and Embron meant to challenge their older brother over the crown, but evidently Flammos heard them as well. He ordered that his two brothers be cast into space with no supplies, a death sentence that would leave his talons clean. Perhaps he does recall that confession and my silence, for he gives the appearance of trusting me. Perhaps his trust is an illusion, intended to trap me. I cannot say. But he left the arrangements to me and I seized the opportunity to undermine his plan.

I knew that the king would not be easily deceived and I suspected that I would be watched. I planned for the princes, Blazion and Embron, to survive their banishment into space, by contriving that they should secretly be put into stasis. I equipped the ship myself with a prototype of the Fractal Interstellar Drive, but I needed help to send them to their fate.

I confided in one person, solely because I had need of her services. She is, against all expectation, a Regalian and one skilled in sorcery. I heard she was living in the forests beyond Incendium city and I approached her under the guise of imperial investigation. Instead of charging and arresting her, which would lead to her certain death, I offered her the opportunity to survive Incendium's justice. If she cast the spell to shield my actions from the scrutiny of the king and all others, and went with the princes upon their journey, I would ensure that she was not discovered.

She laughed at me. I thought she might decline, but she said she had anticipated my arrival. I couldn't make sense of this for I had chosen to approach her on a whim, but she was confident. Alluring, as well. She countered my offer, expressing her willingness to fulfill it but insisting that her price would be twofold: first, I was forbidden to tell the princes anything about her, and secondly, her spell would place a curse upon my lineage. My son and his son and all through the ages forevermore would be compelled to remember my treason. In this way, we would be the keepers of the secret that could betray us all. I took her wager, for I didn't believe in curses, and it was arranged.

Before taking the post of viceroy, I worked in the engineering labs of Incendium. In order to guarantee that no one could track the vessel carrying the princes after its departure, I added a random number generator to the Fractal Interstellar Drive. There is no telling where or when the princes will make landfall. The witch insisted that the drive was unnecessary, that her spell would bend time as well as impede discovery, but we each made our preparations. The princes are gone, but they remain reliant upon the spell of the witch who journeys with them, and unaware of it. There is much risk in their unwitting adventure, but I console myself that they have some small chance of survival.

I have come to rely upon the witch myself and hope for her success.

I also am haunted by my deeds. As the king becomes more dissolute and more demanding, I fear for the future of Incendium. Perhaps my deceit is part of a sickness that will claim us all and reduce this once-mighty kingdom to ruin.

I believed the witch's curse was nonsense, but as I write this confession in the counting room of our family home, my son is writing it verbatim in another chamber of the house. When I halt, he halts. When I resume, he resumes. He has no knowledge of what I am writing, I didn't even tell him that I was writing, but he showed me his copy of my confession when I went to the kitchens for refreshment. It chilled me to read my own words in his hand, when he could have no knowledge of them. The witch was right. My will be my apprentice and I will hide the two scrolls in the cellar as she suggested. I suspect she was also correct that each viceroy after me will keep silent for the sake of his own survival and that we will be complicit for generation after generation.

The dragon kings of Incendium have long memories and no tolerance of treason. They will not suffer the discover of it in the family that serves in the most trusted role of their administration. If this truth is ever uncovered, I would hope that the king is held by a more temperate dragon than now, and that the preservation of the royal lineage will be rewarded.

In these dark days for Incendium, I am reassured by the hope that the princes live on in another land, with the honor and integrity that their father instilled within them.

I sign this confession of my own guilt in the ninth month of the year 589 in the city of Incendium.

Narkam

Viceroy of Incendium

Arkan read it twice, then ran a fingertip across the signature.

Could it be true? It seemed fantastic.

And yet, he had no idea where these words had originated.

He thought of the hiding place in the cellar and Narjal's book and frowned. He took the scroll and the book and headed for the palace. There was only one person who could tell him more, and that was his Uncle Kraw.

ARKAN CAME.

Night was falling over the city of Incendium, and Kraw watched the light change outside the windows. It was his favorite time of day, when Incendium went to sleep, the sky changed hue, and the starport shone high above with new radiance. He had been brought to his apartment and settled in bed. He had been examined and fussed over and had managed to reveal nothing of the shock to him of the ShadowCaster's message.

King Ouros didn't understand the message now, but Kraw was certain his king would dig deeper and discover the truth. The king was persistent and would dig into the records until he was satisfied. The old secret would be revealed.

Would he die first? Kraw didn't know. He had no desire to die, but at the same time, he didn't want to face the fury of a dragon king who realized he'd been deceived. Ouros was inclined to rage first and be temperate later.

When his nephew's arrival was announced, Kraw felt a relief to his very toes. He was glad to no longer be alone in this responsibility. Arkan had always been clever. Maybe the younger man would find an alternative solution. Kraw was tired and the prospect of having an apprentice cheered him.

"Are you well, Uncle?" Arkan asked with concern, no doubt surprised to find Kraw in his chambers and in bed.

"I am better now that you have arrived." Kraw sat up with an effort. "Secure the door and silence the comm, please."

Arkan's eyes narrowed. "Then you know."

"I have been waiting."

When his instructions had been followed, the younger man presented a scroll of paper to his uncle. "How did I do this?"

"It is the curse."

"But there are no curses and there is no magic..."

"That's what I thought, until it happened to me."

Arkan sat back with a frown. "I don't like it. I don't trust it."

"It doesn't seem to care. You've been chosen as my apprentice..."

"No! I thought one of my brothers..."

"And you thought incorrectly. Neither Ranaj nor Saraw have the skill or the inclination that best serves a viceroy. Ranaj is too outspoken to be in close service to a dragon king, while Saraw is not burdened by integrity. Leave them to manage the family trade, while you serve the kingdom. My life has been spent in service to Incendium, and gladly so. I know the demands of the post, and I think it is a position that will suit you best of my three nephews."

"Tell me why, Uncle." Arkan held Kraw's gaze. "The real reason why."

Kraw saw no reason to be coy. "Because you are due to have your toes held to the fire. No woman will do it, not since Jalana's death, so it will have to be dragons."

"But the children..."

"Will be raised as if they were royalty themselves. They would have every opportunity to improve themselves. I think it would be ideal for them."

Arkan's lips set. "They could find an infinite amount of trouble."

Kraw smiled. "Yet they would have thousands more eyes upon them." His nephew appeared to consider that. Kraw nodded. "I'm glad you were chosen, Arkan. I never wanted to have to train Ranaj or Saraw."

"But they're older. Surely..."

"You have been chosen." Kraw shook the piece of paper at him. "It's uncontestable." He shouldn't have said it that way, he realized as much as soon as the words left his mouth, because Arkan's expression turned stubborn.

"What if I don't want to do it? What if I decline?"

"No one declines. Why would you?"

Arkan grimaced and leaned closer, lowering his voice when he spoke. "Because of Narjal. She found what she calls a book of spells, but when she gave it to me, its pages were blank."

"So, it isn't a spell book. Children are fanciful."

"She opened a hidden door in the wooden wall in the cellar with one of the spells she'd learned. There were scrolls within it, and smoke emanated from it, and the seal of the dragon kings burned on the door before it disappeared. She even closed it with a flick of her hand, from across the room. I saw it all."

Kraw was taken aback. Surely there couldn't be a witch in his own family? Was this a new manifestation of the curse? It seemed as if the secret was determined to be revealed, given his dream and the ShadowCaster and now Narjal. He knew his tone sharpened. "Who else saw this?"

"Only Tarun and me." Arkan sat back. "She'll do it again. Why wouldn't she? And I'd rather she didn't break Incendium's law in a place where there are thousands of eyes watching her." He shook his head. "I must decline, Uncle. In fact, I think I should move out of the capital city with the children, just in case."

"But where will you go?"

"I don't know." Arkan shoved a hand through his hair. "It was only when I entered the palace that I realized the peril of the situation. All this power. All these ears and eyes. I have to protect her, Uncle."

"Of course, you do." Kraw cleared his throat. "But have you considered that the safest place for her might be here, in the palace?"

"How could that be?"

"It is human nature and that of dragons, too, to offer mercy to those they love."

Arkan's gaze locked with Kraw's. "Then why do we keep this secret?" he asked, indicating the scroll.

It was a good question. "Because the mercy may be preceded by fire."

Arkan rose to his feet and paced the width of the room, then sat down to confront Kraw once more. He had made a choice, and while Kraw admired that it was made quickly, he hoped it was the decision he desired most. "There can be no more curse from the past. There can be no more secret."

"What do you mean?"

Arkan flicked the scroll with his fingertip. "I will not leave this legacy for my children. Either we show this to the king and his inclination for mercy is proven to me for once and for all, or I will leave the city forever."

Kraw's stomach churned at the suggestion. "What about becoming my apprentice?"

"I'm still thinking about it. I need to be sure before I give my word."

Kraw didn't know what to say. While he admired Arkan's need to protect his children, he didn't think the curse left a lot of choice to the intended apprentice. He could see that his nephew was determined to proceed his own way and wished he could convince him to make a promise first.

He might confess all to the king then still be left without an apprentice. He could lose everything.

Why did the curse make such demands now?

Kraw might have argued but there was a knock upon the door to his apartment.

"Can't you ignore it?" Arkan said with an echo of his own frustration.

Kraw smiled. "I am at the disposal of the king, remember. Will you go?"

"Of course." Arkan strode to the door, his impatience clear, and Kraw wondered what King Ouros would make of his manner. It was far from respectful. Perhaps the king would refuse to have Arkan as viceroy.

But then his nephew opened the door and a woman's low voice carried to Kraw's ears.

"Uncle Kraw!" Narjal cried, racing to his room and casting herself across the bed. "You're sick!"

"I'm just having a nap," Kraw said, not in the least bit surprised that Tarun climbed onto the bed after his sister. "And having you two visit is the very best way to wake up."

Arkan didn't return, nor did his voice rise in anger. Kraw listened and realized it had been the Princess Enigma who had brought the children to his apartment. That Arkan lingered to speak with her was a very, very good sign.

Enigma might change Arkan's mind as Kraw could not.

He decided to give the boy as much time as he needed and invited the children to settle in on either side of him.

"We followed Pater," Narjal confided. "He took my book."

"Oh? Was it a good book?" Kraw asked, knowing exactly which book she meant.

"The very best book," she agreed. "I want it back."

"Perhaps it should be a secret," Kraw suggested quietly and her dark gaze flew to his.

"He told you about it."

"He did, and I remember a story about it."

"There's a story?" Tarun asked, his eyes alight.

"There's always a story," Kraw said. "Let me tell you this one."

"I hope it has velocitor," Tarun said.

"I hope it ends happily," Narjal said.

"It does," Kraw acknowledged to Narjal, even as he tried to think of a way to satisfy Tarun, too. "You see, once there was a witch from Regalia and she was all alone on Incendium." He raised a finger. "Except, of course, for her velocitor, which was very fast..."

ARKAN HAD ALWAYS wondered whether a hint of dragon had crept into his family bloodline over the centuries. There wasn't enough of it that any of the viceroy's relations could shift shape or breathe fire, but Arkan had always known his family was different.

He had that certainty again when Uncle Kraw spotted the scroll. For a brief moment, there was a gleam of surprise in the viceroy's eyes, followed quickly by satisfaction, and then the older man's expression had become inscrutable. That look put Arkan in mind of a dragon guarding his hoard. Kraw held his gaze steadily, without revealing one increment of his thoughts, for what seemed like eternity.

As usual, Arkan blinked first.

He had been shocked to find his uncle in bed in the early evening, but supposed he was getting older. As a boy, he'd been awed by Uncle Kraw's elaborate mustache, his pride and joy, and it was still perfectly groomed. The older man seldom visited the family home, but when he did, his summary of his activities at the palace left everyone wide-eyed in wonder at his efficiency and the scope of his responsibilities.

Arkan had always been pretty sure his uncle confessed only a tiny increment of what he did, which only made his need to rest more reasonable.

"Because you are due to have your toes held to the fire. No woman will do it, not since Jalana's death, so it will have to be dragons."

There had been a glint of humor in the older man's eyes, a dare and a challenge both, and something that again reminded Arkan of dragons. He was tempted, very tempted, but he was afraid for Narjal, too.

His thoughts were spinning when the rap came at the door. He was both glad to have something to do, even as simple as answering a door, and irritated to have their conversation interrupted. He felt a need to choose immediately, and a sense that it would be prudent to delay.

"Yes?" Arkan said as he opened the door.

"Pater!" Narjal cried, hugged him, then pushed past him in search of Kraw. Tarun shot after his sister, moving quickly enough that Arkan barely managed to brush his fingertips across the top of the boy's head.

"I do apologize," the woman accompanying them said, and Arkan looked at her for the first time. Her hair was long and dark, falling in waves over her shoulders. Her eyes were dark and thickly lashed, her lips curved as if she enjoyed a private joke. There was a glint of amusement in her eyes yet a bit of concern as well. Her voice was low and luscious, her beauty enough to make his heart stop cold.

Sultry was the word that came to his mind.

Mysterious.

Belatedly, he realized who he was speaking to. "Your highness,"

Arkan said and bowed. "Princess Enigma, the vid doesn't do you credit."

She laughed a little. "Oh, you flatter as Kraw does. Are you related?"

"I am Arkan, Kraw's nephew."

"I am pleased to meet you. Will you be his apprentice then? My father has been wondering when Kraw would choose."

"We are discussing it." Arkan glanced back without meaning to do so, and looked at the princess again to find understanding in her dark gaze.

"You are concerned about the children," she guessed. "But many children have grown up happily in Incendium palace."

"I wouldn't mean to suggest otherwise..."

"She told me about her book," the princess said, interrupting him smoothly. "I know Incendium's laws as well as you do."

Their gazes met and held. Arkan swallowed, knowing it had been a long time since he had been so aware of a woman.

A dragon princess.

He should take the children and leave the city, for the sake of all of them.

Enigma smiled, just a little. "I was interested in her story, actually," she said. "I have a fascination with the intersection of the rational and the irrational, the meeting point, if you will, between magic and science."

"Is there one?"

"Of course there is! So often, what is labeled magic is simply science we have yet to understand. Is it magic to change shape from a woman to a dragon by force of will?"

"No, it's a perfectly reasonable transformation, more than adequately explained."

"Here on Incendium. On other planets, in other systems, I might be perceived to be a magical being." She smiled and Arkan couldn't argue with a single thing she said.

"I suppose there are other examples," he ventured.

"Like recognizing someone's role in your life at first glimpse?" she said, then reached out her hand. A spark leaped from her fingertip to him, sizzling when it touched him. Arkan jumped, then a warm heat spread through his body, as if he had been illuminated from within.

Or had his toes held to the fire.

He cleared his throat. "If I take this apprenticeship, I'll insist that your father learn an old secret."

"One that has been kept from him?" Enigma watched as Arkan nodded. "That may make him angry. I suggest you take a dragon with you for that event, so you can meet fire with fire."

Arkan found himself smiling. "Good idea. Do you know one who might be interested?"

She smiled back. "I do, especially if it means you remaining at the palace."

They stared at each other, the heat growing between them with every passing second, and Arkan couldn't think of a single reason to decline an apprenticeship with his uncle. He would train to become the viceroy of Incendium, under his own terms, and have the protection of a dragon princess, too.

He wouldn't have been the man he was if he hadn't hoped for even more.

ARKAN DIDN'T remember.

Enigma didn't know whether to be disappointed or relieved. It had been twenty years, just the blink of an eye for her, but she knew that men perceived time differently. It could have been yesterday, the memory was so clear in her mind. Arkan was more of a man than a young rebel, more concerned with convention, more responsible—more attractive.

And less drunk. That could explain a lot.

He wasn't her HeartKeeper, she knew that, and he wasn't the Carrier of the Seed for her. He was just a delicious temptation, and one that Enigma couldn't deny now any more than she'd been able to then.

When Kraw took him to her father, she couldn't stay away. She followed at a distance, blending into the shadows as she could do so well, making sure neither of the men were aware of her.

It would be more tricky to deceive her father.

But she had to know what Arkan was going to do, whether she'd see him again, whether he would be living at close proximity. She had to know whether there might be another interlude like that first one.

His children were cute, although she wasn't particularly maternal. Kraw found a maid to watch them with his usual ease of sorting out details and they seemed happy to go with her. Enigma hoped they would be similarly occupied after Arkan took up his post as Kraw's apprentice.

She slipped into the audience chamber after Kraw and Arkan, no more substantial than a ghost, and neither noticed her silent presence. Her mother was there, as were Thalina and her HeartKeeper, Acion. Thalina looked as pleased as Ignita, and Enigma guessed that they had been talking about the child she carried. Her sisters and mother always shared the same little smile when there was a young dragon on the way. Acion's hair had grown long enough to curl over his collar, though she couldn't forget his origins. He still seemed passionless to Enigma, though Thalina might be sufficiently lively for both of them.

Maybe it was true that opposites attracted.

Enigma remained back against the wall, listening as the entire story of the viceroy Narkam and his deception was explained to the king. Her father listened, a frown marring his brow, but she knew he was more puzzled than angry.

"Who was the Regalian woman?" he asked when Arkan fell silent.

"Witch," Ignita corrected.

"No witches on Incendium, Ignita," Ouros said under his breath, the words so low that Kraw gave no sign of hearing them. Arkan, however, appeared to be startled for a moment, perhaps taken aback by her father's bluntness.

"We don't know, your majesty," Arkan said. "We have only the contents of this confession for reference."

Ouros rose to his feet. "So, we don't know where Blazion and Embron went, much less whether they survived. We don't know the woman's full role, and we don't know whether she truly could bend time. They haven't come back, and neither have any of their descendants." He lifted his shoulders in a shrug. "The matter seems to be resolved."

"With respect, your majesty, it has always been anticipated that the crown would perceive my forebear's actions as treason."

"Defiance of a tyrant in the hope of saving the realm isn't my definition of treason," Ouros said mildly. "If it reassures you, I'll issue an official pardon, but I would like to keep the tale a state secret."

"Of course!"

Ouros glanced at Thalina and Acion, both of whom nodded agreement. Then he wagged a finger at the viceroy. "But here is what I want to know. The ShadowCaster showed me a vision of this incident, presumably to spark my curiosity and your confession. Why has the truth become of import now?"

"Perhaps it has taken the ShadowCaster centuries to reach your hand, sir," Arkan speculated.

"I don't think so. It was just sent to me, in quite an expedient fashion, by the Hive of Cumae. Is that the correct name, Acion?"

"It is, sir. The Hive is a sophisticated maker of androids, housed deep beneath the surface of Cumae."

Ouros nodded, evidently having been told this already. "And this Hive sent the ShadowCaster to me, after the Warrior Maiden Arista retrieved it from Regalia."

"There is no telling how long it was upon Regalia, your majesty," Kraw observed. "It could have been diverted from its destination by Queen Arcana."

"And we will never know the truth of that, now that both she and Urbanus are dead." Ouros held up a hand. "No, I have no regrets about that situation, but it does leave room for questions. Why did the Hive send the

ShadowCaster to me? What interest has the Hive in the affairs of Incendium? What result did the Hive hope to provoke?"

Acion frowned in concentration. "There are myriad possibilities, sir, and it would take me some time to tabulate a list from which to calculate probabilities."

"Then you had best begin," Ouros said. "I will also need as complete a list as you can create of the Hive's capabilities and known facts about it, from which I would like you to speculate upon the obstacles the Hive might present to a party who infiltrated it."

"Father!" Thalina protested.

"And," Ouros continued. "Some suggested strategies to counter these obstacles."

Acion blinked, then nodded. Enigma had the sense he had already begun.

"The wisest strategy might be to appoint Acion a role in the landing party," Thalina suggested.

"My thoughts, exactly." Ouros turned to Arkan. "Do you mean to take the post of viceroy?"

"I do, your majesty, if it pleases you."

"It does. You have six months to learn your duties, memorize the laws of Incendium, study its protocol, and prepare to depart to Cumae as part of the diplomatic mission being dispatched to learn more about the Hive and its intentions."

"But..."

Ouros turned a sharp eye upon Arkan. "Arguing with the monarch is a poor way to begin your new responsibilities."

"I cannot go to Cumae, your majesty. I have children."

"And they will have more than adequate care in your absence. Kraw must remain here to administer the government and I will need a second of command on the mission."

"Ouros! You can't mean to lead this mission yourself!" Ignita protested, but there was no question in her tone. Enigma guessed that her mother already knew her father intended to do just that.

"I must, my dear." Ouros took Ignita's hand and pressed a kiss to its back. "I have been informed that in matters of some delicacy, I am unrivaled."

Ignita flushed. "That's not the same, Ouros..."

"But I can't delegate this and I won't. I intend to go, Ignita, and I will spend these six months in rigorous training to ensure that I am as fit as possible for the task."

Ignita's lips thinned. "And I will spend it trying to convince you to assign someone else to do it."

Their gazes locked and there was a sizzle in the air, one that promised a battle of wills. Enigma doubted that either would change the mind of the other, and guessed that they both knew as much already.

"No one tickles the belly of this dragon and evades the consequences," Ouros said with resolve. "We will convince the Hive, one way or the other, to cease its meddling in the affairs of Incendium. Are we all in agreement? In exactly six months, we depart."

Ignita sighed. "And I hope we have word of Anguissa before then." Ouros took her hand again and the others filed out of the chamber, departing to begin their assigned tasks.

Enigma followed Arkan at a distance, wondering if she could persuade him to indulge in pleasure before his departure. He had changed and was less predictable than he had been twenty years before.

More reticent.

But then he turned to look back just before he escorted Kraw into that man's apartments. When his gaze brightened, Enigma knew he had seen her. She stepped out of the shadows, as if she'd intended to do as much all along, and felt his heart skip. He smiled slowly and she smiled back, her confidence in her success growing until he turned his attention back to his uncle.

Two months, at the outside, and she would have him again.

Enigma couldn't wait.

Deborah Cooke sold her first book in 1992, a medieval romance called ROMANCE OF THE ROSE published under her pseudonym Claire Delacroix. Since then, she has published over fifty novels in a wide variety of sub-genres, including historical romance, contemporary romance, paranormal romance, fantasy romance, time travel romance, women's fiction, paranormal young adult and fantasy with romantic elements. She has published under the names Claire Delacroix, Claire Cross and Deborah Cooke. THE BEAUTY, part of her successful *Bride Quest* series of historical romances, was her first title to land on the New York Times List of Bestselling Books. Her books routinely appear on other bestseller lists and have won numerous awards. In 2009, she was the writer-in-residence at the Toronto Public Library, the first time the library has hosted a residency focused on the romance genre. In 2012, she was honored to receive the Romance Writers of America's Mentor of the Year Award.

Currently, she writes the *Dragons of Incendium* series of paranormal romances and the *Flatiron Five* series of contemporary romances under the name Deborah Cooke. She also continues to write medieval romance as Claire Delacroix. Deborah lives in Canada with her husband and family, as well as far too many unfinished knitting projects.

Subscribe to Deborah's monthly reader newsletter:
http://eepurl.com/reIuD

Visit Deborah's websites:
www.deborahcooke.com
www.dragonsofincendium.com

www.ingramcontent.com/pod-product-compliance
Lightning Source LLC
Chambersburg PA
CBHW031608180726
48284CB00005B/1454